Anna M. Hellier, John Benjamin Hellier

Benjamin Hellier

his life and teaching - a biographical sketch, with extracts from his letters, sermons,

and addresses

Anna M. Hellier, John Benjamin Hellier

Benjamin Hellier
his life and teaching - a biographical sketch, with extracts from his letters, sermons, and addresses

ISBN/EAN: 9783337390785

Printed in Europe, USA, Canada, Australia, Japan

Cover: Foto ©Andreas Hilbeck / pixelio.de

More available books at **www.hansebooks.com**

BENJAMIN HELLIER:

HIS LIFE AND TEACHING.

A BIOGRAPHICAL SKETCH, WITH EXTRACTS FROM HIS LETTERS, SERMONS, AND ADDRESSES.

EDITED BY HIS CHILDREN

Ἐμοὶ γὰρ τὸ ζῆν Χριστός.

WITH PORTRAIT AND ILLUSTRATIONS.

London:

HODDER AND STOUGHTON,

27, PATERNOSTER ROW.

MDCCCLXXXIX.

BUTLER & TANNER,
THE SELWOOD PRINTING WORKS,
FROME, AND LONDON.

PREFACE.

OUR object in the first part of this book has been to give a picture of our father as he appeared in his daily life, rather than to attempt a detailed analysis of his work and character. In the second part, in like manner, we have not tried to give an exhaustive illustration of his theological views, but simply to present what seems to us to be most characteristic of his teaching, both as to choice of subject and mode of treatment.

How little our pages can make him live again, how little the collation and printing of his manuscripts can reproduce the words of his lips, none know better than ourselves.

Our heartiest thanks are offered to all those who have taken part with us in this work.

A. M. H.

J. B. H.

LEEDS.

CONTENTS.

PART I. THE LIFE.

Chapter III. Richmond, 1857–1868.

PART II. THE TEACHING.

SECTION I. CHIEFLY EXPOSITORY.

SECTION II. THE IDEAL CHRISTIAN LIFE.

LIST OF ILLUSTRATIONS.

THE LIFE.

THE authors of the following Biographical Sketch have expressed a wish that I should write some words of introduction. It has been my privilege repeatedly to bear my testimony to the singular worth of my honoured friend, and I should gladly have joined my reminiscences to those contributed by others on later pages of this volume. But the peculiar relation in which the authors stand to him of whom they write may seem to demand that an independent opinion be expressed, not of Mr. Hellier only, but of their presentation of their father's character and life. If this request carried with it the necessity of my assuming the position of an impartial judge, I must have stood aloof. I am too deeply in Mr. Hellier's debt, my life as I look back over thirty years owes too much of its colour to his warm-hearted, faithful, generous friendship, for me to attempt to be coolly critical. But a friend may stand so near as to appreciate excellence, and yet so far off as to gain more comprehensiveness of view. Words unaffected by the glamour of filial reverence and love may seem more worthy of being implicitly believed. If I can answer any such purpose, the privilege is not small.

After reading every word of this testimony to a

father's excellence, I am prepared from my own intimate knowledge of his life to endorse the whole. My
ten years' association with him at Richmond College
involved fellowship as intimate as can exist between
colleagues. A man's character cannot fail to reveal
itself without disguise in the multitude of minor
actions and relations which with us filled up the life
of every day. Term after term we had a hundred
different arrangements to discuss, each year introduced new companies of students whom it was our
duty to study and to provide for, devotional meetings
and schemes for religious work brought us together,
I met my friend in his family, I consulted him on all
my own affairs, our conversations ranged over all the
wide field of our common interests ; and I can hardly
be thought presumptuous if, after years of such fellowship, I am persuaded that my view of Mr. Hellier's
character is accurate and worthy of trust.

As I look back, the chief impression made on me
is of a character of wonderful unity and singleness of
aim. His loyalty and love to the Lord Jesus Christ
were not shown by frequent mention of His name,
but by habitual, unwavering devotion to His service.
When duty was ascertained, then without talk or
question obedience followed : that what was right
must at once be done, was the axiom of his life, an
axiom not often expressed, but ever present. How
simple and unaffected, how free from parade, this life
of duty was from first to last, only those nearest to
him can know. I do not remember to have observed

in him a single trace of self-seeking. Popularity he valued as a means of usefulness, his kindly nature responded to all kindliness, he appreciated the commendation of those who had a right to speak words of praise ; but I cannot imagine him as doing anything, as avoiding any course of action, for the sake of winning favour for himself. The general plans of his life gave the impression of a man of very definite convictions and of strong will. He had carefully studied himself, and knew well what he could do, and in what way it was best for him to do it. These plans of action, well thought out and matured by long experience, he never willingly laid aside. His godliness, singleness of purpose, steady consistency, and unselfishness furnished as fine a type of Christian manliness as it has ever been my privilege to witness.

His single-minded devotion was seen in the whole of his official work as a Christian minister and tutor. " This one thing I do," might have been inscribed on each sermon and lecture ; and the " one thing " was the fulfilment of the Divine purpose in assigning to him this and that act of service. In his Richmond days his preaching had in it more of the element of teaching ; later, along with this, there was manifest more of the longing to convince and persuade. During the former period, when my opportunities of hearing him were not unfrequent, I learnt to admire and deeply to reverence the preacher for his clear and full exposition of Scripture, his strong

II.   *b*

practical teaching, his calm reliance on the Spirit of truth to give success to the proclamation of the truth. In his latest years his preaching became more and more impassioned ; he seemed unable to take a denial, as he urged his Master's message. John Bunyan has given us "the fashion of the picture " of such a preacher. "It had eyes lift up to Heaven, the best of Books in his hand, the Law of Truth was written upon his lips, the World was behind his back ; it stood as if it pleaded with Men, and a Crown of gold did hang over his head."

His preparations for the lecture-room were made with great care, but with the same practical aim. He did not seek even scholarship for its own sake : on the other hand, he thought no labour wasted that might enable him more accurately to bring out the meaning of Holy Scripture to his students. His chief aim was to train them to a wide and deep and spiritual study of the Bible, as their life-long work. In his own studies he was keenly sensible of the limitations imposed on him by his physical constitution. During the whole period of my association with him, though usually he might appear a strong man, he was incapable of severe and protracted work. He had trained himself to do thoroughly that which he was able to attempt, and without a murmur to leave undone many things towards which he felt a strong attraction. But for the disabilities of which I have spoken, it cannot be doubted that he would have made many valuable contributions to sacred literature. His grasp of principles was firm, his interest in the subject intense ; and he possessed in no ordinary degree the gifts of clearness of thought and precision of language. We who knew him can only think regretfully of what might have been, had he been gifted with physical strength. The selections from his MSS. in the latter part of this volume reveal his powers in part, but only in part.

As a minister amongst ministers in the Church which he loved so well, Mr. Hellier's influence was great, and was steadily increasing up to the last. Many of us looked forward with confident expectation to the time when he would be elected to the highest position in our ranks : had he been spared a few years longer, such would no doubt have been his lot, and a worthy leader would he have proved in all departments of the spiritual work of Wesleyan Methodism. But this was not the will of Him at whose feet our dear departed friend laid every work and every purpose of his life. We bow to His unerring wisdom ; but we are permitted to mourn our loss.

To him is given " a life that bears immortal fruit." He serves Christ still.

WILLIAM F MOULTON.

The Leys, Cambridge.

BIOGRAPHICAL SKETCH.

CHAPTER I.

EARLY YEARS.

1825–1844.

B ENJAMIN HELLIER was born at Bourton, in the parish of Wick St. Lawrence, Somerset-shire, on May 9th, 1825.

Wick St. Lawrence is a little village, distant about eighteen miles from Bristol, and five from Weston-super-Mare; and its inhabitants were so few that Mr. Hellier's father could take its census with ease while sitting at his own fireside.

In a letter to a friend, dated from Wick in 1865, Mr. Hellier thus describes the home of his boyhood:

"You can hardly conceive what a quiet, sleepy place this is. Suppose you get out at the Banwell station.[1] There are a few houses, not more than ten at the utmost, dotted about here and there. Then you walk down a green lane, and turn your steps towards Wick St. Lawrence. Behind you is the long and high range of the Mendip Hills, about five miles distant. On your left an offshoot of these hills sweeps round in a curve,

[1] This station is now called Puxton.

and forms the southern boundary of the bay on which Weston-super-Mare is situated. On the right another offshoot makes a like bend, and at its extremity is Clevedon, with its old church memorable as the burying-place of the two Hallams, and therefore celebrated in *In Memoriam.* The church stands quite solitary on a bluff green headland overlooking the sea, and here you may stand and watch hour after hour

> '——the stately ships go on
> To their haven under the hill.'

"Before you all this while rises on the distant horizon a line of long blue hills. These are in South Wales, about ten miles distant, and separated from you by the Bristol Channel. So you see that the district in which Wick is situated is a semicircular tract of level rich land, Mendip and offsets forming the semicircle, and the shore of the Bristol Channel the chord, the extremes of which are Clevedon and Weston.

"After a walk of two miles across green fields, and certain primitive bridges formed of single poles four inches in diameter, you come in sight of my father's house, with magnolia, bignonia, clematis, vine, and other plants covering its whole front from top to bottom. As you approach it, you can readily fancy that its inmates are all sleeping, there is such an air of repose about the place."

The old farmhouse has been much altered of late years, but the roomy, cheerful farm-kitchen existed in its original state within our own recollection, with

settles in the old-fashioned chimney-corner ; while behind the wood fire which burned on the hearth Shad-
rach, Meshach, and Abednego, portrayed in cast iron,
perpetually survived the flames. This curious work
of art is dated 1665. Beyond the garden, orchards
and flat meadow-lands, with many a green ditch between, stretch to the sea wall, so often washed away
by the tides of the Bristol Channel. On one occasion,
indeed, its waters so flooded Wick, that a boat was
rowed down the village street.

The Helliers have lived in Bristol or Somersetshire
for at least 250 years. One of them was Sheriff of
Bristol in 1638, and Mayor in 1653. They have been
for the most part a race of country gentlemen, fond
of their hunters and their dogs, and of the society of
their neighbours, and in days gone by have held
somewhat extensive landed possessions. At certain
traditions as to the still greater antiquity of the
family Mr. Hellier would often laugh, saying that
those who took pleasure in tracing their descent
through many generations are apt to give themselves
credit for what is in reality no credit to them at all,
and that for his part he never cared to go farther back
than his grandfather, for whose memory he had a
great respect.

This John Hellier, a man of distinguished stature
and appearance, was a devout Churchman, with
strong Methodist sympathies, and an upholder of
the cause of Christian missions in days when its
friends were few. In the first years of this century,

when the invasion of the French was daily expected, and beacons lay ready to be kindled on every hill, he raised a volunteer regiment in defence of his native shores.

His third son, John, Mr. Hellier's father, was characterized by sound judgment and great natural sagacity; he was punctual, methodical, prudent, and exceedingly generous; and his spotless integrity and high sense of honour inspired an unusual degree of respect and confidence in all who knew him. When he married he gave up his hunters, and settled down to the life of a farmer.

His wife, Mary Ann Griffin, belonged to an old Methodist family. Her grandparents were friends of John Wesley, whose *Journal* contains more than one reference to visits paid to Chew Stoke, where their house was both his home and preaching place. She became a Churchwoman on her marriage, but she brought her Methodist hymn-book with her to her new home, and it was to the hymns she sang from it with her children that her son Benjamin owed his first religious impressions. Their favourites, strangely enough, were nearly all hymns on the Judgment, sung to exceedingly quaint and mournful tunes, which never ceased to haunt his memory.

She had great influence over her husband, whose temper in his youth was very fiery. For her, however, in his most passionate moments he had none but gentle words ; and the beautiful, old-fashioned courtesy which distinguished him was nowhere more

strikingly exhibited than in the deference and devotion paid to her whom he cherished with unfailing
love during a married life of fifty-eight years' dura-
tion. This passionate disposition made the perfect
patience and gentleness of his later years the more
noteworthy. He lived till his ninety-third year, his
mental faculties unimpaired, his interest in life still
fresh ; while his unselfishness, his touching humility,
and his unconscious goodness, made his old age very
lovely, and endeared him inexpressibly to those about
him. No one who saw will readily forget the fine
venerable figure, the snow-white hair and beard, and
the strangely blue eyes that gleamed so kindly
from under his white, shaggy eyebrows. The tie
between him and his son Benjamin was very close
and tender, and they were not long separated. He
died on November 24th, 1884.

Mr. John Hellier had eight children, one of whom
died in infancy. Benjamin was his sixth child, and
the youngest of his four sons. He is described by
his eldest sister as a child full of life and intelligence, and of mischievous fun, very tender to dumb
animals, very affectionate, and always open to spiritual influences.

An early recollection of his, and one that he
delighted to recall, was a visit paid to an uncle living
at Yatton. His uncle had a small collection of
books, which excited his deepest interest. Though
he had not then learned to read, he would steal
into the room where they were kept, and stand gazing

at them with a great love for them in his heart. They seemed to him the greatest treasure that a man could possess, and he wondered if he should ever have as many.

This visit took place during the general election of 1831, and his family, all of them ardent Tories, were eager in support of Mr. Miles, their local candidate. But it so happened that Mr. Miles was a slave owner, and the proprietor of large plantations in the West Indies. Hearing from his uncle of the cruelties inflicted on the slaves, and identifying in his childish mind Toryism with oppression, the six-year-old politician returned home a staunch Liberal, and a Liberal he remained despite the arguments and persuasions of his elders. Probably at that time he was the only one in the parish.

Another incident, characteristic of his tenderness for sufferers, is recorded by his youngest sister. When, during an illness of hers, he was given the choice of a holiday treat, he could ask nothing better than permission to carry the little invalid downstairs, wrapped in a blanket, that she might have an hour's enjoyment of the family circle.

It must not be supposed that in this remote country village he was surrounded by an atmosphere of rustic purity and Arcadian simplicity. On the contrary, the influence and conversation of his father's haymakers and ploughmen, with whom he was in daily contact, was too often gross and sensual in the highest degree. He was saved from contamination at first by his innocence and then by his virtue, but the peril was great.

His first day school was at Worle, two miles distant from his home. Here, seated on his teacher's knee, he learned his letters at what would now be deemed the advanced age of seven. The only school in Wick was kept by an old dame, celebrated for the readiness with which she disposed of the literary difficulties of her scholars. For when in their reading the children stopped short at a long word, her stereotyped answer was, " Skip thic." The phrase became a favourite quotation in Mr. Hellier's family, and he generally used it if in our reading aloud we came to anything that he did not consider "edifying."

He was for a time profoundly impressed by the learning of his first teacher, Mr. Brickman. " Shall I ever be rich ?" he asked his father ; "shall I ever have as much as two hundred pounds ? Then I will give it all to Mr. Brickman, to make me as great a scholar as he is." So eager was he to acquire knowledge, that neither authority nor persuasion could keep him from school. On one occasion he overheard some one say that he was to stay at home the next day. To avoid this deprivation he rose early in the morning, and hid in the shrubbery until the family were seated at breakfast. Then he made his escape, and remained all day at school without food. When he failed to return at his usual hour in the evening, his mother and sister set out to search for him in great alarm,

and at the end of the village met a thatcher carrying
their truant home on his back.   He had found him
fainting under a hedge about a mile from home.

Mr. Brickman seems to have parted with his store
of knowledge on easy terms ; for his scholar, when
twelve years old, concluded that the learned man
could teach him no more, and asked to go to another
school.   He was accordingly sent to reside in Bristol,
for the purpose of attending a day school there.
He first lodged with his uncle, Mr. William Hellier,
and afterwards with Mrs. Brice, a noted Methodist
class-leader.   Of his next master, Mr. Norton, he
always spoke with gratitude as the man who first
taught him to *think ;* and he seems to have been
equally fortunate in Dr. Day, with whom he ended
his school-life.   The first class in this last school
consisted of himself, his cousin, now the Rev. Henry
Hellier, Rector of Nempnett, Somersetshire, Dr.
Davis, afterwards Principal of a Welsh College, and
Dr. Adam Farrar, the present Dean of Durham.

For a short time he, with his cousin and Dr.
Farrar, attended a Bible-class together, but the
minister who conducted it soon discontinued it because these three boys were his only scholars.   Once
when one of us talked of giving up a scantily attended class, Mr. Hellier referred to this circumstance,
and said that if the minister had foreseen the positions which they would be called upon to occupy,
he might have thought it worth while to instruct
them a little further.

From a journal which he kept while a schoolboy
we learn the story of his conversion. He was very
early convinced of sin, and his religious impressions
were received from many sources. His mother's
singing, his eldest sister's influence, the Baptist
ministry which he attended during holiday visits to
Dundry, and the Sunday-school anniversary services
at Chew Stoke, all had their share in leading him
to Christ.

"I remember," he writes, "that one Sunday especially, after I had gone to Chew Stoke to hear Mr.
Illingworth (1835), the thought was suddenly impressed on me that I should die in the night, and
I then made a solemn promise to be God's servant
if my life were spared. But my resolution was made
in my own strength, and therefore vain. I shortly
afterwards returned to a far different home from what
it is now. We had then little of the form and less of
the power of religion amongst us. My father was to
some extent a *servant* of God, but not a *son*. For a
short time I was a little more regular in my devotions
than the rest, but could not long remain 'singularly
good,' since I depended on my own strength. While
speaking of my home I cannot but reflect how
wonderful a change has been wrought in seven years.

"In the fall of 1837 God in His good providence
brought amongst us the Rev. John Betts as curate
of the parish. I first saw Mr. Betts at our missionary
meeting; but, thinking it would appear too religious
to go inside the school-room where the meeting

was held, I only saw him through the window. His appearance, and the earnest manner in which he delivered his address, struck me very forcibly, and gave my mind such a prepossession towards him as, I doubt not, was a thing not unimportant in its results."

This interest deepened into strong affection, which was heartily returned, and under Mr. Betts' teaching he made rapid spiritual progress. Mr. Betts gave a course of lectures on St. John's Gospel soon after his arrival in the parish, and Mr. Hellier writes: "It was while attending one of these that I first believed to the saving of my soul. . . . My faith, however, was weak, and my peace, therefore, not of long continuance. I was harassed with doubts concerning the sincerity of my repentance, but was greatly relieved from this snare by my sister's remarking that the desire to feel more sorrow on account of sin was an evidence of the truth of my repentance. I was also tempted to think I had never yet believed, but was at last able to silence this doubt by saying, ' If I never *did* believe, I *now* believe.' After this my faith and joy increased." He was then twelve years old.

In the following year, when he went to lodge with his uncle in Bristol, he accompanied him and his family every Sunday to Portland Chapel, and as regularly attended St. James' Church in the afternoon. One Sunday, however, on his way thither, he met his uncle's servant, Hannah Badman, and she,

like the good Methodist she was, invited him to go
with her to her Class-meeting. After a little hesitation, he consented to do so ; and that afternoon, while
listening to the conversation of the little Methodist
company, he felt that he had found the very thing
for which he had been longing—communion with
the people of God, and for this reason he decided to
become a Wesleyan Methodist. Concerning this step
he writes: "I did not come to this determination
finally without first counting the cost. I thought it
very probable that I should displease some whose
good opinion I highly valued, and incur the ridicule
of others whose opinion, however, was a matter of
comparative indifference. But I thought by so doing
I should please God, and whose approbation is to be
weighed against His? I chose Wesleyan Methodism
because, in the first place, as far as I could discover,
its doctrines were in accordance with the Bible, and,
what is the same thing, identical with the doctrines
of the Church of England. I chose Methodism, in
the next place, because I considered its ordinances
and discipline preferable to those of any other
society." He was admitted as a member by the
Rev. Charles Prest in March, 1839, being then in
his fourteenth year.

At this time his eldest sister was his chief spiritual
friend and counsellor. From his earliest childhood
she had striven to win him for Christ, and they had
been in the habit of praying together in the quiet
retreat afforded them by their father's hay-mow. She

had shared with him the blessing of Mr. Betts' ministry, and helped and encouraged him in the difficulties that beset his new-born faith. His correspondence with her throughout his school days was one of his greatest religious safeguards, as was once proved, he always considered, in a very striking manner. She had just despatched her usual weekly letter to him, when she felt impelled to write to him again, under the impression that he was in some kind of danger—an impression which grew stronger as she tried to resist it. Finally she wrote, saying that he would doubtless be surprised to receive a letter from her in the middle of the week, but that she had for a day or two been burdened with the conviction that he was in great danger. She had no idea of its nature, and could therefore only exhort him to look well to his ways. He would know how to apply her warning. The next time they met, he told her that his study of the Greek drama had created an almost overpowering desire to see a play acted. While this feeling was at its height, the walls of Bristol were placarded with the announcement that one of the first actresses of the day was to appear in one of Shakespeare's plays, and he resolved to go and see it. On the morning of the day that he would have gone to the theatre, her letter arrived, and it contained a warning too plain to be disregarded.

Writing to her years afterwards when he was Assistant-Tutor at Didsbury College, he says:

" You will remember my going to Bristol. I was

exposed here to great temptations. My dear Jenny's counsels followed me in her letters, and were a great check upon my wayward tendencies. Then, too, he who is now your best friend became mine, and my obligations to him for his kindness at this time cannot be over-estimated. Scarcely any one thing was more calculated to preserve me from evil company, and so from evil ways, than his kind patronage and the acquaintance which I gained through him with his family. You ought not to be ignorant how imminent my danger of falling away from God at this time frequently was. I had often very little left of religion besides its profession and form, and in looking back I now marvel greatly how I could have so far forsaken God without departing from Him altogether. I should once or twice have gone sadly wrong but for your wise counsels."

The friend here referred to was Mr. Thomas Harper, whom his eldest sister married. He was four years older than Mr. Hellier, and the rare steadfastness and integrity of his character and principles made him an invaluable companion. His father's house, too, became a frequent resort for his friend ; and it was in these days that Mr. Hellier first felt for the eldest daughter of that house the regard which he cherished in silence for seven years, until the time came when he might fitly seek for its return.

We add an extract from another letter to his sister, written during his school days, and exhibiting a combination of piety, philosophy, and common sense, not often to be found in a lad of seventeen :

" But that which I esteem to be the greatest bless-ing of Providence was my coming to Bristol. To the God of all grace I give the praise, and in a secondary sense feel unfeigned gratitude to my father, through whose kindness I was so situated. I do not regret my going to Mr. Norton's. I believe I could not then have had a better instructor. Least of all the events of my past life do I regret joining the Methodist Society. I feel truly grateful to God that He in His good providence directed me to this place of abode. And I will say upon the whole that I am convinced that everything connected with my edu-cation and circumstances during the past years of my life has been directed by God's providence, and has been *all for the best*. As to my present circum-stances, I am on the whole perfectly satisfied, because I am satisfied it is as God would have it to be. I am at Mrs. Brice's ; it is well. I go to Dr. Day's ; it is well. I have few friends ; this is well. But two suits of clothes, and one much the worse for wear ; this is well. But eighteenpence in my pocket ; this is well. (It would be better if I were paid the three-and-elevenpence-halfpenny that I'm owed.) All is well. It is well with my soul also, though it may be better. I love God more sincerely now than ever I did. I have greater simplicity, more faith, and more charity than ever I had, but these are but 'the droppings of a shower.' I do daily what

I conceive to be my daily duty, and can adopt the words of the poet to a good degree and say,—

> 'With "me" no melancholy void,
> No period lingers unemployed
> Or unimproved below.'"

Though he played as heartily as any schoolboy, he never talked like one. He was boyish in his sports and in the simplicity of his character, but far otherwise in his modes of speaking and thinking.

One more influence upon his life at this time remains to be noticed. The Revs. John Lomas and Isaac Keeling, two Wesleyan ministers, were then stationed in Bristol, and their ministry was most powerful in the formation and development of his Christian character. Only the few who still remember Mr. Lomas can fully understand the peculiar influence that a man so saintly and a thinker so profound would exercise upon a young hearer full of spiritual and intellectual cravings. "To him as a preacher," said Mr. Hellier in later years, "I owe very much more than to any man I ever heard."

By the end of 1842 the four boys who formed Dr. Day's first class had advanced so far in their studies beyond his other pupils that they were in danger of absorbing his whole attention. He therefore requested them to withdraw, and advised Mr. Hellier's father to send him to Cambridge as soon as he was old enough to go. He was then but seventeen.

Though the University was not then open to Dissenters, and he was bent on remaining a Methodist all his days, he felt no difficulty on this score. The separation between Methodism and the mother Church was then so little realized that he would have declared himself a Churchman in all good faith, and in a letter written at this time he describes himself as " no Dissenter from the Church of England, although a member of the Methodist Society."

But amidst the doubts and conflicting counsels that rendered this period of his life a season of great anxiety, his call to the ministry made itself felt with increasing distinctness. And in finally responding to that call he renounced his University prospects. His decision caused bitter disappointment to his family, who at that time were all members of the Church of England, and ambitious for his distinction at Cambridge and in their own Church. Dr. Day, too, was highly indignant, and said, " Hellier is a fool to throw away such talents as his upon Methodists, who will never appreciate them ! " He little guessed upon how wide a sphere of influence his pupil was about to enter.

For two years after he left school, he acted as tutor to his two youngest sisters, and of this period his surviving pupil cherishes a very happy and tender recollection. His own journal gives striking evidence of the religious care and pains devoted to his sisters' education, to their physical, intellectual, and spiritual welfare. Nor did his efforts cease when he left home. He still took an interest in their studies, and watched over their health and their religious life. And of Mary Anne, who died in her sixteenth year, he has left a very full and loving little record, which, with her own letters, show how tender and intimate the relation was between them.

"The terms 'brother' and 'sister,'" he wrote in one of his letters, "are so absolutely perfect, when rightly appreciated, that nothing which can be added in way of epithet can make them more endearing."

Those were the days of a large home circle, when father, mother, three sons, and four daughters gathered round the table. At breakfast-time the talk ranged over science, theology, and history, and often lasted till some imperative call of duty broke up the reluctant party. Benjamin was called the "Moderator," and had a bearing of unusual gravity, though keenly enjoying the wit of his eldest brother. On one occasion, when the uppishness of some one had been made the subject of prolonged comment, the Moderator took advantage of a pause to observe quietly, " Well, let us all pity poor ——, and be very thankful we have no pride ourselves." This ended the discussion.

The influence of his country home remained with him throughout his life. He never forgot that he was a farmer's son, nor lost his interest in farming pursuits. " I have great sympathy with the farmers," he was fond of saying. " I was brought up on a farm, and should have been quite content to remain there all my days, if my conscience would have allowed me."

Methodism was then unknown in Wick, and Mr. Hellier joined the nearest society, at Worle. He sometimes asked himself why he should leave his own parish church, and trudge the two miles to join the little handful of Methodists there, and as often felt that he found among them something that he could not do without—genuine Christian fellowship. One by one all the members of his family followed him to the Church of his adoption.

While living at home he laboured earnestly to make Christ known among the scattered and densely ignorant rustic population, and also began to preach in the little chapels and farmers' kitchens in the villages round. One of his early services is thus recorded by his sister :

" I shall never forget, after our walk over the hill, the sight of the pretty cottage on the side of the valley, the well-filled flower border in front, the clean kitchen. After tea our hostess said that she had invited in a few neighbours, hoping that Mr. Hellier would give them 'a little lecture' on the occasion. They soon arrived, carrying their seats, and the little sister acted as precentor. Across the valley lay a field of waving corn ; through the open door came country evening sounds—the lowing of cattle, the even-song of birds, and children's laughter. And in har-mony with it all rose that pleasant voice expounding a scene from the life of Christ. How solemn and sweet and mournful it all seems now ! "

With these early happy associations, what wonder

is it that he had special sympathy with village Methodism? He greatly enjoyed preaching in country chapels, and had a very kindly feeling for small and struggling societies, helping them whenever he could. He would often dwell on the peculiar value of Methodism in rural districts, not only as a spiritual and refining influence, but as affording interests of the highest kind to people who greatly need them. " It gives them something to *do*," he would say, " and something to *think* about."

In 1844 he was accepted as a candidate for the Wesleyan Methodist ministry. For those who are unacquainted with the somewhat protracted stages of preparation and probation by which ordination to this ministry is approached, we offer a few words of explanation ; and it is the more fitting that we should do so, seeing that the greater part of his life was spent in the work of training ministers.

Candidates are only selected from those who are already "local preachers" in some "circuit." A "local preacher" is an unsalaried lay preacher. A " circuit" is a Methodist parish, and a group of " circuits " form a " district." If the Quarterly Meeting of ministers, local preachers, and circuit lay officials agree to recommend such a candidate, he is examined by the ministers assembled in their District Meeting, held in May. If accepted, he is then examined at a central examination by a committee appointed by the annual Conference, which is the supreme legislative assembly of the Wesleyan Church. This examination is held in London, and in recent years at a second centre in Manchester also, and it is of a very searching character. It includes written and oral interrogation in both literary and theological subjects, and a careful investigation of the character, preaching ability, antecedents, and purposes of each candidate. The verdict of the July Committee is formally confirmed, with few alterations, by the Conference, which then decides the destination of the accepted candidate, whether for home or foreign work, and whether he shall enter upon immediate work or be sent to one of the Connexional training colleges. Of these there were then two—Richmond College in Surrey, and Didsbury near Manchester. There are now four, and the cases in which the Institution training is omitted are now very rare. The period of residence is usually three years, though exceptional circumstances may shorten or prolong it.

On leaving college the student has still a four years' probation to undergo. (In Mr. Hellier's time it was a year less.) During this period a course of study is prescribed for him, and he has to pass an annual examination. The missionary students are ordained before they go abroad, but those who enter the home work have to await the end of their probation. In connection with this long course of preparation at least three " trial sermons " have to be preached.

The following letter to his eldest sister describes his experience at the District Meeting, and shows in what spirit he entered upon his ministerial calling :

" BRISTOL,

" *May* 15, '44.

"I am truly obliged to you for your communication, and should have replied to it sooner had I not had the District Meeting in anticipation. I have it now in remembrance. At about twenty minutes to four this morning I rose, cleaned my shoes, etc., and was in Ebenezer Chapel a little before five o'clock, heard one of the young men who has already travelled a year or more preach a very passable sermon, and at six went into the vestry, which was soon filled with the preachers of the District, who were altogether nearly fifty in number. After singing and prayer the examination of myself and another candidate (Mr. Willis, of Cheltenham) commenced. Mr. Stanley was, of course, in the chair. He began by requesting me to give an account of my conversion, present religious experience, and the reasons which induced me to think that God had called me to the ministry. The same question was then proposed to my companion. After this we were asked whether we believed in the doctrines of the Trinity, Divinity and Eternal Sonship of Christ, Divinity and proper Personality of the Holy Spirit, etc., etc. Scripture proofs were also required. These I gave without much trepidation or hesitation, as did my companion. I did not think I should be much dismayed, nor was I. I was asked how I distinguished between regeneration and sanctification. I replied: 'By regeneration we are born

again and become babes in Christ Jesus ; in sanctification we grow up to the full stature of a man
in Christ Jesus. In regeneration our principles are
changed ; in sanctification they are fully acted up
to. In regeneration our souls' affections are turned
towards God and the things of God ; in sanctification
they are fully absorbed by them.' I think I may
venture to say that Mr. Leppington was pleased
with this distinction, for he was sitting close by
me, and immediately asked, ' Was that your own ? '
I said, ' Yes.'

"When Mr. Stanley asked, ' Do you offer yourself,
if accepted, to be employed in any part of the world,
or do you restrict your offer ?' I answered, ' I do not
make any distinct offer for foreign service, but still am
willing to place myself entirely at the disposal of the
Conference.' ' Then if the Conference choose to send
you across the seas, you would not object to go ? '
' No.' You need not be alarmed at this. The Conference never sends a young man abroad against the
consent of his friends. After divers other questions
we were dismissed to the chapel, and found that our
examination had occupied about an hour and a half,
and in ten minutes more we were recalled. ' I have
great pleasure,' said Mr. Stanley, ' in acquainting
you that you have been accepted. I trust that God
will make you able ministers of the New Covenant,
and not only useful, but eminently useful.' "

The reason of the ready answer recorded above is
simple. He had made a practice of writing short

essays on all the principal doctrinal questions, in
order to define his ideas and test his knowledge. The
letter continues :

"I begin to feel more than ever the responsible
office I have undertaken. May God make me faithful! Pray for me. My happiness in this life and in
the life to come, my usefulness to others will greatly
depend on the principles and resolutions which I now
adopt. There is a high way and a low one in the
Wesleyan ministry, and I may walk in the low one
without being excluded from the Connexion. There
is a path of self-denial, diligence, and zeal, often to
be trodden at the risk of offending those who are accounted sober Christians, and those perhaps 'leading
men'; but its reward here is certain ministerial success, and in the world to come a hundred-fold.

"On the other hand, I may make the life of a
minister subservient to the life of a scholar, and pass
my time in literary ease, and compose sermons to
gratify my own taste and that of a few select friends,
while the poor would no longer have the gospel
preached to them. I may drink wine, and feast with
them that 'make provision for the flesh to fulfil the
lusts thereof'; I may laugh with jesters and be
esteemed a merry companion—yes, and without going
out of Methodist company either. Again I say, pray
for me ; pray that I may live with eternity, God, and
a 'world that lieth in wickedness,' constantly in view ;
that love to God and men may constantly fill and
rule my heart and life ; and then, if I thus honour

God, He will honour me, and I shall shine as a star
for ever and ever.   Once more, *pray for me.*"

At the July examination it is customary for each
candidate to present a list of the principal books
that he has read, and some of those who stood
side by side with Mr. Hellier as candidates in the
Morning Chapel at City Road still remember the
amusement that his list gave the examiners.   He
felt it his duty to name *every* book he had read ; and
when the long enumeration ended with the Bible,
the Hymn-book, *Punch*, and the *Pickwick Papers*,
the assembly broke into hearty laughter, in which
he himself joined.

In after days he became a member of the July
Committee, and for thirty successive years was
never absent from it.   His carefully preserved "July
Records" are fully annotated, and the character of
the candidate's book-list is constantly remarked
upon as indicating the degree of his anxiety for self-
improvement.

CHAPTER II.

COLLEGE AND CIRCUIT LIFE.

1844–1857.

IN the September of 1844 Mr. Hellier entered the Wesleyan Theological Institution at Richmond.

The Institution staff consists of a "Governor" and two or more "Tutors." If we were to substitute for these terms those of "Principal" and "Professors," they would not indeed be strictly applicable, seeing that the Governor is of no higher standing than his colleagues, and possesses no manner of jurisdiction over them ; but they would probably convey to the general reader a more accurate idea of the nature of these offices.

Mr. Hellier's tutors were the Revs. Thomas Jackson and John Farrar ; and as he himself testified, he "owed them for their instruction and example a debt of gratitude, which it was as pleasant to acknowledge as it was impossible to discharge." [1]

He is described as being at this time intensely shy and diffident in manner, even to awkwardness. In appearance he was noticeable for his shock of fair

---

[1] *Memoir of Rev. M. C. Taylor*, p. 23.

hair, his fresh complexion, and very blue eyes. But
his expression seemed to some to be wanting in animation ; and when for the first time he took his seat
at the College table, this fact provoked an unfavour-
able comment from one of the other men. "Stop,"
said another of keener vision, "you are mistaken ;
there is something in him." "You always do say
that," was the retort, "if a man looks more unpromising than usual." His defender was Michael
Coulson Taylor, soon to become his most intimate
friend.

The following picture of him as a student is from
the pen of one of the few fellow-students who still
·survive him :[1]

"He looked about the youngest of his year, while
in manner and general character he was anything but
a *young* man. His attainments when he entered Richmond were considerably higher than those of the
average of the students of that year, and he at once
took his place in the classes for advanced studies.
From the first he was a general favourite, attracting
to himself, without art or effort, the love of all the
brethren. Among the senior students in residence
at that time the most prominent was M. C. Taylor.
There was between him and Mr. Hellier a strong
intellectual and spiritual affinity. They became
friends at sight, and were 'lovely and pleasant in their

[1] Letter from the Rev. John Walton, M.A., formerly missionary in South Africa, President of the Wesleyan Conference,
1887.

lives.' Grave, courteous, and sympathetic, wise and
devout, they did much for Richmond during those
years. Nothing could be more excellent than the
administration of that period when the saintly Thomas
Jackson and John Farrar ruled the college. It must,
however, be remembered that in such men as I have
named they had powerful auxiliaries, who contributed
not a little to their success—men whose character
gave strength to the best order of the college, and
elevation to its general tone. Some of us who were
partakers of the benefit have never forgotten our
obligations. The solid attainments of these men
commanded our respect, while their unvarying
brotherliness won our warm affection. At the same
time there was about Benjamin Hellier a gravity
beyond his years, and also a certain reserve. With
a few friends he lived in close intimacy—somewhat
apart. He was equable, cheerful, happy, but little
addicted to fun. A sufficiently keen sense of the
humorous he certainly possessed, and his enjoyment
of a good joke kindled into expression all over his
remarkably fine face, but was never suffered to break
the bounds in a ringing laugh. His relations with
his brethren did him much honour. His wise
counsel and encouraging sympathy, and the sort of
practical help it was so easy for him to render to men
whose advantages had been fewer than his own,
enabled him in various ways to lighten a brother's
care. One could not enjoy his friendship without
conscious self-improvement. His devout spirit made

him an acquisition in our weekly meetings for fellow-ship and prayer.   In the Class-meeting especially, his robust intelligence and rich experience found expression in refreshing testimony, which harmonised with all that we knew him to be as we observed him in daily life, and was greatly to our edification.

"The week-night preaching services in the old chapel at Richmond were conducted by the students, in the alphabetical order of their names.   The governor, the tutors, and the whole body of students were present. The sermon was an element in the probation of the young preachers.   Mr. Hellier's preaching I distinctly remember.   I suppose even then that men of insight discerned in him more than the germ of all that he subsequently became as a preacher.   Twenty years afterwards I heard him again.   I listened to the same man, the same voice, as the same vigorous mind set forth in luminous exposition the great themes of experimental and practical godliness.   Instructive teaching and forcible application were the charac-teristics of his riper ministry, and these qualities were very apparent in his early efforts.   In his Richmond days he was noticeable for his habitual use of the Greek Testament, and to the last it was his constant companion."

The friendships that Mr. Hellier formed while at college with his fellow-students were an inexpressible gain to him, and notably that "triple friendship" which he shared with Mr. Taylor and Mr. Geden.   It was there that he first realised the sense of brother-

hood which is such a distinguishing feature of the
Methodist ministry, and which became one of the
greatest joys of his life. No one, as he often said,
took more delight in the company of his brethren
than he did. Certainly no one could be more loyal
to them or love them better. He was generous in
his estimate of their gifts and character, jealous for
their reputation ; and to hear them unkindly criticised
or disparaged was one of the few things that could
make him look unhappy.

There is in his journal a brief character-sketch,
appreciative, candid, kindly, of every one of his fellow-
students, and many of these give striking proof of
the truth of his dictum that men rarely fail to justify
the estimate formed of them at college. Here, for
instance, we find descriptions of W M. Punshon as
" an eloquent preacher," J. D. Geden as " an incipient
Biblical scholar," and Samuel Coley as one " whose
ambition is to be a theologian."

One portraiture, however, he abandons in despair,
saying of Mr. Taylor, his closest friend of all : " But
I cannot describe thee, Michael ; and there is no need,
for I shall never forget thee, or my own vast obligations to thee."

" How many," he says, in the memoir already
quoted, " will remember the hours spent in Taylor's
study as some of the very happiest of their lives ! "
Almost every day, after dinner, " Taylor's levée " was
held there. There, on Monday afternoons, papers on
theological questions were read and discussed. On

Thursday mornings the arrival of the *Watchman* (the
Methodist newspaper of that day) filled the study
with men eager to learn the news, and after supper
the knot of talkers again assembled.   When all the
rest had gone, and the lights were out, Mr. Hellier
would often remain with his friend and talk on in the
dark.   It would be difficult to conceive of a friendship
more perfect than theirs in its mutual and deep affection, its unbroken trust, and the constant interchange
of intimate thought.

He deeply felt the responsibility of his college
associations, for as he once said : " Every student
exercises an incalculable amount of influence on the
spiritual state of all the rest."   And we find in
his journal expressions of deep anxiety lest he
should have done any of the men "an irreparable
injury " by the unprofitable nature of his intercourse
with them.   To the testimony already quoted we add
that of another fellow-student,[1] who says: "Without a thought of setting a superior example, he was
a beautiful pattern to us all.   Respected and beloved
by his fellow-students from the beginning, nevertheless, he was sometimes so preoccupied or absorbed
in thought as to prove their entertainment ; but he
was quite ready to laugh with the rest at the blunders
into which his absence of mind sometimes betrayed
him, as, for example, when he appeared at breakfast

---

[1] Letter from the Rev. E. J. Robinson, formerly missionary
in Ceylon, now a supernumerary minister at Bath.   He left
Richmond in 1846.

without his cravat, or with his black stock upside
down."

We learn from his journal that he considered his
absent-mindedness a serious fault, and laboured
earnestly to overcome it. There are other failings
named there which left no trace on his after-life, and
which we had never suspected. Of the habit of early
rising, for instance, which we thought a natural virtue,
he says, after repeated failures : " I see I shall never
accomplish it without much perseverance." He speaks
in one of his letters of " a slothful, slovenly habit of
mind which prevented him from doing anything
thoroughly or well." He complains of unguardedness
and want of charity in his conversation ; and of his
sermons he says : " The sentences have often been
loose in their construction, inelegant, and ungram-
matical. They have been wanting in lucidity of
arrangement, in illustration, but especially in application. Worst of all, I have been guilty in the pulpit
of gross misquotations of Holy Writ. The cause of
all my failings in sermonizing and in study generally
is *want of patience.*"

Unlike the students of to-day, he had abundant
time while at the Institution to pursue an independent course of study, without in any wise slighting
the college curriculum. He devoted this leisure to
acquiring a greater mastery of Latin, Greek, Hebrew,
German, French, English grammar and composition,
and Biblical literature ; being guided in his choice
of subjects by the maxim he had laid down, to do

only at the Institution what he could not do so well elsewhere.

He was then, as always, a great student of his Bible. He devoted a whole year while at college to a very careful and comprehensive study of the Epistle to the Romans. His sister remembers that he was able to recite almost, if not quite, the whole of this Epistle from memory. In his study of the Greek Testament he in later years constantly used Scrivener's edition, and accustomed himself to carry a visual image of each page in his mind, so that every quotation from it might recall the context as well. One of his friends, who tested his memory in this particular, could not find it at fault in a single instance.

In a letter to his father written from College, he makes a characteristic reference to an address delivered to the students by the President of that year, the Rev. William Atherton :

" He told us amongst other things that we ought to be ambitious to be *fit for* the very best places in the Connexion, but at the same time not to be over-anxious to *get* them. ' It is enough for you to know,' said he, ' that you are fit for these places ; whether you have them or not, is not of so much importance.' He then proceeded to say that such was the nature of our Society, that it was impossible for any one to be kept *under*, or kept *above*, his proper level. What the President stated is, I believe, the truth ; and if you live long enough you will see that if your son Ben deserves an important position in the Methodist

Church, he will have it ; and if he does not deserve one, then I am sure you would not wish for him to be placed in it. For my own part I am determined by God's grace to follow the President's advice. I will strive to deserve the very best post, but endeavour to be content with the worst, if that should be assigned me. At present I am well content. I would not, if I could, change my calling, my situation, my pro-spects, for those of any man living—not the Arch-bishop of Canterbury himself. I am quite sure that I am called of God to preach His ever-blessed gospel ; I am as sure that the body of the Wesleyan Metho-dists are as truly a part of the universal Church of Christ as any religious body whatever, and that there are as many of the true servants of Christ belonging to it as to any other Christian denomina-tion under the sun. I shall therefore consider it the highest honour I could enjoy, if I shall be accounted worthy to continue to serve Christ and this people to the end of my days."

It is interesting to read his estimate, from a student's standpoint, of the gifts required for an office he was afterwards destined to fill :

" The *House-governor* should be a man of no ordi-nary qualifications. His piety ought to be *eminent*, because he will inevitably determine by his own char-acter and conduct what the standard of religious attainment shall be in the Institution. With deep, fer-vent piety, he should unite a judgment uncommonly sound. His opinions on very many points, especially

H   3

Methodistic, will often be regarded as oracular ; and
if he errs, all the Institution will err with him. Besides, a sound judgment and an accurate knowledge
of human nature are essential in one who has to
govern young men ; for without these, characters will
be mistaken, and dealt with after a wrong fashion.
Kindly feeling towards all the students, and strict
impartiality, are equally necessary. Then it is exceedingly desirable that these advantages should
be recommended by rare intellectual endowments.
Young men are idolaters of intellect ; and if a man
is intellectually the superior of those who are in this
instance under his care, he can do with them anything
he pleases. A House-governor cannot do everything ; but if he be everything he ought to be, the
good he may do is incalculable. To form to habits
of piety and usefulness, of correct thinking and wise
action, the guides, in some cases the founders of
Churches—this is a great work indeed, and requires
great and uncommon qualifications."

In 1847 Mr. Hellier finished his College course,
and was appointed Assistant-Tutor at the Wesleyan
College at Didsbury, about five miles from Manchester. Dr. Hannah, Mr. Bowers, and Mr. Thornton
then constituted the College staff. Two years later
Mr. Thornton was succeeded by Mr. Crowther. The
great kindness shown by all of them to their young
colleague was never forgotten by him ; and his personal experience of the work and difficulties of his
office brought him into fuller sympathy with the suc-

cession of Assistant-Tutors, with whom he was for thirty years so happily associated.

He was at first greatly hampered and discouraged by his want of experience in teaching, and by his excessive diffidence and shyness; and his journal, even more than his letters to his friend Mr. Taylor, shows that he laboured under a constant sense of incompetence. To Mr. Taylor he writes:

> " DIDSBURY,
> "*Dec.* 13*th*, 1847.
>
> "Sometimes I feel thankful I am here; at other times I am melancholy, and sigh for the Conference. My greatest trial is that I appear to myself to have undertaken responsibilities to which I am incompetent. You can imagine what a miserable thing it is to work hard all the while, and still be oppressed with a constant feeling of shortcoming. Of course I do not tell the men that I am incompetent, but they must have found it out ere now; yet they are most kind and respectful. I marvel at it. They are in truth, take them as a whole, a fine-spirited set of men. The majority, I should say, are very good preachers. Many are very diligent students; though some study more according to their own device than after the plan of the Institution, which is of course a mistake. Of some it may be said (to quote Crook, our Irish brother) that 'they might be lawfully married to hard study, seeing they are in no wise near akin to it.'"

Turning from his own testimony to that of the pupil
quoted above, we find that the incompetence he
laments was less evident to others than he supposed.

"I was among the first band of students who were
privileged to be under his care.

"I was in the classes under the care of the Rev.
W. L. Thornton, M.A., but was in the Hebrew class,
and also another, conducted by Mr. Hellier, and
thus was in constant intercourse with him. He was
a model tutor, wakeful and deeply solicitous as to
our progress, truly kind, and full of sympathy. He
encouraged the asking of questions in the class on
points of difficulty, and I never remember to have
seen him at a loss for a satisfactory answer. He
left the Greek Testament in the hands of Mr. Thornton, and seemed to prefer the Hebrew, in the teaching of which he was even then a master. I am
quite sure that none of his surviving students can
forget his devoted efforts to awaken in them a love
for the study of the sacred text, like that which
glowed in his own bosom.

"It so happened that I occupied a seat next him
at the dining-table on his right hand, and thus
became very familiar with him from day to day.
He frequently brought me to his study and also to
walk in the neighbourhood around Didsbury, and
spoke many words of encouragement from time to
time, which I hope were not altogether lost. I was
appointed to a circuit in 1848, and hence ceased to
know him in the capacity of tutor; but the intimacy

which commenced at Didsbury deepened into a
warm, loving regard in after-years, when I frequently
met him both in Ireland and England, and always
felt better as I grasped his friendly hand, and realized
the inspiring power of his look.   When at Didsbury
he was truly brotherly in his intercourse with the
students, and they all loved him.   In after-years,
when I saw him again and again as House-governor
of Headingley, like a father among his children, I
felt that if ever a man had found the sphere of
action which he was pre-eminently qualified by
nature, culture, and tone of character to fill, Benjamin
Hellier was that man.   It was a rich blessing to
the Methodist Church that for so many years, so
large a number of the rising ministry were brought
up under the devotional power of the spirit and
example of so noble a man.

"I sincerely hope that a goodly number of his
sermons have been left so far finished as to admit
of publication.   I well remember a series of sermons
on the Parables, which were remarkably fresh and
interesting, and also some sermons on Sanctification
preached in Dublin, which attracted great attention
for their clearness, richness, and great force of style.
He was a man whom none who knew can ever
forget."[1]

We quote again from his correspondence with
Mr. Taylor.

---

[1] Letter from the Rev. W. Crook, D.D., Newry, Ireland.

M. C. Taylor to B. Hellier

"*Jan.* 17*th*, 1848.

"I have at home two letters of yours from Didsbury unanswered. The impression they have given me is that you are not so comfortable as at Richmond. I expect, however, to hear less and less of this tale the longer you stay. You know well how unapproachable and incomprehensible you are until some one 'grasp the nettle, like a man of mettle,' and then you 'soft as silk remain.' I hope some of your pupils or companions will make the experiment; it would be a happy thing for the adventurer and yourself. But it were a better thing if you would assume the aggressive. Mark out your man, and make him your friend. Your victory is certain, if you will only *come out* and show yourself. You told me once, we were to expect grace would conquer nature. Pray get grace, or set nature against nature—your heart against your face,—and create friends, even at Didsbury, as you want them."

B. Hellier to M. C. Taylor.

"DIDSBURY,

"*Oct.* 21*st*, 1848.

"Again and again I think of Richmond, and live over and over its happy hours; and often, while I think of you especially, I 'feel my heart strangely warmed.'   I have sometimes thought thus : 'How frail I am! how prone to sin! How ready

to forget God and to depart from Him! It may
be that some day I shall go astray.' Now when I
have had these thoughts, it has occurred to me that,
next to the stirrings of the Holy Spirit, nothing
would tend to reclaim me from sin, or from any
degree of departure from God, more readily than
the warning and reproof of that friend whom I love
as my own soul. Now, my dear Taylor, I most
sincerely and earnestly conjure you that whenever
you hear of my growing cold towards God and
His cause ; whenever you hear anything said of me
discreditable to my character, be it truth or calumny,
tell me at once. I think you cannot offend me. I
know you, and can bear from you what I could
hardly bear from another ; and therefore I again
beseech you that should any occasion arise such as
I have indicated, you will not spare me.

" My own reading of late has been very limited.
I have to work very hard at classical and other
studies in order to do my work as Tutor with any
show of decency. I am entirely responsible for
Hebrew and Euclid, beside [taking classes in] Latin
and Greek. I read no theology, but give a good
deal of time to the English, Greek, and Hebrew
Scriptures. Within the last three months I have
read through the Greek New Testament, examining
every word which presented difficulty with Liddell
and Scott's Lexicon. I intend to go over the ground
again with Bruder's Concordance (a glorious book),
Robinson, and Schleusner. I still follow the plan of

'getting up' the different Scripture books, and some-
times write an outline of an epistle from memory.
I find this practice the most valuable I ever adopted.
I have lately read in German the first volume of
Neander's *History of the Planting of the Christian
Church.* It is not all gospel ; but I never read a
work from which I gained more light on the New
Testament."

                    " Didsbury,
                        "*Jan. 29th,* '49.

"I believe I am in some measure growing in
grace. I am at least more impressed with the necessity of oneness of aim—of studying the promotion
of God's glory, and of being indifferent to my own.

"Of late I have thought frequently of those words :
'The Lord thy God is a *jealous* God.' Is it so ?
Then if I seek my own glory, God regards me as His
rival, and will disappoint all my purposes. I find
it a difficult thing to aim at doing good for the
sake of doing good, and not for the sake of being
thought good ; but still I try, and hope that I am
more content than I once was to be just what God
would have me be. I have considerable comfort in
my work in the Institution. I have learned a secret,
that if I ask it at God's hands He will help me to
meet a Hebrew class. Of my preaching I will say
nothing, except I say what Naaman did : 'The Lord
pardon thy servant in this thing.'

"You will be glad to hear that I have recently
commenced a class at Heaton Mersey. One Sunday

afternoon I went to the Sunday school, delivered an address, and invited those who wished to save their souls to meet me in the vestry, that I might take down their names for meeting in Class. I obtained about a dozen names. I have now on my book seventeen—sixteen never met before. Their ages range, I suppose, from twelve to eighteen. A good work has been going on in the place. Last Wednesday, after Class, we held a prayer-meeting. There was a spiritual whirlwind, but I trust the Lord was in it. Three found peace. I shall not rest until they all find mercy, and have good hope that all will soon."

Writing to his sister, in reference to this class, he says :

" Need I say I am greatly interested in my work ? They come right away from the factory just as they are. Am I to slight them because they are young ? I love them all the more ; for I am young too, and I intend to be young as long as I can."

He also visited all the Methodist Society at Dids-bury, and many of the neighbouring poor, and did not omit the students from his pastoral care. These last he invited from time to time to accompany him in his walks, with the view of engaging them in profitable conversation ; although his shyness, and his tendency at that time to self-absorption, made the duty peculiarly difficult. And his journal records a further obstacle :

"I find my want of good conversational powers. I must try to cultivate a talent. Much may be done by persevering effort, and I am strongly persuaded of the vast advantage which a Christian minister possesses who is able to render his conversation generally agreeable."

During his residence at Didsbury he had a serious and prostrating attack of hæmorrhage from the lungs, and for nine months was unable to preach. With regard to the uncertainty of his life at this time he writes:

"I have both a natural desire of life, and a wish to live, that I may glorify God and serve the nation and age in which I live; but God only knows whether by continuance here I shall be useful to others, or rather, stand in the way of better men. I am resolved therefore in the strength of God's grace to be anxious about one thing, and only one: to strive to give up myself fully each day to the service of God, to glorify Him with all my powers, and to do all possible good to those about me. Thus I shall be prepared for every event of God's providence—for life or for death."

At the Conference of 1850 he was ordained, and in reference to this event says in his journal: "I mentally vowed to God two things: to be much in prayer, and to visit the poor. May the Lord give me grace to be faithful!"

In the April of the year following he was married to Miss Harper, in Portland Chapel, Bristol, where he had worshipped when a boy, and where her family had been members for five generations.   On her mother's side she was descended, like himself, from John Wesley's friends at Chew Stoke.   Of her we are not allowed to speak as our hearts would dictate.   Suffice it to say in his own words that the happiness of their marriage "not only equalled his expectations, it surpassed them."   We may also apply to his experience the words he used respecting that of his friend, when writing under similar restraint : " The married life then commenced was an exceedingly happy one.   I believe it may be said with confidence that its happiness was never marred by one word of unkindness or one moment of distrust." [1]

By his marriage, Mr. Hellier had three daughters and two sons.   One son died in infancy.   His wife and four children survive him.

And now began his brief experience of circuit life. Those were anxious and troubled days for Methodism. The spirit of disaffection and complaint agitated a very large proportion of her people, and thousands seceded from her ranks.   Much bitterness of feeling existed against many of her ministers, and " Stop the supplies ! " became a popular cry.   The Methodists who remained true to their allegiance exerted themselves even beyond their power to supply their brethren's lack of service, while the ministers felt their straitened means to be the least momentous phase of these times of peril.   Mr. Hellier shared with

---

[1] *Memoir of Rev. M. C. Taylor*, p. 79.

his brethren an intense anxiety for the fate of their Church, and he took his share of privation also. It has sometimes been asserted that he knew nothing of the hardships of circuit life, but though his experience of them was short, it was none the less real ; and while it is quite true that he knew far less of them than many of his brethren, it is equally a fact that he acquired a personal knowledge of the work of a circuit, of its toils and difficulties as well as its delights, which did much to aid him in the task of preparing young men for labour in the same sphere. In the first eight years of his married life he had eight different residences, and the first three years were spent in lodgings. Then, and for many years after he went to the Institution, he experienced the cares and straits that are occasioned by a very narrow income, and his duties were frequently discharged under the heavy burden of feeble health.

His first circuit was Birkenhead (Sept., 1851, to Sept., 1854) ; his second and last, Islington (Sept., 1854, to Sept., 1857). The following letter to Mr. Taylor shows with what feelings he entered upon his new life :

" SEACOMBE,

" *Sept. 8th*, 1851.

" I am allowed by the circuit £120 a year, and out of this I must find everything. We shall, I believe, contrive to make this do. I have been very kindly received by the people, and there seems to be a prospect of doing good. I was very much blessed during

the first service at Birkenhead. When giving out the
first hymn in the morning's service, a view of the
awful solemnity of the work to which I had committed myself seemed at once to open before me. At
that moment I felt, more deeply I think than I ever
did before, how weak and worthless I was. I could
not refrain from tears, and found some difficulty in
proceeding with the service. What a blessing it
would be if I could always feel my own weakness as I
felt it then ! My dear friend, I purpose to give myself
anew to God's great work. What have I to do but
to teach and preach Jesus Christ ? Everything else
is impertinence and folly."

It was upon entering on circuit life that Mr. Hellier
began to aim more especially at being " an economist
of time," and to cultivate those systematic habits
which became to him afterwards a second nature.

On Monday morning he made a plan of the week's
work, choosing at the same time the text from which
he intended to preach at each service. This plan,
when corrected at the end of the week, served as his
diary. It was his invariable rule to preach his new
sermons on the Sunday to his largest congregation.
This insured adequate pulpit preparation for the week-
night appointments, and enabled him to visit among
his people until the hour of service, with a mind free
from anxiety about his sermon. He kept a list of
the members of his different congregations carefully
drawn up according to their residences and by setting

out each afternoon, and visiting those who were in his line of route to the chapel, he was able, even in so wide a circuit as Islington then was, to visit all his flock with some degree of regularity. His calls were never purposeless, but strictly pastoral ; and in cases of serious illness he paid daily visits. He had a very high estimate of the value of this work, and his constant advice to his students when they were about to begin circuit life was : "Visit your people, or you will not know how to preach to them." His excessive shyness made the duty at first a very difficult one, but experience taught him to regard it as a privilege.

"I love this work," he writes ; "I find visiting our people in all their vicissitudes of health and sickness, sorrow and joy, to be admirable moral discipline. It cultivates one's best feelings, and is a preservative against selfishness."

He spent his mornings in his study ; and during these hours, as the only means of securing him the uninterrupted leisure necessary for his pulpit-work, his wife saw all his callers for him, except his colleagues. From twelve to one o'clock was his hour of prayer, jealously guarded from all encroachment. When he became a tutor, the time was necessarily changed, but the habit continued ; and one of the earliest facts impressed upon our minds was that at a set time the study door was locked, and no one might disturb him.

He always aimed at finishing his preparation for

Sunday by noon on Saturday, and made the rest of the day a holiday. When in London, he and Mr. Taylor constantly spent their Saturday afternoons together, and of one of these occasions we quote his pleasant account :

"Last Saturday, Taylor and I went to Hampstead Heath, a lovely spot. The day being very fine, we greatly enjoyed our excursion. Amongst other things we discussed the question : Who was the most eminent man in Christendom in each century since the beginning of our era ? We afterwards agreed upon a list of names which has since been forwarded to Geden and Mottram for their comment and revising. Upham's works, Christian perfection, and American society and manners were some of our other topics. After tea we read together the first chapter of the first Epistle of John."

Mr. Hellier took deep interest in every department of his circuit work, in its financial affairs and the work of extension, and in the day and Sunday schools, which he regularly visited. He held Bible-classes for the young people, and took especial pains with the missionary prayer-meetings.

This routine of study, visitation, preaching, and other duties was maintained, as we have already said, amidst much physical weakness. He was never at any period of his life a robust man ; and, although generally presenting an appearance of vigorous health, he seldom knew what it was to feel perfectly well. The hæmorrhage from which he suffered at Didsbury was twice renewed soon after he went to Richmond in 1857 ; and hence, for many years, he expected his course to be brief, and would watch his children at play with a pleasure chastened by the sad foreboding that he should have to leave them in the world while they were still young. Even when suffering from no defined ailment, his spirits were often depressed, and his work hindered by a languor which frequently made continuous mental application an impossibility. To be so continually checked in his beloved studies, and rendered unable to use to the utmost advantage the time which he so carefully economized, was one of the principal sources of his life's discipline. Not the least part of the trial was the feeling that others might judge him indolent, while he himself was conscious of having gone to the very end of his strength. Touching this uncertain state of health and the imputations of idleness it might bring upon him, he writes :

" I thank God that all this discipline has proved beneficial to me. It has led me, I trust, to aim more simply than ever at one object—the glory of God. I must 'please all men for their good,' but the end aimed at in all things must be to please God. Milton calls the love of praise 'that last infirmity of noble minds'; but Paul could say, ' Neither of men sought we glory.' My ambition is to be free from ambition. It seems to me, God means to bring me to this point of aiming at His glory, and at that alone. It is not necessary that I should be strong in body, or in mind, in order that God may use me as an instrument to accomplish His purposes, but it is necessary that I be strong in faith, and pure in motive."

The later ' years of his life were also the most vigorous, but at no period was he able to bear any extraordinary strain upon his energies ; and it was only by confining himself to his proper routine of work that he maintained a moderate degree of health. We have felt it necessary to emphasize this fact, because it is the explanation of his having made so few contributions to our Methodist literature.

While yet a student at college, he had devoted much study and careful thought to the subject of preaching, with a view to determine the kind best calculated to do good ; and he acted throughout his ministry upon the conclusions at which he then arrived.

Persuaded that preaching ought to be "eminently scriptural," he adopted for himself the expository style ; and this he further defined as "the development of the leading thought of the text." There was no rule of preaching to which he adhered more resolutely. Not merely did he judge it the surest means of securing that logical method which Coleridge defines as "unity with progression" (a saying he loved to quote), but he felt that in choosing the leading thought of any portion of the inspired word as the leading thought of his sermon, he was submitting his own judgment to the wisdom of God. Acting upon this principle, he never isolated a passage from its context, nor gave it an interpretation which he did not believe it was originally intended to bear. Every text moreover, he was wont to say, contains truth not to be found elsewhere in the Bible under that precise aspect; so that conformity to this rule secures for a man's preaching variety of the best kind—the variety of Scripture.

His expositions were never hazy, partly because he never undertook to explain to others anything not perfectly clear to his own mind.

A further conclusion of his was to employ much illustration, since, in order to instruct, it is necessary to interest. The example of the great Teacher made him feel the duty of acquiring this practice, and experience and observation also enjoined it. The power to illustrate was not one of his natural gifts, but he cultivated it carefully, and used it with good effect.

He considered the most effective, and therefore the best style to be "the simple and direct." That of Addison had a great fascination for him, but he refrained from taking it for his model, because it seemed to him too elegant and finished for use in the pulpit, where the object is to arouse and excite. He had no ambition to be eloquent, but he was exceedingly anxious to be understood by every member of his congregations. And though style was never to him an end in itself, he devoted much pains towards making it the clearest possible medium for his thought. With this object in view he studiously avoided Latinisms, and made his sentences short, and

simple in structure. He attached great importance
to this latter point, saying that a preacher often
failed to make himself understood by uneducated
people, not because his ideas were beyond the reach
of their intelligence, but for the simple reason that
he placed the verb too far from its nominative case.
Very welcome was the tribute once paid to him by
an old woman, who thanked him for his sermon with
special fervour, on the ground that her own ministers
were so learned she could not understand them and
was glad of a change! It was a great pleasure to
him to find that little children enjoyed his ministry,
and many of them remember him as the first preacher
who ever interested them. "The best preaching of
all," he often said, "is *common preaching;* that is, the
preaching which commends itself to the understanding
and conscience of all classes of hearers."

When making a sermon, he usually began by
writing out his text in full in the original, and he
found the practice a safeguard against errors of exposition. This done, he defined in brief terms the
object of his discourse. The introductory notes to
the sermon on 2 Corinthians v. 13–15 (contained in
this volume) illustrate to some extent his methods of
preparation.[1] Then there frequently followed a complete analysis of the discourse, constructed on strictly
logical method. He thought the study of logic the

---

[1] See Sermon on "The Purpose of God in Christ as Taught
by the Apostle Paul:" Part II., Section i.

best means for securing sequence of thought, and said that it was easy to tell from any sermon whether the preacher had ever studied the art. He wrote out his sermon in full, because the process helped him to define and clarify his ideas; but he never preached it exactly as it was written, nor took notes of it into the pulpit, nor did he commit any of it to memory. The first sentence and the last were always determined beforehand, but for the rest he held himself free to incorporate any fresh matter that came to him while preaching. It was his aim to combine by this means the advantages of careful preparation and arrangement with the freshness and interest of extempore utterance.

He never ceased to make new sermons. Those of earlier date are very closely packed, full of carefully wrought out exposition, with many subordinate ideas clustering round the central thought of the sermon. In later years he usually expanded, applied, and illustrated this to the exclusion of all the rest. Then too, as he appeared but seldom before the same congregation, a deepening sense of the importance of each occasion directed his attention mainly to the fundamental truths of the gospel, and he sought more and more to secure their instant acceptance by the unconverted. Repentance towards God, faith in our Lord Jesus Christ, life and religion co-extensive and identical—these were the prevailing themes of his ministry.

He was not what is known as a "successful revi-

valist," and to his deep and abiding regret saw but
little immediate fruit of his preaching, although it
was not entirely wanting. In preaching repentance
he seldom gave invitations to the "inquiry room";
but he did constantly urge his hearers to decide
then and there for Christ, and to give immediate
and practical evidence of their decision by an act of
restitution if needs be, or of forgiveness and reconciliation, or by communicating their resolve to some
friend or member of their own household, before the
day closed. We believe this method to have been
followed with the best results ; and we remember one
instance in particular when an only son, acting on
this counsel, told his parents, on his last Sunday at
home before entering on business life, that he had
also entered the service of Christ.

He paid great attention to elocution, and the
importance he attached to the art is evident in the
following letter written to a friend who had failed to
make himself distinctly heard by his congregation :

"You have hitherto thought it beneath your dignity
to attend at all to elocution. It might do well enough
for Demosthenes and Cicero to attend to such trifles,
but you think it beneath you ! I ask, Is that a trifle
on which the salvation of immortal souls is dependent?
'Faith comes by *hearing*, and hearing by the word
of God. How shall they hear without a preacher?'
And how shall they hear a preacher, who satisfies
himself with preaching, without inquiring whether he
is heard or not ?

"I shall not be satisfied until you do all that in you lies to become a great orator. You have. better reasons for labouring to be so than Demosthenes or Cicero ever had. Did you ever take as much pains to cultivate the mechanical part of the art of speaking, as any second-rate pleader at the bar ? If not, I call upon you to give me one sound reason, at least, why you have not done so."

His own study of elocution did not, however, result in any kind of mannerism. He had no distinctive pulpit-manner, and in voice and gesture was perfectly simple and natural. At the same time, the reverence and the heartfelt interest with which he conducted public worship were always impressive, and gave unity and life to the service. Nothing was perfunctory, nothing dragged; and where the preacher was so full of quiet energy, and manifested such delight in praising God, it was difficult for the congregation to be apathetic. He often arrested attention by his manner of giving out the opening hymn, invariably one of praise. He did not declaim it, but in clear, natural tones that easily filled the chapel, read it deliberately, so entering into its spirit that the congregation was stirred also. He had made a thorough study of our Hymn-book and its history, and in his selection of hymns was careful and critical. In his view a hymn, strictly so called, must have the fervour of intense feeling superadded. to poetic power ; and any that lacked this lyrical quality, and only consisted of statements and descriptions in verse, he did not admit to be hymns at all.   It was on account of their lyrical power and pathos that he so peculiarly prized Charles Wesley's compositions, and as a hymn-writer judged him unrivalled.

He held very defined views about what is some-times called "the dignity of the pulpit," and dissented from those who considered it impaired by the use of anecdote, homely illustration, or every-day language. The one point on which he insisted with all possible emphasis, was that whether matter or manner were concerned, that only was beneath the dignity of the pulpit which conveyed the impression that the preacher was wanting in moral earnestness.   Nothing, he said, is more fatal to a man's usefulness in the pulpit than a suspicion that he is not intensely in earnest.

But earnestness is not incompatible with a degree of humour, and the frequent touches of it with which his home thrusts were accompanied, were very telling and characteristic.

It was an early resolution of his "to make the doctrine of Christian holiness particularly prominent " in his preaching.   And in making a selection from his manuscripts on the subject for this volume, we have been struck with the fact that *all* his sermons bear upon it more or less directly, while of a very large proportion it is the express topic.

The subject of Christian holiness was in a very special degree under his consideration during his life in Islington.   He speaks in his journal of being "intently and continually occupied with it," of "reading, conversing, praying, and preaching much upon the doctrine," and he seems there to have obtained more definite views and more definite experience with regard to it.   He continued to study it throughout his life, and greatly desired to write a work on holiness.   Indeed, he accumulated much material for the purpose, but pronounced and defined as his views were on the most essential features of this subject, he never, we believe, considered that he had reached his full and final conclusions on the whole question, and the project was therefore abandoned.   Practically he defined holiness as the fulfilment of the Divine precept : "Whether therefore ye eat, or drink, or whatsoever ye do, do all to the glory of God" ; and he often quoted one of Charles Wesley's verses as containing as good a "working definition" of it as could be wished :

> "End of my every action Thou,
>   In all things Thee I see :
> Accept my hallowed labour now,
>   I do it unto Thee."

And to this idea of literally doing everything for Christ we find constant references in his journal. "Surely," he writes, "if I do every work with this thought in my mind—'I must do this for Christ, I must offer it to Him when done'—I shall feel bound to do it as well as ever I can.   I must not offer to the Lord a slovenly service or a limping sacrifice.   I must not preach slipshod sermons, or make foolish and empty speeches."

Here we find the reason of the careful preparation he made for every meeting, however small and unimportant. With the Master, rather than the occasion in view, he felt it impossible to do other than his best.

He did not, within our knowledge, ever profess to have attained entire sanctification, and yet no one would have more readily accepted such a statement than the members of his own family. And he himself records that he enjoyed "constant victory over inward and outward sin, perfect freedom from anxious care, and implicit trust in God." But he considered this experience to be negative, rather than positive. "In one sense, I think I am perfect in the love of God, inasmuch as I do not willingly allow myself in what is contrary thereto ; but in another sense, I am not perfect in love,—it does not produce in me all its legitimate fruits." He felt that the perfect state demanded an intenser joy, a more fervent faith, a more consuming zeal than he was conscious of possessing. He says, for example, respecting this last qualification : "I fear that I am, in one sense, too contented, too little troubled about my own defects and the want of prosperity in the Church. And yet the interests of God's cause are never out of my thoughts."

He was especially careful to keep this subject of holiness uppermost in the Class-meeting. He always

continued to prize the institution that first won him
to Methodism, and throughout his ministry was never
without a Society-class of his own.   There was no
part of his work that he enjoyed more.

On the first morning of the year 1856 his beloved
little son, Coulson Taylor, died suddenly.   " This," he
writes, " is the heaviest affliction I have ever known.
I feel resigned to the will of God, but there is a
keen sense of privation, a vacancy in the home and
in the heart which nothing can fill."   Henceforward
each new year came to him "with a reminder of
the uncertain nature of the tenure with which we
hold all our choicest gifts," and to his latest years he
loved to think of this little child as "treasure laid up
in heaven."

A few months later, his sister Harriet died also.
For all his sisters he cherished no ordinary love, and
she, through long years of illness, had become an
object of special tenderness, so that his letters to her
are quite remarkable for the intensity of affection they
express.

During Mr. Hellier's ministry in Islington, Dr.
Bunting was a member of the Liverpool Road congregation.   The young preacher felt a natural awe of
this great man, but in their frequent intercourse was
always received by him with a fatherly kindness and
generous appreciation which were very encouraging.
Dr. Bunting said more than once, that while he would
not choose to be shut up to the ministry of one man
only, yet if such were the case, he would as soon have

Mr. Hellier for his pastor as any man he had ever
known. And when the post of Classical Tutor at
Richmond was about to be vacated, Dr. Bunting
(then President of the Institution) at once nominated
him for the office. This nomination did not pass
unchallenged. Some members of the Committee had
misgivings about his scholarship, his energy and
liveliness, his power to maintain authority in the class-
room ; others thought his pulpit ability " not quite up
to the mark," and one friend expressed a fear lest he
should prove altogether too absent-minded for a tutor.
Mr. Hellier records all these objections in his journal,
with the quiet comment, " I find these criticisms very
edifying."

With regard to his powers of discipline and teaching, he writes :

" I do not think a tutor need be very much excited in the lecture-room, if only he secures the great
result of stimulating to energetic action the minds of
those whom he has to teach. This I am persuaded I
could accomplish. Besides, I greatly mistake my own
character if I did not, when placed in such a position,
feel a great deal of enthusiasm in my work. I have
a fear lest that enthusiasm for mere learning should
abate in any degree the higher enthusiasm which I
would ever cherish in all that relates to the service of
Christ and His Church. On the point of discipline, I
told the Committee that I could fully trust myself, if
they could trust me."

He was, however, disposed to shrink from a post

for which he did not feel himself fully equipped,
especially as his state of health at that time made
close application to study very difficult. Moreover,
the appointment involved a change in his life-work,
and he was very unwilling to give up his pastoral
charge. "On the other hand," he writes, "I magnify
the office of a Tutor in such an establishment as our
Institution. Just because I love Circuit work, I shall
be qualified to sympathize with those who are looking forward to it. If I have one qualification for
Richmond which is unquestionable, I think it is this :
I do not *over-value* learning. My love of learning
has not ceased ; but I regard it now, more than I did
formerly, simply as an *instrument*, valuable beyond
expression when wholly sanctified to Christ and used
only in His service, but worse than worthless when
sought and used in a selfish spirit and for selfish
ends."

We should like to draw attention here to the
manner in which many of his characteristics as a
young man were modified in after years, and in some
cases completely reversed. We have recorded his
regret that his lack of patience prevented him from
doing anything thoroughly or accurately ; but it is
not too much to say that thoroughness became
the pre-eminent characteristic of every part of his
work. He has been described as singularly grave
and absent-minded, with little or no powers of general
conversation, yet he became quite as noticeable for
his habitual cheerfulness; and though he did not

wholly lose his pre-occupied habits of mind, he exerted himself when in society to converse and give pleasure. And no one who has seen him in his happiest mood, among friends whom he trusted, especially his brother ministers, will easily forget the power of story-telling, the zest and kindliness, the frank enjoyment and hearty laughter, that made him the life of the party. "I think," said a busy professional man, with whom he came into contact for a few hours, "Mr. Hellier seems to have less on his conscience than any man I ever met with."

Of his cheerful mode of viewing life, we could give many illustrations. He never, for instance, admitted that there was such a thing as "miserable weather." Any one who met him in a drizzling November fog, with the comment, "What a miserable day!" was liable to the cheery but unexpected rejoinder: "Oh: no; it is nothing of the kind. The day does not feel miserable, I do not feel miserable, and if you do, you have no right to feel so."

He often took exception to the view of Christian service presented to us in a well-known and popular hymn. There the question is asked :

> "If I find Him, if I follow,
> What His guerdon here?"

The answer given is :

> "Many a sorrow, many a labour,
> Many a tear."

"This," he said, "is too melancholy a view of life

for me ; it smells of the cloister.   I very much prefer
the view taken by our own Charles Wesley, when he
says,—

> ' The Master of all
> For our service doth call,
> *And deigns to approve,*
> *With smiles of acceptance,* our labour of love.' "

Mr. Hellier had a certain reserve of manner, which
led some to fancy him unapproachable, though
children never made such a mistake.   He was quite
unconscious of it himself, and expressed surprise
when told that any one stood in awe of him.   When
such persons learned to know him, they shared the
surprise themselves, and to some who were in trouble
he seemed the first to whom they could go.

"He was," writes one, "a friend in need.   I am
acquainted with a minister, who, wondering how to
reach his new Circuit for want of means, secretly
determined to get to Richmond, and to reveal to
Mr. Hellier his lamentable straits.   'I happen to have
some sovereigns here,' remarked the kindly Tutor,
immediately opening his cash-box, and without the
slightest change of face turning the conversation to
other subjects.   To my knowledge, never was cheerful loan more gratefully received and repaid."   Of
course Mr. Hellier only did here what any Methodist
minister or layman would have done, but the way
in which the kindness was rendered was entirely
characteristic.

Others, again, thought that his serene, equable

temperament was due to a nature self-sustained, and independent of others ; but if he had any earthly ambition, it was for the love of friends, and their affection was indescribably precious to him. He was very valiant for his friends on occasion, ready to exercise in their behalf what one of them termed the "chivalry of his friendship." The only person he did not know how to defend was himself, and adverse criticism, instead of rousing his self-assertion, silenced and depressed him. On the other hand, few perhaps realized how greatly he was moved and cheered by words of kindness. His heart was exceedingly tender ; and though oratory that was designed to work upon the emotions stirred him not a whit, he could seldom relate a fine action, or an instance of fine feeling, without a falter in his voice. Above all, his deepest feelings were called forth when dwelling upon the theme of Christ's love as manifested in His tenderness to little children, and His compassion for sinful men. One of the most vivid pictures of him our memory retains is as we have often seen him in the pulpit, when he " stood as one that pleaded with men," his face lit with eager love, his hands out-stretched, his tones tender, solemn, beseeching, his vivid sense of the Divine love and pity thrilling many hearts besides his own.

CHAPTER III.

I N September, 1857, Mr. Hellier returned as Tutor
to the College endeared to him by the memories
and associations of his student days.[1] Mr. Geden
was appointed at the same time Classical Tutor at
Didsbury ; Mr. Taylor was already Secretary of the
Wesleyan Normal Training Institution at Westminster; and these three College friends, thus early
claimed for the teaching óffice, found in it their true
vocation, and never left it until their day's work was
done.

Mr. Taylor laboured at Westminster, with singular
power and self-devotion, until his strength was spent,
and passed away in the prime of life, many years
before his two friends, on March 8th, 1867.

Mr. Geden lived to attain distinction as a Biblical
and Oriental scholar, and he was elected a member
of the Old Testament Revision Company. Like

---

[1] A view of Richmond College is given on the opposite page.
The foot-path crossing the lawn leads to the Tutor's house.

4

RICHMOND COLLEGE.

From a Photograph by MR. SEELEY, *of Richmond*

Mr. Taylor, failing health compelled him to lay down his office, and after many months of illness he too entered into rest, on March 9th, 1886.

Two years later, and on the twenty-first anniversary of Mr. Taylor's death, the third and last of these friends was called home to God.

Mr. Hellier had scarcely begun his new Richmond life when he was obliged to remove to the Institution House, owing to the illness and death of the Governor, Dr. W M. Harvard ; and until the next Conference, he united the Governor's office with his own.

In September, 1858, he had the happiness of welcoming as the new Governor the Rev. Alfred Barrett, and as Assistant-Tutor the Rev. W F (now Dr.) Moulton.   Dr. Moulton's appointment was secured at Mr. Hellier's suggestion, and by his efforts, at the Conference of that year.   He was fond of speaking of this as "perhaps the best day's work he ever did in his life."   Mr. Thomas Jackson, his old Theological Tutor, still held office, and upon his retirement in 1861 was succeeded by the Rev. John Lomas, one of Mr. Hellier's first and best teachers in Divinity.

It is an easy matter for a Methodist preacher to find good colleagues, but surely in this respect few men have been so singularly happy as Mr. Hellier. In the specially close associations of College life it was his privilege at Didsbury, Richmond, and Headingley to labour with men whom he greatly loved and honoured, and in an unbroken harmony, with a unity

H.   5

of spirit and aim that gave peculiar force to their common influence over the students. And though we have only to speak here of the work of one of the Institution staff, we by no means forget his fellow-workers. Many of them are still in our midst; but from among this band of colleagues, Thomas Jackson, John Lomas, Alfred Barrett, John Farrar, and Samuel Coley have, with him, joined the Church above.

Of the first named of these we give a picture in Mr. Hellier's own words, a life-like picture; and yet in reading it we cannot fail to recognise traits common to them all. It is taken from a sermon on the First Psalm, preached on the Sunday following Mr. Jackson's death:

" But the good man's character as here described is not only steadfast and strong, it is also beautiful —'like a tree planted by the rivers of water.' What a beautiful object such a tree often is! Deeply rooted in the earth, and towering aloft in very majesty of strength, it is a shelter from the storm of winter, a screen from the heat of summer. We repose beneath its shadow, we refresh ourselves with its goodly fruit; we delight to listen to the sweet melody of the birds which sing among its branches.

" But lovely as such a sight is, that of a truly good man is still more lovely. Such men I have known. Such a man I lately knew. He has passed to his reward, but in my mind's eye I see him now. A venerable man with a hoary head, which is indeed 'a crown of glory.' He has been my teacher, my

example ; he is now my friend. He has grown strong
in virtue amidst many a storm, and in principles
of goodness is rooted like the oak. But he is not
sternly good. He wears the bloom of a Christian
character, untarnished by reproach during a religious
profession of more than seventy years. To look
upon his pleasant, happy countenance is a delight ;
to converse with him is a means of grace ; to join
in his prayers is to gain a new stimulus to run the
heavenly race. Some of you will know that I speak
of the venerable Thomas Jackson, who on Monday
last was gathered home to God. He has entered
into rest, but in generations to come there are scores
and hundreds that will call him blessed. Why are
such men beautiful in their character? Why are
they full of good fruit? Why even unto old age do
they maintain the vigour and loveliness of their piety?
The text answers the question. They are 'planted
by the stream'—they live in constant communion
with God, and the Divine Spirit whom they seek
dwells in them. He it is who sheds over their
character the bloom that delights the eye ; He it is
who produces in them that good fruit of theirs by
which the Church and the world are blessed."

It is at Richmond that our own first memories
of our father begin. Our home was in the College
grounds, a little ivied house, with trellised porch
overhung with jessamine, roses, and clematis, sheltered
by lofty elms and chestnuts. On either hand were
the wide, well-kept lawns, beautiful in spring with

their wealth of flowering shrubs, in summer with their brilliant flower-beds and borders, and at all times with their stately trees. An indescribable charm of peace pervaded the whole place, and to us it was an earthly paradise.

Just beyond the College gates lay the entrance to Richmond Park, and in this park he took no common delight. It was his daily and favourite resort, and he never wearied of its most beautiful scenery. Very often he was there at sunrise, and we have sometimes walked with him, watching the eastern skies brightening into day, while he recited to us from *L'Allegro* Milton's description of the dawn. Milton was a great favourite of his, and oftener quoted by him than any other poet except Charles Wesley. His other favourite was Homer, of whom he was wont to say, "As a poet no one has ever equalled him."

Our walks with him in the park were part of our education. He taught us there the names of the trees, and how to distinguish the birds by their various notes, and by many and pleasant devices tried to open our eyes to see and our minds to think.

In a letter written to Mr. Taylor, who was at that time ill at Westminster, he thus describes one of these walks, for the amusement of his friend :

"Yesterday I had a pleasant walk in the park with Lizzie, Sarah Anne (brother William's child), and Alice. Few visible signs of spring. There are crocuses in the grounds, fructification on the elms;

the lilacs are budding; but oaks, limes, beeches,
sycamores, and most other trees look as dead as
in December. The songs of the birds were very
pleasant. Thrushes sang famously, and we heard the
notes of the linnet, lapwing, starling, jackdaw, and
wood-pigeon. We looked into one of the farmyards
in the park, and saw hens and turkeys and geese
enjoying themselves in the sun, appearing to approve
of the warm spring day as well as ourselves. When
we came to the lakes we found them brilliant and
still as a mirror, and all the neighbouring trees were
most perfectly reflected. Here, there was a stately
swan, and some ducks were amusing themselves by
burying their heads under the water and turning
their tails uppermost at an angle of 90° with the
surface of the water.

"We had various amusements, such as my telling
the Latin names of all the objects which the children
could name. I did pretty well till Lizzie requested
the Latin for 'button.' I could only declare the
Romans had none (aren't you sorry for them?). Then
we guessed the distances between trees, I promising
to forfeit a halfpenny if any one was nearer than I.
We finished with a game of *cat*, which you probably
do not understand. But see the history of John
Bunyan in *Grace Abounding*."

He showed in many ways how much a busy man
can do for his children's education, without devoting
any stated time to the purpose. It was his constant
study, for instance, to make the conversation at table

both profitable and pleasant. In our early days he often asked us at tea-time for the "new ideas" we had gained during the day, adding something fresh and interesting of his own to whatever elementary statement of facts we could muster. And at all times we were encouraged to reproduce what we had read, and describe what we had seen. As a result of this, the thought of him was present wherever we went, leading us to note more carefully what we heard and saw, that we might enjoy everything over again by retailing it to him. And we knew well that if we missed from mere want of enterprise a sight worth seeing, in what accents of mingled surprise and disappointment he would say, "I wonder at you!" So far as we could observe, he never himself lost an opportunity of acquiring knowledge. He always took pains to draw out those with whom he conversed, on the subjects they best understood, and it was a constant interest to us to see how much information he managed to obtain from them. This was especially noticeable when his old students came to see him. Then, whether his visitor were from a poor Circuit, all the more interesting to him by reason of its poverty, or from a mission station in a distant land, he plied him with sympathetic and comprehensive questions that showed with how much attention and interest he had studied the nature of the work there.

One of his frequent injunctions to us was, "Always make sure of your facts." He never spared any pains necessary to verify his facts before asserting

them, and had an uncomfortable facility for finding
out when we had omitted to do this. Hazy statements and inaccurate conclusions were speedily
exposed by his searching questions.

It was a fundamental rule with him that conversation should be cheerful. His journal records
his desire "to glorify God by a holy cheerfulness."
Therefore, while he did not shrink from dealing
with disagreeable facts if the necessity arose, he
tolerated no useless or morbid canvassing of the sins
and sufferings of others. If any notorious case of
evil-doing were named in his presence, he would say
sorrowfully but promptly, "It is lamentable; do
not let us talk of it any more." Uncharitable conversation he hated, and we never saw him look so
thoroughly uneasy as when ill-natured remarks were
made by those whom he knew not how to silence.
Ministers, above all, were sacred from criticism. Once
in his lecture-room, when he was condemning some
form of pulpit mannerism, one of the class named a
certain minister as a case in point. "I think, sir,
you forget yourself," he answered instantly. "It
shall never be said that in my lecture-room my
brother ministers are held up as examples of defects."
Of course he never told us the name either of the
minister, or student, in question. Once or twice, when
much exercised in mind by what he held to be
neglect of duty on the part of some one of his
brethren, we have known him go so far as to say,
"I cannot at all understand Mr. ——." But we

do not remember any severer or more extended censure.

He was careful to enforce upon us the principle of strict obedience, but his direct injunctions and prohibitions were very few indeed. He said little to condemn " the world," but did much to commend Christ's service; and instead of hedging us about with restraints, made the Christian life attractive, and its happiness conspicuous.

The following description of him as a tutor has been furnished by one of his old students : [1]

"It gives me sincere pleasure to recall a few particulars concerning the Rev. Benjamin Hellier, in his capacity of *Classical Tutor* at Richmond.

"From the first it was evident that he set before himself *a definite aim.* It was not his object merely to make his students classical scholars, and fit them for academical distinctions. He never forgot that they were students in preparation for the Christian ministry. And consequently he bent his energies and adapted his instructions to the great object of fitting them for the pulpit and the pastorate. While leading them to the highest attainments they could reach in learning, he kept steadily before their view the thought, which doubtless acted as a powerful stimulus, that the final object of it all was to make them well-instructed and ' able ministers of the New Testament.'

---

[1] The Rev. Silvester Whitehead, of Southport, who left Richmond in 1866, and was ten years a missionary in China.

" In the class-room he was not the professor, but
eminently the tutor. He did not pour out his learning in the form of lectures, which every one could
appropriate, or otherwise, at pleasure, but grappled
with the minds of his students catechetically—not
only instructing, but exercising and drawing them
out. He welcomed their intelligent questions ; occasionally permitted discussion ; and from time to time
tested their ability and their progress by paper work.
He thus endeavoured to educate as well as to inform,
and to supply to each mind the necessary stimulus
and help in its growth and development.

" In all his work he gave the impression of *strength*.
The ease and confidence with which he dealt with
every subject made one feel that he possessed a considerable reserve of power and resource. He guided
the mind with a firm hand and a sure tread. Quick-
ness was not so much an object with him as thoroughness. He consequently bestowed care on minute
particulars. No particle in language could escape
him, nor would he permit it to escape a student. I
remember this particularly in his teaching of Hebrew.
He would sometimes trip up a man, who had managed to read and translate well enough, by some
point or accent, by ' dagesh lene ' or ' dagesh forte.'
It was evident that his aim was to lay the foundation
broad and deep, as for an enduring edifice, rather
than rapidly run up a flimsy structure of showy but
ephemeral scholarship.   ·

" In *manner*, Mr. Hellier was deemed somewhat

phlegmatic. And if any qualification must be admitted to tone down his tutorial excellences, so
many and sterling, it will be in this direction. Nevertheless he did not fail to evince real interest, and
sometimes even zest, in the subjects of study with
which he had to deal. A warmth of tone, a flashing
glance from beneath the beetling brows, or a significant movement of the massive head, would often
indicate his depth of feeling and excitement of mind.
But the impression conveyed by his general aspect
and demeanour was one of calm conscientiousness.

"Mr. Hellier treated his students as gentlemen, and
took it for granted, until the reverse was shown, that
each was conscientious and diligent. But he was not
slow to detect relaxed effort or any sign of heedless-
ness, and not pointless as to the way in which he
marked it. He could be quietly severe, though never
unkind, calm and yet cutting in his rebukes. There
was nothing of acerbity in his disposition, and his
temper was scarcely ever even ruffled, but his dis-
approval was on that account all the more painful.
It was like a reproof from the lips of passionless
rectitude. And sometimes it was pointed with
irony. Once, in his Rhetoric class, when criticizing a
student's sermon, which gave evidence of hasty and
slovenly preparation, he simply said, 'Well, brethren,
it would not be wise to spend more time in criticizing
the sermon of last night than the brother did in
making it, and therefore we will go to our Rhetoric.'
On another occasion, after pointing out the mean-

inglessness of some flowery passages in a sermon, he concluded with the words, 'Now we must preach differently from this, or we must cease to preach.' His words have been signally justified by the fact that both the brethren referred to have long since left the ministry, and I believe, 'ceased to preach.'

"These, however, were exceptional and extreme instances. Nothing could be more considerate, gentle, and dignified than his normal treatment of his students. Under a somewhat bluff exterior, one felt that he carried one of the kindest, warmest hearts. Though slightly reserved in manner and speech, he was nevertheless frank and unsuspicious in his spirit, and took a lively interest in the men who were under his care. One word against his character I never heard breathed. Expressions of admiration and approval were frequent. For myself, the more I knew him the more I revered and loved him, and his teaching, character, and example made such a powerful impression upon my mind, that I can never recall his name but with sincere and grateful affection."

To this we add the testimony of another Richmond student :[1]

"Among many benefits received from Mr. Hellier during my student days here, I may mention the

---

[1] The Rev. J. Agar Beet. Student at Richmond 1862–1864. Appointed Theological Tutor at Richmond, 1885 ; Fernley Lecturer, 1889. Author of Commentaries on Romans, Corinthians, etc.

following. He taught me the value of a consecutive study of Holy Scripture, of a deliberate and sustained effort to follow the writer's train of thought. The effect of reading with him in Greek the Epistle to the Ephesians has been with me ever since, and has moulded my entire subsequent thought and life. He called my attention to the importance of studying the *words* of the Bible, and especially of tracing the significance of New Testament Greek words to their Old Testament, Hebrew representatives. As an example of such words, I remember his treatment of ἅγιος in the light of its Hebrew representative, and, in some sense, ancestor. A marked feature of his teaching was his constant use of the Greek text of the New Testament as a means of developing the spiritual life. Words of his of this kind live in my memory to-day, and have often been to me a spiritual force. Above all, I was much impressed by the transparent reality of his whole life. In this there was a quiet grandeur, and a subtle power, worth more to me than words can tell. He raised my entire conception of the possibility of human excellence. To exert such an influence on my students would be my highest ambition, if it were within reach of my hope.

" He required time to grasp a matter ; but in the end gained a view of it deeper and broader than do ordinary men. He ever traced details to great principles, and he saw the far-reaching influences of principles. This method of study was a great gain to me.

" This is a poor recognition of a debt I can never pay, a debt due to the common Lord of teacher and pupil."

Mr. Hellier's life while at Richmond was congenial and happy, and its chief events, apart from its quiet routine, were his visits to Conference and to his old home at Wick St. Lawrence. While visiting his parents there in the summer of 1860, he had the happiness of uniting with his brother, Mr. William Griffin Hellier, to introduce Methodism into their native village. His brother, to whom he had expressed a wish to preach at the village cross, suggested his own kitchen as a more convenient place, and here the first service was therefore held. More than a hundred people assembled in the kitchen and the adjoining passage, and Mr. Hellier preached from the text : " The sluggard will not plough by reason of the cold ; therefore shall he beg in harvest, and have nothing " (Prov. xx. 4).[1] Among his audience was "old Lambert," oldest among his father's farm-servants, who seems by his comment on the occasion to have found the sermon disappointing : "I did expect that Mr. Benjamin was come back a great man, but I did understand every word he did tell about ! "

From this time forward, services were held regularly in the same house on Sunday and Wednesday evenings, and Wick St. Lawrence was added to the Banwell Circuit. Within a few months a chapel was

---

[1] See Part II., Section v.

being planned, for which Mr. W. G. Hellier gave the
land, and a tea-meeting held in his wath (a meadow
by the sea), was attended by the extraordinary number of 2,000 persons. The chapel was opened on
August 18th, 1862, and the following record was
entered by Mr. Hellier in the minute-book belonging
to the trustees of the chapel :

"On this occasion the Morning Service, according
to the Liturgy of the Church of England, was read
by the Rev. B. Hellier, of Richmond College, and the
sermon was preached by the Rev. Charles Prest,
President of the Conference.   The Rev. W M.
Punshon preached in the evening in a large tent
erected in an adjoining field. .   .

"Methodism having been introduced into Wick St.
Lawrence in no spirit of opposition to the Established
Church, and with no purpose to hinder, but rather to
aid and supplement the means of grace established
there, it is only just to add that from the beginning
of the undertaking to the present time, the Wesleyans
of the parish have received the most valued help
from their neighbours, and their efforts to do good
have been met on the part of the minister of the
parish, the Rev. Aubrey Townshend, in a spirit of·
most kindly sympathy and co-operation."

Mr. Hellier in many cases had very friendly relations with Evangelical clergymen of the Church of
England. He often met them, also, at the meetings
of the British and Foreign Bible Society, an association in which he felt a very special interest. On one

of these occasions, at Richmond, a clergyman present, in expressing his pleasure at meeting his Wesleyan friends on the same platform, took occasion to remark that he liked them well, always excepting their doctrine of Christian Perfection. "I think," said Mr. Hellier, who was the next speaker, "that all the perfection I hope for is found in the answer to this petition : 'Cleanse the thoughts of our hearts by the inspiration of Thy Holy Spirit, that we may *perfectly* love Thee, and worthily magnify Thy holy name ; through Christ our Lord.' I presume, sir," he added, turning to the clergyman, "that you have no objection to that." The clergyman rubbed his hands with satisfaction, much delighted at the aptness of the reply.

From his letters to Mr. Taylor during his Richmond life we gather a few more of his thoughts on preaching, and obtain some glimpse also of his inner history.

"*March* 30*th*, 1865.

"This is our Quarterly Fast-Day, and we keep up the usual observances. Do you remember the days we spent here together, under like circumstances ? We had some good days. Many of our companions have left us, some for other service, and some for the better country. How solemn it is to think of them ! I do not much dwell on death, but I continually feel how rapidly life is going, and I seem to have done just nothing.

" Do you ever write in your diary now ?   I think
that when at Richmond you used on these fast-days
to set down a three months' review of your experience.
It must be a long time since I wrote anything of the
kind ; I have so little leisure, that I seem to want all
my time for acting, and have none left for review.   I
think, however, that I may here record that God has
been blessing me of late.   I have often prayed for
the gift of the Spirit, and my prayer has been so far
answered that I feel I desire nothing so much as to
be filled with the Holy Ghost.   Another gift of God's
grace is, that I really care about nothing but what I
regard as my work and duty.   I have been chastened,
checked, and humbled so much, that I am cured of
ambition, and now feel that what I have to guard
against is indolence.   I must put forth all my strength
that I may please Him who has called me into His
service."

" *June 16th,* '65.

" If spared to spend another year at Richmond, I
believe I shall come into your notion of criticism
lessons for the students, in preaching.   There are
men here now, completing their second year, whom
I have not heard preach yet.   I have proposed the
thing to my colleagues, but Mr. Lomas fears lest we
should make preaching seem too much an art.   But it
is an art; and the fact that it is of greater importance
than any other, is no sufficient reason why the study
of it should be neglected.   I know you will be glad

to think that I am becoming practical at last. I feel that I move slowly, and as to the great business of preaching, I seem to myself to have been most stupidly dull all my life in this one thing—thinking only of the substance of the truth to be presented, and neglecting the form. But a difference of form determines whether the truth shall enter the minds of the hearers or not. I might as well try to push my fist down the neck of a pint-bottle, as try to get some discourses down the intellectual throat of the majority of hearers. My dear Taylor, I feel brimful of good intentions."

Undated.

"   The substance of the discourse did not seem to me to be quite up to the mark. There was no concentration on a practical object, no driving home. I fear we preachers, with exceptions here and there, have a poor idea of our business. We think too well of our hearers. We talk as if they were all wide awake, when more than half of them need to be roused out of sleep ; we think that if we clearly show them the way, they will certainly walk in it, when we ought to collar them and 'compel them to come in.' Every now and then I seem to myself to wake up as from a dream, with the melancholy reflection that I have been nominally a preacher all these years, yet am only an apprentice to the art."

" This brother has hitherto had the reputation of

being able to preach, though he could do little besides.
I get to be more than ever distrustful of such
men.   It is clear that if a man cannot study, he is
hardly fit to be the guide of men that can, and such
hearers a minister will always find now-a-days in his
congregation."

The above quotation has reference to one of the
trial sermons preached by the students in turn, during
their College course.   Mr. Hellier's diary contains
brief, suggestive comments on the long series of
these sermons to which he listened, and his remarks
are interesting as showing the detailed attention he
paid to each one, and the readiness with which he
seized upon every point which told in the preacher's
favour.   Some of them, concerning men whose names
have since become known in our Church and beyond
it, read to-day as fulfilled prophecies.   But the censure when deserved is unsparing.   Of the discourse
of one student he writes : "A smooth, poor sermon.
Wanting in pith, power, and pathos ; otherwise un-
exceptionable."   This brother did not long remain in
the ministry.

"BRISTOL,
"*Aug.* 14*th*, 1865.

"I left Birmingham on Friday afternoon, had a very
hurried look at Worcester Cathedral, and arrived here
about nine.   Yesterday I heard Gallienne preach a
plain, useful sermon on the Parable of the Talents, and
myself preached at King Street in the evening, on

2 Corinthians iv. 18.   My brother-in-law thinks I am
improved in elocution, energy, matter, and every way;
and his two servant-maids were, I am told, delighted
—they could understand every word.   Here is encouragement.   I do not think praise does me harm at
present.   Whatever others think, I do often entertain
an infinitely mean opinion of my own performances,
and think I am one of the greatest fools alive.   Yet
my humility is more of an absolute than of a relative
kind, for I often hear sermons which do not satisfy me
a whit more than my own.   . I have come to
the conclusion that my calling is to preach Holiness,
and to live it.   I very much wish to be a revivalist,
but am afraid I never shall be, unless in this way."

"RICHMOND,
" *April*, 1866.

"The first meeting of Headingley trustees is held at
Leeds to-morrow.   I am summoned, but do not go.
I am thankful to say that I have no anxiety about
the future, touching any personal matter.   I have in
times past been brought so low by affliction, and so
thoroughly humbled into submission to the will of
God, that I feel bare life to be a mercy, life with
health another mercy, and the addition to these of
any place of usefulness in Christ's Church a crowning
mercy.   I feel just now that the whole world can do
me no harm, and that whatever lot is given me will
be the best.   I am only anxious to see where duty
lies.   As between Institution life and Circuit work,

I am very evenly balanced. Whatever is to be, will be *best.*   When I retire from office I hope I shall not be praised like Mr. ——. Would anybody believe the report?

"The praise of men is very vain, but the love of one's friends is unspeakably precious. I feel as if I *did* want a few people really to love me, and this secured, *odi profanum vulgus et arceo.* Ah! truly, says M. C. T., too much of that '*arceo.*' I am afraid it is so ; but I do *try* to be civil. My lack of politeness arises not from *malice prepense,* but from obliviousness.

"I was at Woolwich on Sunday. I went to Mrs. White's Bible-class in the afternoon—a dozen girls. They sang, and that rather upset me. Then I sat down and looked at them ; then I had a good cry ; and I daresay they all thought I was very stupid. I wished for your tact, for then perhaps I might have brought some to decision there and then. It has been my special ambition to be somewhat of a revivalist, but now I fear I never shall."

"WICK ST. LAWRENCE. THE OLD HOUSE AT HOME.
                                   "*Aug. 27th,* 1866.

"Here once more, in a room which has many associations. It is our bedroom for the present, rather remarkably spacious for a farmhouse. In the days of my great-grandfather and bachelor uncle (our folks have lived here about a hundred years), it was the ball-room, and opened with glass doors on the garden.

The part of the garden on which you formerly descended from it is now occupied by the new portion of our house. The room is now lighted by two windows, in the west end of the house; and from where I sit I can see the trees of the neighbouring orchard, *et præterea nihil.* In this room my two brothers and I used to sleep. Here they persecuted me when I wished to say my prayers, and for a time teased me out of my prayer. Here they fought with bolsters, and I looked on in amazement. During the two quiet and profitable years which passed between school and Richmond ('42-'44), this was my study. Here I read, had day-dreams, made *very* crude sermons, read Foster's *Essays*, and for a time forswore the classics. Here yesterday my son John occupied part of his Sunday by grinding tunes out of a barrel-organ, which used to be in the parish church, and singing hymns the while. Now you will think I am very idle to write all this; and so I am, and judge you will be idle enough to read it.

"Yesterday I preached at Worle to a very small congregation, but had a very good one here in the evening. I never preach at Wick without wishing for something of William Dawson's power. Abstract truth makes no way with these poor rustics. They need allegory, fable, parable, simile, or something of the sort, from beginning to end."

It was, as has been already stated, on March 8th, 1867, that Michael Coulson Taylor passed to his rest.

Shortly after his death Mr. Hellier was asked by
Mr. Taylor's friends to prepare a brief memorial.
This was subsequently published by the Wesleyan
Conference Office. A few sentences from the pre-
face may be appropriately quoted in this volume, for
no words could better express the feelings of the
authors of this sketch in regard to their attempted
delineation of Mr. Hellier himself.

"Those who knew Mr. Taylor well will probably
feel that the following pages do not give an adequate
picture of their departed friend. I would remind such
readers how difficult it is for any words of a biographer
to do full justice to such a life. There are some men
whose characters appear to us perfectly lovely; not
because they are frequently performing noble and
generous deeds, for which indeed circumstances may
furnish no occasion, but because the multitude of
actions which make up their life are all marked by
the same character of goodness, and there is absolutely nothing to be placed on the other side of the
account. Such was the case with Mr. Taylor, and
how weak the impression made by the words of another, when compared with the effect produced by
his daily conduct on those who were the constant
witnesses of it!

"Other readers who were strangers to the subject
of this memoir may suppose that the portraiture here
given is overdrawn; and that all virtues have been
exaggerated, and all faults carefully kept out of sight.
I can only say in reply to such possible objections,

that I am wholly unconscious of having done either
the one or the other. It will perhaps be said, Were
there no faults ? My honest answer is, that I did not
detect any. I could indeed have made my friend a
witness against himself, but I have not thought it
right to do so. What a person says to his own dis-
paragement in private records is often true when
regarded as an expression of *his own feeling;* but it
becomes false when accepted by another and used
against him. It is true, as exhibiting his sense of
the wide distance between his ideal standard of perfection and his own actual attainments, but utterly
misleading if regarded as a statement of what he
was as judged by the standard of attainment ordi-
narily reached by other men."

CHAPTER IV

HEADINGLEY.

1868-1884.

THE new branch of the Institution, to which allusion has already been made, was opened at Headingley in 1868. The Rev. John Farrar was appointed as the Governor, and Mr. Lomas was transferred from Richmond as Theological Tutor. Mr. Hellier also was removed to Headingley, where he held the office of Classical Tutor for nine years longer.[1]

This change deprived him of the daily intercourse which he had so long enjoyed with his friend and colleague Dr. Moulton. From the correspondence which then ensued we have been enabled, through Dr. Moulton's kindness, to make the following extracts.

"ABBEVUE, HORSFORTH,

"*Sept. 5th*, 1868.

"I hardly yet realise the fact that my Richmond life is at an end. I have many and various thoughts as I begin to look back upon it ; but one thing is certain, that there is nothing I shall remember with the same unmixed satisfaction as my intercourse with

---

[1] A view of Headingley College, taken in April, 1883, is reproduced upon the opposite page.

LONDON STEREOSCOPIC CO

PHOTO-MEZZOTYPE.

HEADINGLEY COLLEGE.

From a Photograph by MR. SACHS, *of Bradford*

yourself. I have never had one thought or feeling
towards you that has had in it any approach towards
unkindness, and so far I have not been undeserving
of your confidence ; but in other respects I believe
you have thought of me far better than I deserve. I
shall be always greatly your debtor, and am content
to be so."

"HEADINGLEY,
"*Sept.* 14*th*, 1868.

"I like the look of these Yorkshire people very
well. I have no doubt I shall sometimes find them
blunt, but I believe they are honest and kind. One
or two countenances struck me very much : they
seemed so evidently brightened and refined by grace
Divine. I am *not* impressed as yet with indications
of great spiritual life and earnestness in the people
generally ; but then I fear my flint may not strike
well on their steel. I shall be greatly vexed if I
cannot find the way to the Yorkshire heart."

"*Oct.* 19*th–26th*, 1868.

" I wish you would feel it upon your conscience
to bring about a revolution in our Methodist singing.
Could you not, by writing to the *Times*, or in some
other way, carry these points ?—

" 1. To have all organs played with modesty.

" 2. To abolish payments to leading singers.

" 3. To employ money so saved to pay a professional man to teach large classes of the congregation during the week.

"4. To get a perfect Wesleyan Tune-book, with hymns and tunes on the same page.

"Just carry these few points, and then you shall write as a line for your own epitaph (if you have a fancy that way), '*Exegi monumentum ære perennius.*'

"It vexes me in my inmost soul to think what grand opportunities of doing good we Methodists throw away from us by not taking more pains with our singing. I am sure the singing of this Brunswick congregation might be made one of the grandest things in the whole kingdom."

"HANLEY,
"*July* 30*th*, 1870.

"Yesterday was a grand day in Conference. Bishop Simpson addressed us; and whilst I greatly admired the speaker, I was impressed still more with the magnitude of that American Methodism which he represented. I hope that when the papers reach you, you will read all that he said, for every word was weighty. His view of Methodism as the antagonist of the Papacy struck me as very important. I have now heard two of these Methodist bishops speak, and they both made one impression in particular: these men know the value of words. No doubt they feel that their utterances are official and responsible, and they consider well beforehand what they mean to say. Their careful avoidance of anything that could wound our susceptibilities as Englishmen is also notice-able. I think we shall have to 'get up' American

Methodism more carefully than we have done" (vide
Herzog).

" HEADINGLEY,

" *Nov. 7th*, 1870.

" It vexes me exceedingly that you should have
all this trouble and worry ; but comfort yourself in
this : you must have *something* to exercise your
graces, or patience could never 'have its perfect work.'
This is your trial. Can you not rejoice that you
have ' fallen into divers temptations ' ? "

"*June 22nd*, 1871.

" I have a great dislike to Ovid as a text-book for
our men. *Metam.* xv., it is true, is quite harmless ; as
to *Epistolæ ex Ponto*, I know nothing of them ; but
I dislike the *name* of Ovid.

" I do not take kindly to Cicero *On Divination.*
The whole book is employed in slaying the dead ass
of Roman divination. Should we not choose, if we
can, subjects which are valuable *per se*, as well as
good for teaching Latin ? "

" *May 6th*, 1872.

" I can see good likely to result from all conversation which shall pass between you and Bishop
Ellicott and Canon Westcott respecting the Church
and Methodism ; but all schemes of union seem to
me impracticable.

" How can any formal declaration of union in any
sense be of value, unless we are prepared to declare
our approval of the Articles of the Church of England,

and of her ritual as laid down in the Prayer-Book?
Now whatever individuals amongst us may be prepared for, as a *community* we are no more prepared
for this, than to go over in a body to the Church
of Rome.

"Then, if we are prepared for any expression of
approval on our part, we shall expect some from the
other side. What chance is there that the *community*
of the English Church will express approval of *any
one thing* wherein we differ from the Church itself?
Union *with* accord is an impossibility; and *without*
it, no advantage. It seems to me that the one thing
to which good men should now bend their efforts, before all others, is to bring about a harmony between
Science and Revelation. Huxley says that every
clergyman, every time he repeats the Fourth Commandment, is saying what is not true, and what he
knows is not true. Huxley 'would never do a thing
like that, and would rather go to a hell of honest
men than to a paradise of shams.' I think the Church
is bound to give him some answer. Can you direct
me to one?"

"*Jan.* 20*th*, 1871.

"I have not the vanity to think that I can mention
a single point that you have not discussed already;
and if my jottings have any worth, it can result only
from the fact that they show you 'how it strikes a
stranger.'

"I am disposed then to demur to your retaining

the termination *-eth* [in the Revised Version of the
Scripture]. It certainly is against present usage, and
I suppose in another generation will look and sound
more obsolete than it does at present. Does one man
in a million say, ' My friend loveth me ' ?

" You will be prepared to hear that I attribute no
more sanctity to words than to places. Third persons
in *-eth* sin against the *summa lex* of language. Sins
are sins ; therefore should be absent from Bible and
sermons. Why should I say anything in the pulpit
which I would not say out of it ? "

" *May 9th*, 1873.
"I am this day forty-eight years of age, and it is
a curious coincidence that in reading the class work
of to-day I found myself catechized by our old friend
Horatius Flaccus on this wise :

' Natales grate numeras ? ignoscis amicis ?
Lenior et melior fis accedente senecta ? ' [1]

" I hardly expected to be taken to task in this
way by this old Epicurean worldling, but I have
no objection. One thing I can answer confidently. I
do get ' *lenior.*' I feel more kindly, I think, towards
all sorts and conditions of men, and it is one of the
most comforting signs of grace I have."

" You cannot imagine what a hunger I often feel in
my soul for the love of friends. Those whom one

---

[1] Horace, *Epist.* ii. 2.

can love with all one's heart are so very scarce. To think I have a continued place in your regard is one of the greatest consolations of my life."

To Another Friend.

"*May 7th*, 1878.

"I very much sympathise with Mr. ——, but not in any degree with his opinions, if they are what I suppose them to be respecting future punishment.

"This is a case in which, I confess, *authority* has great weight with me. Eighteen centuries have passed, and on this solemn subject the whole Church of Jesus Christ has been practically unanimous. The names on the other side are so few and inconsiderable that, weighed against the authority of the catholic Church (in the best sense), they are worth *nothing*. Greek Church, Roman Church, Protestant Church, all agree. The Reformers gave up much in Luther's time, but held this. The Puritans rejected much that the Reformers held, but retained this. There have been men of the profoundest intellects, who have made theology their lifelong study, men like Hooker, Owen, Howe, Baxter, compared with whom Canon Farrar is a mere child, who have all rested in the same belief.

"I admit that I do not regard this authority, overwhelming as it is, as finally decisive. But I shall pause very long indeed before I conclude that the *whole* Church of Jesus Christ during eighteen centuries has gone astray on this, or any other vital point.

"When as a staunch Protestant I lay authority aside, and (as far as I can) all prepossession, and ask, What saith the Scripture? then too I reach the same conclusion. No voice in Scripture has spoken so clearly or so often on this subject as the voice of Christ Himself. I know no master higher than He. And unless I am bold enough to say, 'The disciple is above the Master; I know better than He,' I *must* believe, as it seems to me, that at the judgment of the great day some men will enter into everlasting life, and others into a punishment equally everlasting.

"Again, I ask myself, Why should I not receive this doctrine?

"If I look at my personal relation to it, there is no difficulty. The same word which tells me of the danger of everlasting death, brings me the offer of everlasting life. I can never know what the death is except I reject the life; and if at the last I lose what I have put from me, and receive what I have chosen, can I complain that the award is unjust?

"'But surely you think of others as well as of yourself?' Certainly. And these others divide themselves into two classes: (1) Those who have received the offer of salvation in Christ; (2) those who have not.

"As to class 1, the answer already given will suffice. What applies to me, applies to them.

"As to class 2, I acknowledge a great *speculative* difficulty, but no practical one. There are two things which I do not know. (1) I do not know how God will deal with those to whom the offer of salvation never came. I know that He will not deal with them as with those who reject the gospel. 'Go ye into all the world, and preach the gospel to every creature. . . He that believeth not shall be damned' (or condemned), *i.e.* finally. 'Believeth not'— *what?* That which he believes who is saved. But a man does not disbelieve or reject a statement never made to him! Christ Himself has taught us that all men's responsibility respecting His truth does not go beyond their knowledge of it. 'If I had not come and spoken unto them, they had not had sin.'

"(2) I do not know how God will justify to the intelligent universe His own dealing with class 2. That He will justify it, I doubt not. 'The Judge of all the earth' will 'do right.' He who has given me every true sentiment of justice that I have, cannot violate them by His own action.

"So that my difficulty is this: I do not know what God will do, or how He will justify what He does ; but then it is no part of my *duty* to know the one or the other. As to what I ought to *do* in reference to my own salvation, I have not the shadow of a doubt. I must receive Christ and follow Him. What I ought to do regarding the salvation of others, is equally plain : I must make Christ known as soon as possible, and to as many as I can. Here I rest. It is enough for me if I fulfil my duty. I do not aspire to be the counsellor of God."

At the Conference of 1870 Mr. Hellier was nominated for the Legal Hundred[1] by the Rev. E. E.
Jenkins (now Dr. Jenkins), and at once elected. A
prompt and cordial vote at these elections is specially prized by a Methodist preacher as a mark of
his brethren's confidence ; and as such Mr. Hellier
valued it.

In 1877 he succeeded Mr. Farrar as Governor of
the College, and in this office continued until his
death.

Nearly thirty-five years of his life, therefore, were
spent in the service of the Institution, four of them
as Assistant-Tutor at Didsbury, twenty as Classical
Tutor at Richmond and Headingley, and rather more
than ten in his final position as Governor. During
this period nearly seven hundred students were
brought under his teaching and influence. Many of
them have "fallen asleep" ; some are labouring in
other Churches; and others, alas! have fallen from the
ranks : but the greater number are with us to-day,
at work in many fields and in many lands—in Great
Britain and Ireland, in India, Ceylon, China, South
Africa, the isles of the Pacific, Australia, New Zea-
land, and the West Indies.

Many changes took place in the staff at Head-

---

[1] The hundred ministers who, according to Mr. Wesley's
Deed of Declaration, legally constitute the Conference. A
quorum of forty must always be present in the Conference,
and their vote is necessary to confirm its decisions as a whole.
The President is elected from their number.

H.   7

ingley during Mr. Hellier's long residence there,
changes by which he lost colleagues whom he loved
well, to gain others of like spirit ; and his affection
for them they heartily returned. One of them, on
hearing of his death, wrote thus to us :

" Even at this distance, and though I did not hope
to see him in the flesh again, the world seems somehow emptier without him. You know what he was
to me : next to my own father, the best friend
amongst my elders ; kind, wise, faithful, frank ; his
life a continual stimulus to holiness. How good and
kind he was to me in my own great sorrow ! I don't
think he ever knew quite how much I loved him,
but I did and *do* love him very deeply. To have
known him and lived with him seven years is a
privilege which I shall always be thankful to God
that I enjoyed. Since we began work here his
example has often been present with me ; if I can be
to these men anything like what he was to me, I
shall be happy indeed." [1]

Concerning his relations with the other members
of the staff, the Rev. J. S. Banks thus writes :

" It was my privilege to be Mr. Hellier's colleague
nearly eight years at Headingley. The relation of a
Governor in one of our Institutions to his colleagues
is a delicate one, inasmuch as the office carries with

---

[1] Letter from the Rev. E. H. Sugden, B.A., B.Sc., Master
of Queen's College, University of Melbourne, Assistant-Tutor at
Headingley 1874-1881.

it no primacy, much less authority over the other
members of the staff. Looking back now over those
eight years, I can see that the duties of the office
were in this respect met as perfectly by Mr. Hellier
as they ever can be by human faculty. His invariable rule was to leave the decision of all questions
affecting the work of the Tutors almost entirely with
them, only himself offering the advice which his long
experience suggested. Not only so, but in all matters
within the Governor's own province, he always sought
the counsel of his colleagues. In this way unity of
College administration was secured. I remember
that several times, when compelled to act without
consultation, he carefully explained the circumstances.
Mr. Hellier himself attributed our unbroken harmony
of counsel and action to the weekly Tutors' meeting,
and even more to the Tutors' breakfast by which the
meeting was preceded. The strength of his faith in
the social virtues of the breakfast was often almost
puzzling to me at the time. Probably Mr. Hellier
was right. He once told us that the only piece of
advice he gave to a newly appointed Governor was,
' Take care to have a Tutors' breakfast every week.'

" With all the kindness and charity, which were
Mr. Hellier's both by nature and grace, he was firm,
and when necessary, inexorably resolute in maintaining discipline and vindicating law. More than once
I had reason to admire and be thankful for his
clearsightedness and firmness in this respect. His
abhorrence of compromise where moral right was in

question was intense. I shall only be repeating what others have said in adding, that the secret of his influence as Governor, and in every other capacity, was weight of personal character. Of Mr. Hellier's most generous references to his colleagues on all fitting occasions, it is scarcely for us to speak, but we cannot forget them."

The title of *Governor* Mr. Hellier considered a misnomer, apt to convey the impression that its owner must do a great deal of governing in order to justify his existence. "Governing," he would say, "is a mere accident of the position. The men are, or ought to be, 'a law unto themselves.'" This view of his finds expression in an address from which we now quote. It was delivered at the beginning of a College year to the incoming students.

"I am called your 'Governor,' but I am not much in love with the title. I could wish it were something else, because it is suggestive of a more active exercise of authority over you than I wish for. In John Wesley's days those whom we now call Superintendents were called Assistants, and the Junior Preachers were called Helpers. And Wesley somewhere asks: 'What is the duty of an Assistant towards his Helpers?' The answer is: 'To see that they behave well, and want nothing.' I am quite willing to take this definition of my relation towards you. I shall be glad to 'see that you behave well.' It is not a very laborious thing for me to look on and see your good order. Then I have to take care that you 'want

nothing.' I have no objection to accept this obligation. Only in certain cases you must allow me to
judge of your wants. It is conceivable that a brother
may have what he thinks a want, but I may think
it a whim. I will not promise to meet his views in
such a case.

"I shall treat every one with great confidence,
proceeding on the supposition that he deserves my
confidence. I shall steadfastly believe that every
brother is incapable of acting otherwise than becomes
a Christian, until he robs me of this belief by his
misconduct.

"If any one should be so foolish as to take it into
his head that he will outwit, or in any way *do* the
Governor, I tell him beforehand that he will almost
certainly succeed, because I shall never suspect him
of being capable of it.

"If you were boys, I should feel it my duty to be
constantly on the alert, because boys, even when they
have a good and wise master, sometimes think it will
serve them to get their own ends in opposition to the
will of the master; they think that they have interests
opposed to his, that his interests are opposed to
theirs: but to suppose anything of the sort in the
relation subsisting between you and me is obviously
absurd. What interests have I, opposed to yours?
What interests have you, opposed to mine?

"As to your relation to one another, I sum up all
when I say with St. Peter, ' Love the brotherhood.' If
you want a comment on the text, read 1 Corinthians

xiii. I am anxious that you should be Christian gentlemen, and any one who should embody in his conduct
towards others that charity which is there described,
would be the most perfect gentleman the world ever
saw.   In judging one another, have a sharp eye
for a brother's virtues, and a dull eye for his faults.
Those are the truest judgments that lean to the side
of charity.   There is so much in human nature that
tends to envy and unjust depreciation of others, that
if you lean to *that* side you are sure to be unjust.   In
leaning hard to the other, you may perhaps keep the
balance straight."

The following recollections of Mr. Hellier as a
college governor have been written for this memoir
by an old Headingley student : [1]

"In the opinion of his own students, Mr. Hellier
was the very ideal of a college governor ; and this
is not merely a judgment they have formed after his
death, but it was also a current and unquestioned
article of faith during his life, taught by the men in
residence to every new student who entered Headingley, and confirmed by each one's personal experience during his College life.   And it means, not only
that he succeeded in making his men love him, but
that he led them on to a nobler Christian manhood,
so that to-day he 'lives again in lives made better
by his presence'—lives of Christian ministers, who

---

[1] The Rev. W. Bradfield, B.A., York.   Student at Headingley College, 1880–1884 ; Sub-Tutor for two years.

learned from his example how themselves to tend
and feed the flock of God.

" It was no easy success that he won, nor one that
is easy to estimate. We cannot tabulate and report
upon Christian influence, nor say how great and far-
reaching was the effect of his downright goodness and
ripe wisdom. But we can see that he realised the
full significance of his office, and used thoroughly its
large opportunity of blessing Methodism and the
world through the men who are called into the work
of the ministry.

" These men come from the most varied positions
and circumstances. They are gathered from the
country villages, from the shops and offices of the
towns, from the factory, the mine, or the teacher's
desk. Some are raised in social status by entering
the ministry, while others forego comforts and
luxuries to which they have been accustomed. Some
have received the training that is to be got in moving
among masses of men and sharing a common life
with them, and some have lived where they have
never measured themselves against their equals.
They have all been preachers with a considerable
measure of popularity in their own circuits, and have
been encouraged by the very genius of Methodism to
independent and self-directed effort ; a fact which
does not make it easier for them to learn the habits of
discipline and self-suppression which the College life
and studies require. They are bound together by
their common Methodism, and their call to preach the

gospel, but are often diverse in all other things. And they are sent up to our Colleges to be knit together in the brotherhood of the Wesleyan ministry and to be trained for its work. They are to live together, apart from ordinary society, to change many past habits, to study hard, and to develop the Christian graces. Such men may be relied on, in the main, to do their work and to observe in their conduct ' the weightier matters of the law,' without making any great tax on the resources of their Governor; but for him to assume the direction of their social and religious life, to take advantage of all the circumstances that offer to correct their faults, call out their virtues, and raise them to higher conceptions of character and usefulness, demands—what Mr. Hellier possessed—all the tact and judgment of a thoroughly wise man, as well as the genuine sympathy of a mature Christian.

"Mr. Hellier knew well how to take advantage of the impressibility of new students during the first days of their College life. At the first gathering at the beginning of each new College year, he used to read the rules and explain his own position in a way that always won the new men's confidence, while it called out all their self-respect. He told them that he regarded them all as Christian gentlemen, and trusted to their honour for the maintenance of the College rules. He assured them that he would never suspect any man of wrong-doing, nor withdraw his confidence from him until confidence was no longer

possible. And he kept these promises most faithfully. He told them that if anybody wanted to
cheat the Governor, it would be very easy, because
no one would try to prevent him : a way of looking
at things which took all the point out of the esca-
pades and practical jokes which another system of
government might have fostered. And in response
to the Governor's confidence, public opinion among
the students frowned down all but the most venial
rule-breaking, and proved itself able to keep order
in a way that no mere personal vigilance of the
authorities could have secured.

" A favourite principle of Mr. Hellier's government
was that of educating subordinates to work. ' Never
do yourself,' he would say, ' what you can get
another man to do for you equally well. One of the
finest sentiments ever expressed in Latin is *Qui
facit per alium facit per se.* This is the only way to
carry out the complementary principle, Do what no
one but yourself can do.' Illustrations of his working out of this principle can hardly be given in the
limits of this paper ; but all Headingley men know
that it worked admirably in many important details
of College life.

" He was peculiarly successful in correcting petty
faults in such a way as to effectually insure their
amendment, without giving them too much importance, or unduly humiliating the offender. If, for
instance, the monitor's book showed that some brother
had been reporting himself sick without any great

cause, Mr. Hellier would make anxious inquiry after his health in a good-humoured tone that was far more effective than either a sneer or a scolding. And one day, when in the lecture room a student had several times restlessly looked at his watch, he paused, and inquired with interest, 'Well, what *is* the time, Mr. ——?' One favourite saying on these matters was: 'A word to the wise is enough. If the word is not enough, what is the inference?'

" On the few occasions when grave faults had to be condemned, Mr. Hellier could be very severe. And yet what made a rebuke from him so much dreaded was, not the sting of keen words, so much as the evident dislike and repulsion roused in him by anything mean or base. He could make a man feel the stain of sin and the degradation of character which results from it, because he felt these things so deeply himself.

" He presided always at the breakfast and dining-table, and the morning monitor during his week of office sat next him on his left, a plan which resulted in bringing every man in turn into his company for a week. The other seats at the head of the table were eagerly coveted, for 'the Governor' proved most excellent company. He was an un-rivalled teller of a good story, and could thoroughly enjoy one in turn; but a story with any unworthy suggestion, or trace of unkindness, or mean idea of any sort he never was heard to tell, and he listened to such with obvious pain. So far as the students

saw him, he bore St. James' mark of a perfect man,
he did not 'offend with his tongue.'

"The Sunday services of his men were subjects of
great interest to him. He would carefully inquire at
Monday's dinner table after the state of the Societies
the men had visited and the results of their labours,
and he was always ready to 'rejoice with those that
rejoiced' in visibly successful work.

"No one could be in his company without being
deeply impressed by his love of goodness. He had
manifestly 'set his affection' on the things of Christ's
kingdom. His interest in deeds of obedience, self-
denial, and charity, in 'whatsoever things are true,
honourable, just, pure, lovely, or of good report,' was
unfailing. We all knew that, whatever topics might
fail to interest him, these never would. And indeed
he often remarked in the last years of his life, that
while there were many interests that necessarily grew
duller with advancing years, his own interest in the
kingdom of God increased year by year, and was
never so great as at present.

"He took great pains to make the morning and
evening family prayers thoroughly profitable, and
gave careful attention to every detail about them.
He insisted on the importance of good Bible-reading,
and by his kindly criticisms helped the men to a
more correct and intelligent style. If ever a piece of
bad reading seemed to arise from misapprehension of
the passage read, he would after prayers give a most
lucid and helpful exposition of it. He greatly disliked

hurried reading, and would say that rarely, if ever
in his life, had he heard the Bible read too slowly.

"But the centre of Mr. Hellier's influence over the
students of Headingley College was the Society
Class-meeting. Many learned there for the first time
what a Class-meeting could be, and old Headingley
men now speak to one another of those meetings with
a warmth which shows how deep was the impression
made by them on their hearts and lives. When each
new College year brought its quota of fresh faces
into the meeting, he began by asking all the new
brethren to tell how they first 'came into the way.'
Stories of early trust in Christ especially delighted
him ; and when men told of conversion in youth or
early manhood, he always carefully inquired if there
were not seasons of deep religious impression in
childhood, and beginnings of Christian life dating
farther back than the crises of which they told. The
effect of these inquiries was, as he well knew, to
increase, in the future pastors of Methodism, their
regard for early piety and their sense of duty to the
children.

"It was his custom to begin the meeting by
reading a few verses from his pocket edition of
Scrivener's Greek Testament, giving his own trans-
lation, which often threw a flood of light upon the
passage he was rendering. There was one set of
expositions on the Sermon on the Mount, given in
Class in this way, which have been especially remembered for the ripe wisdom with which Christ's

words were treated and brought to bear upon present
personal needs. Then he would open the Class-book,
and call upon some of those present, sometimes in
one order, sometimes in another; and he would sit
swinging his watchguard, as his habit was, listening
carefully to the varied experiences of the Class, and
replying with words of kindliest counsel and encouragement. In these replies he showed that he
possessed in large measure the gift of 'discernment of
spirits.' Sometimes it was but a word that he said :
as when once a brother had been speaking in a
most despairing tone of self-depreciation, he quietly
asked, 'Is that all true, Brother —— ?' 'Yes,' was
the gloomy reply; 'and I'm afraid it is much less
than the truth.' 'Then one thing is certain,'
answered Mr. Hellier ; 'Brother ——, *you must mend.*'
The effect on the whole Class, as well as on the
brother himself, was electrical. At another time
he would point out the bearing of some passage
of Scripture upon what had been said, and show
how it met the difficulty or the need that was expressed. Thus, when some one, speaking of lack of
success in seeing conversions, had said, that he would
sooner die than have an unfruitful ministry, Mr.
Hellier asked if any one could remember the chapter
in which Isaiah describes the vision of the Lord in
the temple. Somebody began, 'In the year that
king Uzziah died,' etc., and others went on with
verse after verse till the commission of the prophet
was reached : 'Make the heart of this people fat, and

make their ears heavy, and shut their eyes ; lest they see with their eyes, and hear with their ears, and understand with their heart, and convert, and be healed.' 'And now,' said Mr. Hellier, pausing, ' we have a new reading proposed : *" And Isaiah said, Lord, I'd sooner die than do it."* '

" Every now and then, as might be imagined in a class of theological students, doctrinal subjects came up, and the Class showed a tendency to argue them rather than dwell on experimental religion. While he was never too prompt to close such discussions, Mr. Hellier took care not to allow the meeting to be altogether turned from its proper purpose. And he loved most to dwell on those practical aspects of Divine truth which are out of the reach of controversy. Thus when the topic of Entire Sanctification threatened, as it sometimes did, to let loose a strife of tongues, he would say : ' Entire sanctification is the sanctification of everything. It means, if you have the corner seat in a railway carriage, and a woman gets in with a little child that wants to look out of window, that you give her your seat.' Another favourite remark upon this topic was : ' It ·is so easy to tell entirely sanctified people what you conceive to be their faults, because you are so sure that you cannot offend them, but will only make them feel grateful to you.'

" Another characteristic of his was his keen interest in whatever concerned the kingdom of God in any part of the world. He had the warmest sympathy for the successes of all branches of the

Church of Christ, from the Church of England to the Salvation Army. He would bring before us the work of Miss Ellice Hopkins among the working men, or of Miss Weston among the sailors, and praise with generous appreciation all that he could approve. He carefully collected information on all such work for this very purpose, and would often bring to the Class-meeting a letter from some mission station, perhaps from some old Headingley student, and would dwell upon his work and prospects.

"But concerning Mr. Hellier's Class-meetings, and indeed concerning all his work, it is difficult to speak, because when all is said one feels that the essence of his character is still unspoken. It was not a sharply defined policy, or special development of any one side of his work, that made him what he was, but the all-pervasive influence in his life and actions of 'the wisdom that is from above,' which 'is first pure, then peaceable, gentle, easy to be entreated, full of mercy and good fruits, without variance, without hypocrisy.'

"The best memorial of his Governorship is the loving reverence with which his memory is treasured among his old students. His work is to be found in the love of goodness, and meekness of wisdom, which his example has made them earnestly covet, and his best eulogy the thanksgivings which they offer that they ever knew him."

He was at any time ready, as Tutor or Governor, to

help students in their difficulties. When one of them came to him with a question for solution, his first reply would usually be, " Have you carefully thought about this question yourself?" If the man said "No," he was probably dismissed with the advice that he should do so. If, on the contrary, he was involved in real perplexity, no trouble was spared in helping him.

Those who came to him in their sorrows know how fully his sympathy was given. One has recorded that, when seeking leave of absence on account of his mother's death, he looked up, and saw that Mr. Hellier was himself moved to tears.

His interest in his students followed them in all their after life, and twenty years and more after they left, his recollection of their individuality often seemed to be as fresh as ever. Every week when the *Methodist Recorder* came, it was searched for tidings of old students and their work. And in their appointment to Circuits, that most important question for Wesleyan ministers, his influence and recommendation were exerted on behalf of his students, and sought by the Circuits. He always spoke of them with kindness in the homes that he visited, and we know well a student could hardly rouse his indignation more than by any words of disloyalty to his brethren when in the company of strangers.

" Former students," he once said, in addressing the men, " have won a high reputation for us ; you have to care that at the very least that reputation shall not go down. Try. if possible, to raise it higher by word and deed. Never say anything to disparage the College. 'He was very scant of news who told that his own father had been hanged'; and that student must be woefully deficient in profitable topics of conversation who entertains people by disparaging his own College."

He strongly encouraged the students to give due attention to physical recreation and athletic exercises, for he recognised the importance of such relaxation in the sedentary life of a student. He would often watch their cricket matches with great interest. He himself greatly enjoyed a game at bowls, at which he was expert. He was also fond of a game of chess, provided the play was rapid.

Mr. Hellier was accustomed to vary the monotony of College life by frequently inviting to the hall table any one whose words were likely to interest the students. A returned missionary was perhaps the favourite guest, and any old student was sure of a cordial welcome. Many eminent Wesleyan and other ministers and laymen were found there from time to time. Here is an instance, taken from a conversation with Mr. S. D. Waddy, Q.C., M.P., which he kindly allows us to quote. It is characteristic alike of host and guest.

"I knew your father well. While he was at the Theological Institution he came to stay at Wesley College, Sheffield, during one of the vacations, as a supply for my father. I remember how fond of him

H.   8

we all were, and how speedily and thoroughly he
became quite a member of the family.   I next met
him after my removal to London.   He was then at
Islington, and I was a young local preacher in that
Circuit; and I was much pleased to be able to renew
our former intimacy.   He visited frequently at my
house, and I specially remember his coming one day
to tell me that he had been nominated Classical Tutor
at Richmond.   We were close friends, and I jokingly
asked him whether he knew any 'classics,' or had
forgotten all he ever knew.   I remember being struck
at the time by the mingled modesty and courage
with which he acknowledged that classical studies
had not been kept up to the highest point of late
years, but that he would give no man opportunity
to find fault with the thoroughness and energy with
which he would soon refit.   His object in calling
upon me was to borrow books from my library.   He
was beginning to read up at once, and industriously,
so as to fit himself for the appointment, if Conference
should make it.   The fact was, he was better fitted
for the post than he ever claimed to be, or than most
people knew.

"If I had to describe him in a word, I should call
him a *reliable* man.   You were absolutely sure
that he would do thoroughly well any work he
undertook, and that he always meant what he said,
without guile.

"After he came to Leeds, I seldom saw him except
on my ordinary professional circuit; but there were

two occasions which I recall with interest. On one
of these he came to me at the Assize Court and said,
'I wish you would come up, and have dinner with
the students and me, some day this week.' Something in his manner made me think that the *dinner*
was not all that he contemplated, and I looked at
him and said, 'And then?' 'Yes,' he replied, laughing; 'and then I want you to give an address to
my boys.' 'But I am a layman. What have I to
do to address theological students, young clerics?
That is not at all in my line.' 'That is just why
I want you to come; I am tired of *lines*.' 'But
you don't want me to preach to them?' 'Certainly
not; I can do that myself.' 'Then tell me what
kind of thing you want me to say.' 'Indeed I shall
not; that would spoil it all. I want you to say
what I cannot think of. They have heard all *I* have
to say many times over; I expect they sometimes
think they hear too much of what I have to say.'
'Well, I am a Circuit-steward, you know. I could
tell them what kind of sermons we want ministers to
preach in our chapel, and what kind of men stewards
like to invite to their Circuits.' 'Just the very thing;
nothing could be better.' 'But I can't talk seriously
about that.' 'Don't talk seriously; make them laugh.
Only when they are laughing, take them unawares
and give it them—give it them under the fifth rib.'
So I went up, and, as nearly as I could, did what
I was told to do, and talked to the students, to the
best of my ability, about ministers from a layman's

point of view. 'Thank you,' said Mr. Hellier afterwards; 'you have done just what I wanted. You
have said what no minister would have ever thought
of. And,' he added with a twinkle, 'what not one
in fifty would have ventured to say, if he had thought
of it. And the very things they would like least
to hear will be the hooks that will fasten it all in
their memories. Do you know,' he said after a
pause, 'I believe people generally consider that I
am such a quiet, steady-going person, that they do
not suspect how much I enjoy getting quite *off the
line* occasionally ? '

"A short time after this I was appointed lay
member of the Missionary Deputation to the Leeds
District. Amongst other duties devolved upon me,
was an appointment to preach in Brunswick Chapel
on the Sunday evening. He was in the congregation ;
and I shall never forget the kindness and tenderness
with which he spoke to me after the service, and the
earnest and gracious way in which, while his eyes
were wet through his hallowed emotion, he exhorted
me and cheered me in my work."

The foundation stone of Headingley College was
laid upon Ascension Day, and when Mr. Hellier became Governor, he instituted the custom of observing
the festival as a College Commemoration Day. It
was a great pleasure to him to welcome year by year
the old students, who came from far and near to aid
in its celebration, to strengthen old friendships, and

review the sacred and happy memories of the past. He wrote for this occasion the verses which we quote below; and though he himself did not think them worthy to see the light, they will serve to show how thoroughly he entered into the spirit of the day, and on this account will be valued by his old students.

JESUS, we Thy servants are,
Objects of Thy kindest care,
Called to serve the heavenly Lord,
Called to preach Thy glorious word.

What, O gracious Lord, are we,
What our father's house to Thee,
That Thou dost this honour give,
That to serve our Lord we live?

We are sent in Jesus' name,
All His mercy to proclaim,
Preaching grace that pardon brings,
Heralds of the King of kings.

Labour, sorrow, toil, and strife
Meet us on the path of life ;
Hatred of the worldly-wise,
Prudent men in their own eyes.

Hope deferred, and trust misplaced,
Cold suspicion soon embraced,
Conflicts fierce with open foes,
Secret malice us inclose.

Yet our hearts shall never fear ;
Jesus will His servants cheer;
We will triumph in the word,
" I am with you, saith the Lord."

Jesus' friends their love will give,
Us into their hearts receive ;
Those whom we have won to faith,
Shall be ours in life, in death.

Friendships formed 'mid studious hours
Bless with unexhausted powers ;
Fervent prayers, triumphant praise,
Still unite us all our days.

Think of us who think of you,
Love with faithful hearts and true,
Fight with us the glorious fight,
Friends of Christ, and truth, and light !

We are travellers to the skies,
Thither we with you shall rise ;
We from many fields shall come,
Bring our sheaves with triumph home !

During Mr. Hellier's College life he preached as a
rule twice every Sunday, and formed in some sense a
circuit of his own, in which some places were visited
annually, and others two or three times a year. Usually
he preached to upwards of forty different congregations in the year. His " circuit " was a very wide
one, and included among other places Selby, York,
Hull, Scarborough, Morecambe, Bridlington, Newark,
and Cambridge.

" I never heard your father preach," said the Rev.
R. Posnett to one of us ; " but I was much struck with
the fact that, when he had preached for me in Wake-
field, my people all seemed in the week following to
be full of the sermon, especially the old people, the

parents, the thoughtful men and women. They spoke
of it with a smile and a relish ; and I seem to know
some of his sermons quite well, such as the one on
' the leaven hid in the meal.' "

He never travelled by train on Sunday, although
the rule involved a considerable sacrifice of time ; and
thus the close of the week generally found him a
guest in some Methodist home. It was always a pleasure to him to acknowledge his indebtedness to the
hospitality of the Methodist people in all parts of the
country ; and although his hosts naturally differed
widely in their social position and surroundings, he
felt at home and happy wherever the cause of Christ
was held dear. With those who left our Church for
the sake of what are called "social advantages," he
had no sympathy whatever. He never affected to
despise wealth, and certainly did not undervalue
culture; but his one social ambition for himself and
his family was, that we should know good people.
"What is good society," he would say, "but the
society of the good? What is the best society but
the society of the best? And where will you find
people who have a greater love for Christ, or take
greater interest in the work of His kingdom, than
are to be found among our own?" In good society
as thus defined he took great delight, and by
social intercourse strengthened his pulpit influence.
Those who best knew his daily life most felt the
power of his preaching.

These Sunday appointments afforded many oppor-

tunities for the incidental gratification of his strong
antiquarian tastes. Before visiting a fresh place he
studied its name, origin, and history, and would now
and then perplex his hosts by inquiries about the
birthplace of some great man, of whose connection
with their town they had never heard. It was seldom that castle or camp, abbey or ancient church,
escaped his notice. On one occasion he sallied forth
from York to find the field of Marston Moor, in spite
of many assurances from his York friends that it
could no longer be identified ; and he came back
triumphant, having secured a handful of bullets from
"a very intelligent and obliging farmer," who had
ploughed them up on the site of the battle. A railway journey with him was always enlivened by the
store of historical and topographical details he produced relating to the places that lay in the route, and
many of his sermons contain striking illustrations
derived from the scenery and historical associations
of the neighbourhood in which they were preached.

He also made it his practice wherever he went, to
learn as much as possible of the local origin, history,
and progress of Methodism. Every detail of the history of his own Church had a charm for him.

The following quotations are from letters written
by some of his numerous kind hosts :

"Your father's first visit to us was early in our
married life, and I still remember the two sermons
he then preached. In the morning the text was,

'Blessed are the pure in heart : for they shall see God'; and in the evening, 'Were there not ten cleansed ?' Those sermons lived with me, and helped me in my spiritual life for weeks afterwards. I felt believing to be easier, and calm, rest, and peace followed.

"The last time I heard him, his theme was again his favourite one, 'Entire Sanctification,' from I Thessalonians v. 23. It was at Bridlington Quay, in September, 1885. It was a time of great blessing to many of the congregation ; several of the visitors to that neighbourhood who were present in the chapel spoke to me about the service during the week.

" I shall never forget one Sunday which your father spent with us. He was not well, and having come to us for rest, refused to take the morning service in our large chapel. During the afternoon, however, he found out that I had an evening appointment some five miles away, in an agricultural village. It had no chapel, because the squire, influenced by the clergy-man of the parish, had persistently refused land for the purpose. But moved, on the other hand, by the influence of his own woodman, he abstained from in-terfering with the service held in one of his tenants' cottages. This woodman by his godly, consistent character won his master's respect, and, it is said, had even been fetched to pray with troubled ones at the Hall in times of sickness. The good man walked seven miles every Sunday morning to attend the Newark

chapel, and was always ready to receive the minister
at night at the little cottage sanctuary. Here he
would start the tunes and lead in prayer at the
prayer-meeting; and he *could* pray. It was his custom
to read the Bible through every year, and I am not
alone as a local preacher in saying that I am indebted
to him for many a new thought upon my text, while
listening to his prayers after my sermon. It was to
this good man, and this little Methodist congregation,
that your father preached for me. There was no
pulpit, but a sort of chair-desk was placed in one
corner of the room ; and as he stood behind it, his
head nearly touched the ceiling. It was a melting
time, in more senses than one ; and he had repeatedly,
not only to wipe the perspiration from his brow, but
the tears from his face, as he talked of Christ's power
to cleanse the lepers still. The people thanked him
again and again ; for the preacher's tears had moved
theirs, and they said it had been good to be there.
The woodman would fain have kept us till late hours ;
for after service he got your father into 'the preacher's
chair' and corner, and I well remember how the good
man's face lighted up as he began to tell of all the
great and good Methodist preachers he had heard,
and how honoured he felt that night.

"Since that time some better accommodation has
been found for the congregation, in a barn which has
been partially adapted for their use ; but the pious
village woodman and the College Tutor and Governor
now worship together in

> 'The house of our Father above,
> The palace of angels and God.' "[1]

"During the sixteen years that Mr. Hellier fre-
quented my house, we were always delighted to see
him. When at the Manchester Conference [1871] I
first invited him to be one of our guests, it was with
a little misgiving, as we were strangers to one
another; but he made himself so thoroughly one
with us in the home life during the month of his
stay, that he never entered our home without bringing sunshine and pleasure. There are two features
in his character which I think should be specially
emphasized.   I never heard him say any word which
reflected upon any of his ministerial brethren.   Here
he 'hoped all things' and 'believed all things' which
were good, true, and excellent.   He delighted much
in their society when with us.   The other feature
is the interest he took in the spiritual welfare of
the servants, making it a rule to speak to them of
the soul's best interests."[2]

"Mr. Hellier's genial, cheerful repose of manner
was one of his greatest charms, and it made every
one feel at home with him.   There was such a
sweet simplicity and homeliness about him, that his
visits were looked forward to by young and old

---

[1] Letter from W O. Quibell, Esq., J.P., Newark.
[2] Letter from W. H. Strawe, Esq., Colwyn Bay (late of
Manchester).

alike, and by none more than our domestics, whose
long, faithful service he fully appreciated, and
whom he treated as members of the family, always
going into the kitchen to speak with them before
he left.

" It was an evident pleasure to him to impart information. He often gave us the outline of a book he
had been reading, or brought with him one which
he thought likely to be useful. But this was done
without any parade of learning, and his manner
in answering questions never made his questioners
painfully sensible of ignorance, but rather encouraged
them to bring forward further difficulties. We felt
that he gave us always of his best. He greatly
admired our old Abbey-church; and one day after
standing and looking at it for some time, he turned
to Mr. Foster and said : ' That church does my soul
good ; I like to look at it. It was built for God ;
they put their souls into their work.'

" He rarely missed giving an address in the Sabbath
school, and generally came on the Saturday evening
in time to attend the 'Band-meeting.' On one of these
occasions several new converts were present, and I
well remember his counsel to them to avoid judging
of their state by their feelings. ' Supposing,' he said
to them, they had been shipwrecked, and buffeted
by the waves before the lifeboat picked them up,
and some one went to them as they were laid on the
shore, and asked them how they felt. One perhaps
was sick, another bruised, and all of them very wet ;

but that was not the point—they were on land, *they were safe.*'

"At another time, when dwelling on the fallacy of making *feeling* a test of progress, he said that his own test was willingness to do work for Christ, to do the duty of the moment. Once when showing how religion should enter into all the little details of life, he said : 'Sometimes I get a letter so carelessly written, that instead of being able to dispose of it in a few moments, I have to spend half an hour trying to make it out ; and even then have had to cut out the man's name and address, and paste them on my envelope, in the hope that the postman in his neighbourhood might be better able to decipher them. What right has one man to waste the time of another by carelessness like this?' One Saturday night he gave a touching account of what he considered a crisis in his earlier religious life. He was taken very ill; his future seemed all uncertain ; the thought of his wife and young family added to his distress. Then came the question, Could he submit to God's will, even if his worst fears were realised? After an agony of conflict, faith triumphed, and he entered into a rest which no after trial in life had greatly disturbed." [1]

"I hope," writes the daughter of one of his hosts, "that mention will be made of Mr. Hellier's ministerial care for the children in the homes where he stayed.

---

[1] Letter from Mrs. John Foster, Selby.

He was so gentle in his dealings with them, and so wise. I remember that once in my Headingley days, when I met him in the village, he was so wonderfully kind and encouraging, that he left me almost speechless and in tears. The last time that he visited us, he asked me, 'L——, are you an out and out Christian?' That question of his I shall remember as long as I live. If our home be a fair specimen of his work among young people, he must have done a great deal of good."

This last letter touches upon a leading feature in Mr. Hellier's ministry. No part of the Church's work interested him more deeply than that which is done among the children. He wrote and thought much upon the subject of their early conversion and Christian training, and did his utmost to promote a more general and prayerful observance of the Sunday in October now commonly called "Children's Sunday," and devoted by a large proportion of the Christian Church to special intercession and effort on their behalf. In connection with this day, his diary contains records such as these :

(Selby.) "Special services for children. Very good day" (Oct., 1881).

(Woodhouse Grove.) "Met the Grove boys in the afternoon with Vinter. Met the boys after the evening service. Several promised to join Junior Society Class" (Oct. 21st, 1883).

(Halifax.) "Afternoon at Sunday school. Eighteen

or twenty gave in their names for Junior Society Class " (Oct., 1884).

His interest in the Woodhouse Grove School and in the Leys School, Cambridge, was very great. He was often invited to preach to the boys, and on returning from either place would speak with special pleasure of the meetings he had held with them. Here and there, we find noted in his diary, beside his Sunday appointments, the Christian names of the young people in the family where he had been staying ; and the interest that he took in their spiritual welfare many of them have reason to remember.

Children always recognised in him a friend, and it was often amusing to see the friendly ease with which they conversed with him, treating him with confidence as their equal. And on his part, he greatly delighted in their artless talk and quaint sayings. He believed in their having plenty of play, and when we were staying at the seaside he would with great satisfaction stand and watch them digging in the sands, saying it was "so pleasant to see them enjoy life." Mrs. Ewing's fresh and vivid pictures of child-life gave him no ordinary pleasure.

The influence diffused through so many homes was most strongly felt in his own. It pleased God to shelter that home to an unusual extent from the ills of this life. It had few sorrows and many joys, and in its affections, aims, and interests was wholly undivided. Our intercourse with him was a daily, unfailing source of profit and enjoyment ; and the

best hour of the day was the after-supper time, which
he always spent in the family circle. Then, as we
gathered round the fire, all " unsociable " employment
forbidden, the day's experiences were retailed to him
with zest and frequent gaiety. As long as we can
remember, we were accustomed to treasure up all
the entertaining things we met with to relate to him,
never feeling that we had fully enjoyed their fun
until he had heard them, and they had evoked his
hearty and delightfully infectious laughter. We
brought out our questions and difficulties to discuss
with him at this time, or else he himself led the
conversation to the subjects he had been studying.
If there were any question raised touching the deriva-
tion or definition of a word, he would send one of us
at once to the bookshelves for the proper authorities ;
but if an interesting point of Biblical criticism were
raised, he made for the study himself forthwith, and
re-appeared, perhaps twenty minutes later, with the
fruit of his investigations. In these fireside hours the
perfect serenity of his countenance was very delightful to witness ; and often in a pause of our cheerful
talk he would say, " Come, children, let us sing."
His favourite hymns were many, but most frequently
of all, perhaps, his choice fell upon one " describing
the pleasantness of religion " :

> " Happy the souls to Jesus joined,
> And saved by grace alone,
> Walking in all His ways, they find
> Their heaven on earth begun."

Mr. Hellier often dwelt in his sermons and addresses upon the duty and privilege of *systematic giving*, and in his own life he acted in this matter according to a well-defined principle. On one occasion, when asked a favour which most certainly would not have been pressed upon him, and which he felt involved a great degree of sacrifice, we remember how promptly an appeal to this principle settled the matter: "The Scripture says, 'Give to him that asketh.' Of course the limits of right and power to do so are understood. So the only question that remains is, *Can we?*"

At times the application of the rule was a matter of more perplexity. Occasionally we have found him, in the middle of a busy morning, with manuscripts, Greek Testaments, and German commentaries spread out on table, desk, and chairs, and in the midst, some itinerant vender of combs, or gas-burners, who with the craft of his species had somehow managed to penetrate to the study, and who, with his wares displayed on the open volumes, would be unfolding the usual tale of woe; while his auditor would be listening, greatly begrudging the precious moments, largely incredulous of the narrative, yet profoundly anxious to deal with the intruder on the highest Christian principles. Very summary ejectment followed our discovery; and yet, when we come to consider the matter, we are far from being satisfied that we did right in depriving these vagrants of an opportunity of spiritual profit, probably not common in their experience.

Once, on or near Christmas Eve, he called upon a poor woman, and found she had no prospect whatever of a Christmas pudding ; proceeding at once to the grocer's, he made various purchases on her behalf. Whether the ingredients were of the exact nature and proportion prescribed in the cookery book we do not know, but we do not doubt that the pudding had a satisfactory flavour.

CHAPTER V

LATER HEADINGLEY DAYS.

1884-1888.

A T the Conference of 1884 Mr. Hellier delivered the Fernley Lecture for that year, taking as his subject *The Universal Mission of the Church of Christ.*[1] His action with regard to this lecture was very characteristic. It was the product of an extraordinary amount of reading and thought; but it was suggested to him before its completion that his simple and popular mode of treatment was out of keeping with the preceding lectures of the series, and would probably be compared unfavourably with them as regards its learning, profundity, and general style. "I am perfectly aware of that," he answered quietly "But my object is to serve the cause of Missions, and I think I can do it better in this way than in any other."

In the autumn of this same year, his youngest daughter sailed for India, to marry the Rev. W H. Findlay, M.A., Wesleyan missionary, of Negapatam.

---

[1] *The Universal Mission of the Church of Christ.* A Discourse delivered at Hanley, Staffordshire. Being the Fernley Lecture of 1884. By Benjamin Hellier. (London : T. Woolmer.)

He bade her farewell upon the deck of the *Dacca*, in the Thames, at Tilbury, and they never met again.

These two events intensified his already profound interest in the work of Foreign Missions. He felt, and often said that it was the duty of every intelligent Christian to keep himself thoroughly well informed in the things pertaining to the kingdom of God, and for him the study had a growing fascination. In the last days of his illness, after he had ceased to read the newspapers, he wanted to know the contents of the *Missionary Notices.* The preparation and delivery of a course of lectures to the students upon Missions was to him truly a labour of love.

Another congenial task was that of lecturing to them upon Methodist History. His love for Methodism and his faith in her future were almost unbounded, and his regard for her founder amounted to a strong personal affection.

The following extract from one of his lectures will show, however, that he was far from regarding Mr. Wesley's authority as infallible. It will also illustrate his views on the relation of the Methodist Church to the Church of England :

" That the present relation of Methodism to the Established Church is a right one needs no elaborate demonstration. That position I understand to be one of friendliness, but also of thorough independence. We owe much to the Church of England in many ways. We have never been her enemies, and I hope we never shall be. But we have not the slightest hesitation in maintaining, that in all that is necessary to constitute true Churches of Jesus Christ, having His approval and working for His glory, the Methodist Churches have as good title to this designation as any Churches in the land. We are resolved not to oppose other good men in doing the work of the Lord, but we will never allow them to hinder us in the work which He has committed to us.

"As to what High Churchmen tell us about our departure from Wesley's principles on this subject, our answer is plain. We know that we have departed from them, and should have been very foolish if we had not. We greatly reverence Wesley's memory; but we have never held him infallible, and on this matter we know that he was mistaken. Wesley said, 'If the Methodists ever leave the Church, God will leave them.' We have left the Church, but God has not left us; He is with us, as surely as He ever was with our fathers. And this is to us demonstration that on this point Wesley was in error.

"As to the idle dream of the re-union of Methodism with the Church of England, there is one short but sufficient objection : 'New wine must not be put into old bottles.'

"When any one has patience enough to look at the question of the union of Methodism with the Church of England, with a view to a practical solution, he very soon finds himself confronted with a succession of impossibilities :

"1. It is impossible, at least in my judgment, for

the two Houses of Convocation of the Province of Canterbury to agree on the terms on which they would unite with the Methodists, and then for the Convocation of York to agree with that of Canterbury. This some may think possible, though I cannot conceive that men with any moderation of views would ever agree to the terms which the High Church party would wish to impose.

" 2. It is impossible that the Methodist Conference should ever agree on terms of union. This impossibility I think is absolute.

" 3. Supposing all this to be surmounted, it would be impossible to harmonize the terms of the two Convocations with those of the Conference.

" 4. Supposing this also surmounted, it would be impossible to prevail on the Methodist people to accept either set of terms.

" 5. Supposing all these impossibilities surmounted, it would most likely prove impossible to obtain an Act of Parliament to sanction the transaction.

" These things considered, and without saying what may or may not be possible one hundred years hence, when you and I shall no longer be dwellers upon this earth, we may say that the question of organic union between the Methodists and the Church of England is one which belongs to the region of pure speculation ; and as a question on which practical men can take action, it has not yet come within the field of vision."

In another lecture in this course we find the

following expression of opinion, on a question which is now much under discussion, that of the conditions of membership in the Wesleyan Church :

"The foregoing historical sketch prepares us for considering the question which has been often asked in late years, and must be asked again and again until it receives a deliberate and satisfactory answer : Ought a Methodist Church, in every place where it is established, to be considered co-extensive with the Methodist Society in that place ?   On this question I offer you my own views ; but you will remember that opinions on this subject are divided, and my own may be opposed to those of high authority in Methodism.

" I. As a matter of fact, from the very beginning of Methodism, persons have been admitted to the Lord's Table who were not members of Society—*i.e.* did not meet in Class.   At City Road in John Wesley's time there were many communicants who were not members of Society, and these were ad-mitted by ticket to the Lord's Supper, the tickets being renewed quarterly.   This practice agrees with what has been the standing rule of Methodism to this day : 'No person shall be suffered on any pretence to partake of the Lord's Supper among us, unless he be a member of our Society or receive a note of admission from the Assistant, which note must be renewed quarterly ' (*Minutes of Conference*, 1796).

" II. Ought these communicants to be considered members of our Church ?   My own view is, that they ought to be so regarded. I cannot conceive how any minister can deliberately and formally authorize a person to come to the Lord's Table, and then declare that he is not a member of the Church of Christ in that place, and therefore in effect not a member of the Church of Christ at all. For this is the only legitimate conclusion. In many parts of the world, as for instance in the Friendly Islands, in Fiji, and in South Africa, there are many spots where the Methodist chapel is the only place of Christian worship within reach; unless therefore such persons are members with us, they are members of the Church *nowhere*. Practically it is the same all over England. We have many families who are attached to us by family descent. They never attend any place of worship but ours, never think of doing so. Now if any one of these were to come to me and say, 'I have insuperable objections to meeting in Class, but I wish to partake regularly of the Lord's Supper; will you admit me?' I should feel (1) that I dared not refuse admission on the ground of his not meeting in Class; (2) that I had a right to satisfy myself by conversation with the applicant that he was a proper person to come to the Lord's Table; (3) being so satisfied, I should give him a note of admission; (4) I would renew it quarterly; and I should be ready to renew it constantly, unless proof were given that such person conducted himself in a way inconsistent with his Christian profession.

"III. There is another thing which, if I could, I would get enacted at the next Conference, and have strictly carried out everywhere:

"1. In connection with every separate Society there should be a Church-roll kept, according to a form prescribed by Conference.

"2. Such Church-roll should contain the names of all the members of Society, and of all regular communicants.

"3. It should be carefully revised and written up once a year, in a meeting of the ministers of the Circuit.

"4. I should regard all whose names were inscribed in this roll as constituting together the Church of Christ in that place, as connected with Methodism.

"As to all these points, I am fully satisfied in my own mind.

"A more debatable question remains: Would you regard the regular communicants who did not meet in Class as eligible for office in the Church? I certainly should *myself;* but you must bear in mind that in saying this I give my own opinion merely: no doubt it is an opinion which would be deemed erroneous by men of the highest weight in our community. Let it stand for what it is worth.

"You must not suppose that by anything I have said I intend to disparage Class-meetings. On the contrary, I hope I have made it evident that I regard the social intercourse of Christian people, the communication of Christian thought and feeling, of mutual

instruction and encouragement, as an inseparable
adjunct of every Christian Church in which there are
the pulsations of vigorous Christian life; and I have
never heard of a method for the cultivation of such
Christian communion better than that of our Class-
meetings. I never heard of any so good ; and I
think it not too much to say, that were Class-meetings
to cease Methodism would have lost the very reason
of its existence. At the same time, as I have said
before, I could not exclude from the Lord's Table
those who did not attend Class, if such non-attendance
were the sole reason for their exclusion. Methodism
has never assumed this power. The whole question
is narrowed down to this, Are all communicants
Church members? I should say *Yea;* others will say
Nay. We must wait for wise men to decide this question, and I hope they will decide it ere very long."

For the practice of nominally insisting on a membership test, and yet allowing it to become a dead
letter, Mr. Hellier had no sympathy. "We must be
honest in this matter," he used to say ; "we should
do more, or less, than we do at present. To say one
thing and do another, is not to be tolerated."

We must not omit to mention, among his other
interests, Mr. Hellier's great love for music. He
sought earnestly to encourage the study of music,
and especially of psalmody, among the students, that
they might take a more intelligent interest in the
musical part of public worship. In this effort he

found a valuable coadjutor in the Rev. E. H. Sugden,
for seven years his colleague, and in a goodly succession of talented students. Music and singing took
a prominent place in College life, and the College
" musical evenings," with their appendix of aphoristic
criticism from Mr. Hellier and his colleagues, form
very pleasant memories for those who were permitted
to enjoy them. He was not himself a trained musician ; but his voice, though of limited compass, was
sweet and tuneful, and when conducting public
worship he joined heartily in the singing,—a simple,
but very efficacious means of promoting the devotional character of congregational singing. Until
recent years he had never heard a first-rate performance of an oratorio; but at the Leeds Musical Festival
of 1877, Mr. Sugden persuaded him to attend the
performance of the *Elijah.* Under the conductor-
ship of Sir M. Costa, with the leading principals
of the day, and the famous Yorkshire chorus, the
rendering was almost overwhelming. " I never heard
anything like this before," said Mr. Hellier. " It has
been a great means of grace to me. Is there nothing
else that I can go to?" After this he occasionally
attended similar "means of grace," and listened with
great delight to Macfarren's *Joseph,* Spohr's *Last
Judgment,* Haydn's *Creation,* and especially to Men-
delssohn's *St. Paul,* which involved him in many
pleasing speculations as to what the great apostle
would have thought of it, could he have foreseen the
day of its performance.

While he was a Tutor he habitually declined all evening engagements, because the work of his classes demanded so much of his time ; but as Governor he felt a little more free to take part in the religious movements of his town, especially those connected with Temperance and Social Purity.   His appointment in 1886 to the chairmanship of the Leeds District drew him further still into a more active public life, and his last years were filled with multiplying interests, which in all their variety possessed as their common end the welfare of Christ's kingdom.

The following extracts from his correspondence with his daughter in India and her husband will help to complete our picture of these closing years of his life, and will exhibit, better than any words of ours, his detailed and vivid interest in the work of Christian Missions :

> *To Mrs. W H. Findlay.*
>> " HEADINGLEY,
>>> " *Oct. 2?rd,* 1884.

" I thought about sending you a list of prospective engagements, before I heard the mention of this in your letter :—*Oct. 26th,* Selby, Children's Sunday (of course the proper day was last Sunday, but the Selby people resolved to have the services a week later, that I might conduct them).   On *Oct. 29th* I am to open a new chapel at Darrington, in the Pontefract Circuit, and shall stay with the Oustons ; *Nov. 2nd,* I am appointed to St. John's in the Manningham Circuit ; *Nov. 9th*, at Birstal, Chapel Anniversary sermons ; *Nov. 10th*, I go from Birstal to Alford to preach Missionary sermon in the afternoon, and attend the Missionary Meeting in the evening ; *Nov. 16th*, Ilkley; *23rd*, Calverley ; *27th*, attend Holiness Convention at Sheffield, stay with the Pratts ; *Nov. 30th*, Garforth Missionary sermons ; *Dec. 7th*, York (Centenary) ; *14th*, Harrogate ; *21st*, Woodhouse and Roscoe Place. I think that is enough for the present. Last Sunday I was preaching at St. John's, Halifax. I went to Sunday school in the afternoon, and had a fairly good service. The Monday morning following I attended a breakfast of Nonconformist ministers at East Parade Chapel. Was elected a member of the Association, and promised to read a paper at the next meeting."

To the Rev. W H. Findlay.

" *Nov. 26th*, 1884.

" Yesterday I learned by telegram that my dear father had passed away. His illness was short. On November 1st he gave his vote at the Municipal elections.

" I am very glad that I saw him last week. Though very feeble, his mind was quite unclouded. I know of no one who, during the last few years, has lived more habitually in the exercise of prayer. One day last week I repeated the words, ' The Lord is nigh unto all them that call upon Him,' and he added immediately, 'I hope I call upon Him *faithfully*,' showing that he remembered the close of the verse.

"I should like you to have known my father, for I am sure you would have admired him. A more thoroughly righteous man I never knew. I should no more have expected to see him do a dishonourable action, than to see the heavens fall. He was truly generous. He had worked hard for all the money he had, and knew how to value it; but he helped, where need was, without stint or grudging. I never knew any one spend less on himself in the way of personal gratification. His care and thought were constantly for others.

"Mr. Farrar is buried to-day in Abney Park. There was a funeral service at Headingley Chapel; Mr. Young gave the address. There was a very large congregation. To-morrow I go to Bristol to father's funeral."

To Mrs. W H. Findlay.

"*Dec.* 18*th*, 1884.

"I incline more and more to the view that school work, such as that at Negapatam, is the best mission work. The teaching of the truth is more thorough; it is more continuous; and it is accompanied by the example of Christian life kept constantly before the minds of the students. The Christian teacher is really influencing for good the minds of his scholars through every hour of school work.

"I have lately preached on the Parable of the

Sower, and it seems to me that its lesson for preachers and teachers is twofold :

" 1. As to many hearers, our labours will be in vain. Small comfort in that, you will say. True ; but it is well to recognise the fact that this has been true of all labourers in the Church, from our Lord downwards ; so that it is clear that there may be want of success as to many whom we seek to benefit, and yet the fault may not be ours *in the slightest degree.*

"2. When the seed of truth grows and comes to conversion in *one* soul, all our labour is repaid, for the increase is a hundredfold. Take, for example, such a case as that of Bannerjee, educated by Dr. Duff, and now an ordained minister of the Free Church of Scotland. (See his speech in the *Report of the Calcutta Conference,* p. 175.) Where is the good effected by such a conversion to end ?"

" *Feb. 5th,* 1885.

" Looking at the whole matter from this distance, and with the very imperfect lights I have, I am ready to conclude that in India we have suffered from impatience. I see more and more that missionary work requires patience, and the workers must be above all things set on doing their duty, but must not be impatient for tangible and visible results. In Ceylon, I apprehend, we have exercised more patience; and we have our reward. As to school work, it seems to me very plain that if God has so wrought with us in His providence that Hindu parents are willing to commit their children to the care of Christian teachers, we are bound to accept the trust, and to do our very best for the children, being quite sure that, sooner or later, large and lasting benefits will result from it. What I want to hear of is a larger number of Christian native teachers, who are competent to walk worthy of their profession. For this we must labour, pray and wait."

"*Feb.* 19*th*, 1885.

"You are quite right in saying that I give a good deal of time to missionary matters, for these are now my chief study. I mean to take up all the mission fields in order, and will write papers on them (not for publication). . I try to get a view of the operations of all the Societies. To survey the whole seems necessary, in order to understand the work of any one.

"I have been thinking lately about the possibility of sending out missionary colonies. Why should it seem a thing incredible? When Gregory the Great began a mission in England 1,200 years ago, he sent forty missionaries. If this could be done so far back in the history of the world, why not now? But we need not ask this. It was done the other day. Bishop Taylor is now on his way to the Congo with a missionary colony of forty. . How far would it be practicable for earnest Christian artisans to follow their trade in India and do mission work? I suppose it would be almost impracticable, except in connection with railway or other engineering work. Would it

be possible for Mr. ——, for example, to encourage
English workmen to come to India with the prospect
of employment ?   This may be only a dream as to
India, but it is surely practicable in some other
places."

> To the Rev. W H. Findlay.

> "*Feb. 24th*, 1885.

"Nothing is more desirable than a perfectly honest
presentation of missionary affairs. When I read the
account of the Calcutta Conference, I greatly admired
the downright honesty of the men and women present. Instead of over-praising their work, they seem
bent on finding out and pointing out all the weak
points in it. At the same time, true success is thankfully acknowledged. There was a book published
some years ago called *Realities of Irish Life*, and it
occurs to me that you might serve your good cause
by sending to the *Methodist Times* papers headed
' Realities of Mission Work.' . .

"Unless you could secure a large number of
Christian teachers, this work of forming village
schools may just as well be left in the hands of the
Government. I am quite one with you in thinking
that the best way is to strengthen and extend the
work of existing stations. In England our cathedral
cities represent original mission stations. This is
very well known with respect to Canterbury, York,
Rochester, London, Ripon, Durham, Chichester, Lich-
field. These stations were made strong, and their
influence spread rapidly."

To Mrs. W H. Findlay.

" *March* 13*th,* 1885.

" I don't know whether I have told you that I have adopted the plan of writing in my diary (*Methodist Desk Diary*) a verse out of the Psalms for the day as the day's motto. I find it very useful. I now usually write it in Hebrew, to get it off by heart. You might do the same with the Tamil. Yesterday the verse was, 'Blessed is the people that know the joyful sound.' The 'joyful sound' I take to be the sound of trumpets on festival days at Jerusalem. This is a Scripture in favour of Church music, and plenty of it. I should like to see the day when in our large chapels we should have choirs of two hundred people. If they all sang 'with spirit and understanding,' lustily and with a good courage, would not *that* be a joyful sound ? Happy the people who in the future will *know* it."

" *May* 7*th,* 1885.

" My verse for the day was Psalm xxx. 5. There *is* an advantage in reading the Hebrew. There is in this language a condensed energy and picturesqueness of expression that is lost in the English version. This verse, literally rendered, runs thus :

'For a moment in His anger;
Life in His favour :
Weeping lodges for a night,
But in the morning—shouting !'

" How rapidly and vividly you are carried back for

more than 2,500 years, and witness the alternations of sorrow and joy in a good man's experience! How much religion there is in the thought that the happiness of life depends on our relation to God! The *parallelism* teaches much. In the four lines above given, there is a correspondence between

anger—weeping—night ;
favour—joy—morning.

"There is a strong contrast between the shortness of God's anger—a *moment*, and the endurance of His favour—a *life*. Your husband might make a good sermon with such heads."

"*May 28th,* 1885.
"I have to preach at Hull on June 9*th.* I think of taking for a text Acts xv. 3. I intend to set forth,—I. Difficulties in the way of converting the heathen. (1) Language—difficulty to both preacher and audience. (2) Antipathy of race. (3) Diversity of modes of thought. (4) Ancient religions to be overcome. (5) Special difficulties in India resulting from the fact that the old religion moulds the whole life. (6) *Add* to these all the difficulties that we find in England—love of sin, frivolity, procrastination, unbelief, stumbling-blocks of various sorts and sizes. II. Conversions are numerous and are genuine, as proved by their fruits. III. Our own duty.[1]

---

[1] An extract from this sermon will be found in Part II., Section iv.

"June 11*th,* 1885.

" I am reading and thinking about Missions every day, and find you and your husband constantly mingling with all my thoughts. We all miss you very much continually, and could not reconcile ourselves to your absence, unless we believed that you were engaged in doing a good work.

" Sept. 3*rd,* 1885.

" Mr. Little has sent me Newman's *Indian Bradshaw,* which, I have no doubt, will give me much help in understanding the distances of one mission station from another. The relative position of all the stations I have in my mind already, with tolerable completeness."

" Sebt. 2*nd,* 1886.

" I have read and heard so little about the Southport Convention, that I can give no opinion on it. I believe such gatherings do good ; but I fear that harm sometimes arises incidentally. Unless great care is taken, they tend to foster the idea that ' holiness ' is something different from practical religion, and make people fix attention too much on a blessing given at a single moment.

" Holiness means righteous eating, drinking, sleeping, buying, selling, talking, and playing. Holy talking does not mean talking always about the most solemn things, but talking in such a way that there shall be nothing incongruous between our talk and our prayers. We may talk very earnestly on some political question, and there need be nothing contrary to holiness in so doing ; but we must not lose our temper, or slander our opponents, or impute base motives to honourable men. Gossip and mirth are in themselves quite consistent with entire sanctification ; but spitefulness, backbiting, and profanity are not. My dear Alice, we do not serve a hard Master ; we serve one who has pleasure in the happiness of His people. The only thing needful is to keep the heart right with God. Then everything is pure and good —jokes and fun included."

"*Nov.* 11*th*, 1886.

" I had a talk with my host, Mr. Skilbeck, about Methodism in the villages. He feels anxious about this part of our work, and so do I. Unless we are watchful, doors now open there will be closed against us. I have a project of going about to see as many of the villages where we have preaching as ever I can, but do not know whether I shall be able to accomplish much in this way. My duties here re-quire me to be at home on most days. The pre-paration of lectures on Missions takes up a great deal of time ; but I do not regret this, because I am never tired of the subject."

" *Dec.* 16*th*, 1886.

" I have been busy with my lectures on Missions. In the last that I gave, I endeavoured to relate a thousand years of the history of India in an hour ! I indicated the great names in the history of Mohammedan power, and pointed out the abiding results of Mohammedanism ; the coming of the Portuguese ; the rise and fall of Dutch power ; origin of English power, and history of English acquisitions. I think I gave a clear outline. Now I must apply myself to survey India as a mission field, and to give a particular account of our own missions.

" I am still anxious that something should be done to revive and extend Methodism in the Leeds District, but at present have no clear light on what is best to be done. It would be a very good thing if we could induce the laymen to raise a fund, and have a committee, for securing suitable sites for chapels in Leeds and in the villages. Perhaps we shall accomplish this.

" But I feel that another thing needed is to deepen and intensify the spiritual life of our people. We as ministers must begin with ourselves, I with myself. I feel that I ought to be more deeply affected by the things which I profess to believe. I say to myself: True religion is the work of God in the soul of man, or it is nothing. But if a *Divine* power works in me, there ought to be more Divine results.

" I believe also that more would be accomplished in Methodism if ministers would set themselves to play the part of good generals. Particular examples show that many people are willing to work, if set to work ; but they need to be set in motion. The next ministers' meeting will be held at the College ; probably on the second Friday in January. I shall then try to 'insense' the brethren with some of these ideas."

The foregoing letter contains the germ of a project which resulted in the formation of the "Leeds Wesleyan Methodist Extension Society," which is now doing an invaluable work in Leeds.

"*Feb.* 17*th*, 1887.

" I don't know whether it would be good for you if I were to tell you of all the tender thoughts about you that often come into my mind ; but I may at least say that you are now dearer to me than you ever were before.   As to experience, you have need to say what I often say over to myself : We are responsible only for those things which are within our control ; all virtue is voluntary. I am not to blame, because I am not so tall as some other men. I think I could not have been taller, if I had tried ever so hard. I am not to blame, if in me the gift of imagination is not so great as in others. So also, if on an intensely hot day my body and mind are incapable of doing what they could and would do in a more temperate climate, I am not to blame on that account. Everything is religion belongs to the moral sphere, and it is only by what is moral—*i.e.* by that in which *will* is concerned—that I can satisfy moral obligation. When the *will* is perfectly right, everything is right, though we may be incapable for a while of vigorous effort of *any* kind. I have my own trials and perplexities every day, and often conclude thus : All

religion is summed up in two words, *trust* and *obey*.
I do now, with all the sense and sincerity I have,
submit myself to God, and trust in Him. I can do
no more. ' Rest in the Lord, and wait patiently for
Him.' "

"*May* 5*th*, 1887.

" I hope you are enjoying yourselves in the hills.
By the way, here is a note on Psalm cxliii. 10 : ' Lead
me into the land of uprightness '—a threefold error in
the Authorised Version. (1) The Hebrew preposi-
tion=not *into*, but *in*. (2) It is not *the* land, but *a*
land. (3) A material noun must not be qualified by
a spiritual adjective. The proper rendering is, ' Lead
me in a land of evenness,' *i.e.* in a level land, where
travelling is safe and easy. The psalmist has been
in a *land of weariness* (*v.* 6). He wants a change.
When the material image is complete, *then* you can
spiritualise. To you, a hilly country is no obstacle to
your being led ' in a land of evenness '; you may have
' a good, refreshing time.' "

For some months previous to the Manchester
Conference of 1887, Mr. Hellier had ceased to enjoy
his usual health ; but it was not until the time of his
departure to Manchester that the serious nature of
his illness was first apprehended. On the Sunday
following his return, and the day before the consultation was held that changed apprehension to certainty,
he preached twice in the East Parade Congregational
Chapel, Leeds. The text of his morning sermon was,

"Be careful for nothing ; but in everything by prayer and supplication with thanksgiving let your requests be made known unto God. And the peace of God, which passeth all understanding, shall keep your hearts and minds through Christ Jesus." He said to his wife when setting out for the day's work, "I intend to preach to *myself* this morning." He was never able to preach again.[1]

But though the nature of his symptoms prevented him from taking pulpit work, all his other duties were efficiently performed until shortly before his death. He was able, for instance, to preside as usual at the September District Meeting, and to take the chair at a meeting held at the opening of the new chapel at Woodhouse Grove, on October 12th. His address on this last occasion was very happy, and delivered with his usual animation.

He suffered much from depression, the direct physical result of his disease. He was also deeply depressed at ceasing to preach, and at the prospect of separation from his family. Especially he was concerned at the anxiety and distress that he knew they had to endure. But for himself, he knew neither concern nor apprehension. His correspondence betrays little or no change in his spirits, and his students were struck to observe the continued cheerfulness of his conversation with them at the table. Even in his family circle, where sadness was inevitable, and his

---

[1] This sermon is given in Part II., Section v.

eyes would sometimes fill with tears at the thought of
leaving us, his self-control never once failed him, and
his efforts to spare us as much distress as he possibly
could were most touching. He even made gentle
apology once or twice for being "such dull company."
How resolutely he continued to occupy himself with
his former thoughts and interests is seen in the letters
he wrote during his illness to his daughter in India.
The first of those we quote from is especially worthy
of notice, because it was written when the shock of
discovering the fatal nature of his illness was still
fresh to us all.

"MATLOCK,

"*Aug. 25th,* 1887.

"Since we came here I have been poorly, and have
not done much to sight-seeing.   Every day
I have read the Psalms for the day in Hebrew. In
Greek I have diligently read St. John's Gospel, and
have been trying to commit to memory the contents
of every chapter. This I find very profitable. Then
in French I have read some of Sabatier's *St. Paul*,
the book which Anna is translating. In German I
am reading a book which professes to give some
account of all the Protestant mission stations in
the world. When you consider that these stations
are counted by thousands, and that the book has
only 338 pages 12mo, you will readily believe that
no long account can be given of any one station.
I turn to 'Nagapatnam' and I find this record:
'Nagapatnam (formerly a Dutch colony); 1,235

souls, with 295 Lutherans. Here is also a Wesleyan little flock, 52 Church members.' That is all; but the book was published in 1881 : a new edition will doubtless say more about you. This German book is useful in showing the wonderful variety of mission work carried on all over the world. It shows that the faith, zeal, labours, sacrifices of missionaries in this century have been very great indeed. The results, such as may be counted and tabulated, are in many cases small in proportion to the labour bestowed ; and yet I think they are very encouraging, when all the mighty obstacles opposing the pure religion of Christ are taken into account. The history of Missions in India is very encouraging, in showing how widespread may be the influence of one good man. The examples of Schwartz in the last century, of Dr. Duff and John Wilson in this, are very striking in this respect. So also instances of civilians and military men like the Lawrences. My book tells of an old Sikh, who said, 'If all Christians were like Macleod (a civilian), we should all of us become Christians.' When I think of all the good work which has been done in India by the English Government in putting down flagrant iniquities and tyrannies, by just laws and by education, and combine with this all the good work accomplished by the thirty-five or forty missionary societies, I feel that we do well to 'thank God and take courage.' We see now only the small beginnings of a wonderful work, that is surely to be accomplished. And *you* have a share in this

work, and a very important one.   It is impossible for
you and your husband to live the lives which I know
you live in Negapatam, without producing a very
powerful effect.   You are witnesses for Christ, witnesses of His power to save.   What can we do better
in this world than bear witness for Him ? "

" HEADINGLEY,

" *Sept. 29th,* 1887.

" You are studying *Ephesians,* and want to gain
light on it.   You know already what I consider the
best method—that of getting up, not the very words,
but the substance of the Epistle, by going through
again and again, a self-catechising.   As thus : How
many chapters in this Epistle ?   What do I remember
of the first chapter? of the second ? and so on.
Try to remember *something* to be found in each
chapter.   Then piece the fragments together.   Take
one chapter for study.   How does it begin ?   What is
the first complete thought ?   What follows ?   What
is the transition from one thought to another ?   Do
I follow the apostle's line of thought?   In pursu-
ing such a method of study, I do not advise you to
spend a long time on it on any one day.   You want
to be wide-awake and to concentrate attention ; but
you need far less time than is often spent to little
purpose in reading commentaries, or in reading the
text over and over *without* such an effort to trace the
course of thought.   The intellectual exercise is good,
and the total religious effect of the very best kind."

"*Jan.* 10*th*, 1888.

"I am very glad that you and Willie have enjoyed reading Telford's *Life of Wesley*. I think it is well written, and will make Wesley better known and better liked. The philanthropic side of his character is well brought out. As Methodists, we have not followed Wesley closely enough in promoting all schemes for men's temporal welfare whilst caring supremely for their spiritual good. We are learning to follow him better just now. The only thing which needs to be guarded is this: let everybody understand that we place the preaching of the gospel far above everything else, and that we abhor the idea of introducing any substitute for it; but then, as flowing from the prime source of all good, let us have as much sound reform and philanthropic effort as possible. Can we improve on Wesley's rule that we should do 'all sorts of good to all sorts of people'?"

One of his principal sources of interest during his illness consisted in a prolonged and critical study of the New Testament use of the *Names of Christ*, made with the special view of obtaining fresh light upon the Pauline authorship of the Pastoral Epistles, and upon the relative value of the leading New Testament MSS.[1]

His Hebrew Psalter, the inseparable companion

---

[1] The principal results at which he arrived will be published shortly in the *Theological Monthly* (Nisbet & Co.).

of many years, interleaved and closely annotated
throughout, afforded him very special solace.   In
these last months he studied in particular the Songs
of Degrees, and committed them to memory in
Hebrew.   His final notes upon them were written
in his Psalter a few days before he died, when his
hand was almost too feeble to hold the pencil.

Throughout his illness, when all other topics failed
to arouse his interest, it always responded to a question on the exposition of a Psalm, or of a phrase in
the Pauline Epistles.   Touching his inner life he
wrote to his youngest sister as follows.

"*Jan. 3rd,* 1888.
"I have not a triumphant faith.   Indeed I am
ashamed that my faith is so weak, and that my inward consolations are not greater.   And yet I know
not how to blame myself; for I believe as well as
I can, and do not knowingly cherish one rebellious
thought."

Although he had much weariness and languor and
distress, and even pain, he never had to endure the
worst possibilities of his condition.   We give these
details of his illness, partly that his friends may know
that he died, in almost every respect, as he had lived
—that he was spared the worst suffering ; and also
in the hope that comfort may perchance be found for
some others, whose friends are found to suffer from
the same conditions.   The onset of cancerous disease

is not necessarily incompatible with months and even
years of life, and life from which usefulness and a
degree of enjoyment are not entirely excluded. Acute
suffering is not inevitable, and a comparatively pain-
less release is sometimes seen. It would be well
if this were more widely known. Too often, the
sombre consolations of sympathising friends, who
have learned the nature of the malady, destroy much
of the possible cheerfulness and hopefulness of such
patients. This was not the case in the present
instance. The thoughtful kindness of many friends
during these last months is something that can
neither be expressed in words, nor repaid with thanks.

Fortunately we had unusual facilities for obtaining
all the resources of medical knowledge. It happened,
too, that Mr. T. Pridgin Teale, the surgeon, whom
Mr. Hellier esteemed and trusted as much as any man
in England, lived within five minutes' distance from
his door, and his skilful services were rendered with
the most assiduous care and generous kindness. And
among the many others who showed him kindness,
we remember with special gratitude the two skilful
and devoted trained nurses, who ministered to him
during the last stage of his illness.

On February 10th Mr. Hellier presided as usual
at the monthly meeting of the Leeds Wesleyan
ministers. No one present realised that it was his
last farewell to his public labours, and to the brethren
he so greatly loved; and yet his ministry could not
have had a more fitting close. We are indebted for

the account of it that follows to the Rev. Stephen Cox, who moved a resolution of sympathy on the occasion of his resigning the chairmanship of the District.

"Mr. Hellier greatly enjoyed fellowship with his brethren in the monthly ministers' meeting. Shrewd, genial, and devout, his presidency ever gave cheerfulness and elevation to the conversation upon the state of the work of God in the several Circuits. Taking his accustomed seat, but, as it proved, for the last time, he gave in some detail the reasons which had led him to place in the hands of the President his resignation of his office of Chairman of the District, reviewing the past with much humility, and yet with grateful satisfaction. He then dwelt upon his failing health and probable retirement from active service, with calm and thoughtful acquiescence in the will of God. A resolution of sympathy was passed, and the mover in presenting it added, 'You know, Mr. Hellier, and must feel sure that your brethren *love* you; and while in your retirement from the office which you have filled with usefulness and honour, they recognise and bow to the Divine will, they assure you that their loving sympathy and earnest prayers will ever accompany you.'

"'I thank you,' said Mr. Hellier, replying with deep emotion; 'next to the favour of God, I value the love of my brethren.' Here his feelings gained the mastery. For some moments he stood silently struggling to recover self-control. Then breathing the words, 'Forgive me,' he resumed his seat. Those present will not soon forget how solemn and tender was that farewell."

A few days before he died, Mr. Hellier dictated to one of his daughters a letter for insertion in the Methodist newspapers, which we give in this place, because it represents the last service that he strove to render to his Church.

"CIRCUIT BOUNDARIES.

" *To the Editor of the ' Methodist Recorder.'*

" DEAR SIR,—

" I shall feel obliged if you will allow me to place before your readers a project on which my thoughts have been occupied for some time past. It is to obtain for each of our Methodist Circuits a complete definition of its boundary; first of all in writing, by resolution passed at the Circuit Quarterly Meeting, and then by an exhibition of the same boundary upon an ordnance map. The need of this may be exemplified by the fact that in this (Leeds) District there is not, I believe, a complete boundary laid down for any Circuit ; and it is very remarkable that a portion of the very centre of Leeds, lying between Briggate and the river Aire, does not belong to any Wesleyan Methodist Circuit. This state of things, doubtless, has many parallels throughout the country.

" The advantages of carrying out this proposal are the following :

" *Firstly.*—It will greatly facilitate the division of any circuit where this becomes necessary.

H.   11

" *Secondly.*—It will prevent disputes about eligible sites for new places of worship.

" *Thirdly* (and principally).—It will enable us to make use of the parochial principle, which has been found so powerful in the Church of England.

"The circuit boundaries, having been fixed by the Quarterly Meeting, and accepted by the District Meeting and Conference, should be delineated on a well-prepared map, which should be placed in one of the vestries of the principal chapels of the Circuit. The effect of this will be, that the official and other workers will have constantly presented to their minds the fact that Wesleyan Methodism is doing nothing to secure the salvation of the unsaved in various portions of the Circuit territory. And this will surely suggest the very practical question, 'Cannot we do something, where we are now doing nothing ?' May we not anticipate that the very best results will follow the thorough organization of all the circuit forces to bring about this end ? Is it not likely that such efforts will often prove more effective than special services, begun and ended within a fortnight ? These latter have often proved of incalculable benefit; but the advantage of the former is, that they can be continued throughout the year, and that all the agents have a permanent interest in the work accomplished.

" Yours sincerely,

" BENJAMIN HELLIER.

" HEADINGLEY, LEEDS,

" *Feb.* 25."

In a sermon on Luke xii. 35, Mr. Hellier thus describes the state of preparation in which death finds the Christian man :

"If he has been a faithful and wise servant, the work will all be finished, and he will be found waiting. There will be no hurry, no alarm, no confusion, no running to put things in place at the last moment. That has all been done long before. He has long been looking for the Lord's return ; and now that the knock is heard, he opens immediately, and has only gladly to say, ' Come in, my Lord, come in.' "

Thus it was in his own case. When his hours were numbered, and he was asked whether he had any directions or wishes to give, he answered, " No ; we have arranged everything." His affairs were always in order ; but months before, he had re-arranged every detail, with a view to giving as little trouble as possible to others. He had examined all his manuscripts, destroying many in the process ; every paper relating to public or private matters was found in its place, and after his death his outstanding liabilities amounted to fifteen-pence.

It was only a day and a half before he died that a sudden relapse showed that the end was near. When he saw that he had to die, he said simply, " The sooner the better," and lay down with a sigh of relief. His first thought, as always, was for his wife ; and she, remembering that not long before, his mind had been shadowed and distressed by questions touching the unsaved world, asked him if it were now perfectly at rest and in peace. He answered with gentle but unmistakable emphasis: "*Perfectly.* As I have said hundreds of times before, I would say now, 'Other refuge have I none.'"

Then he asked for the picture of his absent child, and kissed it, and gave his blessing to the children who were with him. He sent his love too to many friends, remembering those that were left of the old home circle in Wick and Bristol, friends in distant lands, some who had shown him kindness in Circuit life, others whom he had learned to love at Richmond and in later days, the colleagues whom he loved so much, and the students for whose welfare he had lived. To these last he sent a special message: "Give my love to the students, and tell them that my last words to them are to preach Christ; not themselves, but Christ, the good news of salvation, salvation from sin; to *preach Christ.*" And he did not forget to bequeath his Hebrew Psalter to Dr. Moulton. His one request was, that when he was gone he should not be over-praised. "I have tried to do my duty," he said, "but do not let them praise me."

No words can describe the quiet confidence with which he drew near the gate of death that leads to life eternal. Of death itself he seemed to take no notice. His thoughts were with Christ instead.

He even showed touches of his old humour to the last. When he found himself no longer able to command his thoughts, he said : " I consider that I kept my common sense till four o'clock. After that, I am not responsible." This attitude of mind, unconcernedly analysing its own failing powers, is intensely characteristic. Not less so were words, almost his last, expressing a fear that he was "giving a great deal of trouble." And when unconsciousness was finally stealing over him, his wandering thoughts even then clothed themselves in the words of the Apostle Paul, " Whether in the body,   .   .   or out of the body, .   I cannot tell." This was his last whisper.

Early on the morning of March 8th, 1888, he entered into rest, in the 63rd year of his age.

The ground was white with snow, and the day was wet and bitterly cold, when his body was borne to its last resting-place, followed by his friends and colleagues, by the students and the servants of the College, by many old students who, with other ministers and friends, came from the town and district and from all parts of the country to show their love for him.

The first part of the service was read in the Woodhouse Moor Chapel, which was crowded with friends ; and the flowers which covered the coffin had been sent from many homes far and near, by those who loved him well.

The Rev. E. E. Jenkins, M.A., and the Rev. J. S. Banks conducted the service, and the Rev. Dr. Moulton delivered an address upon the life and work of the friend whom he had known and loved for more than thirty years.

In the Woodhouse Cemetery, at the open grave,
amidst the falling snow, we joined in singing,—

" Give me the wings of faith to rise
Within the veil, and see
The saints above, how great their joys,
How bright their glories be."

The stone which now marks the spot bears, beneath his name, these words : " Even so let your light
shine before men, that they may see your good works,
and glorify your Father which is in heaven."

In the above brief memoir of Mr. Hellier, we his
children have tried to place on record the facts of his
life, leaving, as far as possible, to others the description of his work, his influence, and his character.
Of his love and goodness to us we have no words
wherewith to speak ; we are mindful also of his last
request that undue praise should not be given to him.
But they of a man's household watch his daily life
as no others can, and we have a special testimony,
which it is our part to bear. Looking back from the
last hours of his life to the earliest memories of our
childhood, we cannot remember that we have ever
known him do a wrong action, or say an unkind or
unjust word, or yield to unrighteous anger, or neglect
a known duty, or do anything unworthy of his Christian profession. Between what he taught and what
he practised, we detected no difference. For us the
explanation of his life is found in his teaching, and
we ask for no better exemplification of his teaching
than what we have seen in his life.

The old students of the Richmond and Headingley Colleges have, since Mr. Hellier's death, placed mural tablets in the two Colleges ; and have endowed two annual prizes to be given at Headingley College, in Mr. Hellier's name, for proficiency in the study of the Greek Testament and of Methodist History and Polity, subjects in which he had been accustomed to give prizes himself for several years past. The tablet at Headingley was unveiled by Mr. Findlay, on the first Commemoration day held at Headingley after Mr. Hellier's death (May 31st, 1889). The other was unveiled at Richmond shortly afterwards, by Dr. Moulton.

The tablets, which are duplicates, are of polished brass, mounted upon red Mansfield stone ; the design is chaste and simple. The inscription which they bear is as follows :

IN MEMORY OF

THE REVEREND BENJAMIN HELLIER,

TWENTY YEARS CLASSICAL TUTOR AT RICHMOND AND
HEADINGLEY COLLEGES,
ELEVEN YEARS HOUSE GOVERNOR AT HEADINGLEY.

HIS LAST MESSAGE WAS : "GIVE MY LOVE TO THE STUDENTS, AND TELL THEM TO PREACH CHRIST—THE GOOD NEWS OF SALVA- TION, SALVATION FROM SIN—TO PREACH CHRIST."

VIR GRAVIS, MITIS, CONSTANS ;
PIETATE, PRUDENTIA, DOCTRINA PROBE INSIGNIS ;
APUD OMNES GRATIOSUS, AMICIS SUAVISSIMUS FUIT.

OB. MART. VIII., A.D. MDCCCLXXXVIII. : ÆTAT. LXII.

We may fitly close this sketch by giving (in substance) the address delivered by Mr. Findlay on the
occasion referred to.

"Benjamin Hellier needs no testimony from us, or
from men. His earthly course, we are joyfully persuaded, is already sealed with the Master's ' *Well
done* '; and his work will abide to speak for him,
engraved deeply, if not conspicuously, on that which
is most vital and spiritual, most soberly earnest and
reverently intelligent and wisely progressive in the
Church he loved so well.

"But we felt it due to ourselves, to the reverence
we bore him, and to this room fragrant with his
memory, to the house in which he taught and ruled
for twenty years, that some visible memorial of what
he was to us should be set up. In expression of this
feeling Mr. Hellier's old students to-day present this
Tablet to the College, and entrust it to the guardian-
ship of his successors in the charge of this Institution.
It is a slight and unpretending monument, neither
sumptuous in cost nor exuberant in language, but of
its kind the best in material and workmanship we
could procure ; and in this respect, I trust, not unworthy of the name it bears.

"It is fitting that Mr. Hellier's last message should
meet the eyes of all future students who enter this
room to join in fraternal and sacramental fellowship,
a message so touching and characteristic, and of perpetual force. It is fitting too, that, in the words that

follow, all men of authority who assemble here should
be reminded of the qualities to be looked for in those
who have the oversight of such a community as this.[1]
Perhaps if there were any text of Scripture that could
be suitably added to or substituted for what is there
inscribed, it might have been this, from the Psalter
which he loved and knew as few men know it : 'So
he fed them according to the integrity of his heart ;
and guided them by the skilfulness of his hands.'

"Surely it is appropriate also, that the three lines
of characterization should be in the Latin tongue ; it
seemed impossible otherwise to give them the monu-
mental brevity and dignity that were desired. Mr.
Hellier was a scholar as well as a Methodist preacher,
and a Tutor in the ancient languages for the best
years of his life, a man of ripe and accurate learning,
full of knowledge of and sympathy with the ancient
world ; and he was the master, and not the slave of
his learning.

"There is in this circumstance another element of
fitness, pleasing at least to my fancy. 'Mr. Hellier
always reminded me of an ancient Roman,' said one
of his students the other day. There was about him
a massive simplicity, a calm strength of mind and
character, a moral robustness, that were truly Roman.
And his nature was stamped with what I may call

---

[1] In the Committee Room where the Tablet is placed the
weekly College " Class-meetings " and the monthly Communion
service are held.

the *Romana pietas*—that union and identity of reverence toward God with human loyalty, that religious order and exactness, combined with freedom and vigour of thought, which were the foundation of what was greatest in the greatness of imperial Rome, and which belong also to the best type of the homebred Englishman. And this Mr. Hellier always was. His mind and memory were redolent and racy of the soil from which he sprang, of the simple tastes, the shrewd wisdom, and the pure, strong, native speech of an English country home.

" How much might be said, how much is recalled to all our minds when we think of Mr. Hellier, that cannot be put into any such inscription ! Did we ever know a man, a preacher, further removed from every kind of affectation and pretence ? a scholar, more free from pedantry ? a Governor of greater authority, and yet more gentle and unassuming ? a saint more blameless and unworldly, yet more pleasant and conversable ?   It was largely, I believe, the great sincerity of his mind, his true 'singleness of eye,' that gave him his rare insight into life and character around him, and imparted to his piety the naturalness, the homely sweetness and indefinable charm that were, after all, his greatest power.

" ' When I am gone,' he said, ' don't let them praise me.'   Well, we cannot observe that wish to the letter; we cannot speak of Mr. Hellier otherwise than in praise, nor think of him, now he is gone, without grateful reverence.   But we are observing the spirit of his wish if we speak of him just as the man he was, with the simplicity and moderation that in him were known to all men. We record his memory to-day, that we may bless God for so worthy and fruitful a life, and so peaceful a departure as was granted him ; that we may stir up any gift of God bestowed or quickened through his influence ; and that we may hand down to others a pure and high example of what a Christian man may be.

" We ourselves, his surviving friends and students, will be his best praise. Who is not a better man for knowing Benjamin Hellier ? I am very sure none is a worse. Who that has known him is not richer in faith and charity, in patience, in knowledge of what is best and hope for what is best in human nature ? That such knowledge and such love may abide and be fruitful in us, and through us in those who shall come after us, will be his praise and his reward in the day of Christ.

" I say to-day to you, friends and fellow-students, on his behalf, standing in view of his finished course, what he would never have said for himself: ' Be ye followers of me, as I also of Christ; in all things commending ourselves as ministers of God, in pureness, in knowledge, in longsuffering, in kindness, in the Holy Ghost, in love unfeigned, in the word of truth, in the power of God, in the armour of righteousness on the right hand and on the left.' "

PART II

THE TEACHING.

INTRODUCTION.

BUT few words are needful by way of introduction to the " Teaching of Benjamin Hellier," embodied in the discourses and extracts which follow. These addresses have been selected from a great number and variety of MSS., chiefly with the purpose of representing as adequately as possible the main lines of Mr. Hellier's public teaching, and the main burden of his message as a preacher and guide of souls, especially during the years of his later ministry. Some of the sermons included belong, indeed, to an earlier period ; and as Mr. Hellier kept to the last an open mind, and held his opinions and interpretations of Scripture subject to revision, the compilers cannot be sure that in every detail the views here set forth express his final convictions. In all essential points they are satisfied that the statements and reasonings of this volume are such as their author would have wished to set before the Church, had he himself contemplated any publication of this nature.

Those accustomed to listen to Mr. Hellier, whether from the pulpit or from the desk of the class-room, will know what to expect in the following pages. They will count on gathering the fruit of sound and exact scholarship, of a manly and cultivated taste, and of ripe, shrewd wisdom and large experience of the things of God. But they will not look for any lofty flights of eloquence, nor for any oracular depths of philosophy. Mr. Hellier's thought and speech were eminently sober and "of the day." He walked with God in "the light of this world"; and a pleasant thing it was to his eyes to behold the sun and to breathe the common air of life. Scholar as he was, he found in home and friendship, in the work of the Church and in the aspect of nature and the every-day world around him, his mind's nourishment, even more than in books and recluse study.

The strength of Mr. Hellier's teaching lay, therefore, in its practical character. The problem that early occupied his thoughts, and pervaded his ministry increasingly as years advanced, was that which is conspicuous in this volume, viz. *the ideal Christian life*, the proper life of the Christian man as conceived in the New Testament, and as it may be realised by ordinary people in the duties of every day. This problem, by the grace of God, he largely solved in his own experience. In this stedfast pressing toward the mark of spiritual perfection, in his practical attainment of "the rest of faith," in the constant sense of the love of Christ and of "the peace of God keeping heart and thoughts" to which he witnessed in word and in life, Mr. Hellier's testimony belonged to the purest type of Methodist experimental doctrine, and stands in the same line with the *Lives of Early Methodist Preachers.* Apart from other considerations, its record appears to us to have a distinct value on this account. To him religion was a personal, matter-of-fact relationship. He continually "yielded himself to God as one alive from the dead," and sought to persuade others to do the same. The presence of God, the authority and love of Christ Jesus were to his consciousness immediate and all-commanding facts, "plain as the sea and sky," to be assumed and declared in all soberness and simplicity of speech. This he deemed the truest reverence. He could not speak the word of faith as though it were "hidden from him or far off"; he felt it to be "very nigh unto him, in his mouth, and in his heart." And anything that was artificial or laboured and far-fetched in the language of religious worship and teaching, affected him with the same distaste as did the posturing and performing of ritualistic art.

With this reverent simplicity of taste there was connected in Mr. Hellier's disposition a peculiar delight in the homelier human virtues. Those qualities of industry and patience, of meekness and affection and goodwill, that make up "the best portion of a good man's life," but which to high-strung, high-soaring preachers are apt to seem prosaic, found in him a frequent and genuine exponent. He saw them in the elevating light of their religious necessity and import, and they wore in his eyes a true glory. Examples of this characteristic will be found in such discourses as those on "The Nature of Christian love," or, "The Centurion who built the Synagogue." Amongst those who most admired and profited by Mr. Hellier's ministry were thoughtful Christian people in the humbler walks of life.

Added to the sterling good sense and practical spiritual insight of our departed father in Christ, there was a vein of kindly humour rarely absent from his conversation, which, while subdued in his public ministry, yet touched with its quiet glow all his utterances, and often threw into bright relief the salient points of speech or sermon.

But amongst Mr. Hellier's many gifts as a teacher and preacher of Christ, perhaps the most valuable and charming was his rare *lucidity* of mind. It was a habit with him, and one of his firmest principles, not to attempt to teach anything that he did not himself sufficiently understand. "We speak that we do know," might have served for his motto. Obscurity was his special aversion ; nothing came nearer to exciting his contempt than the ambitious striving of men beyond their measure, witnessed sometimes in the pulpit, and the noise and vanity of "words without knowledge." Within his own range, he "saw life steadily, and saw it whole." He was not quick in his judgments, but very sure. He possessed the valuable power of fastening upon the fundamental and decisive conditions of a subject, and dismissing the rest from his mind. "The mere thought of consulting Mr. Hellier," writes one who had occasion frequently to seek his counsel, "seemed to clarify any question I was debating. The effort of stating the matter to him and presenting it as it must appear to his mind, served sometimes of itself to bring light and order into what was before perplexed and difficult." How much his friends and younger colleagues owe, directly and indirectly, to the steady influence of this calm judgment and intuitive sagacity in the guidance of their views and the formation of their plans of work and study, it would be impossible for any of them fully to state or express to themselves.

Were any further title needed for the "Teaching of Benjamin Hellier," it might be found in St. Paul's description addressed to Timothy, of that to which every Christian teacher must "consent" and give his best heed,—

"WHOLESOME WORDS, AND DOCTRINE ACCORDING TO GODLINESS."

GEO. G. FINDLAY

HEADINGLEY COLLEGE,
Oct. 1st, 1889.

SECTION I.

CHIEFLY EXPOSITORY

THE CALL OF ISAIAH.[1]

" In the year that king Uzziah died I saw also the Lord sitting upon a throne, high and lifted up, and His train filled the temple. Above it stood the seraphims : each one had six wings ; with twain he covered his face, and with twain he covered his feet, and with twain he did fly. And one cried unto another, and said, Holy, holy, holy is the Lord of hosts : the whole earth is full of His glory. And the posts of the door moved at the voice of him that cried, and the house was filled with smoke. Then said I, Woe is me! for I am undone ; because I am a man of unclean lips, and I dwell in the midst of a people of unclean lips : for mine eyes have seen the King, the Lord of hosts. Then flew one of the seraphims unto me, having a live coal in his hand, which he had taken with the tongs from off the altar : and he laid it upon my mouth, and said, Lo, this hath touched thy lips ; and thine iniquity is taken away, and thy sin purged. Also I heard the voice of the Lord, saying, Whom shall I send, and who will go for Us ? Then said I, Here am I ; send me."—ISA. vi. 1–8.

THE year in which king Uzziah died must have appeared a very noteworthy one to the Jewish contemporaries of Isaiah, most of whom, in all probability, regarded the death of one king and the accession of another as the most important events which occurred in it.

---

[1] A sermon preached at the Wesleyan Chapel, Headingley, on Sept. 6th, 1873, being the first Sunday in the College year.

Yet to us, who know that this was the year in which Isaiah was called to the prophetic office, these occurrences shrink into insignificance when compared with the last named fact, although that would take place without attracting the notice of any one besides the prophet himself. What is Uzziah to us? To most he is little better than an empty name; and those who remember him best think of him as a weak king, who did one very foolish and wicked act, for which he bore a fearful punishment to the end of his days. But Isaiah is still a living and mighty power. His words still largely influence the thinking and conduct of men. He is one of the princes of God's spiritual dominion, and will live and reign for ever. So it is constantly the case, that events which draw all eyes towards them turn out to be barren of results, and the great transactions which largely influence the whole race pass in silence.

When the Roman emperor Tiberius died, his death would for a short season fill the minds of men, and be the subject of talk throughout the whole Roman empire; but there took place in the same year, or at least about the same time, another event of infinitely greater consequence, known only to a very few, the conversion of Saul of Tarsus. Who thinks of Tiberius beyond the circle of a few learned men? Paul daily touches the hearts and influences the lives of tens of thousands.

In the year 1738, on May 24th, the prince was born who was afterwards known as George III. The event would soon be proclaimed all through England. On the evening of the same day, in a quiet meeting in Aldersgate Street, London, another event took place, known only to one man: John Wesley "believed to the saving of the soul," and obtained assurance of sins forgiven. In a few years George III. will become to all but a few a name, and nothing more; but John Wesley will become more illustrious, and the influence of his work will be more widely felt, as the ages roll on.

So it may be that at this very time God is preparing some mighty ·preacher of the gospel, whose appearance amongst us will be regarded by the future historian as the greatest event of this age. And certainly a mighty preacher would not only be a great phenomenon, but a wonderful blessing. I do not mean a merely popular preacher—that is not a very uncommon phenomenon,—but a man able to grapple with and master the peculiar difficulties of this age ; able to rouse the thought of the nation and to guide it also ; one who should be to England now what Luther once was to Germany, and John Knox to Scotland. I do not know that we could do a better thing than pray earnestly that such a man may be raised up and sent among us.

The passage which I have read shows how great instruments in religious movements are qualified for their work ; and we may all learn how we ourselves, though we may not be eminent in service, may obtain qualifications for the work which God has given us to do.

How was Isaiah prepared for his prophetic office? we take it for granted, first of all, that he had uncommon natural endowments. Men may be very pious, and in proportion to their abilities very useful, whose natural talents are small ; but a man cannot do the work of an Isaiah, Paul, or Martin Luther unless God has given him large gifts of nature to start with. Shakespeare, Milton, Lord Bacon might have been mighty preachers, but the majority of men—never.

We take it for granted also, that Isaiah had diligently cultivated his gifts before he was called to office. It is the unalterable rule of God's moral government that "to him that hath shall be given"; and whatever a man's natural endowments, if they are neglected or abused, God will

never give him high place or noble employment, either in
this world or in the next. Every great preacher, every
great man, is a man of ceaseless toil.

All this being understood, we come to the inquiry, How
was this naturally gifted and, we must believe, self-cultured
man immediately prepared for his high office? This
chapter tells us that it was by a vision; and in seeking to
understand the connection of cause and effect here, we must
consider two things: the vision itself, and its effect upon
the prophet.

I. *The vision itself.*

When we fix our attention on this with a view to understand it, several questions start up in our minds, easy to
propose, but not easy to answer. Was the prophet at the
time of the vision awake or asleep? Was the temple on
earth or in heaven? Was he actually in the temple or
not? I profess not to give answers which cannot be ques-
tioned, but will tell you what to my own mind seems most
likely.

Judging by several other examples of visions mentioned
in the Bible, we conclude that Isaiah was awake, that his
eyes were not closed in sleep, but that nevertheless the
ordinary laws of sight were suspended. Had we, at the
time of this vision, been standing beside him, we should not
have seen what he saw, nor would he have seen what we
did; ordinary objects would for the moment have been
blotted out from sight. He would see nothing beyond
what he here describes.

We think the temple referred to was the temple at Jerusalem, but whether Isaiah was actually present within it
must be left undetermined. To his own thought however
he is there, and we must reverently try to see again what
he saw.

Before all, he "sees the Lord," the heavenly King, sees

Him in human form. He is seated on a throne, which rests upon the floor of the temple, but is raised high above it, as the thrones of kings in their audience chambers are usually raised above the level on which the attendants and courtiers stand. Not only has the King a human form, but He wears the appropriate habiliments of a king; and the prophet tells us that the widespread skirts of the royal robe descended to the temple floor and covered it.

The King is surrounded by His attendants. "Above it stood the seraphim," or rather, "Above Him stood seraphim." Their number is left quite indefinite; they may have been four in number, or they may have been reckoned by tens or by hundreds. They stand around the throne, and, since the King is seated, they appear to rise above Him.

But what are these seraphim? We regard them as being symbols of realities, rather than the realities themselves. Like the varied forms presented to the mind of John in the Apocalypse, they represent something very real, but something the actual nature of which passes our comprehension. We are probably safe in concluding that they appear there to represent that host of the heavenly King who "serve Him day and night in His temple"; beings immeasurably above us, infinitely below their Master. How are these seraphim employed? In praising God. They desire nothing to be *given* to God, for they recognise Him to be the proprietor of all things. They declare His character: "Holy, holy, holy." They declare the relation of the earth to Him: "Its fulness is His glory."

Here let us pause for a moment to gather up the lesson which these seraphim teach us. They instruct us in the value of praise, in the dignity of worship. Sometimes when congregations retire from the service of the sanctuary you may hear some say, with much self-complacency, and with small respect for the preacher: "There was not a single new idea in the sermon. Nothing was said that I had not often heard before." Now I will not say there is no foundation for such remarks. Preachers ought often to be more striking and interesting than they are ; but attend just now to some considerations on the other side. " The preacher said nothing new." This may be quite true ; yet the sermon may have been a very good one, because it may have reminded you of what was very important, and what you may be in danger of forgetting. The seraphim said nothing to each other that was new; but it was so important that it could well bear repetition, and could never be too much dwelt upon. Have you duly *considered* all the old truths ? Have you practised them ? Is there not a need that you should be reminded of these things ?

Besides, although the preacher said nothing new to you, he may have said much that was new to others. You, I will suppose, are an advanced and instructed Christian ; but *every one* in the congregation is not. There are constantly coming into our assemblies those who have been neglecters of religion altogether, and need to be taught the first principles of the Christian faith. There are also children who are beginning to listen to sermons and to understand them. Probably hundreds of children will this day for the first time understand what their preachers say. And the preacher of the gospel cannot overlook these. Be not impatient with him whilst he administers milk to babes, for they greatly need it ; and especially if he deals out a portion of strong meat to you in due season.

Once more, remember that the sermon is not the whole of the service. Preaching is infinitely important, but it is not everything. Preaching is a means, worship an end ; preaching is for this world, worship for the next ; preaching will cease, worship will last for ever. In worship you have your own part. Have you well attended to it? Are you perfect herein? Have you prayed with recollectedness, with fervour, with faith? Have you "sung with the spirit, and with the understanding also"? Have you in singing sought only the glory of God? Has there been no self-gratification, no seeking your own honour? Let him that is without fault in these respects cast the first stone at the preacher. And let us learn from the example of the seraphim that we never rise to higher or more blessed employment than when with them we are devoutly crying, "Holy, holy, holy, is the Lord of hosts: the whole earth is full of His glory."

Again, if the seraphim say nothing new, they remind us of something extremely important. They say that "the whole earth is filled with God's glory." Did you know that? Have you considered it? Many, alas! do not. There are many who travel over large portions of the earth's surface; they see lofty mountains and famous rivers, modern cities and ancient ruins, visit palaces and picture galleries, but they see not anywhere the glory of God.

Some men, who make the earth and its inhabitants their special study, some geologists studying the earth's formation, see stratified and unstratified rocks, they see a long chronology written in the records of these rocks; but they see not the glory of God. Naturalists and botanists study and classify plants and animals, but too often see not the glory of God shining out from His own works. Not so the seraphim. They know more of the earth's structure than these men, and have a wider survey of its multitudinous productions and inhabitants; and they see the whole earth filled with the Divine glory. The narrow limits of the temple disappear. The earth becomes a temple, its surface the variegated floor, the heavens above us its glorious canopy, the everlasting hills its mighty pillars, and all creatures, all men, the conscious or unconscious ministers of its service. And as they behold in God the glorious centre and sun of the world, from whom proceeds all beauty and all blessing, so from all parts of this fair creation the Divine glory is reflected back on their far-seeing and adoring vision ; and in a humble rapture of holy joy they cannot help crying out *Holy, holy, holy !*

II. *The effect of the vision on the prophet.*

But now we return to the inquiry which chiefly interests us : What is the effect upon Isaiah of all that he sees and hears ? The voice of the seraphim is a mighty voice : the temple building is rocked as with an earthquake; the threshold near which the prophet stands trembles beneath him ; a cloud fills the temple, indicating the remaining of the Divine presence, but veiling it from his further gaze. And what says the prophet? Suppose we had been left to conjecture here. We might then perhaps have guessed that his first words would have uttered his adoring wonder, or that he would have attempted to join in the song of the seraphim, and to re-echo their " Holy, holy, holy." But if we had thus conjectured, our thoughts would have gone far astray. Scripture and human experience tell us that when to sinful man the Divine presence is revealed as it here was to Isaiah, he who receives such revelation is at first over-whelmed with fear and shame. Thus it was with Job. In debate with his friends he maintained his integrity ; but when God revealed Himself, all his pleas were silenced, and Job said, " I have heard of Thee by the hearing of the ear : but now mine eye seeth Thee. Wherefore I abhor myself, and repent in dust and ashes."

So with Simon Peter in his fishing boat on the Sea of Galilee. When the miraculous draught of fishes was cap-tured, did he give thanks to Jesus? No ; he cried out, " Depart from me ; for I am a sinful man, O Lord." The

Son of man stood revealed before Him as the Son of God, and he felt that he could not endure to be in that awful presence.

And so with Isaiah. As soon as God has revealed Himself he cries out, "Woe is me! I am undone"; *i.e.* "I am a man doomed to death, already as good as dead." He thought he could not live after having looked upon "the King, Jehovah of hosts." The sight of God brings the sight of sin, and the conviction of sin is followed by confession. The confession is personal and appropriate. Isaiah does not confess sins of adultery or robbery or murder, because in all probability he was free from all these. But he felt that he had sinned with his lips. He had often uttered words which he could not dare to speak in that presence, and the recollection of such words filled him with shame and fear. Well might the prophet feel his own sinfulness in such a presence. The seraphim had spoken to tell of God's holiness, and Isaiah felt that his lips had often been employed in unholy purposes, and he found himself surrounded by a people guilty of unholy language. That he, an unholy member of an unholy community, should see with his own eyes the Lord of hosts, seemed to him enough to seal his doom. But God had appeared to His servant, not to destroy, but to save.

After confession comes cleansing and pardon. "Then flew one of the seraphims unto me, having a live coal in his hand, which he had taken with the tongs from off the altar : and he laid it upon my mouth." Here we see the ministry of heavenly beings in the work of man's redemption. But the seraph is only a minister. He cannot cleanse ; the live coal cannot cleanse. It typifies the power of the Divine Spirit, who is the sanctifier of our nature and the witness of our pardon. And as under the gospel dispensation the blessings of pardon and sanctification always come together, and are wrought by the same Spirit, so here Isaiah is cleansed and assured of forgiveness, specially of the forgiveness of those sins the remembrance of which terrified him most : "Lo, this hath touched thy lips ; and thine iniquity is taken away, and thy sin purged."

After pardon and renewal comes the call to service. From out of the cloud comes a voice, no longer the voice of the seraphim, but of Jehovah Himself : "Whom shall I send ? and who will go for Us ?"

The answer of the prophet is unhesitating : "Here am I ; send me." Are you surprised that he should go so willingly? Can this be the man who a moment ago was crying out, "Woe is me"? Yes; it is the same, yet not the same. In a few moments a mighty change has passed over his spirit, and he who felt himself a sinner doomed to death is now rejoicing in a new-found purity and a new-found pardon. So humble and so glad is he, so inexpressibly grateful for the blessing conferred, that he hesitates not, and he makes no terms. He does not ask to what kind of service he shall be sent, whether at home or abroad ; he says nothing about a recompense ; he does not even ask for success. It is enough for him that he is called, called by One whom by every obligation of duty and gratitude he feels bound to obey ; and he feels that he can do nothing less, he can do nothing more, than say, "Here am I ; send me."

Let us endeavour to learn the lessons which this whole passage teaches. Some of these I have already tried to point out. There are lessons of theological truth of great importance, but to these I can now only refer. I agree with those who think that in this revelation of Jehovah in human form there is a foreshadowing of the glorious doctrine of the Incarnation, and that there is also a foreshadowing of the doctrine of the Trinity ; but these points I leave.

Let us return to an earlier inquiry. How is a great preacher, if one appears, to be prepared for his work? How must all true preachers, even if not great, be prepared for theirs?

There must be suitable mental endowments; there must be much hard toil of the preacher's own, even before he becomes a preacher. But *what make* the preacher are the things here brought before us.

He must get an insight into the invisible world. I do not say that he must see visions or dream dreams, though, in the case of some, visions and dreams have had a great deal to do with the work of preparation.

But he who would preach must be able to say with Paul, " We look upon the things unseen." It is sometimes said that a preacher's usefulness to others will ever be in strict proportion to his personal holiness. I think that history shows that that doctrine is not true; but I believe it is much nearer the truth that a preacher's power, especially his power to awaken sinners, will always bear close proportion to the vividness with which he views by faith the realities of the unseen world. When God, Christ, the devil, heaven, and hell are felt to be realities, and he preaches under the full power of the world to come, he is likely to be an awakening preacher ; and when a professed preacher of the gospel continues to preach after these objects of faith have ceased to be realities, he is a hypocrite, a dishonest man, and one of the most miserable shams upon the face of the earth, and the sooner he lays down his office the better for the cause of honesty and for the Church.

The true preacher of the gospel is one who has felt the burden of his own sins. How else could he sympathise with souls in spiritual distress? how could he enter into the depths of their sorrows?

But he has also experienced the joys of pardon. The

"live coal" has "touched his lips." He has felt the cleansing power of the Spirit. There has been contact, conscious contact, between the spirit of the man and the Spirit of God. Deny this, and you deny all revelation. Hold this fast, and you need not wonder that a man so moved should be mighty in moving others.

How tenderly will such a one preach the gospel of Christ! To the penitent sinner he says, "I know all your trouble, for I have felt it." To the desponding sinner, who writes bitter things against himself, and says, "I shall never be saved," he says: "I once used all your arguments against myself, but I found mercy; I came to God through Christ. As I came, you may come; all things are now ready. The Father is ready to forgive, the Son to receive you as His servant, the Spirit to assure you of your pardon. You ought to fear, but you need not despair." And thus he brings him to Jesus. He encourages his hearers to look for the victory over themselves and over the world. He says with Paul, "I know that in me (that is, in my flesh) dwelleth no good thing." But he also says, "I can do all things through Christ which strengtheneth me."

Brethren, pray for us. Pray for the ministers of this Circuit. The more you pray for them, the more you will profit by them. Pray for me, for my colleagues at the College, and for these young brethren who are come to labour and study among us.

Pray that we may be holy and humble; that, like the seraphim, we may have very exalted views of God, very lowly views of ourselves. Pray that we may be courageous, never fearing to speak the truth and condemn sin; that we may be tender and compassionate, intensely hating sin and intensely loving the sinner. Pray especially that we may be men of faith. There are a thousand things which tend to make you and us worldly-minded, to make us live only under the influence of the visible; and God's greatest gifts to His Church and to the age will be the raising up of men who will preach to us under the constant feeling that the present world is the world of shadows, and the world to which we are hastening, that of solemn and blessed and eternal realities.

THE VISION OF THE MOUNTAIN OF THE LORD'S HOUSE.

" The word that Isaiah the son of Amoz saw concerning Judah and Jerusalem. And it shall come to pass in the last days, that the mountain of the Lord's house shall be established in the top of the mountains, and shall be exalted above the hills ; and all nations shall flow unto it. And many people shall go and say, Come ye, and let us go up to the mountain of the Lord, to the house of the God of Jacob ; and He will teach us of His ways, and we will walk in His paths : for out of Zion shall go forth the law, and the word of the Lord from Jerusalem. And He shall judge among the nations, and shall rebuke many people : and they shall beat their swords into ploughshares, and their spears into pruning-hooks : nation shall not lift up sword against nation, neither shall they learn war any more. O house of Jacob, come ye, and let us walk in the light of the Lord."—ISA. ii. 1–5.

IN order to understand these words, as well as the writings of the prophet generally, we must remember that Isaiah was a *seer*, and that the whole book of his prophecy is designated a *vision*. He saw what the natural bodily eye never sees ; and what the eye of the soul never sees, unless it receives strength to see and light to see with, through the inspiration and revelation of God Himself.

Let us first try to see what the prophet saw ; and, secondly, to see farther than he saw : that is, to interpret his words by the bright light which Christianity sheds on them.

1. *Let us try to see what the prophet himself saw.* Let

H. 13

us in imagination take our stand beside him. We will suppose that we stand together on Mount Olivet, and that we are looking westward, looking down on the temple and its surrounding courts. We see the Lord's house, the holy temple of the Jews; we see the mountain of the Lord's house, Mount Moriah, on which it stands. We will suppose that it is the time of the morning sacrifice, and we behold between us and the temple the great brazen altar. We see the priests ministering at it, the flame and smoke ascending from the sacrifice, and the people worshipping in the court below. We gaze upon the glorious temple porch built by Solomon, whose gilded roof flashes back to us the rays of the morning sun. We see the holy place behind the porch, and farthest to the west the holiest place of all. Between us and the temple we look down into the valley of Jehoshaphat, through which are flowing the dark waters of the river Kidron.

Hitherto we see nothing more than any other man could have seen, standing in the same place at the same time. But as we continue to gaze with the prophet, and share, as we suppose, the Divine illumination given to him, the scene before us changes: the near becomes distant, the distant near, and we have a vision shining across the gulf of ages.

Behold a wonder! The mountain of the Lord's house is rising! It rises higher and higher, until it is seen at the summit of the mountains. It is lifted up higher than any of the surrounding hills. It is the highest, grandest object within our range of vision, and a brighter glory shines around it.

And now behold another wonder! Streams are flowing up the sides of the mountain in all directions. As we look more closely our wonder is abated, but our interest increased, when we see that these streams are people, or rather " peoples," the various nations of the earth going up

the sides of the lofty mount. And now our sense of hearing being supernaturally strengthened, we hear what these
peoples are saying, though their voices reach us across a
wide gulf of time. And what are they saying? Are they
moved by hostility as they see the Lord's house upon the
top of the mountains? and are they saying, " Raze it, raze,
to the foundation thereof"? No; their language is very
different. The nations of the earth are all going to school,
and they are encouraging and exhorting one another, saying :

> "Come ye, and let us go up to the mountain of the Lord,
> To the house of the God of Jacob ;
> And He will teach us of His ways,
> And we will walk in His paths."

This is what the peaceful, happy nations are saying ;
and we see that the blessed time is come when the Lord's
house is the great central school of the whole earth.

But the prophet sees better things still. Jehovah is not
only the one great teacher, He is the great lawgiver ; and
from Zion are going forth the edicts which are to govern
the world.

> "For out of Zion shall go forth the law,
> And the word of the Lord from Jerusalem."

This is what he sees. It is a blessed prospect ; but the
vision does not end here. Right laws are good, but they
avail little without a righteous administration ; but in the
grand time which we now foresee Jehovah becomes the
administrator.

> "And He shall judge among the nations,
> And give judicial decisions for the numerous peoples."

So the blessed time is arrived when, not individuals alone,
but nations also have agreed to settle their disputes by arbitration ; and Jehovah Himself is chosen arbitrator.

You can easily foresee what follows when men become
so wise as this. War becomes an anachronism and an
absurdity. The prophet sees the introduction of the reign
of universal peace. He sees armies marshalled for the last
time, marshalled only to be disbanded. The war-horse
is sent to the pasture, the war-chariot is turned to a
peaceful use, the soldiers are all becoming ploughmen and
vinedressers. The prophet sees many forges with their
fires kindled throughout many lands, and the soldiers, intent
on the occupations of peace, are bringing in their swords
and their spears, and the smiths are busily at work, and a
strange but welcome music is heard ; everywhere the iron
is ringing on the anvil, whilst all the swords become ploughshares and the spears are turned into pruning-hooks. The
elaborate science of war is henceforth to be reckoned
among forgotten things of the past.

> " Nation shall not lift up sword against nation,
>   Neither shall they learn war any more."

Such is the prophet's vision. As we contemplate it, does
not every heart say,

> " O long-expected day, begin ! "

2. *But let us now try to see more than the prophet could
see ;* for between his day and ours stands the day of
the manifestation of the Son of God, and by His blessed
light the prophet's words spread out for us a wider and
more glorious scene than he himself ever beheld. The
material gives way to the spiritual, the local to the universal, the earthly to the heavenly. From Mount Zion
in Jerusalem, from the earthly temple, the sanctity and the
glory departed, from the day when Christ uttered the
solemn and affecting words, " Your house is left unto you
desolate." But by the eye of faith we see another Jerusalem,
another Zion, another temple. We see a kingdom estab-

lished which can never be removed, but which is destined to subject all other kingdoms to its sway. We look to heaven itself as the metropolis of this kingdom ; we see Jesus seated on His heavenly throne, advanced in glory above angels and principalities and powers. But whilst the capital and the throne are in heaven, the boundaries of the kingdom reach to earth, and include within them every soul of man that loves and serves the Lord Jesus Christ.

We acknowledge no one earthly centre of this kingdom, but we find a centre whence its power radiates " wherever two or three are gathered together" in the name of Christ. We cast our gaze backwards, and we see this kingdom beginning in great weakness and obscurity, battling with many foes in the long line of centuries, vehemently opposed, bitterly persecuted, but never destroyed. We see it to-day wielding a greater and more commanding power than it ever had before ; and again, helping ourselves by the prophet's vision, we see the spiritual Jerusalem, the Church of Jesus Christ, exalted above the highest hills. We see the time which will surely come, when the Church of Christ will be, and will be acknowledged to be, the greatest power on earth, giving law to all the nations. And we behold all kindreds and peoples and tongues willingly submitting themselves to the rule of Christ.

We see the blessed state of things which this involves. The prophet tells us much when he says that men shall learn war no more. But his words imply more than they say. St. James gives us the philosophy of warfare, when he says: " Whence come wars and fightings among you ? Come they not hence, even of your lusts that war in your members ?"

And we know that before the outward universal peace can come, it must have been preceded by the inward peace, by the reconciliation of man to God, and by the peace of

soul which the Spirit of Christ imparts when He reigns in
men's breasts. "The kingdom of God . is righteousness, and peace, and joy in the Holy Ghost"; and
where the kingdom comes, these come ; when the kingdom
is universal, these are universal. We want nothing more.
Righteousness universal ?—then an end of wars, fightings,
tyranny, oppression, robbery, deceit, lying. Peace universal ?
—then an end of strife and contention ; the race of men
a brotherhood, not in theory, but in reality. And joy universal ?—the joy which must prevail where righteousness
and peace reign. And the righteousness, peace, and joy are
all "in the Holy Ghost." They are the fruit of the Spirit,
recognised as such, and therefore connected with a Divine
source and a heavenly hope and an everlasting inheritance.
When all this comes to pass, we have all that we can
wish. Earth is turned to paradise. It becomes a vast
temple in which every one celebrates the glory of God.

THE VALLEY OF BACA.

"Who passing through the valley of Baca make it a well ; the rain
also filleth the pools."—Ps. lxxxiv. 6.

THIS is a very difficult verse. It contains four words the
meaning of which is uncertain; namely, those which in
the A.V are rendered "Baca," "well," "rain," and "pools."
The rendering given of this verse by Jerome affords an in-
dication of the great divergence of views as to its meaning
found both in versions and in commentaries. He gives
it thus : "Transeuntes in valle fletus, fontem ponent eam.
Benedictionem quoque amicietur doctor." (Passing through
the valley of weeping, they will make it a fountain. The
teacher also shall be clothed with blessing.) Amidst much
that is doubtful, I think it is certain that the Hebrew word

which in the A.V is rendered by "well" cannot have this meaning. In the Hebrew Bible the distinction is always carefully observed between a "well," in which water is obtained by digging, and a "spring," which gushes forth from the earth without help from man's labour. The Hebrew word used to denote the one is never applied to the other; and the word of this verse means a "spring," and is the one used in Psalm civ. 10, where it is said of the Creator, "He sendeth the springs into the valleys, which run among the hills."

Having reached this firm ground, we can safely take a step farther. Men cannot make a spring where none exists *in rerum natura*. Hence when it is said that those who pass through the valley "make it a spring," this can have no other meaning than that they make a place to be in their thoughts or imagination what it is not in point of fact. This interpretation is rendered more probable by the consideration that the Hebrew verb here used is not the most common equivalent of "make," but signifies to "put" or "place" (so *ponent* in Jerome), and sometimes means to "constitute," or to make a thing to be what it was not before. (See Isa. xxvi. 1; Jer. xxii. 6; Ps. cx. 1.)

The meaning of the word "Baca" is very doubtful. The oldest versions render it by "weeping"; others, like the A.V., treat it as a proper name, rendering "the valley of Baca." The primary meaning of Baca is in this case said to be either "mulberry tree" or "balsam tree." I believe we ought to regard "Baca" as a proper name; and the valley here referred to may be identical with the valley of Rephaim mentioned in 2 Samuel v. 23, 24, in which there were "mulberry trees" or (*bekhaim*).

Those who render "valley of weeping" give a figurative sense to the words, and support their view by a reference to the valley of death-shade (or darkness) in Psalm xxiii. 4.

But this interpretation will not in any way accord with the context. If we are in the right in taking "highway" in a literal sense, then it is reasonable to suppose that the writer will lead his pilgrims by a literal highway into a literal valley, and not into a figurative one. Besides, as he further pourtrays the course of the journey, we see how the travellers "go from strength to strength" until "each of them in Zion appears before God." We cannot understand Zion as making the end of the journey in any other than a literal sense, and therefore the road leading to it and the valley through which the road passes must be literal also. Further, if by the "valley of weeping" we are to suppose that the pilgrims when in it weep for sorrow, this is opposed to the whole purport of the psalm, which describes travellers whose joys are to be envied, not those whose sorrows we have to pity.

The valley of Baca has not, I believe, been identified, but the context in which it is mentioned warrants the conjecture that it lay in the route of many of the pilgrims who went up to the house of the Lord ; and we may further suppose that it was near Jerusalem, so that when the pilgrims reached it they knew that they were near their journey's end. If these conjectures are allowed as probable, we may add one more, that in such a place it would be common for pilgrim bands coming from different parts of the country to meet, and the joy of the travellers would increase as their numbers grew.

The word rendered "pools" in the A.V certainly means "blessings" according to its present vocalization in the Hebrew Bible, and this is supported by the LXX and the Vulgate (εὐλογίας—*benedictionem*). The word rendered "filleth" almost always means "to cover with a garment" ; and Jerome here translates it by *amicietur*. The word *moreh*, rendered "lawgiver" and "teacher" by the older versions, elsewhere denotes only the early rain of spring (Joel ii. 23).

The sense of the whole verse may be given thus: "Happy are those" (this is implied in the context) "who, passing through the valley of Baca, make it a spring (or place of springs, *Delitzsch*). The early rain also covereth it with blessings" (that is, of abundant herbage). The main thought is, that the joy of the pilgrims when they reach this valley is so great, that though in reality it is waterless and bare, it is to them as good as one in which there are springs, and which is covered with verdure.

This thought is often verified in experience when the state of our feelings, whether happy or sad, gives its own complexion and character to the scenery which surrounds us. It is thus expressed in one of the Olney hymns:

> "How tedious and tasteless the hours
>   When Jesus no longer I see !
> Sweet prospects, sweet birds, and sweet flowers
>   Have all lost their sweetness with me ;
> The midsummer sun shines but dim ;
>   The fields strive in vain to look gay :
> But when I am happy in Him,
>   December's as pleasant as May."

Think how the religion of a pious Jew gave brightness to his life in the time of king David. It is exceedingly difficult for us to transport ourselves in thought to the time of David, and to enter into the views of the men of his day. How vastly different the outward circumstances from those of our own time ! We have to think of a country without railways, without roads, such as we should call by that name ; a country mostly without trees, lying under the unrelieved glare of the scorching sun ; no telegraphs, no letters, no books (except a very few, for a very few) ; no churches, no chapels, not a single building in all the land

within which the people met for public worship. If this
psalm was composed in David's time, as seems most
likely, there was indeed the tabernacle on Mount Zion,
but the people never entered it ; it was only for the priests.
There were no sermons, and at this time hardly common
prayer.

There were the sacrifices, most solemn, most impressive
and significant, but speaking clearly only to a few. Imagine
what England would be, were the only authorized place
of worship found in the land St. Paul's in London ; the
religious people going to worship three times in the year,
and the worship consisting chiefly of slaying and placing on
the altar bullocks and rams and lambs.

And yet there were truly religious Jews at this time, and
though their outward circumstances were different from
ours, their inward experience was in many respects very
like our own. They rejoiced in the birth of their children ;
they bitterly mourned their loss when removed by untimely
death. They experienced great dejection of mind when
subject to bodily pain; they shrank from death with a
horror greater than our own ; they felt the upbraidings of a
guilty conscience, and felt the need of God's mercy.

Their views of God, though not such as we have been
blessed with through Christ, were nevertheless true and
exalted. When we wish to extol the majesty of God and
His infinite superiority to man, how can we praise Him
better than by saying, "The heavens declare the glory of
God, and the firmament showeth His handiwork"? When
we would glorify God as the Creator and Ruler, how
can we better do it than in the words of Psalm civ.: "O
Lord, how manifold are Thy works! in wisdom hast Thou
made them all : the earth is full of Thy riches"? Their
views of a future state of blessedness were dim and imperfect compared with our own ; and yet what can we say

higher than this, " At Thy right hand there are pleasures
for evermore " ?

The religion of the Jew made his life more bright and
happy. The tabernacle or temple service which he attended told him that God was to be approached by sacrifice, that He was a God ready to pardon ; and doubtless
centuries before Christ uttered His parable of the Pharisee
and the publican there was many a conscience-burdened
sinner who prayed in the temple courts, " God, be merciful
to me a sinner," and " went down to his house justified,"
able to declare to others, from his own happy experience,
the blessedness of the man " whose iniquity is forgiven
and whose sin is covered."

How does our Christian faith give brightness and joy to our
lives ! The firm hope of immortality brightens life as nothing
else can. Suppose from being Christians we were to turn
atheists and materialists. How sadly would the horizon of
our being be contracted and darkened ! How would the
thought of sinking into nothingness harass and torment us
all the way through life. Especially must this be the case
with all who have advanced beyond middle life, and begin
to find in themselves the sure symptoms of failing strength.
They must feel that the best part of existence is for them
gone already, only the dregs left. Whatever arguments there
are against man's immortality, I wonder how any one can
find satisfaction in being persuaded by them. Can you
bear to dwell on the thought—this busy, active, planning,
and forecasting mind will think no more ; this ardent,
loving soul will love no more, will at death be utterly and
for ever extinguished ? How dismal, how horrifying, to
any one who tastes the joy of living ! How different it is
with the Christian ! However old he is, there is one sense
in which he always feels himself young. In respect of the

better life he is but an infant of days; he stands at the
very threshold of his being, and an unbounded prospect
opens before him. He says what, in effect, the Apostle Paul
says to the Corinthians : "In the contemplation of that
future life I feel myself a child, I think as a child, I speak
as a child, I reason as a child; my knowledge is but
partial, I see through a glass darkly; I am an heir of God,
but at present sojourning in a country far from my father's
house. But I shall not always be a child : I shall attain
full age, and put away the childish things of earth; I shall
see God, not through a glass darkly, but face to face; I
shall no longer be an exile, but dwell in my Father's house
for ever."

Thoughts like these give elevation to life at every period,
whilst to Christian old age they give the glory of the setting
sun, which shall soon change into the dawn of endless day.

THE AGE OF MALACHI.

From a Sermon on MALACHI iii. 16–18.

THE age of Malachi was one of religious declension,
following a period of revival and reformation. He
appears to have prophesied about 420 B.C., and consequently
a few years after the godly and patriotic Nehemiah had
completed his reforms in the Jewish state. We might have
hoped to find a condition of religion altogether satisfactory.
But it was not so. We infer that the grievous sin of
idolatry, to which the Jews had been so long prone, had
now ceased, because the prophet makes no complaint on this
account. The sin of the people was not that they were addicted to a false religion, but that they lacked faith and zeal
towards the true. Let us follow the prophet's guidance,
and see the portrait of his people which he draws.

We find that we must begin at the house of God, and with the priesthood itself. It will always be the case, that if we wish to understand the moral and religious state of a people, we must begin with the ministers of religion. As they are, so the people will be. I say not that there are no exceptions, but this is the rule. If the great body of the ministers of religion are faithful and diligent, religion will prosper; if they are unfaithful, religion will decline. In Malachi's days the priesthood were unfaithful. This is very plainly stated in chapter ii. 7, 8.

The root of all the evil was *want of faith.* There were those among the priesthood who had lost their faith in God as an ever-present judge in the midst of His people, and had come to the conclusion, which they did not hesitate to avow, that the righteous had no advantage over the wicked (iii. 14, 15).

Now unbelief amongst the priesthood must always be a terrible evil. It tends to overturn all religion from the foundation. Men who as religious teachers are unbelieving, cannot always disguise their unbelief. They may not avow it in words, but it affects their conduct, it makes their testimony powerless; and it stealthily but surely propagates itself in the minds of their hearers.

One immediate result of this in Malachi's time was, that the priests performed the temple service in a heartless manner, without zeal, without any love for it. They went through the prescribed service; but it was no longer a labour of love, it was task-work, and the sooner it was over the better they were pleased; and when it was finished they said, " What a weariness it is ! " They went so far as even to express by their very gestures their contempt for the service in which they were engaged (i. 13).

They performed the service of God in such a way that what should have been an acceptable sacrifice became an insult to Jehovah. They allowed the people to bring, and they dared themselves to offer in sacrifice, animals which were blind and lame and sick, in fact of such a description, that if they had been offered to the civil governor they would have been rejected with indignation. They allowed themselves to fall into a mercenary spirit. They would do nothing for love; everything must be done for pay. They would not shut a door in the temple, or light a fire, except for the temporal recompense obtained. Their maxim was "nothing for nothing." When this mercenary spirit once invades the minds of the ministers of religion, farewell to their usefulness. It is right that those who serve at the altar should live by the altar; it is right that those who preach the gospel should live by the gospel; but with every true minister of religion the object of supreme regard will be *his work*, and not his temporal support. His work will be the end, his temporal support a means to the end. With the mercenary minister the reverse is the case. He makes religion a means, and his worldly good the end. Never expect such a man to do much good. It is not in him. What was the result of this conduct on the part of the priests? There was, first of all, a sure result to themselves; *they were despised by the people.* They did not fear to make religion contemptible; but they forgot that they made themselves contemptible at the same time (ii. 8, 9).

It is always so. A faithful minister of religion may be disliked, feared, and by some even hated; but he will not be despised. On the other hand, it is difficult to find a character more cordially or more deservedly despised, than that of the minister of religion who shows that he dislikes his work, but clings to it because of the emolument which it brings.

What was the general effect on the people? It was bad every way. The services of religion were either neglected altogether, or they were performed in such a way that they proved an insult to God rather than an acceptable sacrifice. Tithes and offerings were largely withheld, so that God says by His prophet, " Ye have robbed Me.   In tithes and offerings " (iii. 8).

What was the effect on morality ?   Could it be otherwise than evil?   Men have imagined that it is possible to maintain a nation's morality apart from religion.   They have imagined this ; but it has never been done.   History does not furnish a single example, and we believe it never will. How was it in Israel at this time ?   The priests became sceptical and unfaithful ; and family morality at once decayed.   In the families of the priests there were frequent divorces : " the priests dealt treacherously with the wives of their youth."   Need we go any further than that ?   If the priests set the example, would not the people quickly follow ? What then ?   When the purity of family life is no longer preserved, the morality of a nation is poisoned at its fountain head, and evils of every kind ensue.   God by His ordinance, by His severe but most kind ordinance, guards the purity of our homes : and why?   Because He "seeks a godly seed."   But when adultery and divorce become common, what hope is there of a godly seed, what hope of a godly nation ?   Read the general result in the words of the prophet : " I will come near to you to judgment ; and I will be a swift witness against the sorcerers, and against the adulterers, and against false swearers, and against those that oppress the hireling in his wages, the widow, and the fatherless, and that turn aside the stranger from his right, and fear not Me, saith the Lord of hosts " (iii. 5).

You may perhaps say, What is all this to us ? My answer is, that in all ages like causes produce like results.   In my view, the greatest evil that we have to fear is infidelity ; and in every degree in which this evil prevails, it will tend to destroy our nation. What is the source of crime now? Unbelief. Whence come the robbers, the plunderers, the murderers, whose crimes defile our land, the report of which makes us shudder with horror? They come out of homes where there is no family religion.

But now we turn to a more welcome subject: *the pious few* in the days of Malachi. Note their character: "They feared the Lord." To fear the Lord, in the language of the Old Testament, is to be a righteous man. The "fear" here spoken of is that state of mind which arises from firm faith in the existence of God and the revelation of Himself which it has pleased Him to give to mankind. It is not a slavish, but a filial fear. It is not the fear "which hath torment," and is cast out only by perfect love, but the fear which is associated with blessedness and springs from love. It is not the fear of a slave who has a cruel and unjust master; it is the fear of a servant who knows his master to be just and kind, and fears only to do that which would displease him. It is the fear, not of the condemned criminal who is awaiting the execution of his sentence, but the fear of the rebel who has been freely and fully forgiven, and fears lest he should ever again sin against his forgiving lord. It is the fear of the prodigal son; not that which possesses him as he returns home, hoping for pardon, but fearing rejection, but the fear of the prodigal after he has been kissed and forgiven, who once more walks erect and breathes freely in his father's house, and only fears to offend again a father who has dealt so generously with him. It is truly said respecting such a man, "Blessed is the man that feareth alway."

Note the conduct of these men: "They spake often one to another." It is not difficult to infer the subject of their converse. It is very pleasant and profitable to think of these ancient "Class-meetings," as we may call them, in Jerusalem. They probably did not attract much attention from the general community. The merchant as he passed on his way to his business, greedy of gain and unscrupulous about the means, would not tarry to take any part in them. The hireling priest returning from the temple service, heartily glad that it was over, and crying out, " What a weariness it is ! " would find nothing congenial there. But these meetings were not held in vain. There was One who never overlooked them. Whoever else was absent, His sacred presence was always there. He listened to their pious communings. And He judged the matter of discourse so weighty, that " a book of remembrance " was kept for those who "feared the Lord and thought upon His name." Well would it be for some, if no memorial of their foolish and wicked talk was kept. But happy was it for these that " Jehovah hearkened and heard." And further than this, He revealed to one of their number, to Malachi, what His purposes of mercy were towards them, and how glorious their future reward should be :

" And they shall be Mine, saith the Lord of hosts, in that day when I make up My jewels; and I will spare them, as a man spareth his own son that serveth him."

THE KINGDOM AND ITS CITIZENS;

OR, THE TEACHING OF THE BEATITUDES COLLECTIVELY.

MATTHEW v. 3-12.

THESE verses define the constituency of the kingdom of heaven. Other kingdoms can be defined by geographical limits ; this has none. Other kingdoms have been founded by force; this kingdom never gained by force a single subject. And as it was not founded by force, and is not carried on by force, so it never can in any place be made identical with any political organization. All such organizations must employ force, and must exercise their authority over those who submit unwillingly to it. The nation can never be identical with the Church of Christ, until every member of the nation serves Christ from a principle of love to Him.

The kingdom of heaven is not constituted by the association of people together in virtue of the common acceptance of certain religious ceremonies. It is held by some that the membership of the kingdom is made up of people who are baptized, and who partake of the sacrament of the Lord's supper. But this method of defining the kingdom of God is both too wide and too narrow. It is too wide, because it includes many who certainly do not possess the characteristics of members of the kingdom which are here set forth. It is too narrow, because it would exclude many who have these characteristics, but yet have never been baptized and never celebrated the Lord's supper—many, for instance, belonging to the Society of Friends. How then shall we define the kingdom?

I. The answer is contained in the text. It is determined by *character.* All those who have the character which these verses describe, whether Catholics or Protestants, High Churchmen or Quakers, belong to the kingdom; and none belong to the kingdom who are destitute of this character.

And so if we ask, How is the kingdom to be maintained in the world, and how promoted? our answer must refer first of all to the Divine agency which maintains it, the Divine work of Christ and of the blessed Spirit. But so far as our answer refers to the human agency, we say again, We must depend not on force, or political influence, or social rank, or intellectual gifts, but on *character*. The people who in their own tempers, speech, and conduct prove themselves true members of the kingdom of God, must extend the kingdom ; and all others are of little use. What is the first thing in a Christian ? Character. What is the second ? Character. What is the third ? Character.

II. But these verses also teach us a second great lesson. The character is *manifold*. What deplorable results has the history of the Church of Christ experienced, because this has been overlooked! Even now, some, like the Pharisees, make religion to consist of outward observances. Some teach a morality divorced from religious observance, and they speak of people "who are in moral conduct all that we could wish them to be, but who yet neglect religion." Of such people I have heard, but I never met with them, and I do not believe they are to be found. Morality is keeping the commandments of God. What sort of morality is that which neglects the first and great commandment? And there never lived a man who kept the second commandment, and loved his neighbour as himself, if he was destitute of the love of God. We must hold fast these two conclusions : Religion divorced from morality is worthless ; morality, in its highest and best meaning, without religion, is impossible.

How limited, again, are the views of some as to what this term, religion, embraces ! You may sometimes hear a Christian woman, the mother of a large family, who toils all the day long in a self-renouncing spirit, caring for the happiness of all about her, and seeking her own happiness last, who is cheerful and contented in the midst of narrow outward means, lamenting that she has "so little time for religion." But is not such a woman practising religion all the day long, and that of the highest kind ? Everything that a man does is a part of religion, if all the time that he is doing it his heart is right with God.

How one-sided also are the views of those who exalt some one virtue above all the rest, and make religion to consist in that alone! The beatitudes do not describe different classes of Christians, but different features in the character of all true Christians. The teaching of Scripture and the history of true Christian lives show that those who possess one of the virtues here mentioned have them all in some degree, though it is true that one virtue shines more conspicuously in one Christian, and another in another. But some who are strong in one virtue—or who think they are—fall into the error of supposing that they can therefore dispense with the rest. Here is a man *all honesty*. He pays his twenty shillings in the pound. There his religion begins, there it ends. But if such a man be proud, vain, boastful, without meekness, without humility, and without generosity in his thoughts and words towards others or in his dealings with others, we cannot look upon him as a member of the kingdom of God. Here is a man strong in *benevolence*—good-natured, charitable, and free to give. But benevolence, unaccompanied by other virtues, is a very poor thing indeed. It is a mere instinct, and not a principle. The giver by instinct is often too generous by half. He fails to look conscientiously after his expenditure, and the issue often is that he gives away other people's money rather than his own. Let these illustrations suffice.

How beautiful is the complete Christian character—one which answers to the description here given! Such a man is unfeignedly humble, yet free from all cowardice and cringing; submissive to the will of God, patient and contented under the afflictions of life, compassionate towards the sorrows and afflictions of others, ever seeking to lessen human sorrow and to increase human joy, and kind even to the brute creation; he is pure in his heart and pure in his life; truthful and honest as the day; hating all sin with intense hatred, but pitiful towards all sinners; strictly just, yet always generous; striving always to promote glory to God in the highest and on earth good-will towards men; and if reviled and persecuted, overcoming evil with good; ever hoping and rejoicing, knowing that he has in heaven an everlasting inheritance.

III. A third great lesson taught by the beatitudes concerns *happiness.* Christ is much concerned about the happiness of men; but He teaches that it is upon character that happiness depends, and not on circumstances; not on what we have, but on what we are.

The majority of mankind adopt a different theory of happiness, and steadily act upon it. They ascribe their unhappiness to adverse circumstances, and they are ever saying to themselves, "When I have altered this thing, and improved that other thing in my outward lot, then I shall be happy." Thus their whole life is governed by the falsehood that a man's life *does* consist "in the abundance of the things which he possesseth." A thousand living examples prove that a man may be exceedingly rich in possessions, and poor in enjoyment; and that he may be very poor in possessions, but very rich in enjoyment. God has joined character and happiness together, and man cannot put them asunder.

It would require the exposition of all the beatitudes to show this fully, but take the first only for illustration. "*Happy* are the poor in spirit"—happy because they *are* poor in spirit. These are not the abject, the cowardly, the mean, but the truly humble. They do not undervalue their gifts and possessions; they do not, through mock humility, depreciate themselves before others, but they recognise that whatever good things they have, whatever good there is in them, they have received from God, and they know that this is equally true of their neighbour. How much misery does that man escape who is thus saved from all vanity, all pride, all envy! Think of the proud, vain, ambitious man, piercing himself through with many sorrows, because he takes a higher view of his own merits and virtues than other people can possibly take. See him continually fretting and chafing, because men do not give him the honour which he thinks is his due. As you watch his course, you are at a loss whether most to laugh at him for his folly, or to pity him for his self-inflicted misery. " Blessed are the poor in spirit,"—doubly blessed are all their blessings, for the bliss of constant thankfulness is superadded to each.

Yet here we also see that perfect and unalloyed happiness must not be expected in this world. These verses speak of the blessedness of those that *mourn*, and thus remind us that while sin is still present around us we must be saddened by it ; and even as our own holiness increases, shall we be the more affected by the sight of the evil which prevails around us.

And connected with this lesson is another. As Christians in the kingdom of God, we are minors, who have not come into the full enjoyment of our inheritance. We are heirs of God, but under age. The earth is our schoolhouse ; all our lifetime is a time of learning ; our sorrows and our joys are our lessons, and all our life a preparation for the better life to come.

The great happiness which Christ gives to His followers is all summed up in this : "Theirs is the kingdom of heaven " They belong to it, and it to them. They are under Christ's rule, guidance, and protection. They are in fellowship with all the noblest on earth, and with the saints in heaven. This is their present happiness ; yet it is but an earnest and a foretaste of what shall be theirs hereafter.

THE SALT OF THE EARTH, THE LIGHT OF
THE WORLD.

"Ye are the salt of the earth : but if the salt have lost his savour, wherewith shall it be salted ? it is thenceforth good for nothing, but to be cast out, and to be trodden under foot of men. Ye are the light of the world. A city that is set on a hill cannot be hid. Neither do men light a candle, and put it under a bushel, but on a candlestick ; and it giveth light untó all that are in the house. Let your light so shine before men, that they may see your good works, and glorify your Father which is in heaven."—MATT. v. 13-16.

THESE are the verses that immediately follow the beatitudes. Christ says to certain people, " *Ye* are the salt of the earth, the light of the world." Mark, it is not, " Your sound doctrine, your splendid churches, your excellent ritual, your prayers, your charity, your preaching, is the salt of the earth, the light of the world." These things are in no way to be disparaged, they are, or may be, most acceptable to God, but they are not "the salt of the earth." The salt of the earth, the light of the world, are YE. Whom then does YE embrace ? The answer is, those whose character has just been described in the preceding verses, the citizens of the kingdom of heaven.

I. What is implied in the comparison ? Of what use is *salt*? First of all, it makes many things agreeable to the taste which without it are tasteless, *insipid.* This is what religion does for society.

Because earnest Christians do not delight themselves in many worldly amusements, those who give themselves to these things often suppose the life of a Christian to be dull, uninteresting, and insipid. How completely is this the opposite of the truth ! To the Christian the commonest duty is interesting. He has discovered the secret of the great happiness that infallibly follows doing good to others. His ordinary conversation is far more interesting than that of others. I lately looked into the memoirs of an English nobleman, who had seen a great deal of aristocratic society in this country and others. He has recorded in this book some of the most notable conversations held with different people during many years. We may fairly presume that he has told us the best things he had to tell. My opinion of what he records is this: Some things are said which are simply abominable, because of their indecency; others are very uncharitable and spiteful, highly injurious to the reputations of the persons referred to; and as to a great deal of the rest, it is vastly inferior to the talk which you may hear in a Methodist Class-meeting any week in your life.

You find people sometimes suffering from a terrible malady called *ennui*. Of life itself they say, "What a weariness it is!" or they quote the words of Hamlet,—

"How weary, stale, flat and unprofitable!"

The Christian poet says—

"With us no melancholy void,
No period lingers unemployed,
Or unimproved, below."

You find people now-a-days asking one another, "Is life worth living?" and some modern philosophers are reproducing in Europe the doctrine of the Buddhists, that life itself is an evil, and that the sooner we can get rid of it the better.

Is life worth living? To live so as to please God, to make known Christ and His salvation, to make human hearts glad around us, to make homes more sweet and bright, and by the Christian life on earth to prepare for the better life to come—

> "'Tis worth living for this,
> To administer bliss
> And salvation in Jesus's name."

Christians are the salt of the earth, because *they save society from corruption.* We cannot fail to see that these words are prophetic. Consider the circumstances in which they were first uttered. Our Lord was at this time scarcely known beyond the limits of Galilee. His followers were a few poor, despised fishermen and others; and yet He says to His disciples, "Ye are the salt of the earth. Ye are the light of the world."

How marvellously has this prophecy been fulfilled! In the second and third centuries after Christ the moral condition of the Roman empire was such that society tended towards dissolution. What saved it? The rising and growth of the Christian Church. The planting of the Christian Church saved Saxon England from barbarism and a long night of ignorance. It is true that in subsequent ages the Church itself became corrupt, the salt lost much of its savour. Nevertheless, fix upon the darkest period of the Middle Ages in Europe and England, and you find that, however corrupt the Church was, it was still above everything else the one power which saved Europe and European society from relapsing into barbarism. Look at England in the last century. There were powerful causes at work which tended to bring on such excesses as were perpetrated in France in the French Revolution. What prevented this? The rise and growth of Methodism. This is not what Methodists only say; but this is the view taken by the ablest writers who have recorded the history of the last century. So at the present day, in many of the villages in England, the small Methodist society is, more than anything else, the salt of the earth in that place. I say this deliberately and advisedly, and I speak that I do know.

But our Lord reminds us that there is one thing necessary to make character powerful for good. It must be blameless. "If the salt have lost its savour." Alas! what sad facts, what deplorable histories does such a sentence often call to our remembrance! You know a man of whom you have thought highly for years. One day you hear him utter words which you had supposed he never could utter, you see him manifest a temper which you thought he could not manifest, you learn that he has done what you thought him incapable of doing. Never again can he have the same influence over you for good which he had before.

"Dead flies cause the ointment of the apothecary to send forth a stinking savour: so doth a little folly him that is in reputation for wisdom and honour" (Eccles. x. 1). Christian people, be watchful. Guard your character and reputation, not merely for their own sake, but for the sake of the honour of Christ, and for the precious power of doing good by your influence.

How great then is the power of Christian character! how very much may be done by it alone, even when no word is spoken and no direct effort made! But some may be ready to add: "Yes; and how much better is character than talk! Let Christians show religion in their lives; let them talk less, and make less ado, to bring others to their way of thinking. My influence shall be a silent one." Plausible as this sounds, the very next words of Christ correct this mistaken inference from His first example.

II. "Ye are the light of the world." Christians are, and must be conspicuous. But observe, Christ is here speaking not of individual Christians, but of the collective light of the Church. It is not "*the lights*," but "the *light*." Immediately afterwards he speaks of "a city set on a hill." Here our Lord teaches another important lesson. He designs that His people should combine for collective action. In many places in the New Testament we read of the incorporation of Christians. They are compared to a "flock," a "house," a "temple," a human "body," "branches" united to one "vine." Take a single stone from a great cathedral, and throw it on the ground. It is poor, mean, unsightly. In its proper place it supports and is supported, forms part of a great structure, partaking of the glory and beauty of the whole. Too many in the present day pride themselves on belonging to the body of Christians in general and to no Church in particular. The Lord save us from being "Christians unattached"! The Church is an army, and needs to show an extended front, and battalions many files deep; we must march together and keep our ranks. We need large congregations, conferences, conventions, and all things which will impress men's minds with the conviction that the Church is in earnest, and means to win the world for Jesus Christ.

"Yes," some will say, "but there is a danger of carrying this thought too far. Do not some Christian workers neglect their homes? Do not some mothers and daughters busy themselves with conventions, who ought to be showing piety at home?" Be not too hasty in judging. So far as I have seen, most at least of the women who do the greatest amount of service in the Church are, in their own homes, patterns of good works. But admitting the danger, these verses contain a safeguard,—

"Neither do men light a lamp, and put it under the bushel, but on the stand; and it shineth unto all that are in the house. Even so [*i.e.* like the lamp] let your light shine before men, that they may see your good works, and glorify your Father which is in heaven" (Matt. v. 15, 16, R.V.).

Here we have a picture of a household, and it is a small, poor household; it has one lamp, one bushel, one lampstand. One lamp is sufficient to give light to "all that are in the house." One Christian in a family, if there be but one, is to be the light of that house. Here too is a prophecy of Christ, which has been verified thousands of times.

If any ask, What kind of work is meant? we answer, All work that is good. Are you a carpenter? Let the work you do in wood "shine" as good work. Are you a merchant? Let your business transactions "shine" with goodness. Are you a household servant? Let your household work honour God. This, as well as works of benevolence and evangelistic labour, may shine for the glory of God.

See also how the danger of ostentation, of pharisaism, is excluded here. A work, good in itself, may indeed be spoiled by a bad motive; but a good work, done with a good design, is perfected by its good motive. The best, highest motive that can ever influence us is this, "that they may glorify your Father which is in heaven."

THE LABOURERS IN THE VINEYARD.

"For the kingdom of heaven is like unto a man that is a householder, which went out early in the morning to hire labourers into his vineyard.
. So the last shall be first, and the first last: for many be called, but few chosen."—MATT. xx. 1-16.

IN order rightly to apprehend the meaning of this parable, we must take into account the circumstances which gave rise to it.

After the rich young ruler had gone away from Christ, very sorrowful because he could not resolve to sell all, that he might obtain eternal life, Peter called his Master's attention to the conduct of himself and his fellow apostles, in contrast to that of the young ruler. " Behold," said he, " we have forsaken all, and followed Thee ; what shall we have therefore ? "

To this inquiry our Lord's answer is threefold. First of all, He declared that Peter and his fellow apostles should, as the reward of their fidelity, "sit upon twelve thrones, judging the twelve tribes of Israel." Secondly, that not only should the apostles receive this ample reward, but every one, whoever he might be, that had forsaken all for Christ's name, should "receive a hundredfold, and inherit eternal life." But he adds, thirdly, that "many that are first shall be last ; and the last shall be first." Now it is important to observe that the third part of the answer, whilst it certainly does not contradict what has gone before, is nevertheless set over against the former part, and calls our attention to a fact which we were not likely to anticipate. Our Lord says in effect : Although none shall go unrewarded, and although the rewards of every one shall be proportionate to his sacrifices, whilst immeasurably exceeding them, yet some who might be expected to hold the first place in My kingdom in reward and privilege will be the last, and others who might be expected to be last will be first.

It is very evident that this sentence contains the great lesson of the parable which follows ; for immediately after uttering it, our Lord begins this parable, saying, " *For* the kingdom of heaven," etc. And again, after the parable is concluded, this weighty sentence is repeated, as giving us the sum of what has gone before, and fixing our attention on this thought as the one on which our minds should rest. In a word, this sentence is *the text*, the parable is *its exposition ;* and the key to the parable and the sum of its teaching is contained in the sentence with which it is introduced and closed.

As this sentence is found elsewhere, in other connections,

it is important to inquire what light is thrown on it by the context in these other passages.

In Mark x. 31, we find this saying in the same connection as in Matthew xix., but without any parabolic illustration added to it. In Luke xiii. 22, after having exhorted one who asked if few should be saved, to strive himself to "enter in at the strait gate," our Lord pointed to the time when some of His hearers would see "Abraham, and Isaac, and Jacob, and all the prophets, in the kingdom of God," and see themselves "thrust out"; and when men should come "from the east, and from the west, and from the north, and from the south," and " sit down in the kingdom of God "; and "behold," said He, "there are last which shall be first, and there are first which shall be last."

Again we find that at the close of our parable, after our Lord has repeated the words which form its text, He adds to them the declaration that " many be called, but few chosen," and this is introduced with "*for*," as giving a further explanation of the cause why the last are first, and the first last.

Finally, if we turn to chap. xxii. 14, we find this last sentence of all in connection with the parable of the invited "guest," who "had not on a wedding garment," and it forms the conclusion of that parable as well as of this.

Now combining these particulars in one view, I think we must come to the conclusion that when our Lord in this parable speaks of *the last becoming first, and the first last,* He would have us think of those who will, not merely fail to obtain a high place in His kingdom, but will be shut out of it altogether ; according to a mode of speaking common in the New Testament, where that is expressed comparatively which we are to understand absolutely.

But it may be said, If this is the lesson of the parable, how is it taught therein? Are not *all* the labourers admitted into the vineyard? and do not *all* receive a reward? We answer:

(1) Every interpretation of this parable will be attended with some difficulty, if, as is probable, our Lord designed for wise reasons that His meaning should be involved in some measure of obscurity. (2) The equality of reward, whatever that may signify, cannot be the most important point in the parable ; for equality by itself is opposed to the weighty saying which the parable is designed to illustrate and expound. *That* speaks not of equality, but of preference. The parable is in part the explanation of the *fact* which the gnome states, and not precisely the gnome itself in allegorical form.

To prepare the way for its true exposition, it will be necessary to remove some misconceptions associated with this parable.

First. The award of wages here said to take place at the close of the day cannot be the award of the day of judgment. It is inconceivable that at that day the Judge will tender to any the gift of eternal life, whose characters answer to those who murmured against the householder. Still less conceivable is it that any to whom the Judge will then offer heaven will be dissatisfied therewith, or imagine that they have not received an ample recompense, or will indulge any feeling of envy towards those who are fellow heirs in life eternal.

Again, we know that the awards on the judgment day are not equal ; and therefore to interpret the " penny " given to all as the award of that day would be to make our Lord contradict His own teaching in other parables. For the like reasons, the " evening " here referred to cannot be the close of each individual life.

And from this it also follows, that those hired at " the eleventh hour " are not the representatives of those who on

the bed of sickness and death seek and find mercy. For
those hired at the eleventh hour had no opportunity of
serving the householder till the time they were called; and
when called, they obeyed immediately; and after they were
called, they wrought "one hour" in the vineyard. All
which circumstances forbid the application of this part of
the parable to the case of a death-bed repentance.

What then is the " day " of labour here referred to ? Who
are the labourers ? Where is their field of toil? What is the
reward of service given to all? And how does the parable
explain that saying of our Lord with which it opens and
closes? These questions I will endeavour now to answer.

The term " vineyard " itself furnishes a key to the interpretation of the whole parable; for we find that, both in the
Old Testament and in the New, a *vineyard* is the appropriate
symbol of the Old Testament Church. Thus, in Psalm lxxx.
Israel is "the vine which God brought out of Egypt," and
the land of Palestine is the ground where it "takes root,"
and over which it widely extends its "branches." And still
more explicitly in Isaiah v. it is declared, that " the vineyard
of the Lord of hosts is the house of Israel." And in Matthew xxi. we are plainly taught that the Jewish nation are
the ungrateful " husbandmen," who have been entrusted
with the care of God's vineyard, and refuse to "render its
fruits " to the great Proprietor, and "stone " and "kill "
the messengers who are sent to them.

The vineyard then in this parable is not the Church of
the new dispensation, but *of the old.* It is no objection
to this view that it is here said that ' the kingdom of God
is likened unto a certain man,' etc. ; because it is not the
kingdom of God which is compared to the vineyard, but He
who is at the head of this kingdom acts like the owner of
the vineyard.

If the vineyard be taken to represent the locality of the

Old Testament Church, and the labourers its constituent members, it will follow that the "day" of labour spoken of represents a period of about 1,500 years, extending from the exodus from Egypt to the preaching of John the Baptist. "The law and the prophets were until John," and "from that time" the kingdom of God was preached.

Now it is said in the parable that the owner of the vineyard hired the first set of labourers "early in the morning," at the very beginning of the working day; and he agreed to give, and they to receive "one penny" each as the recompense for the day's toil. With the labourers afterwards hired he made no definite engagement, but only promised to give what was "right"; and they having confidence in the character of their employer, left it to him to decide the amount of recompense.

To this the facts of the history of the Jewish Church answer. When God had brought Israel out of Egypt into the wilderness, He entered into solemn covenant engagements with them. They on their part promised faithful service; and Jehovah promised recompense, so long as they were faithful. The wilderness was the place in which they formally engaged themselves to be the Lord's servants to work in His vineyard. After having thus covenanted with them, He brought them into the land of Canaan; or, to use the language of Psalm lxxx., God "brought a vine out of Egypt"; He "cast out the heathen, and planted it."

In this vineyard the Jews continued to labour until the day of our Lord, which was the eventide of the Jewish day. During the course of this long period other labourers were called into the vineyard, proselytes from among other nations. With these God did not enter into covenant engagements in the same manner as with the seed of Abraham, but they came into the vineyard, having confidence that Jehovah was a Master who would not allow His servants to go without just recompense. Some were called into the vineyard, or joined the Jewish Church, just before its dispensation was closed ; and their period of preparatory service was easy and of short continuance in comparison with that of the Jews, who from generation to generation had been subject to the yoke of bondage which the law of Moses imposed.

When the "even" of the Jewish dispensation was come, the owner of the vineyard directed his overseer,—who perhaps represents specifically John the Baptist, and then generally our Lord's apostles,—to pay the labourers their wages. And what was the recompense to the members of the Jewish Church for having laboured in Jehovah's vineyard ? It was, unquestionably, the *privilege of admission to the kingdom of God.* He who had embraced the worship and service of the one true God, and had yielded obedience to His law before the new dispensation was introduced, was, to speak after the manner of men, justly entitled to enjoy the privilege of entering the new dispensation which was appointed to succeed the old.

And this just expectation Jehovah was ready to fulfil to every member of the Jewish Church. But then came that which was wholly unexpected by the children of Abraham. When John began to preach that 'the kingdom of God was at hand' and when our Lord and His apostles declared its actual presence among the Jews, many were greatly offended, because they discovered that all the privileges of the new dispensation were to be equally free to all, that there was to be no difference made between a Hebrew of the Hebrews and a Roman centurion who had but just embraced the faith. Nay, more, it was seen (though this is not strictly within the scope of the parable itself), that those who had never even become proselytes were to be readily admitted into the kingdom of God.

They were greatly offended, and when they received their

recompense—*i.e.* when they were bidden to participate in the blessings of Messiah's reign—they murmured, and especially so when they saw that John the Baptist and our Lord Himself went first to the publicans and sinners, and seemed rather to shun than to seek those whose pretensions were the highest.

The result was, that, disliking the terms of admission to Christ's kingdom, they were excluded from it. Rather, they excluded themselves. *They who*, according to previous standing and privilege, *were first became last;* they were shut out of the kingdom of God. *And those once last became first*, those who were "not a people became a people."

And thus it was that, whilst 'many' among the Jews 'were called, few were chosen.' "The Gentiles, which followed not after righteousness, have attained to righteousness, even the righteousness which is of faith. But Israel, which followed after the law of righteousness, hath not attained to the law of righteousness" (Rom. ix. 30, 31).

This then we apprehend to be the primary application of the parable. The parable, furthermore, *accounts* for the fact declared in the sentence which it is designed to illustrate; in other words, it shows *how* it came to pass that 'the first became last, and the last first.' The reason is found in the announcement on the part of Jehovah of His purpose to treat alike Jew, proselyte, and Gentile, and to admit all on equal terms into all the privileges of Messiah's kingdom. God had a right to 'do what He would with His own.' By this proceeding the proselyte and the Gentile were most bountifully dealt with ; but the Jew was not in the least degree wronged. God was "good," but the Jewish "eye" was "evil."

But has this parable no significance for us ? Unquestionably it has. It contemplates a specific instance of God's

dealing with the Jewish people ; but it also unfolds general
principles of the Divine government which will be doubtless
illustrated in all ages, until the end of time. We cannot
doubt that the parable contains most important instruction
for ourselves.

Its general doctrine is, that long continued enjoyment of
the privileges of the visible Church, and long continued performance of merely outward service, do not of themselves
secure final salvation ; and that many who have maintained
a long connection with the visible Church will find themselves at last thrust out of the kingdom of God's glory,
while others, whose connection with the Church has been
much shorter, will be finally accepted and saved.

This general principle is illustrated by examples both of
communities and of individuals.

We have seen its illustration already in the case of the
Jews. They are now last in regard to the kingdom of God,
the vast majority having no place in it ; whilst, as our Lord
foretold, many have "come from the east, and from the west,
and from the north, and from the south," and are now ' sitting down' "with Abraham, and Isaac, and Jacob, in the
kingdom of heaven."[1] So again we find it, if we look to
the history of some of the earliest Christian Churches. We
see them flourishing so long as they retain a lively conviction of the unspeakable mercy of God in admitting them
into a place in His Church and His favour. But soon they
begin to mistake privileges possessed for privileges used.
They conclude that they are rich in grace, because well
provided with the means of grace, mistake profession made
for service rendered, a knowledge of God's will for obedience to it. They 'have a name to live, but are dead.'
The light once kindled grows more and more dim, until it

---

[1] Luke xiii. 29 ; Matt. viii. 11.

wholly expires, and 'the candlestick is removed.' Thus
it has come to pass with the Churches of Asia Minor and
Northern Africa, of Italy, France, and Spain. Christianity
has either ceased to exist, or there remains little more of
it than the name and the form.

But to pass from communities to individuals. All may
be considered as labourers in God's service, who have for a
longer or shorter time professed their subjection to His will
by their attendance upon the public ordinances of religion.
The lessons of the parable are, however, chiefly for those
who are as yet unacquainted with the higher and more
spiritual privileges of the kingdom of God, to those who
are " called," but not yet " chosen."

To these God offers *a free pardon*, the blessing of *regeneration*, distinct from pardon in nature, but never separated
from it in fact, and a *good hope of everlasting life*. And
these three together constitute the chief good of man, the
richest treasure and highest joy which he can have in the
present world.

This is God's " penny," the wages which He offers to all
who attend upon His service in the use of the means of
grace.

The parable has its separate lessons for separate classes
of persons. It addresses those who for many years have
been satisfied with a merely external Christianity.

You were born, perhaps, of religious parents, and trained
from your infancy to attend to the duties of religion. Still,
there is more in true religion than you have ever experienced.
There is a " joy unspeakable and full of glory," union with
Christ, power over sin, an inward heaven, an antepast of
higher joys to come. All this God will give you, if you will
only diligently seek it. It will be an ample recompense for
all your previous diligence and perseverance in attending
upon the means of grace, and a thousandfold more than

you deserve. And if God forgives the drunkard and swearer and sabbath-breaker as freely and as fully as He forgives you, and makes them quite as happy in His love, you are not wronged thereby, or made any the worse. Thankfully receive the offers of God's mercy yourself; and rejoice that mercy is free for all, even for the vilest.

The parable has a lesson for those "standing idle in the market-place"; that is, for those who have hitherto neglected the form of religion as well as the power.

"Why stand ye here all the day idle?" Those mentioned in the parable to whom this question was addressed said, "No man hath hired us." This statement may represent the case of the heathen and the inhabitants of other lands, but can hardly be true of many in this Christian country, where the calls to enter into God's service are so many and various.

Yet to all neglecters of God's salvation we would cry, *Come, enter the Lord's service!* It is not true that no one hath hired *you*. Satan and sin have hired you. Are you satisfied with the wages they give? What hath Satan done for you that you should serve him?

For you who know the preciousness of Christ's service, the parable has also a lesson. Go to those "standing idle in the market-place." Tell them how pleasant that service is; win them as fellow labourers. The servant that loves his Master, and loves His service, will often commend both Master and service to others. So let us do, that at the last we may rejoice in many fellow servants who have joined the company of the Lord's followers through our invitation. These shall be "our joy and our crown" in the day of the Lord's coming.

THE OBLIGATIONS IMPOSED BY BAPTISM.

"We were buried therefore with Him through baptism into death : that like as Christ was raised from the dead through the glory of the Father, so we also might walk in newness of life " (R.V.).—ROM. vi. 4.

THE sacrament of baptism is an ordinance of Christ around which much controversy has gathered, and is still carried on. It is not my purpose to enter into these controversies, except so far as this is absolutely necessary in subordination to my main purpose. My aim is a practical one; I propose to inquire, What are the obligations imposed by baptism on those who receive it?

The answer, if given in the strictest form, is this *To lead a new life.* But let us see how this answer is expanded, illustrated, and enforced in this chapter. In order, however, to understand this chapter, we must, for a moment, look back on the preceding one. In chap. v. the apostle has been extolling the free, unmerited grace which God has manifested to men through Christ. He has shown that Christ came to "make His blessings flow wide as the curse is found," and in the close of the chapter he declares that "where sin abounded, grace did much more abound."

Paul, however, was well aware that this doctrine of free grace was liable to be perverted, and might be abused, even as an encouragement to sin. In this sixth chapter he sets himself to guard his own doctrine against this danger. Let us read the opening words of the chapter in the R.V., for the new rendering undoubtedly gives his meaning more clearly than the old :

"What shall we say then? Shall we continue in sin, that grace may abound? God forbid. We who died to sin, how shall we any longer live therein? Or are ye ignorant that all we who were baptized into Christ Jesus were baptized into His death." Then follow the words of the text.

I understand the meaning of these verses to be in effect thus: Some one will say, If it is true that where sin abounded grace did much more abound, were it not well for us to " continue in sin that grace may abound "? The apostle names the supposition only to reprobate it in the strongest manner possible. "God forbid," says he: Let not the thought be entertained for a moment! You are to consider that your former life, such as you lived before you became the servants of Christ, has altogether come to an end. As far as sin is concerned, you have become *dead.* And if the question is asked, When? how did we "die to sin"? the answer is: On the day that you were baptized; and by means of your baptism you ended your former life, you began a new one, you then *died to sin.*

By giving this interpretation to the apostle's words, it may seem to you that I concede to Romanists and High Churchmen everything that they ask, and teach at once the doctrine of baptismal regeneration. But it is not so. When the question of baptismal regeneration is raised in the present day, it relates chiefly to the regeneration of *infants* in baptism. But this chapter teaches nothing as to the baptism of infants. It relates entirely to the baptism of adults. This is evident from what the apostle says in the close of the chapter: "What fruit had ye then in those things whereof ye are now ashamed?" He here assumes that all whom he addresses *remember* their non-Christian state, the life that they lived before they were baptized; and this could not possibly apply to infants.

Bear in mind therefore that the language here used is addressed to those who receive baptism in adult years, and had been instructed beforehand as to the obligations which they would incur by receiving it. You will also see plainly that in their case faith in Christ preceded baptism. At this early period of the Church at Rome, no one would receive baptism until he had become a very decided believer in Christ. By accepting baptism he would secure no worldly advantage whatever ; but he would by the very act, by joining the despised and persecuted Christians, render himself liable to loss, hatred, scorn, persecution, and possibly a death of martyrdom. You may be sure therefore that in the case of these persons faith went before baptism, so that the baptism was a sign of the faith which they had being yet unbaptized. Why then, it may be said, does the apostle ascribe so much importance to baptism? and why make the new life apparently begin on the day of baptism? For a very obvious reason. The whole of this chapter is a strong exhortation to a holy life, to live' as becomes professed Christians ; and therefore he refers the Roman Christians in thought to the day when they professed before the world that they were Christ's servants. Whatever their inward, spiritual experience might have been before that day, their neighbours and friends, the world around them, could not know that they were followers of Christ, till they had been baptized. The apostle therefore says in effect : On the day that you were baptized you became openly and professedly Christ's servants. See that you live in a manner consistent with that profession.

What then is the kind of life which accords with baptism in the name of Christ? The apostle's answer involves the negative and the positive aspect of the new life. First of all, as regards everything sinful in their former life, they are to answer that they have done with it for ever. The services of the temples, the honouring of the gods of Rome, with all former vices, intemperance, licentiousness, dishonesty, all were to be forsaken ; but on the positive side, their life was to be one of activity in promoting the

glory of Christ, the extension of the Church, the welfare
of their fellow men.

He illustrates his meaning in the latter part of the
chapter by referring to incidents in Roman life well understood by his hearers, and connected with slavery.

Some of the members of the Church would understand
this only too well, for, no doubt, many of them were
slaves. Now in the Roman Forum a transaction of the
following kind often took place. Here is a slave who
belongs to Julius. His master wishes to sell him to Marcus. A sale takes place, with all proper legal formalities.
Now up to the hour of sale he is the slave, or bondman,
of Julius. Marcus has no control over him whatever.
After the sale he is the slave of Marcus; and his former
master, Julius, has no control over him, cannot control an
hour of his time, cannot exact a particle of service; his
new master has all his time and all his labour under his
control.

See how the apostle draws the parallel. Up to the time
when you became avowedly Christ's servants—*i.e.* the day
of your baptism—you served a master whose name is
Sin; you were bondmen of sin. And whilst you were
bondmen of sin, you were free men as far as righteousness
is concerned. You had nothing to do with that master
whose name is Righteousness. But on the day of your
baptism you left your old master Sin for a new master
Righteousness. You became bondmen to righteousness,
and you became free men in regard to sin. Therefore
hold yourselves as free from the service of sin, your old
master, as you once were from the service of righteousness.
He makes his comparison still more vivid by distinguishing between the bondman and his tools, his implements of
service. By these he means the various faculties of body
and mind which each man possesses. When you were

bondmen to sin, you used hands, tongue, lips, eyes, ears, muscle, nerve, brain in the service of sin. Now you must employ all these in the service of righteousness.

The hand, e.g., must never again be used to smite with violence, nor in an act of theft or forgery ; not to give a bribe, not to take a bribe ; not to write a bad book, or a scurrilous letter ; not to do a single thing which does not form a part of the service of righteousness. Thus Paul understood the obligations imposed on Roman Christians by their baptism. The same obligations belong to us.

Possibly some one may raise an objection of this sort. I do not feel bound by my baptism, because it was not my own act. I was not at the time of baptism a consenting party. That is true. But what say you to-day? Do you renounce your baptism? or do you accept it? You do one or the other, of necessity. If you renounce it, you say : "I am not a Christian ; I have no more to do with Christ, with His service and His people, than if I were a Jew, a Mohammedan, a Parsee." Are you willing to take up that position? If not, you accept your baptism, and are as much bound by it as if you received it only yesterday.

Now let us look seriously at our position.

We are bound to a life of entire holiness. And there is no respect of persons here. All that the apostle here says applies to every one who calls himself a servant of Christ. We have no more business with sin ; our sole business in this world is to serve Jesus Christ. I do not mean that we are to forsake the common occupations of life, but to serve Christ in them ; the ploughman, the shepherd, the carpenter, the mason, the merchant, lawyer, doctor, minister of religion, we have to make everything we do a part of Christ's service. We are His *bondmen.* He has purchased us. Our time, our faculties, our wealth, all belong to Him. This is the true ideal of human life, and the highest conceivable ideal.

The all-important question which remains is, How to make the ideal actual, how to live this Christian life. There are in it two factors, one Divine, one human.

There is the Divine power in our lives. In the early part of the chapter we are taught how the newer life of the Christian is connected with the new life of Christ. Christ died, we die; Christ buried, our old sinful nature buried; Christ raised from the dead, so we. Then our spiritual death, burial, resurrection are said to be associated with that of Christ.

Do you believe that Jesus Christ was raised from the dead by the glory of the Father? If you do, then believe that the very power which raised Christ from the dead will work in you to produce a new life of righteousness. This is a very frequent thought with the apostle : seek to make it familiar to your own thoughts. When you are tempted to say, "It is impossible for me to cease from sinning; impossible to spend all my time and all my strength in the service of Christ," ask yourself, Is it harder for God to accomplish this in me than to raise up Christ from the dead?

There is our own part in this great matter. Our salvation is never without God; never without *our co-working with God*. Note two expressions of Paul used in this chapter. "*Reckon* yourselves dead to sin." The apostle's word is a very expressive one. It is used in reference to processes of thought, casting up accounts, etc. Apply your mind to this whole matter. See what it is which Christ requires. See how just His demands are, and give to those the full consent of a deliberate mind. Reckon that thus it should be, and resolve that thus it shall be. Then the apostle further says, " *Yield* yourselves unto God," (*v.* 13). There is, first, the act of the understanding, then the act of the will. You first see clearly what Christ claims, and then actually give up yourself to Him.

There are many motives to this. It secures consistency of our life with our profession. It will make us to be what we profess to be. Add to this our recollection of the past unprofitableness of sin. "What fruit had ye then?" Past experience shows that to serve sin is unprofitable and degrading. Then there is the comparison of the issue of a life of sin and a life of righteousness. "The wages of sin is death," the second death, the death that never ends. What folly to work for such wages! "The gift of God is eternal life through Jesus Christ our Lord." You say perhaps, "If I live a strictly holy life, I shall have to forego pleasures, to make sacrifices." You will have to forego no pleasures but sinful pleasures. But whatever you have to give up, remember *the gift of God, eternal life.* That is the prize for which we are running. We can give up nothing to be compared with that, even if we should give up life itself; and to allow anything to stand between us and life is infinite folly.

Let us think very much of "the eternal life." Think of it as life with Christ, in which we shall serve Him evermore. The thoughts of this life will have their constant influence on our present life, elevating and purifying it, making it ever more and more noble, more and more happy; and so the present life will anticipate the life to come. Then, if we have been united with the likeness of Christ's death, we shall also be united with the likeness of His resurrection. "When He who is our life shall appear, we also shall appear with Him in glory."

THE LORD'S SUPPER.[1]

" As often as ye eat this bread, and drink this cup, ye do shew the Lord's death till He come."—1 COR. xi. 26.

THESE words remind us of the great evidential value of the Lord's supper. For more than 1,800 years the Lord's supper has been celebrated without interruption. The Acts of the Apostles and St. Paul's epistles show that the practice of celebration was established before A.D. 60 ; the writings of Justin Martyr and Tertullian and others testify to its use in the second century ; and innumerable witnesses speak of its celebration ever since : until, in this present age, there is no portion of the civilized world where the celebration is not constant ; and in the midst of many heathen tribes this simple, solemn sacrament speaks powerfully to the people of a new life begun in the midst of them, and of the prospect of eternal life opening out before them.

This perpetual celebration shows that all followers of Christ have attached the utmost importance to His *death.* The four gospels bear witness to this, in their ample details of the last hours of Christ's life. It proves also that those who commemorated His death believed that He who was once dead was now alive for evermore. Had they believed that He had *not* risen, their hopes must have died in His grave ; they must have regarded Him as a deceiver of the people. Here we have the testimony of millions of men, including the most highly gifted and cultured, for eighteen centuries in favour of our Lord's resurrection. Surely this fact ought to have great weight with the sceptical and unbelieving of our own day. True

---

[1] A sacramental address delivered at Headingley College.

it is that they will say, These facts only prove that these men have believed these things, not that they are true. Still this belief of so many millions, during so many centuries, is in itself a most stupendous fact; and if we conclude that all is a mistake, we may well lose confidence in man's certainty about any fact of history.

But this is not all. The multitudes who have so believed and so testified their belief have been, as a rule, the most virtuous, the most happy, the most beneficent known through all the centuries; and they have all declared that their belief in the great facts commemorated in the Lord's supper has been the great source whence the excellency of their lives and actions has sprung. So that if what they have believed has not been true, we must come to this most appalling conclusion, that the belief of a falsehood has been the source of more virtue and more happiness to mankind than all the truth which men have ever discovered; and if this were so, we had better give up the pursuit of truth as being more harmful than useful.

These considerations show how imperative is the duty of constantly celebrating the Lord's supper, if only for this reason, that we hereby confirm the testimony of past ages, we bear witness to the present age, we hand on the testimony to future ages, of the truth of those great things pertaining to Christ and His kingdom which are most surely believed by us.

But this sacrament has a deeper interest for us. Putting aside all thought of unbelievers, and our duty of testifying to them, we think of what it is to ourselves. It is a great bridge, spanning all the gulf of time, between our Lord's first and second coming. We "show His death *till He come.*" We look back to the one; we look forward to the other. Thus memory and hope have their most sacred exercise. What is the legitimate effect of this memory and this hope? The death of Christ ought to become in us the death of sin. This is the Apostle Paul's view : "The love of Christ constraineth us ; because we thus judge, that one died for all, therefore all died."[1] In the purpose of God, all died to sin, "and that they that live," who after this death to sin and self enter on a new life, "should henceforth live not to themselves, but to Him who died for them and rose again." The extinction of the life of self, the devotion of the whole man to Christ—these are the practical results aimed at by our commemoration of our Lord's death. And as to the anticipation of His coming again, He "that hath this hope in him purifieth himself, even as He is pure." If gratitude for boundless benefits already given is a powerful motive, so also is the hope of the continuance of our being, and of its inexhaustible and endless bliss. It is evident that just so far as we come under the influence of these powerful motives, life becomes ennobled. What is it that degrades life? It is to have all our purposes centred in self and limited by them. "Let us eat and drink, for to-morrow we die," is the appropriate expression of the mind which rejects Christian immortality. A life whose purposes go out constantly in pursuance of Christ's glory in our personal holiness and in doing good to others, which looks upon every part of life as an education for the better life to come, must needs be noble.

In conclusion, I may say to you, do all possible honour to this blessed sacrament. Make not a superstition of it. You are in little danger of doing that. The very way in which we celebrate this sacrament in this place, apart from all surroundings which appeal to the senses in order to increase our solemn feelings, is itself a testimony that we

---

[1] 2 Cor. v. 14, 15 (R.V.).

do not attach too much importance to the outward ceremonial; but on the other hand, let us do nothing to
countenance a hurried, slovenly, irreverent celebration.
For myself I confess that I hope the Lord's supper will
remain to me what it has ever been hitherto, a solemn,
heart-searching service. Here we pledge our loyalty to
Christ; here we own our indebtedness to Him; here we
vow to be faithful to Him in life and in death; here we
dedicate our whole selves to Him. May Christ Himself
give us the strength whereby we may serve Him faithfully!

THE TEMPLE BUILT OF LIVING STONES.

" Built upon the foundation of the apostles and prophets, Jesus
Christ Himself being the chief corner stone."—EPH. ii. 20.

THE building mentioned in our text is the Church of
God, and in this Epistle to the Ephesians, perhaps
more than anywhere else, are exhibited the greatness and
glory of the Church viewed as God's great work in the
world. The great design of Christianity is shown in short
compass, but in words most full of meaning, in the verses
preceding the text. It is there shown that the one grand
purpose of God is to unite all mankind in the bonds of a
common faith, a common worship, a common brotherhood.
Until Christ came, this could not be. Not only did a
multitude of false gods divide men from each other in
opposing creeds and communities, but even that religion
which was divinely ordained and sanctioned, and in the
observance of which the one true God was worshipped, by
the multitude of its rites and ceremonies raised a wall of
partition between its adherents and all the rest of mankind;
and the kingdom of God, as established among the Jews,
was local and limited, its priests confined to one family, its

chief sacrifices offered only in one place, the great body of
its adherents confined within the limits of one small country.
But the death of Christ broke down the middle wall between Jew and Gentile. The law of ordinances, the divers
sacrifices, washings, distinctions of meat, were necessary
till He came ; but when the great sacrifice for sin had been
offered, all other sacrifices were unnecessary, were worse than
useless. The one sacrifice and one priest were as available
for Gentile as for Jew, so that Christ by His death made
them " one " who had been " twain," but He also thereby
made provision for the reconciliation of all men to God, and
this provided for the universal brotherhood of mankind.

As long as any two men are living each at enmity with
God, there is no security for their living at peace with each
other ; but let them each be reconciled to God, and their
enmity becomes no longer possible. And what is true of
two men is true of thousands, is applicable to nations, to the
whole world. So that the peace of the whole world is promoted and secured, as men individually obtain peace with God.

This was the case with those at Ephesus to whom Paul
wrote, and he who was once a bigoted Jew and persecuting
Pharisee felt that differences of race and nation were nothing
when weighed against the common faith in Christ which
united them. And therefore, though he had reminded the
Ephesians of their previous exclusion from the privileges of
God's people, he now says to them, in language he must
have delighted to use, and they must have delighted to hear :
' Ye are no more strangers and foreigners, but fellow
citizens with the saints, and of the household of God ; and
are built upon the foundation of the apostles and prophets,
Jesus Christ Himself being the chief corner-stone."

In contemplating this invisible temple, consider—

I. Its structure. II. Its greatness. III. Our own duty
in relation to it.

I. *Its structure.*—We must begin with the foundation. Once the kingdom of God had one visible representative only. After Christ had been tempted by the devil in the wilderness, He returned full of the Spirit into Galilee. He was about to found His kingdom, but at first He stood alone. He had not as yet received any disciples, and even John the Baptist, His great forerunner, was not reckoned as in the kingdom of God. But very soon He called to Him Andrew and Peter and James and John and others, and these became the nucleus of the new community, or, to use the language of the text, were placed as foundation stones in the new building on which others were afterwards to rest.

I understand the text to mean that the *apostles and prophets* constitute the foundation; others hold that the foundation of the apostles and prophets means *the doctrine taught by them.* But the representation which Paul gives of the Church is that of a building in which human souls are the living stones, and Christ Himself part of the foundation. We cannot conceive of a foundation partly personal and partly doctrinal; and the unity of the figure requires that as the superstructure is personal, the foundation must be personal also.

Two classes of persons are mentioned as foundation members: the one class the apostles,—men called, taught, and commanded by our Lord Himself; the other the prophets,—men filled with the Holy Ghost, who spoke under His plenary influence, and were only second to the apostles in their power to win souls to Christ.

Who were they who were placed on this foundation? We gain light on this question if we consider how the apostles, the very first members of the Church, were introduced to it.

We learn from the gospel history that they became mem-

bers of Christ's Church through faith and love towards
Christ Himself. They heard of Christ, and saw His works,
and believed on His name; they received His call, and
obeyed it. And in the way in which they became members,
in a manner strictly analogous, though not precisely identical,
others became members through their means, and were
built in as living stones. As the corner stone in a building
binds together courses of masonry, so Christ unites His
people to Himself, and in virtue of their union with Him
they are united to one another. The whole structure of the
Church depends on Christ, and the Church without Christ,
not only is a thing impossible, but has become to us a thing
inconceivable.

In a word, the Church of Christ, the holy catholic
Church, is "the blessed company of all faithful people."
It consists of all who believe in and love our Lord Jesus
Christ. Let a man come to us with these credentials, and
we are bound to receive him as a friend and a brother. But
we can acknowledge no man as a living stone in this temple
in whom these signs are wanting. Shall we call ourselves
a Church? If we have these marks upon us, we know that
we are of the Church of Christ. If other men deny our
claims, we are not troubled; enough for us that the Master
owns us, though His professed servants disallow us. Let
others contend for the shadows; we will contend for the
substance. Let others show their zeal for vestments and
altar cloths, for elaborate ritual and imposing ceremonies;
but we will contend for faith which unites us to Christ, for
the love of Christ in the heart, and for the practical evidence of it in the life.

II. *The greatness of the building.*—The glory of the
Christian Church is the topic largely dwelt upon in this
epistle, and is shown in the first place in the antiquity of
the design. When we look upon a building vast in its

extent and venerable for its age and charming in its beauty, we often inquire with interest, Who planned this structure? when and by whom was this wonderful design conceived? When we ask this question respecting the building of God of which we now speak, we are carried back in thought to a time before the earth was framed or the sun shone. "He hath chosen us in Him before the foundation of the world." The whole period of the world's history preceding the coming of Christ may be looked upon as the time during which God was preparing the place and gathering the materials for the building of His Church.

Again, the greatness of this work appears from the widespread influence which it has over the universe of being. All *men* are concerned in it. The Jews had thought that when Christ came, His reign and His benefits would be for them, and all His glory reflected on them. Paul had thought so once; but now to him had been given the grace of apostleship, that he might proclaim among all the nations the unsearchable riches of Christ. But not only is man interested in this work—it has its relation to the *invisible powers of darkness.* A shallow and unbelieving philosophy professes to make light of the awful truths relating to the devil and his angels; but St. Paul, we apprehend, was as competent to speak on such subjects as any man that ever lived—not excepting the wisest of modern philosophers— and he describes the contest which he had to maintain in his advocacy of the gospel of Christ as a contest with the powers of darkness. He had human adversaries not a few; but he makes light of all their opposition when compared to that he encountered on the part of invisible foes : "We wrestle not against flesh and blood, but against principalities, against powers, against the rulers of the darkness of this world, against spiritual wickedness in high places."

Again, this work is one in which *angels* are interested.

To the reflective mind the progress of a great work is deeply interesting as a study, because it is the visible manifestation of a design which has long existed invisibly in the mind of the designer, and we watch with great interest to see how invisible thought obtains visible embodiment. And thus the angels contemplate with deepest and most reverent interest the work of God in His Church, because it gives them new views of the glorious character of Him who made all things. We greatly mistake if we suppose that man's salvation is the only end proposed by God in the work of the Church. The apostle leads us to think of this work from first to last, as serving the great and glorious purpose of more fully revealing God to the adoring view of angelic hosts. The design is that " now unto the principalities and powers in heavenly places might be known by the Church the manifold wisdom of God."

The grandeur of the work is further seen in its *perpetuity.* We sometimes hear it said of a work of man's creation, that it will last as long as the world lasts ; but this is a vain boast. For aught we know, the fire may consume it, or the lightning shatter, or the earth engulf it, or the mere lapse of time bring it to dust. But this building shall be carried on as long as the world lasts, without doubt. Paul speaks of the revelation of God's glory as about to be accomplished through the Church in the *ages which* should *follow* his own. Many ages have already followed ; how many are yet to come I cannot even guess, but this I know, that as long as the world lasts, the building of this spiritual house will go on. Christ has promised to be with His people in their evangelizing work " until the end of the world," and that the end should not come until this gospel of the kingdom shall have been preached in all nations. Kingdoms may rise and fall ; this kingdom cannot be removed. Systems of law and philosophy now in repute may become obsolete and known no more, but Christ's faithful servants will go on gathering in the living stones into this temple, until the great Master Builder shall see the completion of His plan. Then the Church militant shall cease to exist, and Christ's triumphant Church shall reign with Him in glory for ever and ever.

III. *Our duty in relation to this building* falls under two heads: 1, As it regards ourselves; 2, As it regards others.

Our first duty is to secure our own place in this spiritual building. Are you a living stone in this temple? The first members of the Church saw Christ and believed on Him. They received a call from Him, and obeyed it. You have never seen Christ, but "blessed are they that have not seen, and yet have believed." Your outward ear has not heard His call; but have you not heard it in other ways—by His written word, by His ministry, by His friends, by the voice of the Spirit in your hearts? "Come unto Me, ye weary and heavy laden": have you obeyed that call? "Take My yoke upon you": have you taken Christ's yoke? Your choice is left to you entirely free; but life and death depend upon it. "Out of the Church no salvation," says the Church of Rome. In one sense this is a falsehood; in another a most solemn truth. To make connection with this or that visible community essential to salvation is to add terms to God's terms. Who shall dare to make the way to heaven narrower than God Himself has made it? But we must have part in this invisible Church; we must rest on this one foundation, or there is no salvation for us.

2. But our duty in reference to God's great work does not end with ourselves. The text is suggestive of lessons in reference to our fellow believers. Christ says plainly to us: "See that ye despise not one of these little ones which believe in Me." How often are we in danger of breaking

this command! how ready to say of another, especially if
he differ from us in opinion, "He is a man of no account:
his gifts are small, his work amounts to nothing; the
Church could do very well without him"! The Master says
not so. If indeed he rest upon the foundation, a living
stone placed in the building by the Master's hand, then
in the view of the great Architect, the building would not
be complete without him. "Be not high-minded, but fear"
lest he whom ye despise should be found at last a goodly
stone in the everlasting structure, and you who seem to be
a pillar should be cast out as worthless.

Further, there is a duty which we owe to those who are
still far off from Christ. It is to bring them near.

You have gazed with delight at the work of the sculptor.
You have wondered how it is possible to impress on stone
the expression of human thought and human passion; and
when you have remembered that the marble before you
which seemed almost to breathe and live was once a rough,
unshapen block in the quarry, you have been ready to envy
the artist his wondrous power. You need not envy him,
for you can do "greater works than these." There are your
neighbours and acquaintances who are estranged from God.
You need not go far to seek them. These are the rough,
unhewn stones out of which you by God's blessing may
help to build His Church. Apart from Christ they will
never attain true moral beauty and loveliness; but brought
nigh and placed upon the foundation, they will become
polished stones in the temple, and will reflect the glory of
Him who is the light thereof.

The sum of what I would say is this: God's great work
must be our great work. If it be true that the building of
this spiritual temple is the only grand result of this world's
history, that it is His work through all the ages of this world,
and will stand throughout the everlasting ages of the world

to come, then it must follow that if we wish to live to any
good purpose, we must unite ourselves with it and make our
whole lives contributory to its promotion.   No man's life
is worthless or mean, if it furthers God's work ; every man's
life is so, if it does not.   Sever your life from God's cause,
and the end will be that you perish for ever.   Time not
used for Him is time lost.   Time used for Him brings
happy results which will be found in eternity.   Wealth not
consecrated to God's cause perishes with the using ; wealth
given to Him is treasure laid up in heaven.   What we keep
here, we lose ; what we give away, we keep for ever.   For
they that build upon this foundation shall see their work
survive the wreck of nature when the last fires are consuming the solid earth itself, and shall for ever and ever
rejoice in their portion in God's heavenly kingdom.

THE PURPOSE OF GOD IN CHRIST AS TAUGHT BY THE APOSTLE PAUL.

" For whether we are mad, it is for God ; or whether *we are* [1] of
sound mind, it is for you.   For the love of Christ controls us, having
formed this judgment, that [2] one died for all, then all died, and [that]
He died for all, that those who live should no longer live for themselves,
but for Him who died and rose again for them."—2 COR. v. 13-15.

PARAPHRASE OF CHAP. V. *v.* 11 TO CHAP. VI. *v.* 1.

SINCE then we know what it is habitually to fear the
Lord, we are [indeed] still engaged in persuading *men*
[of our integrity] ; but we have already become manifest to

---

[1] ἐξέστημεν is aorist, but to say " we lost our senses " implies *in this
connection,* "we are now of unsound mind."   Alford renders it,
" whether we have been beside ourselves."   But compare the *present*
tense in the parallel member of the sentence, and consider that Paul
proposes two views which may possibly be taken of the same fact.

[2] The evidence for omitting εἰ is, I think, decisive ; so Meyer.

God as sincere, and I have good trust that we have become
manifest as such in your consciences (the conscience of each
one of you,[1] (I say this, not so much for your own sakes
as with reference to our opponents;) for we are not again
commending ourselves, but are giving you an opportunity
to boast on our behalf, that we may have this opportunity
of boasting in opposition to those who boast of their
presence (personal appearance), not of their heart.   For
the fact is,—whether we are mad (as our enemies allege), all
that we do suggesting this notion of madness is done for
God; or whether we be of sound mind (as we are conscious
is the fact), all that may justly be regarded as the product
of sound reason is done in your cause.   And that we are
men of sound reason ought to be clear from this, that we
can give a reasonable account of our conduct.   The truth
is, then, that the great fact of the love of Christ to mankind
exercises complete control over us.   For we have formed
this conclusion, that One died for all, and therefore, as a
consequence involved in that fact, all died (a moral death,
i.e. died in regard to their former selfish and sinful life).
And He who died for all did so with this further purpose
in view, that men having so died and living again should no
longer live to themselves, but to Him who died and rose
for them.[2]

   It results from this that we (ὥστε ἡμεῖς) from henceforth
know no man according to the mere temporal relations of
the flesh; and if previously we knew Christ according to
such temporal relations, we on the other hand now know
Him so no more.   It follows, in fact, that if any man be in

---

[1] For this is the force of συνειδήσεσιν in plural.—Meyer.

[2] I cannot resist Meyer's argument for understanding ὑπὲρ here
for the benefit of, not *in the stead of*—namely, that if we insist on the
latter view, *we make Christ's resurrection substitutionary.*

Christ, he is a new creature; the old things of his pre-Christian life are passed away; behold, all is become new!

But the whole must be traced up to God as its source, who reconciled us to Himself through Christ, and gave to us the ministry of reconciliation, the tenor of our theme and commission being this, that God in Christ was reconciling the world unto Himself, not reckoning against those who compose the world their transgressions, and confiding to us the ministry of reconciliation.

We then are acting as ambassadors on behalf of Christ; and as though God were entreating you through us, we pray you on Christ's behalf, be ye reconciled to God. For Him who knew no sin He hath made a sin-offering for us, in order that we may become the righteousness of God in Him.

OBJECT OF SERMON:

To expound a doctrine and enforce a lesson.

The doctrine : *Christ for us all.*

The lesson : *We all for Christ.*

I.

It is evident from what St. Paul here says, that there were some of his contemporaries who thought him mad, and who spoke of him as such; and not very long after, he was to hear the same reproach from the Roman Felix. In this there is nothing which need surprise us. The apostle's character, conduct, and aims were so different from those of most other men, that they must have felt that if Paul was right, they were wrong. They adopted the alternative which suited best their self-love, and they cast on Paul the charge of madness rather than admit the defects of their own character, and the perverted tendency of their own course of life. Such has been the reproach cast upon the most faithful servants of Christ in all ages. It was first the re-

proach cast on the Master Himself. The people said of
Him, "He hath a devil, and is mad." And certainly one
of the most blessed things that could happen now would
be for many preachers of the gospel so fully to enter into
Paul's spirit, and so closely to follow his example, as to
earn from an unbelieving world this same reproach. Nay,
we would say, may Paul's madness affect us all !

But, after all, *was* Paul mad? How are we to decide
the question? We are usually satisfied that no one is mad
if he can give reasons for his conduct, and if these approve
themselves to our judgment as sufficient. Now this Paul
was ever ready to do. This he does in the passage before
us. And I think that those who are most indifferent to
Christ's religion, and most sceptical respecting its claims,
must admit that it is worth while to hear what such a man
as Paul has to say in explanation of his own conduct. For
Paul was no ordinary man. As far as my own knowledge
goes, I know of no one man who has appeared on the stage
of history who was superior to him, excepting always Paul's
Master and Lord. Consider the character of his mental
endowments, his labours and sufferings in what he judged
to be a just cause, his readiness absolutely to sacrifice every
selfish interest for the good of others, and the large influence which his acts, character, and writings have had on
all subsequent ages, and it becomes a question worthy of
the deep attention of every one—Why was Paul so devoted
to the cause of Christ?

When we ponder this question, let us also bear in mind
the fact that Paul must have been a contemporary of our
Lord. This epistle was written within thirty years of
Christ's death, when the number of Christians was comparatively small, and when almost the whole world was
arrayed against the cause to which Paul devoted himself.
That he was insincere we cannot for a moment believe,

because, by taking the course he did, he had, in a worldly point of view, nothing to gain, but everything to lose. Now this great man, this incomparable man, tells us that his whole mind, his whole heart, his whole life, was ruled and determined by one absorbing thought—the thought of the love of Christ. This, he says, "constrains," *i.e.* "it absolutely controls and governs me." What does he mean? We will follow, and try to enter into his own explanation.

By "the love of Christ" we are not to understand the love that Paul had for Christ, but the love which Christ had for mankind. That Paul had deep and all-pervading love to Christ, we cannot for a moment doubt ; but his object here is to set forth, not his own love for his Master, but his Master's love to him in common with all mankind. And he proceeds to show how that love manifested itself. It was demonstrated by that last sacrifice which it was possible for it to give. *Christ died for us ;* He "died for all." Let us dwell upon this statement. Let us endeavour to comprehend, as far as we can, its vast significance. If we ask, Whom did our Lord intend to benefit by His death? the answer is, "all men"—all men then living upon the earth, and all men who ever were to live, down to the very end of time. In accordance with what Paul teaches here and elsewhere, we believe that there is not a single sinner now living upon earth whom the death of our Lord was not designed to bless. There is not one for whom God does not in the purposes of His mercy design salvation from sin, and the gift of everlasting life. We hold that there is no human creature living between whom and eternal bliss there is any barrier except his ignorance of God's mercy proffered to us in Christ, or his wilful rejection of it.

How the death of Christ was to benefit and save men is explained in the 19th and 21st verses of this chapter. We take the apostle's meaning to be briefly this : the death of Christ was intended by God the Father and by Christ Himself to be a propitiatory sacrifice for sin, in order to show in the strongest possible way at once God's hatred of sin and His love for the sinner. By ordaining, by accepting the sacrifice of Christ, God was "reconciling the world to Himself," devising means by which His anger might be turned away, so that men's trespasses might be no more reckoned to them, but that they might be accounted as righteous before God, and dealt with as righteous. And all this glorious work of reconciling, pardoning, justifying, was, according to the grand view of the apostle, accomplished for *the world*—done once for all—for all men, for every man, for all ages, for every time and place, done once and for ever! So that the one great sacrifice needs no repetition; and we need no other.

In one word, when Christ had died and risen again, all mankind were *provisionally* saved; *i.e.* everything was then accomplished on the part of Christ and God that was necessary to our salvation. Salvation was made possible for every one of us.

Paul does not teach, however, that every man will therefore of necessity be saved; He plainly teaches the contrary, because he says, "There is committed to us a ministry of reconciliation," and we now, as "Christ's ambassadors, beseech you to be reconciled"; nay more, he says, "God is, by us, entreating you to be reconciled." But it still remains for each individual man to make the salvation his own, by his personal acceptance of it through faith.

The door of our Father's house stands wide open to receive every prodigal. The Father Himself waits to welcome every one that returns. But *to return* is the prodigal's own act; he will never be forced to return. If he chooses to remain far off, he must do so. And if he returns not during the day of this earthly life, he will be shut out for

ever. Some object to this doctrine, and say : " It is impossible that God could thus have designed the salvation of
all mankind, for had He done so He would never have
allowed His own merciful purpose to be so largely frustrated as it now is. To all such objections there is a
general and sufficient answer : we poor limited human
creatures are not competent to say what is consistent with
God's wisdom and goodness, and what is not. In some
cases we may be warranted in saying, " The good God
could never do this " ; but there are many in which to say
this is to assume to ourselves the power of sitting in judgment on the Almighty. If we say that God's merciful
purpose can never be frustrated, then the facts of human
life constantly before our eyes prove the contrary.

Is not every human creature capable of wisdom and
happiness? Is not every one designed for these things?
Yet how few attain them ! Think of all the children born
in England during the last thirty years. We think we see
what is possible to all by what is actually enjoyed by some.
These latter have grown up in the midst of all influences
friendly to piety. Almost their first words were words of
prayer and praise, their first thoughts thoughts of God and
heaven. They have healthful bodies, well-instructed, well-
disciplined minds ; their passions are well regulated and
sanctified to God ; and their very countenances are beau-
tified by the smiles of innocence and the joy of religion.
They are happy in themselves and a source of happiness to
others, and they rejoice evermore in the good hope of a
life everlasting. Is not this what God designs? Is not
His purpose fulfilled in them? On the other hand, you
see those who have grown up in ignorance of all that is
good, instructed only in sin,—their bodies diseased through
vice, their countenances made repulsive by the domination
of evil passions. They are wretched in themselves, and

plague-spots in human society, hastening to an untimely and dishonoured grave; and, unless the mercy of God arrest them, and that soon, about speedily to sink into eternal death. Shall we dare to say that God never intended such wretched creatures for anything better than they are? God forbid! But if we reject such a view with abhorrence, what becomes of the argument that God's merciful purpose respecting men can never fail?

Take another illustration. Go back fifty years and visit the Fiji islands. There is not found among the Fijians a single Christian. No one has heard the name of Christ. Their moral degradation is such that no traveller can dare to describe to us faithfully all its revolting features. Visit the same islands now, and you will find there thousands of people who know and love Christ, and are happy in the prospect of a blessed immortality. What has redeemed them from barbarism? What has made them happy? Faith in Christ. But what have they believed respecting Christ? That He died to save them. Have they then believed a lie? Can the propagation of a falsehood produce so many blessings? Surely not. Then it is *true* that Christ died for them. But what of the past generations of Fijians? Did not Christ die for *them?* Was it designed by God that the salvation of the gospel should have no effect, as far as they were concerned, until this nineteenth century? What shall we say of the degraded hordes of Africa? When Dr. Livingstone first crossed the African continent, and first preached to these degraded people the doctrines of the gospel, they said to him, "Did your forefathers know these things long ago?" He said, "Yes." Then said they, "Why did not some one come long ago and tell them to us?"—What answer must we give to this affecting question? Has God provided nothing better than what they have already attained?

Surely the doctrine here taught should excite in our hearts both joy and sadness. Joy that the great salvation is provided for all men; sadness that to so many millions of our race the purposes of God's infinite mercy have not been made known.

Can we doubt what our duty is towards those who have no knowledge of God's unspeakable gift?

II.

This leads us to consider the great design of Christ in this manifestation of His love to us. In other parts of Scripture we are taught how the purposes of God's mercy in Christ stretch far beyond the horizon of time; how the Father, through the Son, designs to bestow on us eternal life. But the design referred to in the text is more limited. It respects our conduct in this life. The passage before us shows what, in the case of each one of us, is to be the practical result of our accepting the salvation of the gospel —a practical result in which that which is made prominent is not so much blessing received, as duty rendered.

"We thus judge, that if one died for all, then all died." That is to say, in the purpose of God, whilst Christ died to sin on behalf of all, the all for whom He died died *to sin.* Here we have to speak of a design, a purpose, not one that is actually realized in all, but one possible in all. The best comment on the words, "Then all died," will be found in Paul's own treatment of the same truth in Romans vi. There he fully unfolds what is here given in a more compressed form. In the purpose of God, faith in Christ's death so unites us in sympathy with Christ, that the death of Christ becomes to us and in us the death of sin. From the time that we believe on Christ, we die to sin. We look upon our old, sinful, pre-Christian life as brought to an end, and we view ourselves as having entered upon a life wholly

new. As the apostle himself adds immediately, "If any
man be in Christ, he is a new creature."

So also faith in our Lord's resurrection introduces us to
a new life. We do not merely die through Christ's death,
but we live again through His resurrection. So that the
apostle does not say that those who are *dead* to sin should
live unto Christ, but that those who *live*,—live the new
life—should "live unto Him." We have been made
familiar with this doctrine of a death unto sin and new life
unto righteousness by various passages of Scripture; but
that which claims our attention as specially taught in this
passage is the strongly marked contrast here given between
a life unto *self* and a life unto Christ. The apostle says that
the great design of our Lord is that we should not *henceforth*
live unto ourselves, but unto Christ ; thus plainly intimating
that all men, up to the time of their believing in Christ, *do*
live unto themselves, and that from that moment onwards
they cease to do this. The actual life on earth is cut into
two portions ; the dividing line is the time of our entrance
into fellowship with Christ : on the one side of that line is
life for self—on the other side, life for Christ. And thus it
is plainly taught, especially if we compare what Paul says
here with his teaching in Romans vi., that life unto self is
life unto sin, and that life to Christ implies annihilation
of life to self. These things are so contrary the one to
the other, that selfishness destroys Christianity, while Christianity destroys selfishness.

To understand this doctrine fully, we must also remember
that living to self would comprehend far more in Paul's
mind than it would in the minds of men generally. The
selfish life, according to his view, is that of *all* who are
not living the Christian life. Men may be in one sense
self-denying, in the service of their families, in the service
of the State, and even in many walks of philanthropy, but

still they are living unto self if they are not living to Christ.
They do not acknowledge the law of Christ as higher than
their own will. And this is the proof. If at any time the
claims of Christ come into conflict with their own inclinations, the claims of Christ are set aside, their own inclinations are followed. With the true Christian, the opposite is
the case; his natural inclinations bow to the will of Christ.
The will of Christ is to him in everything the supreme rule
of life, so that he can say with the apostle, "The love of
Christ controls me." The example of Christ's great and unspeakable love, held constantly before his mind, constrains
and controls every point of his conduct. He believes that
Christ gave Himself for him. That is the very truth.
Through Christ's death he lives, absolved from the curse of
the law, reconciled to God, rejoicing in the hope of life
everlasting. He believes that through every moment of life
he lives by the mercy of God in Christ, and he judges that
the proper sequence to his faith is, that the life which he
owes to Christ should be devoted to Christ.

Hence, too, all his views of life take their colour from
this view of his relationship to his Lord. He looks upon
all mankind in the light of the truth here taught. He
'knows no man after the flesh.' The only distinction
between man and man that is really of great importance,
arises out of each man's relationship to Christ. Is he *in*
Christ through faith, or separated from Christ through
unbelief? The distinctions of Jew, Gentile, Barbarian,
Scythian, bond or free—all are as nothing compared with
this. Is a man, according to the flesh, rich, honourable,
learned? He is in the view of one who sympathizes with
Paul, an object not of envy but of pity, if he is not in
Christ. Is another destitute of all these advantages—poor,
obscure, unlearned? Yet if he is in Christ, he accounts
him happy and a brother beloved. What is true respecting

all others is pre-eminently true in regard to Christ Himself.
Any one of Paul's contemporaries who was not a Christian
would "know Christ after the flesh." When Tacitus, for
example, learnt something respecting Christ, he thought of
Him as an obscure Jew in a distant province of the empire,
who had been put to death by the Roman governor
Pontius Pilate. Paul thought of Christ as Him in whom
God was reconciling the world to Himself; Him through
whom we attain everlasting life; Him to whom entire
devotion constitutes the only life on earth that is worth
living.

Are we to say then that the life of every true Christian is
absolutely devoted to Christ, that it is wholly unselfish,
and this in the highest sense of the word? We dare not
say so, because to affirm this absolutely would be to say
that if the life of any man is in any measure devoted to self,
he is not a Christian. We dare not affirm this. We saw,
when speaking of the purpose of God in the death of Christ,
that we have to conceive first of all of a Divine purpose
embracing all mankind, and then of a limited fulfilment
determined by the measure of human faith in, and co-
operation with, that purpose. In so far as the purpose of
God is believed and embraced by each individual, it is
fulfilled in him. This applies equally to the moral result
here designed. Not every professed Christian becomes
unselfish from the first moment of his professing himself
a Christian; not every true Christian becomes absolutely
unselfish from the first, but he renounces the life of sin, the
life of self, *so far forth* as he is a Christian. In other
words, in so far as the unselfish conduct of his Lord in
giving Himself for the Christian is copied by the yielding
up of himself by the Christian to the will of his Lord.
Here we have the true ideal or model of a Christian life.
Whatever in our lives is done to please ourselves, without

regard to Christ, and still more what is done in opposition to His will, is so much taken from the Christian life; by so much do we fall short of our high standard; to the same extent do we fall back into our former pre-Christian life, the life of selfishness and of sin. But is it possible to realize in actual Christian experience this grand ideal? May the whole of life be devoted to Christ? Can it be made wholly Christian? We answer, Yes. It is an ideal life here proposed, but not an impracticable one.

It is not, however, to be attained in the way in which many in past ages have sought it. If we would devote our lives wholly to Christ, we need not leave our homes for the monastery or for the nunnery. We need not assume any peculiar dress; we need not give up any employment of life, unless it be of its own nature sinful. We may live in the same homes, wear the same clothes; we may plough and sow, plant and build, buy and sell, marry or be given in marriage, as we did before: and yet we may become new creatures—our past life all dead, our present life all new! Does any one ask, How? We answer that the moral value of every single action, and so of life as a whole, does not depend simply on the outward act itself, but on the intention with which it is done. Those who are now servants of Christ know that before they entered His service they loved to please themselves. They bought, they sold, they laboured, they rested, according to their own pleasure; their own will was their law. Now all is changed. They buy for Christ, they sell for Christ, they labour for Him, they rest for Him. If they make gain, they make it for the Lord; if they lay out money, it is for the Lord; if they lay it up, it is also for Him. They have sorrows and trials: they are endured for Christ. They have pleasures and joys; but they are such as the Lord approves, and they desire no others. Thus the Christian lives in a new world.

All things become new. The things around are not
changed in their essence, but they have new aspects for the
Christian. All things to his eyes wear the hues of redemption; he walks in the light of God's countenance, which
brightens his path here, and surely leads him on to everlasting joys in the heavenly world. Say not that the ideal
cannot be realized. It is God's ideal made known to man.
It is not the dream of a heated imagination; it is founded
on facts. The facts of redemption are as real as any in the
universe; and they are everlasting. He who sets before
us this holy life says to us, "My grace is sufficient for
thee." Let us at all events try to realize it; for the attempt
itself is noble, and will elevate us. And let us not dare to
say that the attempt is vain, until we have tried the value of
the promises and the sufficiency of the promised grace, and
have found them wanting.

This life of devotion to Christ we must endeavour to
exemplify in two distinct but never widely separated departments; there must be *life in the world* and *life in the
Church*, both Christian always and Christian only. Paul's
own experience will illustrate my meaning. Paul was both
an apostle, and a tent-maker. To make Christ known
to those who had not yet known Him was his chief work
and unspeakable joy. But he judged it right, for special
reasons, sometimes to engage in tent-making. Was he less
holy, less devoted to Christ when making tents, than when
preaching the gospel? Not one whit. He was in the latter
case not so usefully employed for mankind, and it must be
an everlasting reproach to the Corinthian Church that their
lack of love for their spiritual father drove him to tent-
making; but considering the motives which influenced the
apostle, this work was as holy as any other. And how truly
noble does our life become when we do our ordinary work
in the same spirit! Then there is no drudgery in life; then

no occupation can be called mean, for all that we do is done for Christ.

But the sanctification to God of our ordinary occupations is not all that is required. We must not only live to Christ, we must live for others. Christ's conduct must control ours; what He has done for others suggests what we should do for them. He has procured the great salvation; we must make it known. He has made the happiness of our fellow men a possibility; we must labour to make it a fact. Can we refuse to take our part in helping to spread the gospel if we do indeed believe the gospel? As Christians, we believe that we owe to Christ individually priceless blessings. We say, Take away our Christianity, and you rob us of our most precious jewel—the sanctifier of our nature, the solace of our sadness, the perfecter of our present joys, the parent of our brightest hopes. It is to us infinitely precious. Let me lose all, rather than my interest in Christ. If we say this and believe it, ought we not to suppose that it will prove as great a treasure to others as to us? Our neighbours, many of them, are living in great misery; or, at best, are living a dreary, unsatisfied life because they know not by experience the happiness of religion. Shall we not strive to impart it to them? Shall we not at least invite them to be sharers of our own joys? Our treasure will not be diminished by their participating in it. Rather will it be increased. Christianity is exceedingly generous, and the more we distribute it, the more we have. The five loaves and two fishes in the hands of Christ's disciples only began to multiply, when they began to distribute them to the multitude.

Will you then resolve to devote life entirely to Christ? Life to self, self-centred and self-devoted, is like a stagnant pool—it ever turns to corruption. Life to Christ is like a fountain, always receiving fresh supplies from the secret spring, and sending these forth to brighten and gladden the life of many. No kind of life on earth is comparable to the Christian life for dignity or for joy. Dedicate life to self, look upon this world as a place where you are to make all tributary to yourself, live for pleasure, gain, honour : and you will have your reward. You may succeed in many of your designs ; and if you are successful, " the world will love its own," and men will flatter you and envy you. But you will not be truly happy. All this time you will carry about with you everywhere a heart ill at ease ; because your happiness will depend on the things without—not on the things within.[1]

And the world in which and for which you live will never quite satisfy you. You will never get all you wish. You will never think that the world does you full justice ; and you will have a thousand disappointments and vexations, because men will not award you the full recompense for all your toil. And perhaps when you are able to slake your soul's long thirst with the full cup of worldly enjoyment, it will be dashed from your lips, and the cup of trembling and of death be put into your hand, and you be forced to drink it. Or you may continue till old age, and then worldly pleasures and comforts may leave you one after another, your soul getting more and more contracted and selfish all the time, and the weary, unsatisfied life will be closed at last by a death of darkness and despair.

But give yourself wholly to Christ. Settle it with yourself that you have absolutely nothing to do in this world but what Christ gives you to do, and that you dare do nothing which you cannot do for Him. You will then be saved from ten thousand vexations which harass other

---

[1] " Mirum dictu ut sit omnis eorum virtus velut extra ipsos."— Tacitus, *Histories*, bk. i. 79.

people. You have but *One* to please ; you are safe from all employment that is degrading ; life is at once redeemed from drudgery, and even when you give up your own inclination in order to obey Christ, you know that you forsake an unwise course for a wise one ; that you forsake what is against your happiness, in favour of something that makes for it.

You may lose the world's favour, but against that set the approving smile of Christ. You may lose the company of summer friends and gay companions. You gain the dear love of the servants of Jesus Christ, which compensates a thousand times over for the loss of the world's friendship, and you will be preparing for the blessed society of the noblest of all ages, of those who have entered into the spirit of Paul, and have been ready to say with the dying martyr, Lambert, " None but Christ, none but Christ ! "

Here then are two paths set before us : Life for Christ, life for sin and self. Henceforth, what shall our life be ?

FREE FROM THE LAW [1]

" If ye are led of the Spirit, ye are not under the law."—GAL. v. 18.

THE Epistle to the Galatians is largely occupied in setting forth and explaining two antitheses or contrasts ; namely, those of *the Spirit* and *the Law*, and *the Spirit* and *the Flesh*. But the contrasts are widely different. Between the Spirit and the flesh there is an opposition of nature ; they are as antagonistic as light and darkness ; between the Spirit and the law there is no opposition of nature, but only

---

[1] A sermon preached before the Leeds Wesleyan District Meeting, at Dewsbury, on May 10th, 1886.

one of function. I must refer afterwards to the opposition between the Spirit and the flesh; at present I deal only with the contrast between the Spirit and the law. " If ye are led by the Spirit, ye are not under the law."

In expounding this passage I shall speak, firstly, of the apostle's doctrine ; secondly, of the apostle's safeguards ; and, thirdly, of the advantages of preaching and practising this view of Christian life.

I. *The Apostle's Doctrine.*—The teaching of this passage, and of the epistle generally, is this : That as Christians we are ruled, not from *without,* but from *within* ; not by precept, but by principle; not by the law, but by the Spirit : and that thus we attain to the highest freedom and noblest life that is possible to man. Let us look at some illustrations of the truth here taught.

You are a merchant; two men come into your counting-house the same day, and on each occasion you have on your table a heap of gold coin uncounted. When the first man enters, you have such an opinion of his character that you feel it quite safe to leave your room and leave him alone with the money. You believe he would as soon cut off his right hand as appropriate anything to his own use. When the second man enters, you would not trust him in the same circumstances for a single minute. You would not leave him with uncounted money unless he had a policeman at his elbow watching him every moment. Why this difference ? Because the one man is ruled, and strongly ruled, from within; the other is ruled from without, so far as he is ruled at all. Again: two boys are trained in two different families. In the case of one, the training is by multiplied rules and precepts, by threatening, by fear, by frequent punishment. The restraints of evil come from without. He is not credited with good principles ; is rather expected to go wrong than to do right. The discipline of the other boy is very different. He is not governed by many precepts, but by a few all-important principles : as that God is our Creator and Father, Christ is our Saviour. Sin is above all things to be hated; God is above all to be loved. There is little threaten-ing, little punishment, little fear, but much love. Need I ask which training makes the noblest character ? This boy will grow up to be a law unto himself ; not the other.

If you compare French and English schools together, and look at broad, general facts, I believe you will find this difference. In French schools the children are subject to constant external rule, and are hardly ever out of the teacher's presence. In English schools less reliance is placed on external discipline, though that cannot be neglected ; more reliance is placed on high, self-regulating principle.

If you compare the best-known religions of the world with Christianity, you see the same difference. Hinduism has a rule for its adherents which governs them as to all the external actions of their lives. Mohammedanism has its times and forms of prayer and fasting, which must be rigidly observed. But in these religions there may be, and often is, the most rigid and constant conformity with the outward precept, but an utter absence of any lofty moral principle.

So if we compare Romanism with Protestantism. If a Romanist would attain to the highest perfection of his religion, he must observe a multitude of rules and precepts, and must use just those prayers, and read just those books which the Church appoints for every day of the year, and every hour of the day. Protestantism exacts no such observance, but strenuously insists on the need of having the heart always right with God.

The Apostle Paul makes a wide and deeply interesting application of the principles just dwelt on. He brings before us God's own education of the human race. Up to a given period in the history of the world, the whole race, including the Jews, was in a state of nonage and bondage, as the apostle says, under a *paidagogos.* I venture to use this Greek word, because we have none in our language exactly equivalent to it. It denoted among the Greeks that person in the household to whom a father delegated his authority whilst his children were under age. He might or might not be their teacher, but he was always their governor,—guiding, controlling, punishing; so that an only son and heir differed nothing from a servant, though, in prospect, lord of all, until the time came which was appointed of the father, when he stepped out of his nonage and bondage, ceased to be under the control of the *paidagogos*, and entered into relations with his father such as became a free-born son who was now of full age.

"Even so we," says the apostle, "when we were children, were in bondage under the elements of the world; but when the fulness of the time was come, God sent forth His Son, born of a woman [and thus a partaker of our nature], born under the law" [and thus a partaker of our condition], but thus born with the very purpose "that He might redeem them that were under the law, that we might receive the adoption of sons." The Son of God became man that the sons of men might become sons of God, and His own brethren by adoption. "And because ye are sons, God hath sent forth the Spirit of His Son into our hearts, crying, Abba, Father." The Spirit of the Son of God in us creates in us the spirit of sons of God, establishes to our consciousness the relation of sons, and begets in us the love of sons towards God. "Wherefore thou art no more a slave, but a son; and because a son, an heir through God."

He who knows God as his father, and loves God as his father, becomes, in one view, *a law unto himself;* but, more strictly, is henceforth ruled by the Spirit of God dwell-ing within him ; is led by the Spirit—not governed by law. This is the doctrine.

II. *The Apostle's Safeguards.*—The words, " not governed by law," will probably seem to some the announcement of a perilous doctrine. You will be ready to say, " It is a dangerous thing to tell Christian people, You are not under law ; you are not to be controlled by law ; you must be ruled from within, not from without." And I fully admit that such teaching is very dangerous indeed, unless guarded as the apostle guards it in his own teaching. But we need never be afraid of following the apostle, if we will only follow him fully, and take his doctrine, not in fragments, but in its completeness.

First of all, look at the supposition here made : " *If* ye are led by the Spirit." To those who are led by the Spirit, and to these *only*, the apostle says, " Ye are not under law." Now if any one is indeed led by the Spirit, he is in no danger. We are perfectly sure the Spirit of God will never lead him astray. Yes, it will be said, this is quite true ; but history shows that men have often *thought* themselves to be led by the Spirit when they were not ; and we need to fear lest men should mistake their own wild fancies for Divine guidance. All this we admit. And there is no doctrine, however plainly stated and carefully guarded, that is not liable to abuse ; but if we follow Paul's guidance, we shall not stray. See what precautions he takes against self-delusion.

1. First, *there is no antagonism between the Spirit and the law.* The apostle himself commends the law highly. It is holy, it is good, it is spiritual. The law itself, proceeding from the Spirit, cannot be opposed to the Spirit ; nor is the Spirit opposed to the law. The difference between the law and the Spirit is this : the law commands and prohibits ; it reveals sin, and pronounces on us the sentence of death.

It makes no allowance ; it does not pity ; it cannot forgive ; and it does not enable us to fulfil its own precepts. The Spirit enlightens, animates, controls, creates us anew, and endows us with power which enables us to fulfil the righteousness of the law. The whole work of the Spirit perpetually tends to bring us into harmony with God's law ; and no one who violates the law can ever plead for this the sanction of the Holy Spirit.

2. The second guard is, that *it is the office and work of the Spirit to destroy the flesh.* I need hardly say that in this part of the apostle's teaching the term "flesh" does not denote our bodily nature. I shall not attempt any exact philosophical or theological definition of the "flesh"; it suffices to say that it is the principle, or the source, of evil within man himself. As everything good in us comes from the Spirit, everything morally wrong in us is from "the flesh." And you may safely accept this short definition : by the flesh, Paul means everything in us which is opposed to the Spirit. Here is a sure guard. The Spirit is absolutely intolerant of the flesh. Any one who is governed by the flesh cannot be governed by the Spirit. In whatever degree the flesh prevails in any one, in so far he is *not* led by the Spirit. But further, the Spirit is to destroy the flesh. "For the flesh lusteth against the Spirit, and the Spirit against the flesh ; for these are contrary the one to the other ; that ye may not do the things that ye would" (*v.* 17, R.V.) The meaning very commonly put on these words is altogether wrong. They are understood to mean that this conflict between flesh and Spirit goes on in every Christian, and sometimes the Spirit conquers, and sometimes the flesh ; and moreover that it never can be otherwise. This is the teaching of a vast number of religious teachers and of religious books. I am perfectly sure that it is not Paul's teaching. I am quite sure that he teaches the opposite. Read

what he says in *v.* 16 : " Walk in the Spirit, and ye shall in no wise fulfil the lust of the flesh." Let the Spirit control you wholly, and the flesh shall not control you at all.

He therefore that is under the full control of the Spirit does not in any measure fulfil the desires of the flesh.

3. But the apostle is not satisfied to state the truth in the general and abstract way. There is still a danger of self-deception when we deal only with generalities, and with inward principles of action. To guard us still further, he points out " the works of the flesh," which are the products of the evil principle : " The works of the flesh are manifest, which are these, fornication, uncleanness, lasciviousness, idolatry, sorcery, enmities, strife, jealousies, wraths, factions, divisions, heresies, envyings, drunkenness, revellings, and such like : of the which I forewarn you, even as I did forewarn you, that they which practise such things shall not inherit the kingdom of God " (*vv.* 19-21, R.V.). No one can plead the Spirit's leading for any one of these. If these evils are manifest in our lives, every one has a right to say that we are not led by the Spirit. If we are conscious that the evil passions here enumerated,—wrath, strife, hatred, envy,—have power in our souls, though not manifested outwardly, our subjection to the Spirit is not complete. Therefore no one can persuade others, no one, if he closely follows Paul, can persuade himself, that he is led by the Spirit whilst these evil things have power over him, or have place in him.

4. Still the apostle is not satisfied that he has guarded us enough. He adds another guard : *when the Spirit dwells in a man, He will not be inactive.* The Divine power will manifest itself, not only by abolishing evil, but by creating good ; not only by destroying evil tempers and passions, but by creating good ones. Some will say to us that they have the " witness of the Spirit " within them ;

some will go further, and express their conviction that they are " filled with the Spirit." We are quite ready to believe all this, and to rejoice with you in the great grace given to you ; but at the mouth of two witnesses let everything be confirmed. If, while you make this profession, we see in you " the fruit of the Spirit,"—" love, joy, peace, longsuffering, gentleness, goodness, faith, meekness, temperance,"—then we know that the Spirit indeed dwells in you, and we glorify God on your behalf. But if we do *not* see these fruits in you, and especially if we should mark in you any of the works of the flesh, then we cannot accept your testimony ; and however strong your own conviction may be, we shall certainly come to the conclusion that you are *mistaken*.

III. What advantage is there in taking this view of the Christian life ? Much every way.

1. It brings our life into harmony with our creed. When we repeat our creed, we say, "I believe in the Holy Ghost." But what is the Holy Spirit to you ? An article in the creed ? An abstract conception, and nothing more ? Happy for us when the blessed Spirit is no longer an abstraction, but when He is our Guide, our Comforter, and Sanctifier !

2. It leads to the highest perfection of the Christian life, because the rule of principle, divinely implanted, and sustained, is more far-reaching than the rule of precept and outward restriction. The precept says, "Thou shalt not kill." It is very easy to a Christian man to observe this precept in the letter ; but when we are led by the Spirit, we go much further, and put away far from us these feelings of envy and hatred and malice, which make men murderers in their hearts, though not in act.

The precept says, "Thou shalt not commit adultery " ; but if we follow the Spirit, He will destroy all unchaste desire.

"Thou shalt not steal," says the precept. The Spirit leads us to put away every kind and form of dishonesty. Let me give you an illustration :

Joseph Sturge and his brother were corn-merchants in Birmingham. They sent a cargo of corn to one of their customers in Ireland. It was damaged on the way. The matter was referred to arbitration, and when the award was given, the consignee took no objection to it ; but the brothers were not satisfied, and some time after, they wrote to the consignee to this effect: "We have carefully reviewed the transaction referred to arbitration, and have reason to believe that the award was £250 too much in our favour. We send you a cheque for this amount, and your acceptance of it will terminate the business to our satisfaction." Now some men would declare at once that these men were fools to pay that which they were under no legal obligation to pay. But *we* say that the devil makes fools of those who talk thus. For the inward satisfaction of doing right in the sight of God, according to the principle within, is something which money cannot buy, and for the loss of which untold riches cannot compensate.

3. It leads to extreme watchfulness. If we adopt this as our fundamental view of life, that we must in all things and at all times be led by the Spirit, then we see that it is absolutely necessary that we should not grieve Him whom we have taken to be our guide. Imagine yourself to be passing in the night time through a dark and dangerous forest. You know not a step of the way. But you have a guide with you who knows every step. He is besides so mighty that he can defend you from every danger and every foe. Suppose you offend your guide, and he threatens to leave you? You feel at once you must conform your conduct to his will. You say, If my guide leave me, I perish !

We know that we must not give way to the sins of the

H. 18

flesh, as these are commonly understood. We know that the sins of gluttony, of drunkenness, of unchastity, quench the Spirit. It is absolutely impossible to be led by the Spirit if we yield to these sins. But we must not grieve the Spirit by *evil words.* It is to be feared that many Christians do this, by words not in strictest harmony with truth ; by words not consistent with due reverence for the Divine name and the Divine kingdom,—not consistent with perfect purity of thought. If anything could make me despair of the future of true religion in this country, I think it would be the worse than unedifying talk often uttered by Christian people. We must go further. We must guard our *thoughts.* "The Spirit searcheth all things." If we desire Him to dwell in the inner sanctuary of our souls, we must keep that sanctuary undefiled by unholy desires.

When Thomas Fuller was asked by the Triers to give some evidence that he was a Christian, he said, "I make a conscience of my inmost thoughts."

4. It leads to great *promptness* and *vigour of action.* As we must not grieve the Spirit by doing the things which are evil, so we must not resist Him by refusing to do the good to which He moves us. Here we approach a very difficult subject, which cannot be discussed in a few sentences. How far does the Holy Spirit direct us to the performance of particular definite actions? The Spirit directed Philip to go in a particular road, to address himself to a particular person. Does He so direct us? I cannot fully discuss the question. But ministers of the gospel say that they are "moved " to take upon them the office and work of the ministry. Why should we not expect that He who moves us to the work as a whole will give us much guidance as to the particulars of it? This, I think, we may safely say : the more humble, teachable, pure-minded we are, the more we shall have of the Holy Spirit's guidance. And to be sure

we have it and are acting on it, gives vigour and decision such as are not derived from any other source.

5. If we are led by the Spirit, we shall have *power*, and that of the highest kind : the power of intense conviction of the reality of the truth, and of its infinite importance ; power evinced in the highest moral courage, enabling us to stand forth as faithful witnesses for Christ at all times, in all places, in all companies; the power of Peter and John before the Jewish Council, the power of Stephen before the Sanhedrin, the power of Paul before Felix and Agrippa. Is there anything in this world that we need more, that we should prize more ?

6. To be led by the Spirit leads us to great *peace.* The trouble, the unrest of our souls arises from this very fact, that we grieve, that we resist the Spirit. When we do not grieve Him, when we do not resist, there is no trouble—the stream of our thoughts flows all in one channel. And as the guidance of the Spirit brings peace to the individual, so it brings unity to the Church. If the Spirit works in you and also in me, we cannot oppose one another ; for the Holy Spirit never counter-works Himself. The fellowship of the Spirit necessarily leads to the fellowship of the saints.

7. All this means *liberty.* "Stand fast in the liberty wherewith Christ hath made you free." Liberty from the yoke of a burdensome ceremonial ; liberty from the condemnation and curse of the law ; liberty from the bondage of evil habits, evil passions, evil desires ; liberty from the fear of death and the fear of man—all the fear that " hath torment." What liberty can be compared with this?

Brethren, let us pray for the Spirit ; let us wait for the Spirit. The apostles waited, men in later times have waited, and not in vain. Let us not prescribe to the Holy Spirit how He shall work in us and by us. He will not work in

any two of us exactly alike. "There are diversities of operations, but the same Spirit." Let the tenor of our prayer
always be,—

> "So I may Thy Spirit know,
> Let Him as He listeth blow;
> Let the manner be unknown,
> So I may with Thee be one."

So shall we be filled with the Spirit, and He Himself will
cause us to understand, as no other teacher can, the triumphant words of the holy apostle : "The Spirit of life in
Christ Jesus hath made me free from the law of sin and
death." If we are led by the Spirit, we are not under
the law.

THE NATURE OF CHRISTIAN LOVE.

"Love suffereth long, and is kind ; love envieth not ; love vaunteth
not itself, is not puffed up, doth not behave itself unseemly, seeketh
not its own, is not provoked, taketh not account of evil ; rejoiceth
not in unrighteousness, but rejoiceth [in] the truth ; beareth all things,
believeth all things, hopeth all things, endureth all things."—1 COR.
xiii. 4–7 (R.V.).

THE love here spoken of is the principle which fulfils
the second great commandment of the law, and of
which Paul says in another place, "Love worketh no ill to
his neighbour : therefore love is the fulfilling of the law."
We see the strength of the principle by the evils which it
overcomes.

1. *Impatience.* It "suffereth long." He who is destitute of love is ever ready to take offence. He is irritable ;
every slight thing puts him out. He is not only unable to
keep his temper when he is the object of the intentional
hostility of others, but he often takes offence where none is
meant. He very likely calls this impatience by some well-

sounding name. He says that he is sensitive, or that he has a high sense of honour, and cannot endure insult. Such a man passes a very uncomfortable life—he makes himself many enemies ; and if he has any friends, they need have a great deal of patience with him, because he has so little with them. He frequently says, " I have no patience with this thing or that "—a very true, but very superfluous announcement.

Love cures this evil. It is slow to take offence, unwilling to believe that others can intend unkindness, because this is so foreign to its own nature ; and if the loving man sees plainly that wrong and unkindness are intended, he does not lose his temper ; he pities the offender even while he condemns his conduct, for he knows that the malignant spirit brings upon the offender himself more misery than he can possibly inflict on one who dwells in love. Love suffers long ; it is patient toward the follies and infirmities, the unkindnesses and the injuries of all by whom its patience is tried.

2. *It overcomes and eradicates unkindness.* It " is kind." Men destitute of love are very unkind ; whilst they are so sensitive to their own honour that the slightest neglect or affront, intentional or unintentional, rouses their anger, they are little concerned about the sensitiveness of others. You must not say one word to wound their feelings ; but if you do, they will pour out a torrent of words very well calculated to wound yours. And this with cool self-complacency they call "speaking their minds," choosing to give their ebullitions of bad temper the honourable names of candour and straightforwardness. Some men one would think from their ways must feel a devilish sort of satisfaction in making other people uncomfortable, and they never get through a day without doing this. Love makes men kind ; gentle and courteous in their speech and behaviour, kind in deed and

in word. Their souls dwelling in love, they carry with them
an atmosphere of benevolence, and make all people who
have to deal with them happier for their company.

3. *Love cures envy.* It "envieth not." You tell the
envious man that his neighbour is prospering and successful
in business, and expect him to look pleased, but he looks
vexed ; and he ever has his detracting speech ready. His
neighbour's wealth, he hints, is not honestly come by ; "all
is not gold that glitters," and the success is not so great as
it seems. His neighbour, you tell him, is generous : " More
generous than wise," is his answer.

Love destroys this spirit. It teaches us to rejoice in
another's happiness ; for the man of love wishes good to all,
and the increase of the happiness of another is the fulfilment of his own desires. This is truly a sorrowful world,
but the man who is saved from the pangs of envy, and has
the happy art of finding his bliss increased by the prosperity
of others, will seldom lack occasions of rejoicing.

4. The next evils here referred to as cured by love are
closely related : *vanity, pride, and unseemly behaviour.*
Vanity leads a man to "vaunt himself." Many a man who
has never a good word to speak for another, has ever a
good word for himself. He is boastful. He tells you the
brave things he has done, the clever things he has said.
He boasts of his great wealth, or his great relations, his
supposed great learning, wit, or wisdom.

In another man the evil is not vanity, but *pride.* He
"thinks of himself more highly than he ought to think."
He does not often boast, but nevertheless makes men feel
that he thinks much of himself and little of others. He
greatly overrates his virtues, and is very blind to his own
failings. Now whether pride or vanity prevail, it leads to
the third evil here described—*unseemly behaviour.* This will
happen whether one's station be high or low ; for though

we naturally associate vanity and pride with wealth and high birth, they are by no means confined to these. Poverty and pride may go together. Love removes these evils. What a man has that is good is God's gift, whether strength, or beauty, or riches, or intellect, or learning, or power. If he has received it, 'why should he glory as if he had not received it?' He honours God who gave him his gifts, and not himself for their possession. The deepest humility does not make it necessary for a man to be ignorant of his own gifts; but love is humble, because it is grateful. The same love recognises God's gifts in others, and rejoices in them. Thus love "vaunteth not itself, is not puffed up, and doth not behave itself unseemly."

5. *Love cures selfishness.* It "seeketh not its own." A man void of love lives only for himself. The friends whom he professes to cherish are but the ladder by which he is striving to rise, and which he will thrust aside when it serves him no longer. But love, as was seen in Paul himself, seeks the welfare of others, and labours earnestly to promote it. The example of our Saviour is the most perfect illustration of this form of love, but in the greatness of its self-sacrifice is beyond comparison, and is unapproachable by us. Perhaps we may safely say that he who wrote these words was in this, as in other instances, the most perfect exemplification of his own doctrine. What labours, what perils, what sufferings did he endure! and yet looking for no gain of worldly wealth and honour. He did doubtless covet the love of those for whom he laboured; but so great and perfect was his self-renunciation that he could not be prevented from seeking the good of others, even by their coldness and ingratitude. And writing to these very Corinthians, for whom he had done so much and from whom he had received so little, he says, in language the like of which surely had never been heard before, " I will very gladly spend and

be spent for you; though the more abundantly I love you, the less I be loved."

6. Yet another evil is *anger*. "Love is not (easily) provoked." It does not give way to paroxysms or fall into passions. How very easily some men are provoked! If anything crosses their inclinations or tries their temper, they are ready to fly into a passion even instantly. To have to deal much with such persons is like having constantly to handle gunpowder. Such men sometimes excuse themselves and are excused by others on the ground that though they are quick-tempered, their passion is soon over; but then they forget that the pain and real injury which they inflict on others are not soon over, and their unhappy victims may be smarting with all the pain of a wounded spirit long after these quick-tempered people have recovered their equanimity and are very well pleased with themselves. Sometimes they will tell you, "I am very passionate, but then I am very forgiving." That may be true; but the man who gives way to his temper has much oftener occasion to *ask* forgiveness than to bestow it. In such a case, to offer forgiveness instead of asking for pardon is only to add insult to injury. Love cures this. You may think it impossible; but, by the grace of God, "all things are possible." There is good reason for thinking that not one of Christ's apostles was more quick-tempered than John the son of Zebedee. Yet surely in him, if in any, love was made perfect. And when natural warmth of temper is subdued and sanctified by love, it makes one of the noblest of all characters.

7. Further, love cures *revenge*. It "taketh not account of evil." These words have been variously interpreted; but I believe the sense to be this, that love does not brood over injuries received, with a view to retaliation. The words of Paul might almost literally be rendered, "Love does not put down injury in its account." It keeps no reckoning

of wrongs received. Some men are said to have great
control over their tempers, when it would be more correct
to say that they have control over their countenances.
They do not give way to outward manifestation of passion
when the injury is received, but the secret thought of their
heart is, This shall be paid back with interest when the
opportunity comes. They can smile upon you when they
are bent upon your ruin. They are like the man described
by David: "The words of his mouth were smoother
than butter, but war was in his heart" (Ps. lv. 21). This
also love casts out. It saves from malice and revenge,
as well as from passionate anger. It forgives and forgets,
heartily and utterly. It forgives, even as it hopes to be
forgiven.

8. Again, it cures that hateful disposition which "rejoices in iniquity." It is one of the worst features of the
depraved heart that it can take pleasure in witnessing and
hearing of the wrongs inflicted on others. But to the
loving soul wrong-doing of every kind is exceedingly hateful.
It matters not what form it assumes, whether it be robbery,
or theft, or murder, or adultery; whether that by which a
man is injured in his property, or in his virtue, or in his
reputation. All sin is hateful to love; because while it
dishonours God, it tends most inevitably and directly to
destroy human happiness.

9. And for the same reason love "rejoices in the truth."
"The truth" is but another name for the true religion of
Christ, which first of all blesses men's minds with the knowledge of that truth which is life eternal, and then leads to
a conduct which is characterized by truth and integrity in
every part of it. That man may well rejoice in the truth
who feels that knowledge of this truth is the source of all
his life and joy and comfort, and who knows that as the
truth of God prevails in the world, the happiness of man-

kind follows in its train. His own happiness is inseparably connected with the triumph of the truth.

This last characteristic of love must be borne in mind to save us from giving the noble name of this Divine virtue to something which is in reality very unlike it, but which sometimes affects to wear its garb. The love here spoken of is never separated from the truth. It is not that most dangerous notion, sometimes called charity, which would have men believe that all creeds are alike, and that it matters very little what men believe, provided only they are generous and honest. This was not Paul's doctrine. He believed that there was a system of doctrine which deserved to be called *the truth.* He was willing to forego all personal convenience and ease and honour to serve and save others, but from the truth itself he would not swerve a hair's-breadth; and rather than give up one iota of the truth, he was willing, if need were, to lose every friend and render up life itself.

10. And, finally, Paul, having shown us love in its peacefulness, tenderness, and gentleness, now exhibits it in its *firmness and strength.*

It "beareth all things." It bears up against all things. It is often tried, but does not fail. There are many discouragements to love. Paul found this. His large and loving heart was sorely tried by many things, but surely most of all by the faults and failures of those from whom he had reason to expect better things. He was tried by the fickle Galatians when they were 'so soon removed from Him that called them, unto another gospel'; but this did not quench his love. He was tried by these Corinthians, by false brethren, who belied the confidence which he had placed in them; but his love did not fail—it "bore up against all things." He did not become either soured or gloomy.

"Love believeth all things." It believeth all things that

it ought to believe. "We can do nothing against the truth," and love cannot believe against the truth ; but it cures that kind of scepticism respecting others which is willing to believe nothing good of them. It believes good when it sees fair ground to believe. It does not set out with the principle that "every man is to be dealt with as a rogue until he proves himself honest," but it rather believes all that is good till compelled to disbelieve.

"Love hopeth all things." It hopes that good men will continue good, and that bad men will mend. It has hope for the Church, and for the world.

"Love endureth all things." It is steadfast and unmovable. "Many waters cannot quench" it. Where there is no love, or the love is very weak, the professor of religion is liable to be turned out of the way by slight hindrances. ·He is soon offended and gets his mind hurt, and backslides from God ; but where love abides and abounds, the whole character is strengthened by it. See this in Paul. What afflictions and perils and persecutions he endured ! but nothing quenched his love to God or man. He did not desert the cause of Christ. He ceased not till the latest hour of his life to labour for the good of his fellow men.

Here then is Love, the crowning grace of Christianity. Does love produce all these fruits in all? We answer that these are its legitimate fruits. It never produces the contrary of any of these, and where it has its seat in any heart, the tendency is to produce them all ; but according to the vigour of the tree is the abundance of its fruits. This love may be in us, but may not be perfected in us. If the principle be feeble, its manifestation will be correspondingly feeble. But we may have "love" perfected in us. This we should seek for, pray for, believe for. If our religion bear these blessed fruits of love, it will bring great glory to God, great happiness to ourselves, and great benefit to others.

THE BENEDICTION.[1]

"The grace of the Lord Jesus Christ, and the love of God, and the communion of the Holy Ghost, be with you all. Amen."—2 COR. xiii. 14.

I HAVE chosen this text for Trinity Sunday, because it upholds and unfolds the doctrine of the Trinity. I know that some hearers have little liking for doctrinal sermons. They say to the preacher, Do not trouble us with doctrine; give us something practical. And some are ever ready to say with Pope,—

"For modes of faith let graceless zealots fight,
　He can't be wrong whose life is in the right.'

But in such speeches there is a great fallacy, and those who use them are the victims of a delusion.

They suppose a man's life can be right who has a wrong creed, but it never is. Bad doctrine always leads to bad practice; right doctrine tends to right practice. Take a broad view of the world to-day, and you find that all the world over where men have low and perverted notions of God, their own lives are degraded. The nations that have the most elevated views of God, are themselves the most exalted. Look at India. Here you find a few hundreds of Englishmen ruling many millions of Mohammedans and Hindus. What is the explanation? I have no doubt whatever that the explanation is this : we have a purer faith.

Read the history of India, and what do you find? The individual men who have done most for India, those who

---

[1] A sermon preached on Trinity Sunday.

have shown beyond all others the highest qualities of rulers, have been men of the highest Christian faith. Take, for example, such men as the Lawrences, Edwardes, Montgomery, Bartle Frere, and others. "As a man thinketh in his heart, so is he"; and the higher the thoughts, the nobler and happier is the man.

I. In examining this verse, see first of all how the *doctrine of the Trinity* is taught in it.

There is, in the first place, the distinction of three Persons. The apostle prays that a blessing may be given by the *Lord Jesus Christ;* he asks another blessing from *God the Father;* and a third from *the Holy Spirit.* The three names indicate three distinct givers of blessing; therefore three distinct Persons.

The *divinity* of each Person is also apparent. In the first place, we may be sure that the Apostle Paul would not offer prayer to any person if he did not regard him as Divine. He had been trained as a Jew, and had regarded with horror the idea of giving Divine honour to one who was not God; and there is no reason to suppose that from this part of his belief as a Jew he had ever receded. Besides, the asking of blessing from each Person supposes the divinity of each. It supposes that each Person is acquainted with the spiritual needs of all the members of the Church at Corinth, and has the power of communicating a blessing to each.

The Church by adopting and constantly using this prayer of the apostle, strongly declares its faith in the divinity of Father, Son, and Spirit. This prayer is put up at the same hour for millions of people, and supposes that the Son and the Spirit, as well as the Father, can bless millions of people at the same time. But to do this is to suppose each Person possessed of Divine attributes. The unity of the Persons is not taught in this passage so clearly as in some others, but it is plainly implied. The apostle prays that blessing from each Person may come to every member of the Church of Corinth ; that where one blesses, all will bless. This supposes that the act of one is in harmony with the act of all.

II. Having considered the doctrine of the Trinity in general as here taught, let us inquire into the nature of the three great blessings here sought. 1. *The grace of our Lord Jesus Christ.* In the first place, note the designation here given to our Lord. The writings of the Apostle Paul are remarkable for the number of times which he designates our Lord, and the great variety of titles given to Him. He speaks of Him as *Jesus,* as *Christ, Jesus Christ, Christ Jesus, the Lord, the Lord Jesus Christ,* etc. These are all designations of the same Person, but express various aspects of His person and of His relation to His servants. When the apostle speaks of the *Lord Jesus Christ,* he thinks of Him as the glorified Saviour, seated at the right hand of God, partaker of the Father's glory, and with the Father dispensing blessings to His people.

1. The particular blessing here sought is *the grace* of the Lord Jesus Christ, His favour, or goodwill. The enjoyment of this blessing by any one of Christ's servants implies two things : (1) That the goodwill of Christ is towards the believer in Christ. (2) That the believer is assured of that goodwill of Christ towards him. The knowledge of Christ's favour is obviously necessary to the enjoyment of it. If I am still in doubt whether the relation of Christ towards me is one of favour or displeasure, I cannot rejoice in Christ as my Saviour; but when this assurance is given, my joy is great. For what does it imply ? To me it means that the Lord Jesus Christ, the King of glory, mercifully and graciously regards 'this individual me.' He knows all my circumstances, all my needs. He knows all my

past sins, all the present defects of my character; never-theless He loves me, His goodwill is towards me; He accepts me as His servant; He deigns to call me His friend; He pledges to me His love and faithfulness; pro-mises to be my Protector and Guide even unto death, and after death to receive me to dwell with Him for ever. All this, and much more than I can express, is true of me and you if we enjoy this blessing, "the grace of our Lord Jesus Christ." If I, as a Christian, testify that I have this blessing, that I can say, "I am the Lord's, and He is mine, and I am persuaded that He will be my everlasting friend," does this seem like the language of presumption on my part? If so, I defend myself by the example of the Apostle Paul, who says, in writing to the Galatians, "I live by the faith of the Son of God, who loved me and gave Himself for me." It is a very obvious thing to say that there is a great difference between myself and the apostle. Granted; but the apostle himself would have been the first to admit, and even to contend, that what belonged to him as a Christian belonged to every true servant of Christ. To prove this it is sufficient to quote our text: "The grace of the Lord Jesus Christ be with you *all.*" He wished every believer in Corinth to enjoy what he himself enjoyed.

If any one still thinks that this conviction, "I am the accepted servant, the friend of Jesus Christ," is liable to engender feelings of pride, let him reflect that I claim for myself what every man can claim. I share this honour with millions of fellow Christians; and to be proud of it, as if it implied merit on my part, would be just as reason-able as to be proud because I tread on God's earth and enjoy the light and heat of the sun.

Is this blessing *yours?* Have you the favour of our Lord Jesus Christ? Can you say, humbly but confidently,

"I am the Lord's, and He is mine"? If not, I ask, Why are you living without it? This humble, strong confidence in a man's heart that he enjoys the favour of the Lord Jesus Christ is the greatest treasure any one can possess. It is a constant source of peace and joy, and it is the most powerful and the most elevating of all moral forces; the strongest safeguard against the power of temptation, the most powerful motive to all noble, godly living. Others are enjoying it, and finding in it their greatest happiness. Why should you live without it? Will you not seek it to-day—this hour? Will you not resolve that the sun shall not set this day before you have sought and found acceptance with the Lord Jesus Christ? Remember this is the most important question of any in the world: Is Christ for me or against me? If you say, "Yes, I humbly believe that I am Christ's servant, that He loves me and I love Him, that there is a covenant of peace between Him and me," then to you I say: Walk circumspectly; walk worthily of Christ. You profess yourself a friend of Jesus Christ: do not dishonour your profession; do nothing that tends to break, to mar the friendship. Let this be your resolve: I must, I will keep right with the Master. Come health, come sickness, come sorrow, come joy, nothing shall part between Him and me. Whilst you are faithful to this resolve, nothing can harm you; you pass through life a conqueror of the world.

2. *The love of God.* The full effect of the apostle's prayer is: "May each member of the Church at Corinth be loved by God." Here is a thought greater than any of us can comprehend. We can never think worthily of God Himself, and therefore cannot comprehend what it is to be loved by Him. When we think of our Lord Jesus Christ, though we regard Him as glorified and Divine, still we do not lose sight of His humanity, and we can

in some sort understand how man can be loved by man; but here we have to think of being the object of the love of the Infinite Creator. Here is wonder, mystery, joy.

The psalmist said, "When I consider Thy heavens, the work of Thy fingers, the moon and the stars, which Thou hast ordained; what is man, that Thou art mindful of him?" But to us the universe appears infinitely greater than it did to David. How great it is none can tell. The earth, which seems to us so vast, is but a small part of the solar system; but the whole solar system, including sun, moon, earth, and all the planets, is but a very small part of God's universe. If you could take your post of observation in one of the nearest fixed stars, you would see nothing of our solar system but the sun, and that would be diminished to a mere speck of light, if indeed it could be seen at all.

Our thoughts are confounded not only by the infinitely great, but by the infinitely small. Look down on an ant-hill, with its little world of inhabitants. How insignificant each creature seems! But take up one of them, and examine it with a microscope, and you will find that one of its eyes is composed of more than 1,000 facets, and each more perfectly formed than the most skilled workman living could form it. Not all the resources of all the workshops of Europe could produce the like. Is it possible that the Maker of this stupendous, glorious universe can think of *me*, care for *me*, love *me*? Here the teaching of Christ comes to our help. He shows that the presence of God is everywhere, and that the knowledge of God embraces everything. A sparrow cannot fall to the ground, He says, without our Father's notice.

But another difficulty arises. I may say: "I can believe that the infinite Creator is not unmindful of the work of His hands, and may therefore take account of me. But He

H. 19

is holy, and I have sinned ; His law is strict, and I have
transgressed ; His anger is great against sin, and I have
deserved it." Here again the teaching of Christ and His
apostles comes to our aid : " God was in Christ, reconciling
the world unto Himself, not imputing their trespasses unto
them "; "Being justified by faith, we have peace with God
through our Lord Jesus Christ "; "There is no condemnation to them that are in Christ Jesus." This explains
why in this verse "the grace of our Lord Jesus Christ" is
put first. That obtained, it secures to us the love of God.
Christ Himself has said, "He that loveth Me shall be
loved of My Father.   If a man love Me, he will
keep My words : and My Father will love him" (John xiv.
21–23).

In this blessed assurance, deep, incomprehensible as it
is, our souls may well rest. God, the Almighty everlasting
God, loves me. What have I to fear ? Though I cannot
comprehend His ways or understand all His dealings,
though He may be leading me through a dark valley or
through a dry and thirsty land, yet He loves me ; His will
is to bless me now, and to bring me to eternal life. But,
brethren, this faith involves obligation. If God so loves
me, I must love Him. I must show my love by my
obedience ; by hating and departing from all sin, and by
loving my neighbour as myself. If any man say that he
loves God whilst he hates his brother, he is a liar.

3. *The communion of the Holy Ghost.* We have no
English word which exactly answers to the Greek word [1]
here rendered "communion." It means a *sharing something with others*, a joint participation. The full effect of
the apostle's prayer therefore is : "May all the members of
the Church at Corinth partake of the blessings bestowed

---

[1] κοινωνία.

by the Holy Spirit." What are these blessings? They are the highest kind of blessings ever given by God to man.

Under the Old Testament the gift of the Spirit sometimes resulted in a large and sudden accession of physical strength, as we see in the instances of Samson and Elijah. I will not venture to say that the Spirit does not even now impart such blessings ; but what we chiefly regard as the gift of the Spirit are blessings intellectual and moral.

To describe the nature of these is one of the difficulties of the Christian preacher. If he speak of them to advanced Christians, he feels that their experience is a better expounder than his own words ; if to people who have no experience in the Christian life, he knows he cannot make plain by words what only experience can teach. "The natural man receiveth not the things of the Spirit of God : for they are foolishness unto him."

Yet some effort must be made to show what these blessings are, and there is no more instructive teaching on this point than that of Galatians v. 16 and the following verses. According to Paul, the great antithesis to "the Spirit" is "*the flesh.*" These, as he says, "are contrary one to the other." The flesh is the evil principle of our nature, the immediate source of all that in us is evil ; the Spirit is the immediate source of all that is good. The Spirit has to save us from the flesh. "The works of the flesh," the outcome, the practical manifestations of the evil principle, "are manifest, which are these : adultery, fornication," and the rest.

It is obvious that the less any one knows of the renewing power of the Spirit, the more he is under the power of the flesh. And such a one can understand that to be delivered from all these evils, saved from their outward manifestation in the life, and their inner defilement in the conscience, must of itself be a priceless blessing. And this is what the Spirit of God accomplishes for Christ's servants. The two principles, flesh and spirit, are mutually destructive ; when the flesh has complete sway, the Spirit is quenched ; when the Spirit has complete control, the flesh dies. So the apostle says, "Walk in the Spirit, and ye shall in nowise fulfil the lust of the flesh." Would you not like to be delivered from all these evil things ? Suppose you should never again be brought under the power of unholy desire, never again fall into sinful anger, henceforth be free from 'envy, hatred, malice, and all un- charitableness,' would not that alone be a great salvation ? Well, it may be so. Yield yourself wholly to the Spirit's control, and all is accomplished. But this is only the negative side of the blessing wrought in us. The apostle gives the positive side when he says, "The fruit of the Spirit is love, joy, peace, longsuffering, gentleness, good- ness, faith, meekness, temperance." The apostle speaks of the *fruit* of the Spirit—not the *fruits ;* because the Christian graces here named form a cluster. He who has one has all in some degree, though one grace is more con- spicuous in one Christian, and another in another.

Look at this beautiful assemblage of virtues : *love*—love to God, itself the spring of all virtue, leading to personal holiness and the love of our neighbour ; *joy*—the joy of loving God, and all mankind for His sake, joy of commu- nion with God, joy of fellowship with fellow Christians, joy in anticipation of endless life ; *peace*—the peace of reconciliation, peace with God, peace of conscience, peace of holiness, the internal peace leading to the external peace, making the Christian always a peacemaker, never a peace- breaker ; *longsuffering*—that is, cheerful patience amidst the hardships of life and the provocations received from man, the opposite of fretfulness and passionateness ; *gentleness* or *kindness* —that which makes us treat all around us with due consideration and courtesy, the perfect Christian urbanity, the opposite of rudeness and boorishness; *goodness*—which includes the two ideas of benevolence and beneficence, good-willing and good-doing, the readiness to help and to give, to bless according to our ability; *faith* or *trustfulness*—faith towards God, and trust towards man; *meekness*—contentedness with our lot, cheerful acceptance of whatever is the will of God, because it is His will; and then, lastly, *temperance*—the grace which perfects all the rest: not temperance in the narrower sense in which we now understand it, but something which includes that and a great deal more; it means complete self-control —control of the appetites, passions, and desires, control of the temper, control of the tongue, that which makes a man a law to himself, and saves him from all extravagance, vanity, self-assertion, pride. How complete and beautiful the character in which all these virtues are found! Is it yours? are you striving after it? You say that you "enjoy the inward witness," the consciousness that you are a child of God. That I will not call in question: but let the manifestation of these Christian virtues be to others the indisputable evidence that you have received the Holy Spirit, and that He dwells in you.

Once more. The communion of the Spirit creates the true *communion of saints.* Men may subscribe to the same creed, worship in the same church, and exactly observe the same ritual; and yet the true communion of saints may be wanting. But if in any given community the Spirit produces in each the fruit of the Spirit, then between those who are partakers of the same Spirit there is an inner union which will manifest itself outwardly. The Spirit never contradicts, never counterworks Himself; and if He produces in you and me the same tempers, the same principles of action, we cannot but sympathise with each other. Whence arise quarrels in the Church, whence strife, whisperings, backbitings, coldness and apathy towards the common cause? It is the want of the power of the Holy Spirit in the hearts of its members. Let the Spirit be given to each and all, and then

> "Envy and malice shall die,
> And discord afflict us no more."

In conclusion, let us sum up what has been said. This passage teaches us to believe in Father, Son, and Spirit—three Persons, all Divine, all joined in mysterious, blessed unity. It shows us our deep obligations to each. We enjoy the grace, the goodwill of our Saviour Christ; we are His beloved friends; we are bound to walk worthy of our high calling. Being reconciled to God through Christ, we are assured that God loves us; we are bound to love Him in return, and to show our love by keeping His commandments. We partake of the gifts of the Spirit. He becomes our renewer, sanctifier, guide, the pledge to us of endless life. Our duty towards the Holy Spirit is not to quench, not to grieve Him, but to be obedient to His every monition. Our duty is to give to our fellow Christians and the world the proof of the indwelling Spirit by manifesting His blessed fruit.

Brethren, may "the grace of the Lord Jesus Christ, and the love of God, and the communion of the Holy Ghost, be with you all. Amen."

SECTION II.

THE IDEAL CHRISTIAN LIFE.

THE SCRIPTURAL DOCTRINE OF HOLINESS.[1]

I.

THE true ideal of the Christian life is indicated in the words : "If any one be in Christ, he is a new creature (καινὴ κτίσις) : the old things are passed away ; behold, all things are become new "[2] (2 Cor. v. 17). I observe on this passage :

1. "Any one in Christ" is a perfect definition of *all* true Christians. Every one "in Christ" is a true Christian ; none other is so.

2. Anything which is true of *every* true Christian must be true of him on the *first day* of his Christian life ; otherwise there would be found a true Christian of whom it was not true.

3. The "old things" evidently refer to the state of things existing in the pre-Christian life, which is opposed to the ideal of the new life. The comment on the "old things" supplied by the text is, that in the old state of things men

---

[1] An unpublished essay.—EDS.
[2] The best authorities omit "all things," but this makes no difference ; "all things" is implied in τὰ ἀρχαῖα, "THE old things."

live unto themselves, that in the new state of things they do this no longer (μηκέτι ἑαυτοῖς ζῶσιν), but live for Him who died and was raised up for them (v. 15). In the old state of things they "knew men after the flesh," Christ included ; they now know no one after the flesh—in particular, not Christ.

4. The old things having passed away, there is a new creation. If we refer κτίσις to the act of creation rather than to the product of it, then the act *implies* the product —there is a *new thing* created, a new spiritual subsistence. It is created by the Spirit, and is therefore spiritual.[1]

5. This new product is wholly spiritual, and therefore wholly pure. It is abhorrent to reason to suppose that what is the immediate creation of the Holy Spirit, is partly pure and partly impure.

6. This conception of a pure thing, created by the Spirit of God, and found within the totality of a man's nature, does not of itself exclude the notion of something impure co-existing within the same totality at the same time.

7. It is only too evidently proved by the experience of Christians, that the remains of the old life do co-exist with the new life. The Apostle Paul recognises this fact. In writing to the Corinthians, he greets them as persons "who have been sanctified in Christ Jesus" (ἡγιασμένοις ἐν Χριστῷ Ἰησοῦ); but afterwards he says to these same persons, "Are ye not carnal?" (οὐχὶ σαρκικοί ἐστε; Comp. 1 Cor. i. 2 ; iii. 3.)

8. How are we to understand this apparently contradictory teaching? How can men be wholly spiritual, and yet carnal? There seems to me only one way in which we can explain it ; and the solution offered, if accepted as sound,

---

[1] Πνευματικόν opposed to ψυχικόν in 1 Cor. ii. 14, Jas. iii. 15, Jude 19, ψυχικοί, Πνεῦμα μὴ ἔχοντες : also to σαρκικόν in 1 Cor. iii. 1, 3, 4.

will prove to be a key unlocking many a difficult passage. The explanation is found in the difference existing between the *ideal* and the *actual.* This distinction I will next state.

9. When it pleases God to set before us a rule or pattern of life, that rule will of necessity be perfect. The command, "Thou shalt love the Lord thy God with all thy heart, and thy neighbour as thyself," is such a rule.

In the New Testament the power which is to regulate our life is conceived of not so much under the idea of a law governing us from without, as of an informing spirit ruling us from within; and we are taught that the Spirit of God dwelling within us, *if not quenched*, and *if in no wise resisted*, will *totally* suppress the old life of sin, and produce in us a life altogether new.

This is the only meaning which I can attach to the words in Galatians v. 16 : "Walk in the Spirit, and ye shall in no wise fulfil the desire of the flesh" (Πνεύματι περιπατεῖτε, καὶ ἐπιθυμίαν σαρκὸς οὐ μὴ τελέσητε). These words seem to me as clear as daylight, and they say this: "Yield yourselves entirely to the control of the Spirit, and then no fleshly desire shall have fulfilment in you ; that is, ye shall be wholly πνευματικοί and in *no degree* ψυχικοί, σαρκικοί."

But this conception of life is set before *free agents.* The Spirit dwells in those who are capable of resisting His gracious impulses. Exactly in that degree in which the Spirit of God is resisted, we fail to be *wholly spiritual*, and are *in some degree* carnal.

10. Hitherto I have said what I suppose no Christian will dispute. Now we reach divergent views. And the first to be noticed is one which is found in nine out of ten, perhaps, of all books which treat of the Christian life. It is this : There *always is* and *always must be* in every Christian a great gulf fixed between the ideal and the actual. All Christians always are, to some extent, carnal. The old man

in them is crucified, he is nailed to the cross—always dying, never dead ; never will die till you die ! This is the " Calvinism " towards which we have " too much leaned." [1]

Secondly, there is what I suppose to be the view of very many Methodists. I say nothing here of what is in our standards, or in our sermons, but speak only of what is in the minds of our people. " Nearly everybody has something of the old man in him. The preacher who preaches entire sanctification is not entirely sanctified. The carnal nature in him peeps out here and there. So it is ; so it ever will be ; *so it must be.*"

11. I will now state what appears to me to be the true view of the case.

The ideal, pattern, model of the Christian life set before us in the New Testament is that of *entire death to sin, from the first day of Christian life.* When we enter into Christ's service, we are to leave the old life of sin entirely behind, and enter on a life entirely new. " What is the inward and spiritual grace signified by baptism? A *death* unto sin, and a new birth unto righteousness." " This," we say, " I steadfastly believe." Whatever may be admitted in the New Testament as to the actual state of true Christians, nothing other than this entire death to sin and entirely new life to righteousness is ever set before us as that to which we are to aspire and attain. No other kind of life is treated as *allowable.* This life we are to enter on and maintain *from first to last.*

This conception of Christian life is set before us in a great variety of ways. First of all, we find it in the teaching of Christ. In the parables of the treasure hid in the field, and of the precious pearl, we are taught that if we would possess the kingdom of God, we must " sell all." What

---

[1] *Minutes of the Wesleyan Conference,* vol. i., pp. 3, 95.

can this mean less than this, that he who would be Christ's servant must abandon for ever all that Christ disapproves? When He says in Matthew xvi. 24, "If any one wishes to come after Me, let him utterly deny his own self," [1] He demands such a complete giving up of self as is equivalent to a complete giving up of sin. To the same effect are the passages about "forsaking father, mother, all that a man hath, for Christ's sake." When in any man self is dead, then sin is dead.

In Romans vi. we have the same doctrine. Having taught that God "justifies the ungodly" (chap. iv.–v.), St. Paul judges it necessary to guard his doctrine against antinomianism. This he does most effectually. He himself states the thought likely to occur to some minds: ' Shall we continue in sin, in order that grace may abound?' and meets it by saying, 'Let it not be thought of.' [2]

His next position is, that, according to the Christian hypothesis, we died to sin the day we were baptized; and therefore to continue in sin is to contradict the theory of the Christian life, and to oppose in actual conduct what we professed in baptism. 'We who died to sin, how shall we still live in it?' 'Are you not aware,' he says, 'that *all of us* [3] who were baptized into Christ Jesus were baptized into His death? We were therefore buried with Him by baptism into death.' In *v.* 6 he states more specifically *what* in us, or belonging to us, died: "our old man was crucified with Him, in order that the body of sin might become of no effect (or *inoperative*, καταργηθῇ), with a view to our no longer serving sin." The teaching here as to

---

[1] ἀπαρνησάσθω ἑαυτόν; "utterly deny" is the first meaning given to the verb in *Liddell and Scott.*

[2] This is the proper force of μὴ γένοιτο.

[3] The real force of ὅσοι with first person plural.

God's purpose respecting us, is very plain : from the day
on which by baptism we profess ourselves Christ's servants,
we are to consider that the old, sinful life is dead and
buried, so that we are to live it no more.

Precisely the same view is given in Galatians v. In the
latter part of that chapter the apostle brings into vivid
contrast "the flesh" and "the Spirit." He gives us a very
precise definition (in effect) of what he means by the flesh.
He says in *v.* 17 that these two principles are antagonistic and mutually exclusive. In proportion as one prevails the other ceases. So that by "the flesh" he means
"*whatever is antagonistic to the Spirit.*" Having so
defined "*the flesh,*" he tells us, in *v.* 24, that "they that
are Christ's (=all true Christians) did put the flesh to
death by crucifixion" (ἐσταύρωσαν). The aorist refers to
a past definite act. The time is not named, but, I presume,
as in Romans vi., he is thinking of baptism, as the day
on which the Galatians became Christians *before the world*,
and therefore began to be held by the world responsible
for a certain line of conduct.

12. It will be said, " Suppose we grant all that you ask,
and admit that this is the true and only ideal tolerated in
Scripture, is it actually realized in one true Christian out of
ten thousand ? " Perhaps not.—" Then what advantage is
there in having such an ideal ? " Much every way.

(1) A perfect ideal is better than an imperfect one.
Suppose two men in a workshop, each set to construct a
steam-engine. One has before him a perfect model, the
other an imperfect one. He who has the perfect model
may make a perfect engine ; the man who has an imperfect
model *cannot*. True, the man working after the perfect
model *may* fail ; the other *must*.

A Christian has before him as his model of virtue the
Lord Jesus Christ ; a Mohammedan imitates Mohammed,

and never aspires to be any better than his pattern. The advantage to the Christian is immeasurable.

(2) In the moral sphere, mistaken theories of life always produce bad facts. True theories do not always produce good facts ; but they *tend that way*. Allow, for the sake of argument, that by the grace of God it is possible for a man to gain complete victory over his besetting sin. Then take the case of two men, one of whom believes victory to be possible, whilst the other believes it to be impossible. The first *may* get the victory, but not the second ; because the victory can be won only by prayer, and no man will pray for what he *believes* to be impossible, though the thing itself may be possible all the time.

13. The way to judge a theory of life is to suppose it carried out universally, and then to ask, *What good will come* of it, and *what harm?* Deal so with this theory. It is admitted that it is not likely that it will be fully carried out in many cases ; but if it *were* carried out in all, would any harm ensue ?

Suppose all modern Christian preachers were to teach as I believe St. Paul teaches ; how would this work ? As soon as men became truly converted, and were assured of peace with God, we should address them somewhat to this effect : " By the mercy of God you have obtained pardon. By the same mercy you have access to that grace of God wherein you stand. Your perseverance in the way of life is not at all a matter of course or of necessity. At any future moment of life it is *possible* for you to forsake the right path, to forsake Christ and His people, 'to measure back your steps to earth again.' There is *always* the *possibility* of this, *never* the *necessity*. You will meet with temptations and trials, in one shape or other, all the days of your life ; you *can* yield to any one of these, you *need* yield to none. You have, and will have fierce, spiritual, unseen adversaries; but the Captain of your salvation is mightier than all.   He is able, not only to keep you from falling, but to preserve you even from stumbling.   He gives to you for every day and every hour of life the word which He gave to Paul: 'My grace is sufficient for thee.' If you trust that grace, which is indeed all-sufficient, *as* all-sufficient, it will never fail you.   You feel free from condemnation *now;* you need never come into condemnation again as long as you live.   You are in Christ: abide in Him, trust in His almighty love; and He will make you more than conquerors in all things." Could any possible harm come of counsel like this?

14. Whilst no harm could come of it, much good would, I think, result.

(1) Every one who looked upon constant victory over all sin as *the normal state of Christians* would be greatly cheered by hope, and would be much more likely to succeed in his Christian course than one who looked upon a course of sinning and repenting *as the normal condition of things.*

(2) Suppose him to enjoy such constant victory, he would be in no danger of spiritual pride.   Instead of looking upon himself as somebody special and extraordinary, he would say: "This is just what all Christians may be, and ought to be.   My being as I am is not the thing that calls for wonder or explanation, but why anybody should be different."

(3) Suppose him to fail in his high endeavour, as most likely he would, and fail many times.   Still he would be cheered by hope, not disheartened by despair.   Instead of saying to himself, "It is God's will that I should be overcome sometimes, in order to keep me humble," he would say: "The will of God is that I should conquer always. The grace of God has not failed me; I have failed it."

(4) There would then ensue this great advantage.   Such

a man would *never be content with anything short of complete victory.* He would not say, " You see, it is my way." He would not say, with a light heart and cheerful tone, " You see, I do not *profess* entire sanctification "; because he would feel himself greatly to blame if he were content to stop short of it.

Thus we should get rid of the distinction between the " higher Christian life " and the lower Christian life, as being both *allowable* in the Church. " High Christian life for all, low Christian life for none," would be our rule.

The idea that there is one rule of life for one Christian, and another for another, is to be utterly abhorred and driven out of the Church.

15. It is asked, Can any one be entirely sanctified on the day of his conversion ? John Wesley mentions a case of a woman *awakened, converted, entirely sanctified* on the same day. I would not answer this question by an affirmative or negative, unless I had opportunity to explain my meaning.

(1) It is conceivable that a person on the day of his conversion may make so full a renunciation of self, of sin, and of the world, that he may be said to be "sanctified wholly" *in this sense,* that he *purposes* to devote himself to the service of Christ without reserve, for the rest of his life.

(2) But he could not be sanctified wholly in the same sense in which another man may be after some years of Christian life. He may be compared to a newly born child who is entirely free from disease, but is very weak and ignorant.

(3) The Scriptures, which so strongly insist on the need of a *new birth,* also tell us of the necessity of *growth.* This growth will manifest itself in the formation of religious habits, which can be formed only by repetition of individual acts. It will manifest itself in continually increasing

knowledge of God, of His kingdom, His relations to mankind, and of the extent of man's duty.

(4) A man may, on the day of conversion, adopt as the rule of life, that he will consecrate the whole of his life to God. But there is a great difference between *adopting* such a rule, and *applying* it in every detail. When men are perfectly sincere and earnest in religion, it takes them a long time to find out how every part of life is to be brought under the sanctifying rule. There are some sincere Christians who seem never to apply it to some parts of their conduct. With some the last thing brought under rule is the tongue; with others, it is the purse. A man with a thousand a year, *e.g.*, believes himself entirely sanctified, and gives a guinea a year to aid in sending the gospel to the heathen! This is ignorance. *If he is sincere*, and the mistake is pointed out to him, he will at once amend it.

16. How far is the common Methodist view, that on a given day and moment a man may "receive the blessing of entire sanctification," justified?

I see nothing unreasonable or unscriptural in this notion, *if it be properly guarded.* The matter presents itself to my mind thus: Up to a given day the man has lived in the sincere belief that he never can get the victory over his besetting sin. He believes, perhaps, that he can be saved from every sin except this; but from this, *never.* But by studying the Scriptures, by hearing a sermon, or by conversation with a friend, he becomes satisfied that for him a complete victory is possible. As soon as he believes it possible, he resolves it shall be actual; and on that day does what he never did before—he trusts the all-sufficient grace as *sufficient for him*, and he gets the victory that day, and will continue to enjoy it thenceforward, if he abides in the same faith. There is no absurdity in supposing that such a man from a given day and hour enters on a new phase of

Christian life, contrasting very strongly with what has gone before.

Take another case. A man trained in Methodism, and versed in its doctrine, has long believed that constant victory to him has been possible. But he has never said to himself, "The possible shall be actual." There has not been a want of intellectual conviction, but a lack of moral earnestness and decision. But on a given day, in a well-remembered hour, he says, "I will humbly claim *all* the great salvation provided in Christ, when it is promised, 'He shall save His people from their sins.' There is no limit in the promise; there shall be none in my faith. I trust the sufficient grace of the Almighty Saviour; I will never doubt it more." It is done to him according to his faith. But such a man may have much to learn. He may be careless about the expenditure of his time; he may spend more time in a day in reading the newspaper than in studying the Scriptures; he may use a freedom in speaking about others inconsistent with perfect charity : but when his faults are pointed out, he amends.

The sum of the matter is this : A Christian *ought* to be, and *therefore may be*, from the day that he is found "in Christ," a new creature. He may from the first be dead to sin; but he will of necessity be ignorant of many things which it is important for him to know, and ought therefore to make constant advancement in knowledge, faith, love, and all Christian virtues, abounding more and more in all those fruits of righteousness which are by Jesus Christ to the glory and praise of God.

This is the Christian ideal.

Christians in general do not realize the ideal—

1. Owing to unscriptural teaching.

2. Owing to want of concurrence between their own will and that of God.

H.   20

3. Owing to want of faith in God's promises.

He who has long neglected to bring the actual into agreement with the ideal may do this on any day, at any hour, when he clearly sees his privilege, and resolves believingly to claim it. But such a man will never be perfect *in this sense:* he will never have advanced so far that he cannot go farther. God is always "able to do for us exceeding abundantly above all that we ask or think."

Nov. 23rd, 1883.

THE PREACHING OF HOLINESS.[1]

I TAKE for my text on this occasion two sayings of John Wesley. The first is this, that the great purpose for which God raised up the people called Methodists was to spread scriptural holiness through the land ; and the second, that the preaching of scriptural holiness tended more directly than anything else to revive and enlarge the Methodist societies (see Wesley's *Works,* vol. xiii., pp. 8, 9, 78). Starting from this text, I propose (1) to indicate very briefly the nature of scriptural holiness ; (2) to give reasons why we should preach it.

I. *Scriptural holiness.*

We do well to emphasise this word *scriptural,* because there are many views of holiness prevalent which are *not* scriptural. These I shall not attempt to notice and refute ; it is more important to state the truth which, when received,

---

[1] This address was delivered to a gathering of lay preachers in Leeds, in June, 1886 ; and although it partly covers the ground of the preceding essay, it is inserted here, because it is almost the only account of his views on the subject that Mr. Hellier ever published, and is also less technical in form.—EDS.

excludes them. A good maxim for preachers is : Fill the bushel˙with wheat, and there is no room for chaff. The right starting-point is the fact that every true Christian is a sanctified person—a saint. This is clearly the teaching of the Apostle Paul. If you take up the Epistle to the Ephesians, for instance, and ask, To whom was this letter sent? the answer given in the first verse is, "To the saints who were at Ephesus" (Eph. i. 1 ; comp. Phil. i. 1). "The saints" here mean the Christians; all the Christians in Ephesus were saints—holy persons. The conception of a person who was a true Christian, and *not* a real saint, was one which never entered the apostle's mind. If you need further evidence, you find it in 1 Corinthians vi. 11. There the apostle teaches most plainly that every justified person is also sanctified. "But ye are washed, but ye are sanctified, but ye are justified."

But what do we mean by a saint, a holy, sanctified person? We always mean two things—one negative, the other positive. The negative side of holiness means, purification from sin ; the positive side, dedication to the service of God. Observe, I do not say that every true Christian is wholly delivered from all sin, or entirely consecrated to God. But every Christian is purified from many forms of sin,— murder, adultery, theft, profane swearing, lying, drunkenness, and such like ; and every Christian is in profession, in purpose, and in some degree of fact, devoted to God's service. This is the doctrine of all Christians whose opinion is worth considering.

What then is there special in the Methodist testimony? It is expressed by the one word *completeness.* Our contention is, that we may not only be saved from sin, but saved *fully;* and we found our belief on the very name of Jesus, and the interpretation given to it in the first chapter of St. Matthew's Gospel : "Thou shalt call His name Jesus:

for He shall save His people from their sins " (Matt. i. 21).
Here the promise is without limit; and we do not feel
warranted in introducing a limit where the Scripture places
none. But when we say that we may be completely purified
from *sin*, we use this term in its popular, most common
signification. A man may frame a definition of sin so wide,
that complete deliverance from it in this life is impossible.
He may say, " By sin I mean any and every transgression
of the pure and perfect law of God, known and unknown,
voluntary and involuntary ; and do you think you can be
saved from all sin *in that sense?*"   I answer, " Certainly
not ; it is wholly impossible."

But when I state a proposition, I must be allowed, in
all fairness, to give my own meaning of the terms I use.
When, therefore, I speak of complete purification from sin,
I mean by sin *a voluntary transgression of a known law,—*
whether by deed, or word, or thought.   I mean that, by the
all-sufficient grace of God continually imparted, we may be
kept from all the things which bring on men the condemnation of God and their own consciences.   In other words,
we may "have always a conscience void of offence, toward
God and toward men."

But I do not mean that we can be saved from all mistakes
and errors of judgment ; and certainly I do not mean that
we can ever be saved from temptation and the possibility
of sinning.   As to temptation, I hold that the holiest man
living may be very powerfully tempted to commit great
sins ; and the fact that he is powerfully tempted is no proof
of his want of entire sanctification.   We see this in the
temptation of Christ Himself.   He was tempted to distrust
His Father's providential care, then to presume upon it
unduly, then to worship the devil himself.   How can we be
tempted worse than that?   We may have passing through
our minds a thousand *thoughts about sin*, and yet have not

one *sinful thought.* The difference between thoughts about sins which are not sinful, and thoughts which are sinful, may be illustrated in this way : A number of rude, troublesome people come and knock at the door of your house, and clamour for admission. As long as the door is locked and barred against them, as long as you are able to say, "I have given these people no invitation to come, and no encouragement to stay," then, though they give you much trouble, you are not in the least to blame. But if you are overcome by their importunity, unloose the door, invite them in, and spread entertainment before them, then you must blame yourself for all the annoyance they cause you. Temptations that are not sin knock at the door of the heart, but are not welcomed ; temptations become sin when they are welcomed, admitted, cherished.

I may put the matter more precisely thus : A multitude of experiences arise in our minds prior to any determination of the will respecting them, and before any act of the will takes place they have no moral character. A determination of the will gives them a moral character—good or not. For example : Two men are quietly standing in the street witnessing a procession. A man comes along, and out of mere wanton wickedness strikes each of them in the face. Both men have inevitably the same experience. Both feel bodily pain ; both feel indignation of mind before any act of the will can take place. But very soon there is in each an act of the will. One resolves to return the blow, and does so ; the other resolves to refrain, and does not return it. I cite this example to show how swiftly and unexpectedly temptation may come, and how swiftly the decision of the will decides whether the temptation passes into sin or not.

Another thing follows from the temptation of Christ : the presence of temptation not only does not involve the necessity of sinning, but it does not even prove that our nature is sinful.   Here again some good people condemn themselves, when God does not condemn them.   They say, " I must have an evil heart, or such temptations would not come to me."   You have no right to say that.   See what temptations came to the Son of God, to Him who was perfectly holy.   And therefore it is certain that the very worst temptation may come to the very best of men, and the holiest man living may be tempted to commit the worst of all crimes.

> " Evil into the mind of God or man
> May come and go, so unapproved, and leave
> No spot or blame behind." [1]

These statements, however, need to be guarded.   Without retracting anything that I have said, I may add cautions against the abuse of this doctrine.

1. We must never forget that there *are* such things as sinful thoughts, and we may sin most grievously against God, although the sin of the heart may find no outward expression in word or deed.   A man may be a murderer or adulterer in the sight of God, simply by cherishing unholy passions and desires.   Remember also the words of the psalmist : " If I regard iniquity in my heart, the Lord will not hear me."   Let us all pray, " Create in me a clean heart, O God ; and renew a right spirit within me."

2. Another caution is necessary : whilst temptation in itself may involve no blame, we may be very much to blame for the force which the temptation has at the time when it comes to us.   The habitual drunkard may be practically unable to resist a temptation to drink.   Is he to be acquitted of blame ?   No ; it is his own sinful conduct in days and years past, which has caused the temptation to

---

[1] *Paradise Lost*, bk. v., line 117.

have such power over him. So in our courts of law, when a plea is set up in favour of an accused person, that he did an evil act in a fit of drunkenness, our judges rightly hold that this is no extenuation of the crime. But just as weakness in the hour of temptation is largely due to past sins, so strength to resist is largely due to past fidelity to God. Every instance of yielding to temptation weakens moral power; but every instance of resisting it strengthens moral power. In this life good habits may be so perfected in us, that in regard to many things it may be next to impossible for us to sin; and bad habits may become so strong, that it may be next to impossible for us to do right.

Turn to the *positive* side of sanctification. Entire sanctification means the sanctification of everything. The sanctification, for example, of the daily work; that is, doing it to the Lord, and therefore doing it as well as we can. If a ploughman be entirely sanctified, he will plough a straight furrow,—or at least try his best to do so. If he be a mason, he will put no bad work into his walls; if a doctor, he will care more about curing his patients than about getting large fees; if he be a minister of religion, he will strive to serve the people of his charge to the utmost of his ability. I do not believe in the entire sanctification of any man who does his daily work in a slovenly way, who keeps his books so badly that he contracts debts without knowing whether he will ever be able to pay them, and spends other people's money rather than his own. Entire sanctification means that a man will be perfectly upright in all his business transactions, even in buying and selling horses, and in paying income tax. Entire sanctification means dedicating all our property to God. When Christians ask themselves, How much of my money shall I devote to religious purposes? they do not consider rightly. There ought to be no question of *how much;* all must be devoted to God. The only question is, How much shall I give away? and how much shall I retain in my own power? But that which we keep must be used religiously, quite as much as what we give away. In regard to all we have we are only stewards; "to the last penny" it is the Lord's property,—we have it in trust, and must give an account. If we satisfy the great Proprietor, everything is right; but nothing is right unless we do. Entire sanctification means simply this: spending all our time in the Lord's service; making our religion our life, our life our religion.

Let it, however, be carefully observed, that, whilst we earnestly contend for the completeness of Christian sanctification, there is a very important sense in which we contend for its *incompleteness.* As John Wesley says: "There is no perfection of degrees." No one has so much religion but he may have more. Whatever the degree of our knowledge, faith, love, zeal to-day, we may have more of these to-morrow. The Apostle Paul knew well that he could not obtain the prize for which he ran, until he reached the goal. He could not feel that he was "perfected,"—that he had obtained all that was to be gained by running, whilst the race lasted (Phil. iii. 12). Indefinite advancement in holiness is at once the duty and joy of the Christian. To say that Christian holiness may be at once complete and incomplete involves no absurdity. The perfect sapling grows into a perfect tree; the perfect child into a perfect man. During every moment of our lives God is "able to do exceeding abundantly above all that we ask or think, according to the power that worketh in us" (Eph. iii. 20).

Can we be entirely sanctified on a given day, in an hour, in a single moment? To this question I answer both Yes and No. We may, on a given day and hour, give ourselves wholly to God as we never did before; we may trust the all-sufficient grace with a perfect confidence, and thus enter on a higher Christian life than we ever lived previously. But the work of sanctification is not the work of an hour, or of a day. It extends over the whole regenerate life. Though on a given day we may enter into a state of entire sanctification, we cannot continue therein *as a matter of course.* Hence the importance of the weighty words in the *Large Minutes.* "Does not talking, without proper caution, of a justified or sanctified state, tend to mislead men, almost naturally leading them to trust in what was done in one moment? Whereas we are every moment pleasing or displeasing to God, according to our works: according to the whole of our present inward tempers and outward behaviour" (Wesley's *Works,* vol. viii., p. 325).

II. *Reasons for preaching this doctrine.*

Why do we not all of us constantly, earnestly enforce it? Perhaps it is because we have met with some unlovely examples of people who have professed entire sanctification, but have not lived it. It is a great pity that there should be such; but they are not the only examples. There are those who both profess and live it. Have you not known at least one or two? And do you not know this, that if there is in any town one man who thoroughly and consistently acts out his religion in things great and small, that one man is a great power for good in that place. If there are unworthy professors of Christian holiness, that should be to us a powerful argument to seek to multiply the consistent examples.

Another reason why some do not earnestly preach this doctrine is this: they have not taken a sufficiently practical view of it. Entire sanctification has seemed to them to mean a high state of religious fervour constantly maintained; to be a matter of feeling, rapture, ecstasy, attainable only by a select few. The truth is, there is no difference between holiness and practical religion; and I think it is to be regretted that we call some of our religious meetings " holiness meetings," and not others.   Every meeting to promote religion is a meeting to promote holiness.   Every Sunday morning and evening service, every prayer-meeting, every Class-meeting, every lovefeast, every Quarterly Meeting. They are all holiness meetings.   Why not ?

All religion consists in loving God with all our heart, and our neighbour as ourselves.   But love is not a mere emotion ; it is a principle.   Suppose a man loves his wife and children with a perfect love, what follows ?   This follows : There is nothing in his conduct towards them *contrary* to love.   He never speaks to them an unkind word, because he never has towards them an unkind thought. His love is perfect, and that is the evidence of it.   The man who loves wife and children with a perfect love is not unjust to them, even in his most secret thoughts.   His love to his family as an *emotion* passes through all degrees of intensity, and very often they are not present to his thoughts ; but this love to them as a *principle* rules him always.   We are to love our neighbours *as ourselves.*   Self-love is the pattern.   As an emotion, love of self is very weak.   I do not think I have ever said to myself, " Oh, how I love myself ! " I do not know that I am conscious of love to myself as an emotion ; but self-love as a principle is very strong indeed, and very constant.   I suppose we all know that.   If love to God *as a principle* rules all our actions, that is entire sanctification, whether our emotion be much or little.

There seems to me one imperative reason why we should earnestly preach holiness.   It is the necessary complement to our doctrine of free salvation and instantaneous pardon. We teach that the hoary-headed sinner of sixty or seventy may in one short hour repent, believe, and be saved, and come away a saved man.   We preach this.   You do ; I do. I have no intention of doing otherwise. But it seems to me really dangerous to preach in this way, unless we preach something more. We must constantly tell people, that when they obtain pardon, this is not the end of a religious life, but the beginning ; this is the starting-point, not the goal. Many people before they are converted are very ignorant of moral obligations, and have a very low standard of right and wrong. If we urge them from the first to go on to perfection, and succeed in rousing their enthusiasm for a completely holy life, they are safe, and they bring honour to the Church ; if not, they often bring dishonour upon it. We must remind them, and remind ourselves, that after Romans v. comes Romans vi., and after Romans vii. comes Romans viii. I do not stop to explain ; read the four chapters, and you will see what I mean.

When men are earnest in the pursuit of holiness, they value all the means of grace. If we are intent on any end, we value the means which leads to the end. The man anxious to make money and skilled in doing so, is glad when the market-day comes ; and if our hearts are set on making life all religious, we shall value every means which helps us to do this. The pursuit of holiness leads to the growth of the Church. The one thing needful in the Church of Christ is the complete consecration of all we have and are to God's service. The Church never counted such large numbers, never had so many places of worship and schools and material appliances, never had so much wealth, and culture, and social influence. If all this were fully consecrated to God, what wonders we should behold ! Listen not to those who say that we are not to expect large increases, that the circumstances of the times do not admit of it. Think of our Sunday scholars. In the Sunday schools of the Wesleyan Methodists alone there are over

850,000 scholars ; and only about 100,000 of them Church members.[1] What scope for increase there ! Think of the unconverted people already within our congregations ! Think of the millions of people in England who belong to no congregation. What we want is *consecration,*—consecration of self, of one and all.

If we, and the ministers of Christ's Church generally, resolve henceforth that we will both preach entire consecration and live it, then I have no doubt we shall soon see such a revival of religion as England has never seen yet. What could we wish for better? What greater blessing could come to our nation? If the great mass of our people ever become alienated, the outlook is fearful ; but if we can win all England to God, what joy there will be ! If a great revival of religion could be bought with money, what large sums you would be willing to give ! We well know that no money can buy it ; but it can be obtained by prayer, by God's blessing on Christian lives and Christian work. Is it not worth seeking? Is it not worth working for, living for? Who then is willing this day, this hour, to consecrate himself wholly to God ?

May the Spirit of holiness be now poured out upon us all !

THE JEWISH IDEAL.

CHRISTIAN ideas rest upon a Jewish foundation ; for as the Christian system is the full unfolding of God's great plan of saving men, so the Jewish dispensation prefigured this, and raised the expectation of it before " the fulness of time " came. According to the fine saying of

---

[1] The returns in 1889 are : Scholars, 928,506 ; members, 131,682 ; on trial, 7,867.—EDS.

Augustine : "In the Old Testament the New lies concealed ; and in the New Testament the Old is revealed."

In the Jewish view then, holiness on the part of the creature is devotion or dedication to the service of God. This is the general notion. The whole Jewish people, for instance, are spoken of as "a holy people" when contrasted with other nations, because whilst other people served idols, Israel served the one living and true God (Exod. xix. 6). Again, the priests were called "holy" in contrast with the rest of the nation, because, whilst others were engaged in the ordinary employments of life, they were occupied with what related to religious service (Lev. xxi. 8). So the "tabernacle of witness" and Solomon's temple were "holy places," because not used for any common purpose, but only for the worship of God ; the vessels which it contained were "holy" vessels, and the garments of the ministering priests were "holy" garments.

Here is the foundation of the Christian idea of holiness. But it is only a foundation, on which is built a superstructure much more impressive and glorious. As with respect to other Jewish ideas, so in this instance, the Jewish notion is under the Christian system spiritualized and expanded. The spiritually-minded Israelite doubtless often rose above the letter and outward form of the law, to the inward and spiritual truth signified and symbolised ; but, contrasting Jewish holiness generally with Christian holiness, we may say that the Jewish was official, the Christian is personal ; the Jewish, external—the Christian, internal ; the Jewish, local—the Christian, universal. The Christian minister has no official holiness apart from personal holiness, and if the Christian minister choose to array himself in peculiar vestments, these imply no holiness, and they certainly impart none. He is holy so far as he is made partaker of the grace of the Spirit, and no further. And again, the plough-

man and the collier may, under the Christian system, be as
entirely sanctified as the holiest minister, and their labour
may be as holy as his.

To the Christian there is no holy place, save that where
God manifests His presence ; and the place where he walks
and talks with God is a holy place, be it a palace or a dungeon, be it St. Peter's at Rome or a desolate wilderness.

The Christian holiness differs from the Jewish in its
completeness.   It embraces all our powers, and extends
through all our time.

IS IT POSSIBLE ?

IS it possible to be "entirely sanctified"? We answer
that it is. The apostle prays for this, and he would not
have prayed for anything which he thought impossible.
Do you think the apostle was a madman ?   You say, Surely
not.   But suppose in writing to the Thessalonians he had
said, "I pray God every one of you may live upon the
earth a thousand years." They would surely have said,
"Paul, thou art beside thyself to pray for such a thing."
Why would it have been a proof of madness?   Because the
thing prayed for was impossible.   But if entire sanctification
was impossible, then Paul was mad to pray for it.

Some say this : " I can conceive it possible to be entirely
sanctified for a short time, in favourable circumstances ; but
I doubt the possibility, at least in my own case, of maintaining the condition of complete holiness.   I fear lapses,
break-downs, interruptions."   The apostle anticipates this
objection when he prays for the Thessalonians that they
may be "*preserved* blameless unto the coming of our Lord
Jesus Christ " ; and then adds, " Faithful is He that calleth
you, who also will do it."

In religion we cannot travel faster than our convictions of truth. To any one who believes entire sanctification to be impossible, to him it is impossible. It can be obtained only by prayer, and no one prays for an impossibility.

THE REAL HINDRANCE.

MEN are not holy, because they do not wish to be; men are not entirely sanctified, because they do not desire this. God is willing, if we are willing; but He saves us only up to the measure of our own consent, not beyond. Take the covetous man, the Christian man who is in some degree covetous : suppose him to pray, " Lord, save me from my besetting sin, this love of money "; and suppose that all the time he is resolved to do as he has ever done, to go on hoarding, and to refuse to give in any worthy way : what is the use of such a prayer?

Another man, whilst praying for entire sanctification, is intending all the while to reserve for himself a little license in the use of his tongue. He means to leave himself at liberty now and then to say a few smart things; that is sometimes to break the law of love. Will he succeed in his prayers? If he can succeed in keeping the fact of his desire to be a little uncharitable out of God's knowledge, or cause Him to forget it just while he is praying, then he may succeed; but not otherwise.

Some men plead for one fault as Lot pleaded for Zoar, and say, " Is it not a little one? " Yes, comparatively it is ; but though little, it is quite enough to spoil the perfectness of your peace, and the complete symmetry of your character. A grain of sand is a very little thing, but if it get into the eye, what trouble it causes !

Think of the highest motive of all. Christ says respecting His servants, " And I am glorified in them." This is true of all His servants. All true Christians glorify Christ to some extent ; but some much more than others. Make it your ambition to bring much honour to the Master's name. Let that be your supreme care, and you need have no care besides.

SECTION III.

PREACHERS AND PREACHING.

A STUDENT'S PREPARATION FOR THE CHRISTIAN MINISTRY.[1]

DEAR brethren, the important practical question which you have to ask yourselves, which doubtless in effect you have already asked, is this, How am I to make the best use of the opportunities now put within my reach?

To answer this question rightly you must consider your calling. You are, as you believe, called to be preachers of the gospel, heralds of the glad tidings of salvation. *Preacher* is the highest designation you will ever bear; *preaching*, the noblest function you will ever fulfil. The question above proposed may therefore be put in this form, How can I use the advantages I now possess so as best to prepare for a successful ministry of the word of life?

You have, I repeat, above everything else to be preachers, and I entreat you never for a moment to give way to the mistaken ambition of being distinguished for something else, so as to put that first, and preaching second. Sometimes a man has held our high calling and profession,

---

[1] An inaugural address delivered to the students of Headingley College, Sept. 8th, 1880.

and people have said of him: He can write capital Latin
verse, but he knows nothing about preaching; or, He is
a perfect master in finance, but in the pulpit he has no
power. Now this is like commending a lawyer by saying,
He knows next to nothing about law, but at a game of
billiards he is first-rate. It is as if you should say of a
physician, He shows no skill in curing his patients, but he
can play excellently well on the violin.

I intend in what I am about to say to exalt the office of
the preacher; but before I do so I wish to give you two
cautions. *First,* whilst giving your best attention to your
highest work, never imagine for one moment that you can
afford to neglect or slight any part of the ministerial office.
When you are engaged in Circuit work, you will have to
visit the people, especially the sick and the careless; to
meet Classes; to fill up schedules; to draw up minutes;
to write reports; to look after local preachers, leaders, and
stewards, and to see that they attend to their work; to
interest yourselves in the Sunday-schools and day-schools;
to look after the interests of home and foreign missions; to
attend to chapel affairs, and secure, as far as it depends
on you to secure it, that all the chapels in your Circuit are
kept clean, well lighted, well ventilated, and adequately
insured. To attend to all these things and do them, or
see that they are done, in the best possible way, will be your
duty and a great part of your religion. One can easily
understand how a man through lack of capacity, or through
sheer ignorance, may fall *below* the performance of these
duties; but how by any degree of genius or of sanctity he
can ever be exalted *above* them is, to me at least, a thing
unthinkable.

The *second* caution is this. Never neglect any part of
the studies of this College on the plea that you do not see
how it will help you to preach the gospel. In these things

it is your duty to submit your judgment to ours. We are all perfectly one with you in thinking that preaching is your great work, but we claim to know better than you what is the most needful preparation for it. And in doing so we rely not merely on our own judgment, but also on the accumulated wisdom and experience of the godly men of many generations.

Many studies, which do not immediately help you in preaching by furnishing you with matter for pulpit discourse, are still of inestimable value, because they impart to the mind itself those qualities of clearness and strength which will be useful in every sermon you preach and in every part of your work. So Lord Bacon says: " If a man's wit be wandering, let him study the mathematics; for in demonstrations, if his wit be called away never so little, he must begin again." [1] Whenever any student here is negligent in attending to lectures and class-work, we shall set this down as owing to want of sense or want of religion. Nevertheless always bear in mind that the flower and the fruit, the glory and the crown of all your studies is the sermon.

And I wish you, first of all, to look at what is *possible* to the Christian preacher under the blessing of God. Judge of what may be your own future by recalling the history of the past. Think of the preaching of the Apostle Paul. What were its results ? You must attribute to it very largely, though not solely, the overthrow of the paganism of the Roman empire, the transformation, the purification of society in Europe. Paul is at this day a living power, moving to beneficent action the minds of millions of men. You will say, But Paul was an inspired preacher. True ; yet remember two things : that Paul was a man of like passions with ourselves, often bowed down with bodily infir-

---

[1] Essay L.: *Of Studies.*

mities; and that it is your own fault if you ever preach a sermon unaccompanied by the power of the Holy Ghost.

Think of the preaching of Ambrose at Milan, in the fourth century. To the men of his own generation Ambrose was a great power; but by the conversion of Augustine he has indirectly extended his influence through the whole Christian Church for the space of nearly fifteen centuries. Think of the effects wrought by the preaching of Luther, Calvin, Knox, Latimer, Baxter, Howe, Wesley, Whitfield, and many more whose names will readily occur to you. Think of the possible results of a single religious service. In the year 1630 John Livingston preached at the kirk of Shotts in Scotland, under such a mighty power of the Holy Spirit, that five hundred people were converted to God as the result of that one service. Whitfield, speaking of a three hours' service held amidst the tumults of Moorfields, says : "Three hundred and fifty awakened souls were received in one day; and I believe the number of notes received from persons brought under concern exceeded a thousand."

Who can estimate the value of sermons of power like these? You try to picture to yourself the consequences of *one* conversion. You think of "the mystic joys of penitence," the rapture of the newly found peace, the changed and purified life, the home made happy, the benefits descending to children and children's children through many generations, the saints gathered home to God, their perfect and endless joys in the heavenly kingdom. Then you multiply the single instance by hundreds more, until even the powers of imagination fail, and you can only say, The blessing is unspeakable !

History enables us in some instances to see how widespread are the consequences of one true conversion. In the last century John Wesley was one day preaching out of doors, and amongst his hearers was John Howard. The sermon was the means of bringing Howard to religious decision, and of determining the character of his future life. At this day the fruits of that conversion are found in all the prisons of Europe. A poor slave goes for the first time in his life to hear a sermon. The preacher is a baker, but under that first sermon the slave is converted. His subsequent life shows how genuine was the work then wrought. He is chosen by Mrs. Stowe as the hero of *Uncle Tom's Cabin*, a book which contributed in no small degree to bring to an end the accursed system of American slavery. In 1796 Charles Simeon, of Cambridge, was making a holiday tour in Scotland. The visit which by a seeming accident he paid to a Scotch minister ultimately bore fruit in the conversion to God of Alexander Duff, a man whose work has already brought benefits direct and indirect to untold multitudes of men. So when the seed of everlasting truth falls from your hands into the good ground of honest and believing souls, you begin a work of blessing that never ends.

It will be a great encouragement to you to remember that your opportunities for doing good are far greater than those of most men who have preceded you in this Methodist ministry. When John Wesley was preaching a hundred years ago, the population of England was less than a third of what it is now. You move amongst large masses of people, and these by means of the railroad are much more accessible than the smaller numbers of former years, whilst there is in many instances a far greater preparedness of mind for the reception of the truth than could be reckoned on by our fathers. The people addressed by the first Methodist preachers were for the most part poor and very illiterate. Now, very few of your hearers will be altogether without education; many of them will be highly cultured;

whilst not a few will possess considerable wealth and social influence. Their souls are not on that account more precious in the sight of God ; but if you succeed in moving these, you will move many others with them.

You will have an advantage over many ministers through your connection with an *itinerant* system. If this next year you were to be settled as curate or as rector in some country parish, your congregation might possibly for the next forty years never exceed 200 persons, and would vary very little from year to year. Now you may hope, even during your three years' residence here, to preach the truth to many thousands of persons, and to gather precious fruit of saved souls, who will be your crown of rejoicing " in that day." Several of our students of former years have been greatly blessed in their preaching, and have witnessed whilst still at College scores, if not hundreds of instances of conversion. Their success is your encouragement.

I hope you will all aim at an awakening and soul-saving ministry. I will not, however, dwell on this point, because I believe your own hearts are rightly disposed towards the work, and because all that I would wish to say is admirably set forth by Mr. Spurgeon in a recent sermon on " He that winneth souls is wise," which I earnestly advise every one of you to read.[1]

But whilst anxious to be awakening preachers, never undervalue those services which, though they may not be attended by converting power, are of unspeakable value to the Church of God. The history of the last Methodistic year proves that, however much we need a converting ministry, we need a conserving and edifying one much more. We report more than 43,000 new members added during the year, and yet have a decrease ! What does this

---

[1] *Metropolitan Tabernacle Pulpit*, No. 1292 (Passmore & Alabaster).

mean? It shows that the under-shepherds of the flock have not been as anxious to keep men in the fold of Christ as they were to gather them in.

Think of what is possible in a single service on a Sunday morning. There come together hard-toiling men and women, wearied in body and mind by the labours and cares of the week. There are present invalids, who have not been at chapel for some time, but to-day have ventured forth, chastened and thankful, looking for a message from God. There are the wealthy and prosperous, the gay, the thoughtless. There are those present who are the strength of the Church, the earnest Christian workers who have prayed for the preacher in the early prayer-meeting, and are now hungry for the bread of life. At the appointed time there enters the pulpit a preacher who, like the Apostle Paul, is sure that he comes to the people " in the fulness of the blessing of the gospel of Christ." The way in which he gives out the hymns, and prays, and reads the Scriptures, tells of a man in close sympathy with Christ, and therefore full of deep and broad sympathies with the people, young and old, rich and poor alike. The preacher has "sought out acceptable words," and these are accompanied to the hearts of his hearers with that most subtle, refined, and mighty of all influences, the power of the Holy Ghost. The theme is Christ calling the weary and heavy-laden to Himself that they may find rest. The attention of all is arrested ; the poor man forgets his poverty, the rich man his wealth, the invalid his feeble health ; the frivolous become serious ; whilst all feel that there is a mighty power moving their hearts towards the compassionate Saviour. Best of all, the earnest workers are instructed, strengthened, cheered. They feel that they can do their own work on that day and during the week ten times better for the service in which they have taken part ; and perhaps

some forty or fifty years afterwards a veteran in the Church
will say, when referring to such an occasion, "It was on
that day and through hearing that sermon that I began to
lead a holier and more useful life."

I need not try to paint the sad contrast seen, when a
similar congregation gathers, and a like opportunity is
given, but a preacher comes without preparation of heart
and mind, and with a dull, perfunctory service fills up
the allotted time. When the flock of Christ has such
pastors, the melancholy result is that described in a single
line of Milton's *Lycidas*,

"The hungry sheep look up, and are not fed."

There is another possibility which must not be overlooked.
It may be that some of you at least will greatly extend
your influence by means of the press. The question will
sometimes arise in your minds, Shall I attempt authorship?
Now whether you are called to write books is uncertain ;
but you are called to preach the gospel. Aim at perfection in this work, and it may some day come to pass that
the sermon delivered to hundreds will be read by thousands.
The great examples of Augustine and Chrysostom, of Luther,
Jeremy Taylor, Barrow, South, and Wesley, of Massillon
and Bourdaloue, of Krummacher and Schleiermacher, teach
us that sermons may be amongst the most permanent forms
of literature ; and more modern examples like those of
Chalmers and Guthrie, Robertson, Ward Beecher, and, above
all, of Spurgeon, show how largely a preacher's influence
may pervade his own country and extend far beyond it,
until he gains an audience to be counted by hundreds
of thousands. I am speaking of possibilities, and who shall
say that the words spoken by some whom I now address
may not be a living power in England 500 years hence ?

I hope you will all aim at being very popular preachers.

" What ! " you will say, " court popularity ? "   Yes, in every
possible way ; but not for its own sake.   To make it your
supreme object to win for yourself popular applause, is
despicable ; but to try every legitimate art of pleasing, in
order to gain the ear and win the heart of the largest
possible number for the things of Christ, is noble.   Follow
closely the teaching of the Apostle Paul, and seek to 'please
every one for his good to edification ' ; but also remember
that there is no foe so certainly fatal to the highest perfection in oratory as vanity in the speaker.   As soon as ever
any one begins to care less about what he is saying than
about how he is saying it, the moment that he cares more
about pleasing than about persuading, in that moment he
loses power.   When the audience admire the speaker during
his discourse, he has not attained the highest reach of
his art ; but when they forget both him and themselves
through the intense interest which they feel in his subject,
then his success is complete.   According to my own judgment, I never read oratory more perfect than the speech
of Mark Antony over the dead body of Cæsar, as given
by Shakespeare.   Yet if you suppose that speech actually
uttered in the circumstances imagined by the poet, you may
be sure that none of Antony's hearers would have pronounced
him eloquent, at all events whilst listening to him.   He
moves his hearers to pity and to tears for Cæsar, to indignation, hatred, rage against Cæsar's murderers ; but as for
admiration of Antony's eloquence, that never enters their
minds, and they doubtless accept as simple truth the words,
which the speaker brings in with consummate art, "I am no
orator, as Brutus is."

But it is high time to consider the practical question,
How to make present opportunities contribute to success in
preaching ?   The objects of your study admit of a twofold
division : into substance and form—in other words, *What*

to teach? and *How to present it?* For an answer to the first question you will find your safest guide in the saying of Christ: "Ye shall know the truth, and the truth shall make you free." These words suppose that there is a body of truth so unspeakably important that it deserves to be called *the truth*, other truth being comparatively unimportant; and that this truth imparts a freedom unattainable by any other means. This is, in other words, "the truth as it is in Jesus," of which Christ is not only the great Teacher, but also the great subject; and the test of your success in preaching it will be found in the measure in which you are made useful in bringing men to freedom from the guilt and power and pollution of sin. The success of your ministry will ever depend on the degree in which you are faithful to your commission to preach this truth, and *this only*. There are a thousand truths very interesting and important in their degree, but it is not your business to teach them. You are heralds, sent to proclaim a message from the King of kings; and you are bound to keep within the tenor of your commission.

This truth in its scientific form and various relations, together with the controversies that have gathered round it, will be brought before your attention by our Theological Tutor, whom we now gladly welcome among us, and whom we trust God's good providence will preserve to us in his office here for many years to come.

You will learn this truth by your diligent study of the Holy Scriptures, and you will enjoy the inestimable advantage of reading these in the original tongues. You may hope, whilst resident here, to become tolerably familiar with your Greek Testament, and to gain such an initial knowledge of Hebrew as will enable you to prosecute this delightful study in after years, encountering only such difficulties as patience will overcome. You must, above all, seek to know the truth experimentally. Every true preacher is a *witness*, and every step you advance in the actual experience of the great salvation will increase your power to make it known to others.

Now, as to the *form*, or mode in which truth is to be presented. You have to win the attention of your audience, and to keep it. In order to do this you must avoid, or else cure, all obvious faults of speech and manner; else, when you wish your hearers to be pondering the question, "What must I do to be saved?" some of them will be considering the very different and very unprofitable one, Why does not the preacher get rid of these irritating provincialisms and this grotesque action?

Shun as you would the plague a dull, monotonous delivery. This sends the hearers to sleep, and so renders their profiting a thing impossible. There is another mode of speaking only one degree less deplorable, in which the speaker begins every sentence with a loud note and ends it with a faint one. This is called the thunder-and-whisper style of delivery. It is a great abomination, and to hearers of irritable nerves all but unendurable. Our teacher of elocution, Professor Bell, will afford you most valuable help as to all these matters; but you must supplement his teaching, and seek to make yourselves perfect, by abundant private practice. I especially recommend the habit of reading aloud to a friend who will kindly tell you of all your faults. Ward Beecher is a very popular preacher, and doubtless many causes have contributed to make him so; but certainly this among others, that years ago he spent hour after hour, through many successive days, in the practice of mere vocal drill, seeking in this way to attain a perfect enunciation of every vowel and every consonant. That which in the finished speaker sometimes seems perfect nature, is in reality perfected art.

You must study logic. This is essential to all good speaking. One who is himself a logician soon finds out whether the speaker to whom he is listening has given attention to this subject. Logic gives to discourse what a Latin poet calls the *lucidus ordo*,[1] the perfectly clear arrangement; it furnishes what Coleridge says is essential to right method, "unity combined with progression."

To logic you must add rhetoric. A discourse may be very logical, but very dry. Rhetoric teaches how to marshal and adorn discourse so as to arrest attention at the outset, and to keep it to the end. Lord Bacon understood both logic and rhetoric, and his contemporary Ben Jonson says of him : "His hearers could not cough or look aside from him without loss. He commanded where he spoke, and had his judges angry and pleased at his discretion. No man had their affections more in his power. The fear of every man that heard him was lest he should make an end."

You must cultivate the imagination. In doing this your linguistic studies will be very helpful to you. Trench *On the Study of Words* will show how words traced up to their etymologies become pictures, and contain "fossil poetry." In the present day some of our brightest colours are obtained from coal-tar. By skilful chemistry the colours which once glowed in the forests buried long ages since have been made once more to glitter in the sun ; and you will find buried in words the rich hues of the imaginations of primitive men, who gave names to things whilst the race possessed the vigour of its youth, and abstract truth was seen only through the medium of material analogies.

Read the greatest poets of all ages, in whom the imaginative faculty is seen in its greatest strength. Read Homer, Æschylus, Virgil, Dante, and the great Germans, Goethe

---

[1] Horace, *Ars Poetica.*

and Schiller. As to the two last-named, however, it is to be regretted that, although writing in a Christian age, they are too heathenish ever fully to satisfy the Christian mind. Of course you will read the grand poets of your mother tongue; but do not waste time on poetry that is only second-rate. Some of the finest poetry ever written is found in the Bible itself. Study this in the Prophets, the Psalms, and the Book of Job, using the German writer Herder as your guide. Do not neglect the poetic prose of Lord Bacon, John Milton, John Bunyan, and John Ruskin. These writers will teach you how imagination may illuminate a subject whilst it adorns it, and may be as helpful to the understanding as it is gratifying to the taste. Here the study of science will also aid you. Modern physical science introduces us to new worlds of wondrous magnificence, the vastness and perfection of which excite the imagination to the utmost, yet defy all its powers to scale the heights and sound the depths of the glory which science reveals.

Every man has the gift of imagination, and every one who cultivates it will find how serviceable it is. Listen to a sermon that shows not a particle of imaginative power, and it is like walking along the dry and dusty highway that traverses a featureless country. But to listen to a discourse which in all other respects is excellent, and has been illuminated by the play of well-trained imaginative power, is like walking across Ilkley moors at the present season of the year, when the turf springs under your feet, and an Italian sky is overhead, the air is exhilarating, and the rich and varied landscape exhibits new scenes of beauty at every advancing step you take. If you wish to hold your hearers bound by a spell which they cannot resist, in order that you may sway them towards the highest purposes at which man can aim, then cultivate the imagination.

Cultivate pathos. This is most difficult, but most neces-

sary. A sermon without pathos lacks one of the greatest
sources of power. One of the most stupid criticisms on
preaching ever heard is that of people who make it an
objection to the preacher that "he appealed to the passions
of his audience." Of course he did if he understood his
business. He had been a simpleton if he had not done so.
Unless you excite your hearers to hope, to fear, to love,
to hatred, you do nothing ; or at least you only reach the
point where so many sermons stop short and fail ; you only
convince your hearers that they *ought* to be moved, but do
not actually *move* them.

How can we attain pathetic power ? The study of mental science will be helpful, because it shows how human
passions are aroused and allayed. Much may be done by
reading. History is full of pathos, especially the history
of the early Church, of the Reformation of religion in the
sixteenth century, and of the great struggles for liberty of
thought and worship in England, Scotland, France, Germany, and the Netherlands. Read the history cf Methodism in England and America. Be sure you do not fail to
read the lives of John and Charles Wesley and of the Early
Methodist Preachers. Here you will find records that will
deeply move you, and excite the noblest feelings and
highest aspirations of which human nature is capable.
Read books like *Uncle Tom's Cabin,* and do not despise
little books like *Rab and his Friends,* and *Jessica's First
Prayer.* Read anything that will stir your own souls, and
thus help you to move the hearts of the people.

But there is another means better than reading. *Get
to understand the thoughts and feelings of the people.* Now
in your tract districts, and afterwards in your circuits, talk
with everybody that will talk with you ; and that not merely
to instruct them in what they do not know, but that they
may teach you how to preach by revealing to you their

spiritual wants. To visit your people is on many accounts a duty; to attain to the highest perfection in preaching, it is an absolute necessity. All the great preachers have understood the heart of the common people. They never would have been great preachers if they had not. The best preaching in the world is common preaching—"common," I mean, in the sense in which *The Book of Common Prayer* is so designated. That book has been highly and justly praised, because it contains petitions suitable to all sorts and conditions of men; and he is in my judgment the best preacher who can at the same time interest and profit both young and old, the most illiterate and the most cultured. Such preaching most nearly resembles that of Christ Himself, who spoke to the common hearing and understanding of men, whom, therefore, the "common people heard gladly"; whose parables delight children, and yet contain depths of wisdom which the wisest can never fathom.

There is a kind of preaching which, I suppose, some people like, that is called "highly intellectual." Now, if this meant that high intellectual power had been employed in the production of the sermon, no one would object to that. No sermon is ever spoiled by having too much intellect spent upon it. Of that you may be quite sure. But when a sermon is addressed only to the intellect and has nothing to do with the heart, when it is designed only for the benefit of the select few who are supposed to possess superior intelligence and culture, and when the preacher is ruled by a supreme desire to be thought highly intellectual himself, the result is an abominable monstrosity, as certainly condemned by all wise men, as it must be hateful in the sight of God Himself.

The best way to gain pathos is to live in sympathy with Christ. Fill your minds with the great purposes to accomplish which the Son of God came down from heaven, for which He died and rose again, and now lives for evermore, and your hearts will yearn with pitying tenderness over perishing men, and then it will be impossible for your words to lack pathetic power.

In conclusion, *be willing to take infinite pains with your work.* You will see that in what I have said I have regarded preaching very much in the light of an art in which you have to perfect yourselves. ·It is much more than an art ; but it *is* that, whatever it is besides. And what is true of other arts is true of this, there can be no great success in it, certainly no perfection, without endless painstaking. Look at the sculptor, the painter, the musician : what rigid self-denial they practise, what incessant labour they give that they may attain perfection !

No one expects to play well on any musical instrument without years of study and practice. And the instrument to which you have to apply your skill—the soul of man—is, above all others, the most delicate, complicated, and difficult to handle. You find it but too often sadly out of tune and full of discords. To bring it into tune again, and to educe from it the sweet harmonies of Christian temper and a holy life, is no mean task. In fact, preaching is the most difficult thing in the world. To rouse the dull to attention and the careless to seriousness, to prevail on men to give up the sins they love and to practise the virtues they despise, to forsake the world and live above it, is a work so arduous, that no man has any right to expect to succeed in it unless he is willing to put forth all his strength. You might as well expect that one who has learnt music only six weeks will play Handel's *Messiah* thoroughly well, as hope to preach with great success when you have bestowed little pains on the work. We know that without the blessing of God all our labour is ineffectual, but never delude yourselves by thinking that you may rely on the power of the blessed Spirit to make amends for your own indolence. Supposing the preacher's motives to be pure, the general rule will be that the sermons which have cost the most labour will be attended with the richest blessing from God.

No particle of your toil will go unrewarded. Sometimes, indeed, you will be ready to think that you labour in vain. People whose judgment is not worth a straw will sometimes say that you are shallow because you are clear, whilst they admire others as deep because they are obscure. Some will think you wanting in intellectual force, because you are powerful in persuasion. But the godly people will be greatly blessed, without ever troubling themselves with the question as to whether you are shallow or otherwise. And sometimes, it may be, the wisest man in the congregation will say: "I was so intensely interested in the truth which the preacher brought before us, that until the service was ended I never gave a thought to the admirable skill which made everything so impressive and so transparently clear." Higher praise than that you cannot have.

I have spoken much of possibilities, and as I now pause and think of all the good that may be accomplished if every man here does his very best, and again, of the good that may be left undone if your gifts are not cultivated and your opportunities are not duly improved, I am filled with a feeling of awe which is largely blended with hope, but not wholly separated from fear.

The day will come when the future historian of Methodism will write the record of this year 1880, and perhaps he will write this : The men who were students at Headingley College in 1880 gave themselves to the work of the ministry with so hearty and entire devotion, that they wrought a mighty work in the land, marking out a new era in the history of the Church, and showing what great results can be accomplished by preachers who despise and trample under foot all motives to action which would interfere with the one great purpose of glorifying Christ in the salvation of men. Such a record is a possibility. It is for you to say whether it shall become a fact. Or shall this be said of any of your number?—This man was a Headingley student in 1880. God had endowed him with no mean gifts. He had great opportunities, but he had not wisdom and conscience enough to make a right use of them; and his course through life furnishes one more melancholy comment on the words of the wise king: "Wherefore is there a price in the hand of a fool to get wisdom, seeing he hath no heart to it?"

The record of each life will be written: you will, each one for yourselves, determine its character; and I ask you to ponder seriously and prayerfully this question, What shall the record be?

THE DOCTRINE OF RECONCILIATION.

"God   hath committed unto us the word of reconciliation." —2 COR. v. 19.

BRETHREN in the ministry, this is our commission. It is the most solemn, the most blessed commission ever entrusted to man. We have to tell every one whom we can reach, that there is salvation provided for him, and to urge it on his acceptance. Unless we preach this doctrine, and preach it constantly, we are not faithful to our commission.

Some may say, "The people know it already; they have heard it often enough." Say not so. There are young people in the congregation who may have heard, but never yet understood ; there may be strangers who have never learned the doctrine ; there may be those who have heard and understood, but have not accepted salvation : and these we must, after the apostle's example, 'beseech to be reconciled to God.' We must have patience with others, even as God had patience with us. Perhaps some of us heard the doctrine of reconciliation preached twenty times before we received it to our salvation. How well it was for us that the preacher did not stop at the twentieth time, but went on to the twenty-first !

" But," say others, " we shall weary our people with a thrice-told tale." We shall indeed do this if we are indolent and heartless, and tell the story of the cross as if we had no sympathy with it ; but if our hearts are full of the love of Christ, and we use the best skill we have, we shall not weary our hearers. For more than eighteen hundred years have preachers of the gospel dwelt upon the reconciling love of God to men ; but to the men of this generation the story of the cross is as fresh, as interesting, and as powerful as it ever was. Nay, this is understating the truth. Never before was the doctrine of reconciliation so widely and constantly preached, and never with more blessed results.

Here is one fact which shows how welcome this doctrine is to the heart of man. The last two centuries have produced a multitude of hymns. Many of these have sunk into oblivion. Some live, and will ever live. Which are they? They are "Rock of ages," "Jesu, Lover of my soul," "Now I have found the ground," "Just as I am," and such as these. And the universal acceptance of these hymns is a strong proof that there is no theme more welcome to the universal heart of man than that of Christ crucified for us.

METHODIST PREACHING.

METHODISM has been made by its preaching. So it has been, so it must be still. We cannot attract people by our splendid edifices, by gorgeous ceremonies, by exquisite music, but we can by preaching. But then our preaching must be very good. It must be better than that of the first Methodist preachers. It was an easy thing for them to excel others, because other preaching had fallen to so low a level. It is not so easy now. But we have great advantages which our fathers had not. We have large and settled congregations, and if our preaching is excellent we shall retain and increase them. But *it must be excellent.* Not to dwell on higher motives, this is necessary to our own happiness. We must, if we would be barely comfortable, command the respect of our congregations. We are surrounded by well-educated and clever men. We have constantly among our hearers people who know far more than we do in particular departments of knowledge : lawyers, who understand law better ; doctors, who understand medicine better ; and many better versed in various branches of science and literature than we can pretend to be. This is inevitable, and we are not to blame that it is so. But *preaching* is our special business, and we must convince our hearers that we understand it better than they do, and that in our knowledge of the Bible, and of all that relates to spiritual religion, we are superior to them. When this is the case, it makes all the other parts of our work easy. A pastoral visit is highly valued when made by a man whom the people thoroughly respect. It is easy to manage a Quarterly Meeting if all the members look up to the chairman as their superior.

In order to attain excellence in the pulpit we must spare

no pains. We must regard it as one of the greatest and most pernicious delusions of the devil to believe that diligent preparation for the pulpit stands in the way of the Holy Spirit's guidance and power. I believe that the *rule* is, that the most carefully prepared sermons do the most good, if the aim is right, if the only thing the preacher cares about is to do the people good, and if he cares nothing for his own praise.

I have thought very many times of a sentence which I read some time ago in one of Mr. W. H. Aitken's addresses. He said that soon after he was ordained, an aged clergyman said to him, " You will not do very much good until it is said of you, as of Christ Himself, He was ' moved with compassion toward the multitude.' " There seems to me a world of wisdom in these words. The history of the Church shows that her great and glorious preachers have been men of large hearts and wide sympathies, who have forgotten the distinctions between rich and poor, learned and unlearned—I had almost said the distinction between moral and immoral—who have dared to say with Paul : *There is no difference ;* all are guilty, all are perishing ; all alike need Christ, all are equally welcome.

We must follow up this truly gospel preaching by an earnest enforcement of practical religion, by teaching Christian perfection in a very practical way. This is the necessary complement to the doctrine of a free salvation. Finding peace with God is not the goal, but the starting-point of religion.

THE WORK OF THE CHURCH.

THE CHURCH AND THE CHILDREN.[1]

THE proposition which I wish to maintain is this : *Our children may be saved all the days of their life.* (You will understand that I have in view the children of Christian people living in this country ; for, although my premisses would warrant a wider conclusion, I think the proposition thus limited is large enough for a brief paper.)

Why not? By some it will be said, "What becomes of the doctrine of original sin? Is it no longer in your creed ?" Certainly it is. I believe in the doctrines of universal guilt and universal depravity, as taught by John Wesley ; and I purposely name him, because few theologians have urged them more strongly. But these doctrines must not be looked at alone. Over against the doctrine of universal guilt we have to place that of universal atonement ; and over against the doctrine of universal depravity we set that of the universally bestowed gift of God's prevenient grace. Christ 'coming into the world enlighteneth every man.' And therefore the conception of a human creature

---

[1] A paper read before the Nonconformist Ministers' Meeting in Leeds, October 9th, 1885.

342

living among us on the earth, who is utterly and absolutely bad, is a mere transient conception of the theologian, and not a fact verified in human experience. If every one has in him some of the grace of God, either prevenient or saving, we dare not say that there is nothing good in him.

As to our children, the matter seems to me very plain. In the earliest days of their infancy they are quite safe. As they fell in Adam without any fault of their own, so they are safe in Christ without effort of their own. If to infants you attribute guilt and depravity, you must do so in a highly technical sense; but, whatever these mean in their case, the abundant grace of redemption in Christ is sufficient to countervail them, and our children dying in infancy go to be for ever with the Lord, whether they die baptized or unbaptized. I do not argue in favour of this proposition, because I suppose you all hold it. If argument were necessary, it would be enough to say, Let the proposition be denied, and what follows? We must say that infants perish everlastingly, because they have not exercised a personal trust in Christ, of which they are incapable; or we must say, with Augustine and the Church of Rome, they will so perish unless they are baptized.

But though children start in life in a condition of irresponsible salvation, they cannot continue in this state if they pass the days of early infancy, because they become responsible. At what age does responsibility begin? Does it begin in all children at the same age? These are interesting questions, but who shall answer them?

It is enough here to say that children do not become responsible until they have some knowledge of right and wrong; until they can refuse the right and choose the wrong, and do this knowingly. They do not pass out of that initial state of irresponsible salvation until they are capable of rejecting Christ, until they can, by their own wilful act, thrust from them that Almighty arm that has hitherto upheld them in a state of salvation. But surely on the same day that they are capable of rejecting Christ, they are capable of accepting Him ; on the same day that they are capable of thrusting away that saving arm of Christ, they are capable of clinging to it in loving confidence; so that there is no reason why they should not pass out of the initial condition already described into one of conscious acceptance with God through faith in our Lord Jesus Christ, without any appreciable interval of time. They may therefore be saved all the days of their life : *which was to be proved.* If any one reject this proposition, he is bound, by the inexorable laws of logic, to assert the contradictory.

My proposition is : *There need be no days in the life of our children without salvation.*

He who denies this says : There *must* be some days in the life of our children without salvation ; and this being interpreted means, that there are days in their life when they *may perish* everlastingly, but *cannot be saved.* Who will find chapter and verse to prove that? Some persons may object (I do not mean any present) : "This may be a very finely spun theory, but it is disproved by facts." The objection is illogical. The supposed *possible* is not refuted by alleging the actual. If I say that it is possible for all the Christian ministers in Leeds to become total abstainers, this is not disproved by showing that some of them drink wine ; it must be disproved, if at all, by showing that in the case of some total abstinence is *a thing impossible.* The objection may be put more plausibly thus : That which has never happened is never likely to happen : but salvation all the days of life has never happened ; therefore it is never likely to happen.

To the first proposition, understood to refer to men's experience of the grace of God, I do not object. But to the second premiss, "Such a thing never happened," the objection is twofold. First, no one is competent to affirm such a proposition, unless he knows the lives of all men from the beginning. The second objection is, that this supposed statement of facts is disproved by facts.

To the assertion, "None are saved all the days of their life," I oppose the contradictory, *Some are so saved.* What is the evidence? I quote, first of all, from Mr. Payson Hammond's book on the conversion of children.[1] He quotes the words of an American clergyman, who says, "I speak with assured confidence here, because I can point to the case of earnest Christian men respecting whom I *know* that they were converted in the cradle" (p. 156). Another minister, Dr. Plumer, says of the Rev. Dr. James Hoge, " This venerable man, who died in 1822, often said to his friends that he could not remember the time when he did not love the Lord Jesus Christ" (p. 159). To these testimonies I may add those of some of our own students at Headingley College. I have sometimes asked the question : "Looking back on your past life with your present views of religion, can you remember a period of your life when you were not in a state of salvation?" And more than once I have received the answer, "No, I cannot."

To these instances of salvation from the time of earliest recollection I add examples of very early conversion, and quote again from Mr. Hammond. He gives the case of Phœbe Bartlett, born in America in 1731, respecting whose conversion *at four years of age* a detailed account is given by Dr. Jonathan Edwards (see Hammond, pp. 53, 54). He mentions a boy who was attending a children's service

---

[1] *The Conversion of Children.* By the Rev. E. Payson Hammond, M.A. London : Morgan & Scott.

in Dublin, and was then five years of age. A gentleman said to him, "Do you love the Lord Jesus Christ?" "Yes, sir," said the boy. "And how long have you done so?" "Ever since I was a little boy." At this point in the conversation the child's father came up and said, "That's my boy; he has been a Christian for the last two years, and certainly as good a one, to say the least, as any one else in the house." I quote one story more, which will no doubt amuse you, but I refer to it for a special reason. A boy, who was scarcely four years of age, one day came to his mother, evidently in great trouble, and said, "Mama, I said a naughty word—I sweared, I did!" His mother said, "Then come here, and I will wash your mouth out." She took a piece of rag, soaped it, and first of all carefully washed the child's mouth. Then she began to poke the rag down his throat, and the little fellow felt as if his mother were about to choke him. "What do you do that for, mama?" "Because I want to get to your heart, and wash that out; but I see I can't do that, so that you will have to ask God to do that for you." The child did as he was taught, prayed earnestly to God to wash his heart, and to make him a good boy; and from that time forward, according to his mother's testimony, lived a Christian life. This example shows how very early conscience may be aroused in children; and also that they may very soon be taught the need of forgiveness, and of the renewal of the heart in righteousness.

What do facts like these prove? Even if you set aside the first class of instances, *i.e.* of those who have no remembrance of an unsaved state, then the early conversions prove that if there is any period of life during which salvation is impossible to our children, it must be before they are four years of age. If any one chooses to believe this, then let him believe it.

Yet what is practically the faith of many good Christian people on this subject? It amounts to this: when children are young, say before they are in their teens, they cannot be reckoned as members of the Church, and they cannot be converted; but let them grow up into their teens, and be for some time openly wicked, and then they will make fine cases for conversion. I do not say that anybody has ever formulated this faith in propositions and put it in his creed; but practically that is what it comes to. And this view of the case of children has led, and still leads, to infinite evil. The children themselves are greatly perplexed. They cannot tell whether they are inside the fold of Christ or out of it. By the way in which they are treated, spoken of, and spoken to, they are led to think that they are outside. Hence *they lose the very powerful motive to godly living that they would have if they were recognised members of the Church of Christ;* and every temptation to wrong-doing is strengthened by the thought that older Christians are expecting them to act unchristianly rather than the contrary. Too often, if they are disposed to profess the love to the Saviour which they truly feel, they are wofully discouraged by being told that they have obtained salvation too easily, that there is a great crisis for them to pass through before they can regard themselves as saved. I do not say this as a guess of my own, but from knowledge of facts. Now here is a double error. Older people imagine that the turning of a young child to Christ must be after the same pattern as that of one who has lived many years in open rebellion against God; and, secondly, there is a complete ignoring of the really hard struggle against sin, and the unfeigned sorrow on account of it, that often take place in the minds of very young children. Were the children of godly people encouraged to exercise faith in Christ when very young, admitted into the Church, and recognised as Church members, many would have a bright, happy, consistent, Christian childhood, who otherwise will spend dreary years of doubt and uncertainty, and perhaps at last become hardened against all the good influences by which they are surrounded.

Why are not more of our children saved in very early life? I cannot give all the reasons, but will name some.

1. It is largely owing to *bad doctrine.* In the moral sphere of things bad doctrine always produces bad facts. If parents have no expectation of the conversion of their children before they are in their teens, they will not pray for this; and if they do not pray for it, they will not labour for it. I do not say that the right doctrine always produces the right facts; but it always tends that way, and very often does produce them. I have known several instances in which parents confidently expected to see all their children early saved, and *I have never known one instance in which such parents have been disappointed.* It has been done to them according to their faith. And the right faith of the parents in these cases produces the right kind of training. It is watchful, prayerful, firm, but always loving and hopeful. And when the bond of love between parents and children is sealed and sanctified by the stronger bond of union in Christ Jesus, so that parents and children recognise one another as "heirs together of the grace of life," how much family happiness is secured, how much misery prevented!

2. Another reason is *the culpable reticence* of parents towards children in reference to the soul's welfare. It is often a fault of parents in regard to other things that they do not sufficiently win the confidence of their children; but when they make no attempt to do this in regard to the child's own thoughts and feelings about religion, the consequences are most lamentable. I know that to do this

work aright requires tact and judgment; but as "the heart of the wise teacheth his mouth," so a heart full of true love will teach loving words; and children who can resist everything else, cannot resist love. How sad to think of a child struggling hard to be right year after year, and yet never getting from father or mother a single word of advice or encouragement in reference to such struggles! And the pity, the infinite pity of the thing is, that often there is nothing in the world that the children would like their parents to talk to them about half so much as the love of Jesus. I remember a beautiful boy of five years of age, now grown up to be a useful servant of Christ; but when he was a boy his Christian teacher one day said to him, "Willie, do you love the Lord Jesus Christ?" He had not expected such a question, but looking up into his teacher's face said, with sweet surprise, "Teacher, how can any one help it?"

3. *The coldness, unbelief, indifference on the part of the Church* with which youthful Christians are often treated. I will not enlarge on this topic; Mr. Hammond's book will give you instances.

How are we to bring about a better state of things? I will not attempt a complete answer. If we all hold and teach the right doctrine, this will lead on to the right methods. At present I can suggest nothing better than what has been adopted in our own community—the formation of "Junior Society Classes," *i.e.* classes directly preparing for full Church membership. From these very great good arises, and as far as I know, nothing but good.

I have only one other observation to make. The religion of children may be as real, as consistent, and beautiful as that of older people, if they are properly taught that religion is intended to embrace the whole life; that for them it

means, not only private prayer, singing hymns, reading the
Bible, and going to public worship, but also obedience
to parents, acting justly, courteously, and kindly to everybody; it means being quite punctual at the day school,
keeping all the rules, writing the copies well, doing the
arithmetic correctly, learning Latin nouns and verbs so
as to say them through without a single mistake.   It
means *religion in play.*   How can there be religion in play?
There is evidently much irreligion during play hours; why
may there not be religion?   If Christian children during
play never cheat, never speak an untruth, never lose their
tempers, show that they are as much concerned about the
enjoyment of their companions as about their own, there
must, I think, be a great deal of religion during play hours.
The sum of all is this :

*All the children for Christ; all their days, days of salva-
tion; all their hours, hours of religion.*

WHO BROUGHT THE CHILDREN TO JESUS?

"And they brought young children to Him, that He should touch
them : and His disciples rebuked those that brought them."—MARK
x. 13.

WHO brought the children to Jesus?   It has been
commonly assumed by preachers, painters, and
poets that the *mothers* brought them.   But the sacred
record nowhere states this.   There is rather more to be
said for the supposition that the *fathers* brought them than
for the ordinary view, because the Greek participle which
answers to the English words, "those that brought them"
is not feminine, but masculine.[1]   It is certainly a serious

---

[1] τοῖς προσφέρουσιν.   In the Revisers' text, αὐτοῖς.

evil if in our own time the duty of bringing children to Jesus is thought to belong to mothers only. Why should fathers be released from the obligation of doing this? Why deprived of the privilege?

THE MISSION TO THE HEATHEN.[1]

I. A MISSIONARY'S DIFFICULTIES.

I PASS by many things in a missionary's experience, not because they are trifling or unimportant, but because they are matters about which a true missionary says very little. I dwell not on separation from home and friends, the multiplied dangers and inconveniences of foreign travel, the effects of climate upon health, the loss of the pleasures and amenities of civilized life. All these are taken for granted, though they ought not to be forgotten by us. What chiefly concern us just now are the difficulties which hinder success in mission work.

There is the hindrance of a foreign language, learnt with great toil, and often never perfectly mastered. You have heard foreigners who have lived some years in this country speak English, and if you understood them it was not without much difficulty. Here is a difficulty for hearers as well as preachers: would you like to have a Frenchman preach to you in imperfect English, even if you fully approved his doctrine and admired his character?

There is the antipathy of race. We know something of this even within the bounds of the United Kingdom. Do you find it as easy to love Irish people as to love English people? If you find no difficulty in this respect,

---

[1] From a sermon on Acts xv. 3.

some of the Irish find much difficulty in loving you. Judge of the difficulty in China, where the missionaries constantly hear themselves saluted as "foreign devils."

Then there is the conflict with old-established religions. Our missionaries in India are trying to overthrow a religious system which has held its ground there for 3,000 years at least, and in China they are opposing systems nearly 2,500 years old. Can these old religions be overthrown in a day? The difficulty is intensified by the fact that they form, not merely theoretic beliefs, but laws of custom, which claim to govern, and do actually govern, all the relationships of life. They prescribe to their adherents what they shall eat and drink and wear; they regulate the ceremonies connected with birth, marriage, and death; they extend their jurisdiction over every hour of every day and over everything that a man does. To break away from these religions is indeed for a man to renounce the world, *i.e.* to renounce family, position, employment; to become dead to the world, whilst his former world becomes dead to him.

When you have fully entered into all these difficulties, you have to add to them all the obstacles to true conversion that are found at home: listlessness, worldliness, unbelief, love of sin, hardness of heart. It is not an easy thing to secure true conversions in England, how much more difficult abroad!

There is another ground on which the missionaries require our sympathy. Perhaps you have never once thought of it, perhaps you will be surprised when I mention it,—the difficulty which the missionary has to maintain unimpaired the vigour of his own spiritual life. Perhaps you think that the near sight of the evils of heathenism will be enough to maintain the missionary's fervour, just as the idolatries of Athens stirred the soul of the Apostle

Paul. But experience proves to the missionary how much when at home he owed to his fellow Christians, to abundant means of grace, to Christian sympathy. Here, as it has been well said, Christianity fills the air; it manifests its power and blessed influence in a thousand ways. Amongst heathen people heathenism fills the air, shows itself at a thousand points, and holds too often triumphant sway. I only repeat the words of an experienced missionary, when I say that the trial of faith and character, the strain on a man's physical and moral nature is so great, that in some instances there is failure; even the missionary fails; and the wonder is, not that a few such cases occur, but that they are not more numerous.

Bear all these things in mind, the difficulties besetting the work of the missionary, and the difficulties in the way of those who would forsake heathenism for Christ, and can you wonder that the work of converting the heathen is often slow?

II. OUR OWN DUTY.

The question first to be considered is, Ought we ourselves to take part in the work by going forth to labour amongst the heathen? Some will perhaps say, "What a strange question! I never thought of such a thing in all my life." Very likely not; but do not at once put the question away from you. I do not say it is the duty of any one here to go on foreign service; but do not treat it lightly: consider it in the fear of God, and in the light of your obligations to Christ. We must get rid of the notion that only young men, missionaries, ordained preachers of the gospel, are to go to the heathen. We need large companies of labourers; and we want Christian people to consider whether they cannot go forth to this work at their

own cost.   Not a few have done this, especially in connection with the China Inland Mission, and several of our
own missionaries have acted likewise.

There are Christian people in England whose life is comparatively objectless and therefore joyless, who would be
far happier if they were employed in mission work amongst
the heathen.   They would find full scope for all their
powers, they would have a noble purpose in life.   They
might meet with trials and hardships, but, on the whole,
life would have more interest and more joy.

But suppose you come to the conclusion that it is your
duty to stay at home, that circumstances imperatively
require this.   There is another thing which I would put
before you.   Could not some of you go *by deputy ?*   There
was once a time in this country, I believe, when men were
drawn by lot for military service ; and sometimes when
this happened the friends of a young man drawn would
buy him off and procure a substitute.   Why should not
wealthy Christians in this country do something similar ?
Why should not a man say, " I cannot go myself, but I will
pay the cost of a missionary year by year."   This is what
some are actually doing.   In other cases a Christian in
England provides the salary of a native minister in a foreign
country, or of more than one.   It must be a pleasant
thought to such men that they have their deputies labouring
abroad.

Suppose we cannot do any one of these things, we can
still do much to help forward the good work.   We can
all do three things : read, pray, and give.

First of all, *read.*   Many of us have had friends or relations who have gone to the mission field ; and these are
amongst the noblest, most self-denying, self-sacrificing men
and women now living.   It seems to me that whilst *they* are
making the sacrifices, which are very great, the least *we* can

do is to acquaint ourselves with their work. There is no literature which more deserves to be read by us than missionary literature.

Let us *pray* more, fashioning our prayers more on the pattern of the Lord's Prayer, and let us do this in private as well as in public.

Let us *give* more largely. We flatter ourselves that we do great things ; but we do very little. If you take the wealth of England, the income of the nation, you will find that the contributions to Missions do not amount to more than the one-thousandth part, hardly to a farthing in the pound. I could tell you of one town in Yorkshire that every year spends more on strong drink than the whole of the Christians of Great Britain contribute to the cause of Christian Missions. You say, " But the Christian people, the Methodist people especially, give very liberally." This I acknowledge. There is a steady improvement, but we shall have to do more. Our first duty always is to provide things honest in the sight of all men, to care for the bare necessaries of life. But when this has been done, and there is a margin left, what shall we do with the margin ? Calculate what is spent on self that may be done without : the new coat, the new gown, the book, the picture, the summer excursion. "Ah! but," you say, " these are necessary, things indispensable." And are not the blessings of salvation necessary to the heathen ? How much is your religion worth to you ? For what sum would you sell your present happiness in religion, your interest in Christ, your hope of life everlasting ? You are perhaps shocked and scandalised that I should ask such a question. You say, " My religion is beyond all price; I would not barter it for the wealth of the whole world." Most true. But do you not think that when a Kaffir, a Chinaman, a Hindu comes to possess real religion, it will be as precious to him as it is to you.   And if the gift of your money can help him to obtain this priceless possession, can you make better use of it?

In conclusion, let us think of this great matter in the light of our personal relations to Christ, and our obligations to Him.   He knows what we are able to do, and what we are actually doing.   If He is well pleased with what we are doing, then everything is right.   Is it so?   Does the Master approve?   He once said of a certain woman, "She hath done what she could."   Will He say this of our past?   Will He say it of what we are doing to-day, of what we intend to do?   As He sits over against the treasury, and sees what we put into it, will He approve, as of the widow's two mites?   Whatever we do to-day, let us do it unto the Lord, and may He say now, and say in that day, "Well done, good and faithful servant!"

MAN SAVED BY MAN.[1]

I WISH to address a few words to Christian workers; and, first of all, I draw your attention to the fact that *God saves man by man*, and as far as we know, not otherwise.   Did you ever within the range of your own observation know of an instance in which God brought a man to the saving knowledge of Christ without human instrumentality, direct or indirect?   You may have known or heard of cases where a man at the time of his conversion had no one to help or guide him.   He may have been at sea, without one godly companion in the crew; or he may have been in some remote place, far away from ministers, teachers,

---

[1] An address delivered at a convention of Christian workers in Brunswick Chapel, Leeds, October 31st, 1879.

or spiritual guides, and have turned to God : but in all such cases I believe it will be found that the Divine Spirit then quickened into life and fruitfulness the seed which had been previously sown by human hands ; the words spoken by a father or ·mother, brother or sister, preacher or teacher, or the word of God, long ago read, but long neglected, were brought to remembrance ; and thus the Spirit, making use of human means, turned the man "from darkness to light, and from the power of Satan unto God." But did you ever know, or read, or hear of a sinner being led to Christ without *any* human instrumentality? I have never heard of such a case. It would be daring presumption to say, God could not save a man without help from his fellow man—we dare not say this ; but I will venture to say that, although God might conceivably save without human help, yet so far as I know He never does.

What then follows from this? It follows plainly enough, that, humanly speaking, those now unsaved must be saved, if at all, by those who are already saved. The waters of salvation flow through the Church ; and we have to direct their currents, and to invite men to them. God has put into our hands the bread of life, and we have to distribute it. If we are earnest in inviting men and saying, " Ho, every one that thirsteth, come ye to the waters," it is likely that many will come, and drink, and live for ever. If we hold our peace, those who might have been saved, may perish through lack of the water of life. If, having the bread of life in our hands, we are diligent in distributing it, many will live by our means ; if we neglect to do so, they may perish for ever. In a word, if we, every one of us, do all we can to extend the salvation of the gospel to others, many, very many of those who live at the same time with us, and in the same place, will be saved ; but if we are indifferent, slothful, selfish, caring only to save our own souls but careless about the salvation of others, many may perish around us, and some will perish to whom *we* might have brought the blessing of eternal life.

The second thing I wish to say is this. Not only does God save man by man, but He doubtless designs to use for the salvation of our neighbours *the special social position and influence which in His providence He has given us.* God has so placed you that you have more influence over some who are still unsaved than any one else has. As masters, as mistresses, you have special influence with your servants, especially if you are, as I assume you to be, good Christian masters and mistresses in your own houses, "adorning the doctrine of God our Saviour." You who are parents have special influence with your children. You young people have influence with brothers, with sisters, with parents, that no one else has. God has so placed you, and so bound you together with your dependants, relatives, friends, that you are the very fittest persons in the world to lead them to a saving knowledge of Christ. How will you answer to the great Master if you do not use for Him that special talent of usefulness with which He has entrusted you?

Thirdly, *Let not the sense of your responsibility overwhelm you.* Any view of our responsibility which overwhelms us, which overpowers and paralyses effort, is surely not a thing to be desired. I would wish you to have a deep, keen sense of responsibility, one ever present with you; but instead of paralysing, let it rather prompt you to effort.

It is when we look at the responsibility of *the Church as a whole*, and imagine this to be our own, that we say to ourselves, "The amount of wickedness in the world is infinite; the amount of work to be done before the world is saved is infinite: I cannot do an infinite work, therefore— most miserable 'therefore'—I will do nothing."

Now remember, the work of the Church is indeed infinite;

but *your* work is not infinite. All the work that you have to do in this world, even if you do every particle of the work which Christ requires of you, is very limited indeed. It is limited by the term of your natural life, by your physical strength, by your social position ; and nothing is more certain than that you are well able to do all the work required of you. But do not neglect it. Do not delay it. Set about it at once. Let me give you one plain, practical piece of advice. Resolve that during this mission you will do all that you can to *save one at least*. Get one at least to attend the services. Do your best to get that one interested. See him before the service, get his promise to come. See him afterwards. Do everything that combined wisdom and love can suggest to bring him to Christ. Say, "If I have never saved any one before, I will be an instrument in that man's salvation, if possible." Try to save *one*, I do not speak of more. If you are to save many you must begin with one. If you once begin a work so blessed, I feel sure that you will go on.

Lastly, *think of the never-failing encouragement to labour.* I remember once hearing that good and great man Dr. Livingstone, and I shall never forget what he said. There had been a great deal of stamping and clapping amongst the audience whom he was addressing. He said : " It needs a great deal of enthusiasm to do mission work in Africa ; not the kind of enthusiasm we have here to-day, but that which springs from the conviction which a man has in his heart that he is accomplishing a great work which God Himself has called upon him to undertake." I would I had myself more of this blessed enthusiasm. But there is a thought more stimulating to the Christian than even that of Livingstone. It is the word of Christ, given to His first messengers : "Lo, I am with you alway, even unto the end of the world."

CHRIST AND HIS WITNESSES.

" To this end was I born, and for this cause came I into the world, that I should bear witness unto the truth."—JOHN xviii. 37.

" As My Father hath sent Me, even so send I you."—JOHN xx. 21.

" Ye shall be witnesses unto Me."—ACTS i. 8.

THESE three utterances of Christ were spoken on the three most memorable days of the world's history. The first on the day of His death ; the second, on the day of His resurrection ; the third, on the day of His ascension. They claim our attention on this account, and they combine to teach us two great lessons. First, that *Christ's work on earth was to bear witness to the truth.* Secondly, that now that He has ascended into heaven, *this is the work of the Church.* Committed to us as Christians is the carrying on of the great purpose and work of Christ. We are the trustees of the Lord Jesus.

Let us consider—I. *The trust.* II. *The trustees.* III. *The fulfilment of the trust.*

I. *The trust* committed to us is *the truth.* And here it is assumed that the truth taught by Christ is beyond comparison the most important of all truth. Does any one ask why? Because this truth alone meets our needs as moral and immortal creatures. We do not disparage other truth. It is the utmost folly for Christians to deny or decry scientific truth ; we are greatly indebted to men of science, in a thousand ways. But science cannot answer certain questions, which to us are the most important of all things. These concern facts in our human nature, which are as certain as the shining of the sun. Take, for instance, the fact of human guilt. How terrible it is, often leading even to self-destruction, to the choosing of " strangling rather than life " ! Of what avail is science here? Wonderful are the triumphs of modern science. What, for instance, are more amazing than the revelations of astronomy? It reveals the infinite spaces of the universe; unfolds the solar planetary system; tells us the forms, orbits, distances of the planets,—nay, it actually weighs them for us; and then it tells us, that if the sun with all its attendant planets were blotted out of existence, it would no more affect the universe than the extinction of one little twinkling star. We rejoice in these triumphs of science. But how will this knowledge help a man weighed down with guilt? Man is depraved, sunk to the level of the brutes; yea, sunk lower still. How shall we raise him? Search all the records of science. Has mere science ever made a bad man into a good man? But the records of the Christian Church can show thousands, tens of thousands of such instances; they are taking place every day. "The living know that they shall die." What after death remains?—what can science say? The most sorrowful hour of life comes to us: what relief can science give?

Where all science fails us, the truth of Christ prevails. It avails for pardon, holiness, for hope of life eternal, for strong consolation at our greatest need. This is why we speak of *the truth*,—the only truth which makes us safe, and holy, and happy, and noble, and opens the prospect of endless life. Our present duty is to receive this truth ourselves, and to communicate it to others. This truth is our trust.

II. *The trustees:* who are they? To whom is the truth committed? "Ye shall be witnesses," said Christ. The work is committed to *witnesses*. If we are to propagate the truth, we must know it. How shall we learn it? Christ must take us into His school.

"A wonderful fashion of teaching He hath."

His philosophy is experimental; He makes us understand

His religion by giving us the experience of His salvation.
We can know it in no other way. A man may indeed
say, " I will become a teacher of Christ; I will study the
New Testament, and become conversant with His doctrine," and so on.   But in that way you cannot become a
teacher of Christ's religion.   What Christ wants is, not
a philosopher, a reasoner, an orator; He wants *a witness.*
The first witnesses bore testimony to the great external
facts of Christianity—the death, the resurrection, the
ascension of Christ ; but they also bore witness to facts
of inward experience.   They said, " Being justified by
faith, we have peace with God, through our Lord Jesus
Christ."   " There is therefore now no condemnation to them
which are in Christ Jesus."   " We have redemption in His
blood, even the forgiveness of sins."   Are *you* such a witness?   Can you define true repentance ?   You may give a
verbal definition, but no one can *witness* of true repentance,
unless he has experienced it.   What is saving faith ?   What
is peace with God ?   What is inward holiness ?   What is
the " joy unspeakable and full of glory " ?   How can anybody bear witness to these things without experience of
them ?   No one is qualified to be a trustee of Christ's
truth, a furtherer of Christianity in the world, without experimental knowledge.

On the other hand, every one who has this knowledge is
qualified.   We all agree in saying that in the Church of
Christ there is no such priesthood as the Church of Rome
claims ; but it is sometimes too hastily said that there are
no priests in the Church on earth.   This is a great mistake.
There are as many priests as Christians.   The converted
child of ten years of age is as truly a priest unto God as the
most learned bishop.   But if we claim for all Christians this
dignity, let us remember the corresponding responsibility.
Are you a priest unto God ?   You must have something to

offer ; you must have some sacrifice to present. What offerings do you make ? what sacrifices do you bring ? Do you 'present your body a living sacrifice to God' ? Do you offer God your hands, your feet, your lips, your tongue, your bodily strength, your powers of mind ?

If you are a Christian, you are by calling and profession a witness for Christ. What testimony do you give ? Who hears you ? Who is won to Christ by your witnessing for Him ? If the world is to be won for Christ, it must be won in this way ; not by ministers of religion only, not by official members of the Church only, not by public preaching and teaching only, but by every Christian becoming a witness. And nothing wins men so surely as testimony. I have less and less faith in argument and eloquence, more and more in believing testimony.

III. This leads us to ask, *How may we best fulfil our trust ?* The answer is, that *we must bear witness to the truth.* But here the question arises, What part of Christian truth must be made most prominent in our testimony ? We may say a great deal that is perfectly true about Christ and His religion ; but, unless we bear witness to *the* truth, we may leave our hearers as much unmoved as if we had discoursed about the size and age of the pyramids of Egypt. Let us follow Paul's example at Ephesus. He shrank not from declaring unto them anything that was profitable. He taught both "publicly, and from house to house, testifying both to the Jews and also to the Greeks repentance toward God, and faith toward our Lord Jesus Christ."

We must bear witness to *right practice,* as well as to right doctrine. We must especially bear witness where the world will not, where the newspaper will not, against selfishness, worldly spirit, greed of gain, love of display, inordinate love of amusement. And we must bear witness with our lives. We must not only cry out against these things ; we must show that we are superior to them. We must not only testify that men should be self-denying, generous, noble; we must show ourselves examples of these things. Who of us is free from the worldly, self-seeking spirit? Are you? Am I? You will think that this is a very proper thing for a minister of religion to ask himself. Now suppose I should tell you that I am thoroughly worldly, that I care more for worldly show and splendour, for getting money and spending it on self, than for anything else, what would you say? You would cry shame on me. You would say that I did not deserve to be a minister of religion, if I cared more about money than about saving souls and edifying the Church; and you would be quite ready to tell me what sort of a man you think that a minister of the gospel ought to be. You would draw a picture of a man laborious, self-forgetful, self-denying, so anxious to promote the spiritual welfare of his people as to be indifferent to his own personal comfort, warm in zeal, yet always having a perfect command of his temper even in circumstances most irritating; and having formed this beautiful picture, you would hand it to me and say, "There! that is what I should like my minister to be." And I should take the picture, and admire it very much, and then hand it back to you and say, "There! that is what I should like my people to be." There is no obligation to personal holiness resting on me which does not also rest on you. God's requirement of me is, that I should love Him with all my heart, and my neighbour as myself. He asks nothing more of me; and nothing less of you.

What do you say? Will you be Christ's witnesses? Christ has left the world, but He has left His great work in your hands. He says to you, "Ye are My witnesses." The world needs your testimony for Christ. Men are saved every day by the testimony of others saved before them.

Will you not give your testimony for Christ? You may be sure of this, that whenever you bear faithful witness for Christ, there will be a blessed reaction. Witnessing to your faith will strengthen your faith. You are not answerable for the result of your testimony ; you are answerable for giving it. And whether men are benefited or not, you are blessed, and your Lord is glorified.

Here are three very powerful motives to persuade you to be faithful witnesses : *your neighbour's highest good, your own spiritual advancement, Christ's glory in the world.* Is not that enough ?

"NOT SERVANTS, BUT FRIENDS."

" Having loved His own which were in the world, He loved them unto the end."—JOHN xiii. 1.

IN the last discourses of our Lord with His disciples there is much that fills our minds with astonishment and awe. One of the most astonishing things of all is the way in which our Lord speaks to and of the apostles, and His other followers. We know something of these men ourselves. We know something of the character of Peter, James, Thomas, Philip, and Andrew, and the rest ; and sometimes we do not rank them very high. By birth and training they were Galilæan peasants ; in point of education their attainments were but small. In moral and spiritual elevation they appear to us at this time to be by no means very uncommon men. We call to mind the base conduct of Peter on the night of the betrayal, and the cowardice of them all ; we remember that petty dispute as to which of them should be the greatest ; we think of their narrow and earthly views of Christ's kingdom, after all the advantages of His teaching : and we are ready to pass a harsh judgment on them, and to pronounce them to be, on the whole, rather poor specimens of mankind.

But when in our self-sufficiency we have in our own minds pronounced their condemnation, how startling it is to turn to the estimate which our Lord gives of them! He knew them well; He looked them through and through; where we see one fault, He must have seen a thousand. Yet of these very men we read that, " having loved His own which were in the world, He loved them unto the end." He tells them that He no longer calls them His *servants*, but His *friends*. In His sublime prayer He commends them to the care of His heavenly Father, dwelling with satisfaction on the thought that they have known Him, believed in Him, loved Him, and says that He has been glorified in them; and when He contemplates His own return to glory, and thinks of sharing again with the Father the majesty which He had with Him before the world was, His last request to the Father is that these humble men, with the followers of their faith, might be the beholders and partakers of His everlasting glory.

All this is very wonderful; but to you and me it becomes more wonderful still, when we apply our Lord's words to ourselves. That they belong to us, and are spoken of us as truly as of them, I rather assume than seek to establish by argument. These chapters in John (xiii.–xvii.) show us clearly whom Christ acknowledges as His disciples: they are those who believe in Him and love Him. If this be true of us, then what Christ says of these disciples He says of us: "As My Father hath sent Me, even so send I you." This holds good for us, not because we are preachers, but because we are Christians. These words were not spoken to the apostles only. The two disciples from Emmaus were certainly present also (see Luke xxiv. 33–36), and our Lord here puts on us this high honour, that He brings His mission into connection with our mission, and establishes a parallel between them, making His mission the preliminary of ours, and ours the continuation of His.

CHRIST OUR EXAMPLE.

WE must seek to do Christ's work *in Christ's spirit.* There is an infinite distance between Him and us, and yet He is our best model. The great mystery which we see in Christ helps us to understand and deal with the greatest problem of our own lives. When we carefully weigh what our Lord said about Himself, especially when He spoke of Himself as the Son of man and as the Son of God, we see that He was conscious of possessing both a human and a Divine nature.

He knew that He was a sorrowful, suffering, depressed man, who had to die. He knew that He was the sharer of the Father's glory before all worlds. We see that in Christ the Divine did not efface the human, the human did not degrade the Divine. Though we cannot think of ourselves as Divine and human, we know that whilst we are frail, perishing men, we are possessors of the Divine, for "the Spirit of God dwelleth in us"; and the highest problem of life is, not to destroy the human, not even to suppress anything that is essential to our human nature, but to bring everything into harmony with the Divine within us. Then, like our Lord, we are in the world, but not of it.

Nothing is more encouraging to us, when seeking to solve this problem, than to observe the wide range of our Lord's human sympathies, we may even say, His human pleasures. The scenes of external nature which charm us delighted

Him. He watched and admired the changing aspects of the heavens; He observed the growth of the lilies, and delighted in their beauty; He watched the flight and the habits of the birds of the air. How interested He was in human affairs! He watched the children playing in the market-place, and listened to their innocent prattle. He saw with interest the housewife busy in mixing her leaven with the meal; He sympathised with the poor woman who had lost her piece of money, and who searched diligently until she found it. He watched and followed the sower sowing his field, the ploughman putting his hand to the plough, the shepherd tending his flock, the fisherman casting his net into the sea. He joined the festivities of a marriage feast; He knew the joy of a mother's heart when her child is born into the world. He noted the joys and sorrows of our domestic histories, and has set them forth in the parable of the prodigal son, and has dignified our human experiences by telling us that they have their correspondences even in the heart of God Himself. The best Christians are not those who stifle and crucify their human nature; but those are best, because most like Christ, in whom all that is essentially human is fully developed in harmony with the Spirit of God dwelling in them as in His living temples.

How near Christ came to men! and yet how far He was above them! He hated no man, despised no man, reviled no man. He shrank not from contact with the lowest, nor sought favour from the highest. He hated nothing but sin, had infinite pity for the sorrows of all, and laid down His life for those who despised and rejected Him. We cannot attain, we cannot nearly approach His perfection, but we follow after it.

Another thing very instructive to us is, that our Lord patiently accepted the conditions under which His work was done. His associations were chiefly with the peasant class. His sphere of labour was about the size of Wales, and there is no certain proof that He ever went beyond it. It was a narrower tract of country than we often pass through in a day's journey. His fare was of the humblest. He had no settled home. He had to make His journeys on foot, and knew the fatigues of travel. These conditions He accepted cheerfully, because He knew such to be the Father's will.

I need not point out the lesson. It lies in one word— the greatest life ever lived on earth was one the outward circumstances of which many men think beneath them, and almost all would escape from if they could.

H.   24

THE LIGHT OF THE WORLD AND THE LIGHT OF LIFE.

"I am the light of the world : he that followeth Me shall not walk in darkness, but shall have the light of life."—JOHN viii. 12.

IN these words a great truth is declared, a duty is suggested, and a promise given.

I. The great truth declared is this : *Christ is the light of the world.* Suppose it were possible that you could forget whose words these are, and imagine a preacher coming before you and making this claim on his own behalf, saying in his own name, "I am the light of the world !" with what feelings would you regard the speaker? You would find it very difficult to persuade yourselves that he was in earnest; but if once convinced of this, you would be so offended by his arrogance, that you would not have patience to listen to another word that he said. But it is almost impossible to imagine any preacher, any man ever making this claim, save only that man who was more than man. You cannot imagine any of the sages of antiquity— Socrates, Plato, or Cicero—setting up such a claim. When Moses the great lawgiver, received his commission to go

down into Egypt and deliver Israel, he pleaded his unfit-
ness for the task (Exod. iv. 10–13). You think of the great
prophet Elijah, but you hear him saying, " O Lord, now
take away my life ; for I am not better than my fathers "
(1 Kings xix. 4). Of all the prophets that appeared before
Christ, none was greater than John the Baptist ; but you
hear him saying of Christ : " He   is preferred
before me, whose shoe's latchet I am not worthy to unloose." Of all the illustrious preachers of righteousness
who have followed Christ, there is not one who would not
have ' shrunk with pious horror from the very thought of
·making these words his own.

It is evident then that we have before us a claim altogether unparalleled, and of such a kind that we must
wholly receive or wholly reject it. If we believe that He
who made it was justified in putting it forth, we owe Him
reverence and obedience without limit. If He was not
justified in making it, it is hard to see how we can reverence
Him at all.

Let us endeavour to understand more precisely the meaning of this claim, " I am *the* light of *the* world," *i.e.* the
sufficient light of the whole world. Not of course the
natural light of the visible world ; although we believe as
Christians, that even the sun shines by His power. Not
the intellectual light of the intellectual world ; although we
believe that the light of man's intellect ultimately comes
from Him. Our Lord nowhere appears as a teacher of
purely human science,—I mean of that knowledge which
men obtain by the exercise of their powers of observation
and reasoning, apart from the light of revelation. The light
here spoken of is "the light of life." As in the natural
world, so in the moral, there cannot be life without light.
What the sun is to the natural world, Christ claims to be to
the moral world. Man is capable of a life above that of the

brutes, of a spiritual life, which brings Him into communion with God, and fills his soul with anticipations of the life immortal. This life Christ gives; and He who gives the life, gives the light by which it is sustained, guided, perfected, and which leads those who follow it to the life eternal.

Such is the claim. What is the evidence that He who makes it has a right to make it, and that He can do what He has promised?

This is neither a needless nor an irreverent question, because the claims of Christ are very far from being universally admitted. We find that no sooner did He utter these words than they were met on the part of the Pharisees with flat denial, and even contemptuous rejection. "Thy testimony is not true," they said. Many there are who are now saying the same. In answering the question, we cannot do better than follow in the steps of Christ Himself. How did He support His own claim? Chiefly by an appeal to His own works, as well as to the doctrines which He taught. He said, in effect, that if He had not spoken such words, and supported them by such works, men would have been blameless in rejecting Him; but that after He had spoken the words and wrought the works, they were left without excuse (John xv. 22–24).

While Christ did His works, He put forth certain claims; He said that He was in constant co-operation with the Father. "My Father worketh hitherto, and I work." Saying this, He implied that what He did had the constant approbation of God. He also said that He was the Son of God, and that He and the Father were one. His miracles produced on the minds of unprejudiced witnesses the conviction expressed by Nicodemus: "No man can do these miracles that Thou doest, except God be with Him." They were, in fact, the manifestation of a superhuman, of a Divine power. Hence it follows, either that God put forth

His Divine power to uphold an impostor and to corroborate a lie, or that Jesus was all that He claimed to be.

Thus Almighty God Himself set His own seal on the claims of Christ, and declared Him to be "the Light of the world."

But here some may ask, "Granting, for the sake of argument, that what you say is true, what evidence have we that Christ is now shining in the world?" This is not an unfair question, if only it be remembered under what limitations the evidence which we seek is to be looked for. Now if we turn to the opening verses of this gospel, we shall find two things asserted : first, that the Light of the world is designed for every human soul ; secondly, that for many, often for the majority of men in any given age, He shines in vain. All men, except the blind, see the light of the sun, because they cannot help seeing it ; but when we pass from the physical world to the intellectual, we find that the light of science, though free for all, shines only on those who make some effort to receive it. The many bright lamps which science kindles in this age, for millions of our race shine all in vain. And when we pass on to consider the moral world, we find that something further still is necessary ; not only attention and effort, but the consent of the will. And our Lord has taught us that men are destitute of His light, *because they are unwilling to receive it.* Even in these there may often be evidence of its shining ; but if the light is being quenched, we must not expect to find in its fulness the proof which we seek.

Where then shall we look? The text again gives us the answer. It is in *those that follow* Christ that we shall see the light shining. Not indeed in all the *professed* followers of Christ : since these words were first spoken He has had many millions of followers ; but, alas ! many have been followers only in name, for their conduct has been in flat

opposition to Christ's teaching, precepts, and example.
Even the true followers of Christ are not always equally
faithful in following Him; and therefore the brightness
of the shining light will vary, even as their fidelity to
Him varies.   But when these necessary limitations are
made, we find all the evidence that we can desire. And observe that these limitations are not after thoughts, designed
to account for any comparative want of success of Christianity, but are stated or involved in the very passages
which set forth Christ's claim.

What then is the evidence? It is this. In the centuries
which have followed the establishment of Christianity there
have been thousands and ten of thousands who have shown
a moral elevation above the majority of their contemporaries, and who have ascribed all their virtue to Christ.
Take the most illustrious example of all, the Apostle Paul.
We raise here no question of intellectual power or scientific
attainments; but, looking only at the one point of moral
excellence, we defy the world to produce a brighter example
of virtue than was this Apostle of the Gentiles. Whence
did he derive his excellence? He tells us again and again,
that it all came to him from Christ. On the one hand, we
find him saying, "I know that in me, that is in my flesh,
dwelleth no good thing"; but again he says, "I can do all
things through Christ, which strengtheneth me."

I cannot here adduce one ten-thousandth part of the evidence bearing on this point; but it exists, and is producible.
A most striking part of the evidence is seen in the lives of
those who, prior to faith in Christ, were openly profane or
immoral; and who, after they became believers in Him,
have become conspicuous examples of holy living. Such
instances abound. They are seen in Augustine, John
Bunyan, John Newton, and in hundreds and thousands of
living men.

Another portion of the evidence, of a very convincing kind, is within the reach of most if not all of us. We look around the circle of our own friends, of those with whom we have had the most intimate acquaintance; and we single out those whom we believe to be the best people we have ever known. We reverenced them with unstinted reverence; we gave them the whole love of our heart without mis-giving; we thought of them as persons who could never say or do anything unjust, or mean, or unkind. Admiring them, and wondering how they proved themselves superior to the temptations which overcame us, we have ventured to ask them the secret of their great strength. The answer has been always the same: "It is not in me; it is in Christ." There are tens of thousands of men and women now living on the earth, distinguished above their fellows for the purity and benevolence of their lives, who are all ready to say to Christ, with one consenting voice,—

> "Thou all our works in us hast wrought;
>   Our good is all Divine;
> The praise of every virtuous thought,
>   And righteous word, is Thine."

Is not this evidence enough that Christ shineth in the world?

Some perhaps may reply: "It is more than enough, it is superfluous. We have never doubted it, and no argument of yours can make our assurance more sure than it is already." To such I say, I rejoice in the unbroken serenity of your faith, and pray that it may never be less firm than it is now. But be not offended with me if I endeavour to strengthen weak hands and to confirm feeble knees. The argument which seems unnecessary to you may be very necessary to others; and it is also true that those are " most firmly good who best know why." Perhaps also it

is not too much to say that those who have never regarded
Christ's claim as matter of doubt or of argument can hardly
be aware of the full value of the truth which they admit, or
of the weight of obligation which such admission imposes.
It is indeed a very awful thing to reject His claims; it is a
very solemn thing to admit them, for by allowing Christ
to be the Light of the world we admit that we are bound in
reason and duty to follow Him.

II. *The duty suggested* is that of *following Christ.* If we
would follow Christ, we must make Him our supreme Lord.
He has taught us that "no man can serve two masters";
therefore if we follow Him, we acknowledge no authority
outside ourselves superior to His. If we come to Him and
say, "Lord, I will follow Thee, but——," He will have
none of our "buts." If we say, "I will follow Thee, but
not in anything which father or mother, husband or wife,
disapproves," He will not accept us. If we say, "I will
follow Thee, except in matters which imperil my life," He
will reject us. "If any man will come after Me," says
Christ, "let him deny himself, let him cease to be his own
master, and accept Me as his master." Here it was that
the rich young ruler was tried and found wanting. He
said, "What shall I do to inherit eternal life?" Christ
replied, and everything seemed to promise well until our
Lord directed the young man to do something which very
much crossed his own inclination. Then he went away
sorrowful. The test had been applied: Should the will of
Christ or his own inclinations prevail? He followed out
the desires of his own heart in opposition to Christ's commands, and could not therefore be one of His followers.

If this principle of accepting Christ as our supreme Lord
be once adopted as the rule of our own lives, then the
determination of our duty in any particular case depends
on the just application of the rule. We see at once that it

involves our accepting Christ as our supreme authority in all that affects the doctrines of religion. He has not settled every question of religion in detail; but He has settled so many, that these virtually decide all that is most important. The great doctrines of Christianity are no longer open questions. Christ in reference to them has spoken the last word; and to profess to receive Him as the Light of the world, and yet to dispute the truth of what He has thus taught, is to mock Him with a show of homage which He will never accept.

Many practical questions He has settled for us. Such are questions relating to *divorce, paying tribute to Cæsar, forgiving injuries,* and *relieving our brother in distress.* There are other cases in which it is not so easy to decide what obedience to Christ requires. We sometimes find ourselves in circumstances wherein great difficulty arises, not from an unwillingness to do right, but from an uncertainty as to what the right course is.

It is a question, for example, of change of residence, of marriage, of choice of a profession for ourselves or children. We see nothing morally wrong on the one side or on the other, and yet we feel that it is possible to make a great practical mistake, which will cloud the whole future of our lives. What does following Christ require of us in such circumstances?

We must attend to three things. (1) We must not expect God to guide us in the neglect of those means which we have for forming our own judgment, but in the use of them. You and I would sometimes like to have a revelation from heaven, or the judgment of an infallible pope (if there were such), or the direction of a father confessor so sure and authoritative that we should be saved from all the trouble of coming to a decision for ourselves. But God will not grant us this. He does not thus put a premium upon indolence, but He helps those who help themselves. We must use our own common sense. (2) We must be careful about our motives. Whatever else may seem uncertain, let us make quite sure that we *intend* to follow our Lord in what we do. (3) We must trust in Christ for the fulfilment of His promised guidance. This is following Christ; and if we do not fail Him, He will not fail in His promise to us. He will give us the "light of life."

III. This leads us to consider *the promise to Christ's follower :* he "shall have the light of life."

How does Christ give light? We receive it both directly and indirectly. A very large portion of the light of the sun comes to us as *reflected light.* Much also of that which Christ gives is reflected. We find it treasured in the Scriptures. It is given to us in sermons. Few of these do not give some light, and in hearing them we often get more than we follow. Christ gives us much light by means of His saints. Saints departed instruct us by the records of their lives and by their writings ; living saints will teach us much if we associate much with them. But, above all, Christ imparts the light of life through His own Spirit dwelling in our hearts. We do not in all things agree with the Society of Friends ; but we hold with them that there is "an inward light," and that still "the inspiration of the Almighty giveth men understanding," and we claim our own share in the gracious promise, "They shall be all taught of God."

How far may we depend upon Divine guidance in those perplexing passages of our lives to which I have referred ? To quote the words of a living preacher : "The promise must be understood with some limitation. We shall not always have all the light that we may desire ; we shall have what is necessary. We may not be able to see far before us or very far on either side of us ; but we shall have

light enough to see how to put one foot before another." [1]
But shall we be infallibly guided? Yes, if we are perfectly
faithful in fulfilling the condition. If the *following* is perfect,
the *guidance* will be so too.

There are, it may be said, many seeming exceptions. You
may say, perhaps, " I know a good man who made a serious
practical mistake, and he has suffered for it ever since."
But are you sure that in that very thing he followed Christ?
Religious men have sometimes great reverses in business
because they desert plodding for speculation; but we must
not expect that God will exempt us from the consequences
of our own folly. Others will say, " Even though I am sure
that I intended to do what was right, though I followed
Christ closely according to my best judgment, yet I made a
mistake." Are you sure that you attended to the three
things mentioned above : that you used your own best judgment, with a right motive and believing prayer for guidance?
Perhaps you may say, "I surely did." Then I answer : I feel
quite sure that you *have not suffered loss.* Your *highest*
interests have not suffered. Your motive being pure and
your conduct morally right, your moral character, your life
in the highest sense, cannot have suffered. You say, " But
I have suffered temporal loss." That may be true; but if you
have suffered through following Christ you have still done
right, done wisely; there is nothing to regret. And He
will compensate that loss by everlasting gain in the world
to come, and very probably by temporal gain, even in this
present life.

Are you a follower of Christ? If you follow Him not,
you "shall walk in darkness." To reject Christ is to incur

---

[1] We believe that these are the words of the late Rev. Samuel Coley.
The same thought is found in Cardinal Newman's well-known hymn,
" Lead, kindly Light."—EDS.

deepest condemnation : " This is the condemnation, that light is come into the world, and men loved darkness rather than light." Light from Christ has reached you, light meant for your salvation. It is in your power to quench it ; and, " if the light that is in thee be darkness, how great is that darkness!" The understanding will be darkened, the moral perceptions blunted. Often men become indifferent to various forms of vice and crime, and whether you trace the history of unfaithfulness to Christ in a man, or in a nation, you find it ever followed by a rapid moral deterioration. We cannot help thinking of the man who goes on in life persistently rejecting Christ, as a traveller from whose pathway the light is ever fading away, and on whom there will speedily fall the darkness of an endless night.

But how blessed the portion of him who follows Christ faithfully ! His path " is as the shining light." With him the light is ever growing in his understanding. His moral perceptions become more quick and keen ; his moral judgments more sure ; his whole nature more pure and strong. As purity grows, joy grows ; he has closer and still closer communion with God. There shines upon his path, there shines into his soul, more of the light which comes from heaven and leads thither. And as the light of dawn grows into the light of day, so at last the light on earth ushers him into the everlasting life and everlasting light of the heavenly world.

SELF-RENUNCIATION.

"If any man will come after Me, let him deny himself, and take up his cross daily, and follow Me."—LUKE ix. 23.

LET us imagine that soon after this gospel had been published, it had been put into the hands of a thoughtful Greek or Roman, say those of Plutarch or Seneca ; and he had been told that it recorded the life of a founder of a new system of religion. Let us further suppose that he began to study it with a serious purpose of embracing the new faith, should it commend itself to his approval. He would probably have found that to many of his inquiries the book gave no satisfactory answer. He might have asked : " If I embrace the new faith, where is the temple in which I must worship ? Of what kind is the image of the god ? What sacrifice must I offer ? Who are the priests of this religion ? " He would have found that to these inquiries the answer was : " There is no image to be honoured, no temple in which you are required to pray ; and, in the sense of your question, there is no sacrifice to be offered, no priest to present any." He would probably have thought the answer vague and unsatisfactory. But as he pursued his inquiries carefully, he would find that the book presented him with grand principles of action, and with a most wonderful and glorious example, in which these principles were embodied. We may well imagine that the attention of our supposed inquirer would be arrested with a passage like this : " If any one wishes to come after Me "—in other words, " to be one of My followers,"—" let him do thus and thus." He might have exclaimed : " Here is just what I want. Here is a precise answer to the question, What must I do in order to become an adherent of this new faith ?" And if he had well pondered, and obtained a thorough understanding of these words, he would have made no inconsiderable progress in a true knowledge of Christ's religion.

I think it is not a useless exercise of the imagination to transport ourselves in thought to the standpoint of an inquirer of the first age ; for in our conception of Christianity there is so much that is merely traditional, that it is quite wise again and again to come to the study of

Christ's words as if we read them for the first time. The advantage of doing so in the present case will, I hope, appear as we proceed.

We inquire then, as if for the first time, What must we do if we would be Christ's followers? And the answer is, we must, *first of all*, renounce ourselves.

To understand what this saying means we must rid ourselves of the false interpretation of it which has grown up in the course of ages.

1. Something has been put into our Lord's requirement which was never intended by Him. This may be made plain by an example. If you visit Italy, and pass through Tuscany, you will find in the town of Siena that a certain St. Catherine is held in high honour there, although she has died more than 500 years ago. Why is St. Catherine honoured? Of course for her great sanctity. And when you inquire what this holy woman did that was so meritorious, you are told, among other things, that she did not sleep on a feather bed, nor even on a mattress, but on a hard board, and that she had a block of wood for her pillow, and that she often rose up in the night, and scourged herself until the blood ran down in streams! Now though this may be an extreme case, there are many which approximate to it; and it illustrates a view of self-denial which has been widely spread among Papists, and Protestants also. But, according to our view, it is not in the sense meant by Christ *any self-denial at all;* and we hold, strange and paradoxical as the statement will seem, that this was a piece of *self-indulgence* on the part of St. Catherine, that it was no virtue, but a sin,—a sin of ignorance, but still a sin. Christ has never taught us by precept or example, that we should inflict pain on ourselves for the sake of inflicting pain; or that we must cross our inclinations, merely for the sake of crossing them. If our inclinations are in harmony

with the will of God, it is better to follow them than to go contrary to them ; and we cannot doubt that it was more in harmony with God's will for St. Catherine to lie on a bed, than for her to lie on a board.

Besides, our bodies are God's creatures ; and as it is a sin voluntarily and needlessly to deface any of God's creatures, it is no less a sin because the creatures which we injure happen to be our own bodies. Who gave St. Catherine authority to deface and destroy God's handiwork ? Surely, not God Himself ; and if He gave not the authority, no one could give it. She was following out her own will, not the will of God.

The error I have just dwelt upon is not one into which we ourselves are likely to fall ; but it is important to notice it, because all misrepresentations of Christianity are great hindrances to pure Christianity itself. Because the unreasonable and unscriptural view of self-denial has been held up before men's eyes and highly commended, they have been hindered from practising and seeing the true self-denial.

2. A second error subtracts from our Lord's requirement. It consists in making self-denial or self-renunciation *partial*, instead of total. By the language which we habitually use, we have obscured and reduced to the smallest proportions this idea of self-renunciation ; so that sometimes we talk of "denying ourselves," when in a very trifling matter we have set aside one inclination in order to gratify another. A man says he denies himself the pleasure of a day's excursion, in order that he may attend to his books or his business ; and all the while he would perhaps hardly venture to say that he loved what he chose one whit the less than that which he rejected. If this partial kind of self-denial were what our Lord intended, we should have to rank the sordid miser with the most self-denying of mankind. He denies himself of needful food and clothing ; but who

commends him save those who are as sordid as himself?
We all say at once that his self-denial is worthless, because
he restrains other passions in order to gratify not a nobler,
but a meaner one.

But we may go further than this. You may see a man
deny himself with a view to gratify a very noble purpose;
and yet he falls short of what is here required. He is a
philanthropist, and in order to carry out his benevolent
schemes he refuses to spend money as others do in indulg-
ing his bodily appetites; nay, more, he sacrifices ease,
leisure, the gratification of his tastes: yet he has not renounced *himself.* His temper is imperious; his self-will is
astonishing. He will carry out benevolent schemes, but it
must be in his own way. No one must thwart him or
oppose him. This man, really so admirable, and who really
accomplishes so much good, has a temper so irascible that
to approach him is like walking amongst gunpowder with a
lighted candle. You fear every moment there may be an
explosion. Or again, there is a great show of doing good,
and great sacrifices are apparently made; but when you
search the matter to the bottom, all is done that it may be
seen of men. It is clear that in these cases the apparently
self-denying man has never "renounced himself."

Let us hear again what our Lord says: "Let him deny
himself, and take up his cross daily, and follow Me." He
does not say, "Let him give up money, time, pleasure, sin;
but, Let him deny *himself,* and let him *follow Me.*" We
are not required to give up our own will in this and the
other particular, but to give it up altogether, at once, and
for ever; and this with a *purpose,* that we may follow
Christ.

And this entire renunciation of our own will is not to be
a late attainment in the Christian course, but is to take
place at the threshold of the Christian profession; so that

before we can be Christ's disciples at all, we must be prepared to make this renunciation of self in favour of Christ.

The same thing, in effect, may be stated thus : We "cannot serve God and mammon." Up to the time of becoming Christ's disciples indeed, we all do serve mammon. I do not mean of course that we all worship wealth ; but we trust in the creature, rather than in God. Disguise it as we will, we make ourselves our own centre, our own will our supreme law. When we truly pass from mammon's service to Christ's service, all is changed. We no longer expect to find happiness in the creature, except so far as the creature is subordinated to God and made a channel of His goodness. We make God our centre, not ourselves ; God's will is our law, not our own. The rule of the Christian life, to which every one who professes himself a Christian becomes pledged, is this :

Firstly, I will not follow my own natural inclination in anything great or small, when I believe the indulgence of such inclination is opposed to the will of God.

Secondly, I will not refuse to do anything demanded of me by the will of my Lord, however much it may be opposed to my own inclination.

I referred before to St. Catherine of Siena, and showed how she mistook the rule in its first branch, by opposing her own inclinations when they were *not* contrary to the will of God, and by following impulses that were contrary to His will. It is but simple justice to say that she did most nobly exemplify the second rule which we have laid down. There lived in her day, and in her own town, poor, miserable lepers, whom no one else would approach. St. Catherine visited and tended them. There were women made loathsome by disease, who were equally odious in moral character, and withal basely ungrateful. These she nursed with

H. 25

the perseverance of an unconquerable charity.　Honour for ever to the pitying love that can so act !

The touchstone is this : Self-renunciation stops short of the Christian standard always, when one human impulse is checked only to follow another equally human; it is the true Christian self-renunciation in so far as it opposes an impulse which is opposed to the will of God, in order to obey that will.　"Renounce thyself; take up the cross, in order that thou mayest follow Me."　So far as self-renunciation involves a more perfect following of Christ, it is right and good, and not one iota further.

This is the principle.　Its applications are manifold.　By this touchstone many questions of conscience are at once settled.　I am asked to go to the theatre, to the ball, to the race.　Shall I say Yes, or No?　*Yes*, if I can satisfy myself that by going I can follow Christ, but not otherwise.　Again : I am asked to contribute to a charity, to visit a sick person, to teach in a school, to take a class.　I must not say No, if Christ would have me say Yes.

Yet in truth the difficult matter is, not to *understand* our Lord's requirement, but to *comply* with it.　We may have known a great deal about self-denial in detail, in order to accomplish some object of our own choosing; but self-renunciation in the total, in order that we may fulfil the wish of another—that is above all other problems difficult. Let us ask ourselves why we ought to comply with this command ; or rather, let us first ask, Why should we not?

The first objection, perhaps, which arises in our minds is, " It is such a complete giving up of one's liberty."　True ; and it is a more absolute surrender of it than we can make to any merely human master, even the most despotic.　Yet why should we object ?　We refuse to yield up our liberty to a fellow man, because we believe that no one man has the right, or is fit absolutely to control another.　Slavery has often brought about this intolerable evil, that it has put a wise man absolutely into the power of a fool, and made the virtuous purposes of the righteous subject to the control of the ungodly. But if we resign our personal liberty in favour of Christ, no evil can result from this, but only good. No impulse of our spirits towards good will ever be checked. We shall feel the bridle holding us back, only when we are bent on what is evil. Submit yourselves to Christ and follow Him, and it will involve this : that every foolish purpose will be abandoned for a wise one ; every thought abandoned for Christ will be a worse forsaken for a better. Here then it is evident that when we are most absolutely bound to Christ, we are most free from folly and sin ; we rise higher and higher in all that constitutes the true dignity and bliss of our nature, as we sink lower and lower in humility and subjection at our Master's feet. Search as long as you may, you cannot find one solid reason for refusing Christ's requirement.

A VISIBLE CHRIST A HINDRANCE TO FAITH.

HOW must we come to Christ ? First of all, by a movement of our minds towards Him, by the movement of the invisible spirit towards the invisible Saviour.

This may seem to some a superfluous remark. They may say, "Of course we know that we must come in this way, because there is no other." But when we think of what is passing around us just now, the statement cannot be regarded as unnecessary. There is in the minds of many a craving for a visible Christ. We know that it has long been the doctrine of the Roman Catholic Church that there is a visible presence of Christ in the sacrament of the

Lord's supper ; and now there is largely held by the clergy
and others in the Church of England the doctrine of a
"real presence" in the Eucharist.   It is not always easy to
make out what is meant by this real presence; but it is
held that in some sort, in some sense, there is a bodily
presence of Christ in the Lord's supper: and men seem not
satisfied unless they can have a Christ whom they can
see, and handle, and eat !   Why should men so crave a
bodily Christ ?   Does not the history of our Lord's life on
earth show that men may have our Lord's bodily presence
with them, and yet be none the better for it ?

Probably you and I have thought what a great privilege it would have been to us to have seen Christ, and to
have heard Him whilst on earth ; and God forbid that I
should say that it would not have been a great privilege.
But the sight and hearing of Christ would not have saved
us.   It may seem strange to say so, but is it not true that
our Lord's bodily presence was in some respects a *hindrance* to faith, even in His own apostles ?   Is it not at least
plain that they had a better, a higher faith in Christ after
His ascension than they ever had before ?   Is it not remarkable that our Lord's brethren are nowhere found among
His disciples during His life, but are reckoned with them
after His ascension ?   Remember also what Christ said to
Thomas : " Thomas, because thou hast seen Me, thou hast
believed : blessed are they that have not seen, and yet have
believed " (John xx. 29).

If we had come to Christ when He was on earth, and
had sought for ourselves a miraculous cure, we should still
have had to believe not so much in the visible, as the invisible Christ,—I mean in that part of His nature that was
invisible.   This is well exemplified in the case of the woman
who touched the hem of His garment.   Think again of
blind Bartimæus.   He had never seen Christ ; probably he

had never heard His voice before he came to Him. What was Christ to Bartimæus? He was a name, a character, an invisible person. Yet he believed. So we may come to an invisible Christ and find mercy.

And as we need not a visible Christ to come to, so we do not need an audible voice to pronounce our pardon. Some will not be satisfied without words of pardon falling on the natural ear ; but if we believe we can draw nigh to an unseen Saviour, we may well believe that He can speak our pardon to our hearts in words that the soul can hear. When He said to any one in His earthly life, "Thy sins are forgiven thee," these words would have been spoken in vain, unless they had been spoken to those who already had faith in the invisible.

THE SEARCH FOR RIGHTEOUSNESS.

TRUE righteousness is a blessing above all price, be-cause above all thought. There is nothing which deserves to be sought after with so much earnestness ; and, in fact, there is nothing which men have sought after with more passionate earnestness. Whatever appearances there may be in the case of some men of total indifference as to whether they do right or wrong, I believe that if you could know all that passes in the heart of the very worst man that you ever knew or heard of, you would find that even that man sometimes desires to forsake the wrong and do the right, has some regrets that he has done wrong, and at least some hope that he may do better in the future. But if the desire of doing right is not absolutely dead in the heart of any man, as I believe it is not, in the heart of all the noblest of our race it has been a most intense passion.

To do always what is right, to avoid all that is wrong, to gain a perfect mastery over self, to have all their words and all their actions pure, in short, to be able to carry out constantly in action what their own conscience has approved as right, how eagerly have men desired this! what sacrifices have they made to attain it! Could you have stood face to face with that ancient Greek sage Socrates, and have asked him, "Socrates, what would you give in exchange for the gift of righteousness?" I have no doubt what his answer would have been. He would have said at once, "Everything I have in the world to give." Could you have proposed the same question to that very remarkable man who founded the Buddhist religion, no doubt he would have said the same.

So in subsequent ages, to attain to righteousness, men have been willing to submit to all kinds of self-inflicted torments. They have gone on long and weary pilgrimages, with bare and bleeding feet; they have fasted and prayed, until they have been almost dead.[1] In order to subdue their sinful passions men have rolled themselves in briars and thorns until the blood has flowed out in streams; they have exposed themselves to the extremest severity of cold, until life has been almost extinct.[2] To attain righteousness, ministers of state have retired from cabinets, nobles and princes have abandoned rank and wealth, and even kings have laid down their sceptres and left their thrones to others.

And yet these noble aspirations have often ended in failure; and the eager votaries have reached no further than the experience of the heathen poet who said,—

---

[1] As in the case of St. Bernard. See Mrs. Jameson's *Legends of Monastic Orders*, p. 140.

[2] As in the case of St. Benedict, *ibid.*, p. 8. See also pp. 126, 167.

"I see the right, and I approve it too ;
Abhor the wrong, and yet the wrong pursue." [1]

Or they have expressed themselves in the still more energetic
language which we find in the seventh chapter of Romans :
"What I would, that I do not ; but what I hate, that I do.
O wretched man that I am ! who shall deliver me
from the body of this death ? "

And here some one may ask, " If other men have sought
so eagerly, but yet in vain, are you sure that we may have
what you have spoken of—this complete righteousness of
heart and life ? "

Yes, I am. Those who have sought earnestly but in
vain have not sought in the way which Christ directs.
Otherwise they would have found. He who cannot lie has
promised it, when He says, "Take My yoke upon you,
and ye shall find rest unto your souls."

He promises righteousness, because He promises *rest*.
Rest in unrighteousness He could not possibly promise, for
it never exists ; and the one promise involves the other.
Besides, He gives the promise in more express terms.
"Blessed are they which do hunger and thirst after righteousness : for they shall be filled." " Filled " with what ? With
righteousness. It must be so, for no appetite is filled
unless it has that which it desires. Further, we know that
this righteousness is attainable because it has been attained.
Paul, who so strongly describes in Romans vii. the bondage
of a man struggling in vain with sin, declares in the next
chapter the glorious liberty of a man who conquers sin :
"The law of the Spirit of life in Christ Jesus hath made me
free from the law of sin and death " (Rom. viii. 2).

And there are many living witnesses to the same expe-

---

[1] " Video meliora proboque ;
Deteriora sequor."—*Ovid.*

rience, many who will tell you modestly, but most truly, that they have a constant triumph over all the temptations which once triumphed over them. And whilst they give this testimony concerning themselves, others will bear testimony as to their outward life.

I have known some men most intimately, watched them from day to day, seen them in circumstances of great trial and provocation, and yet have seen nothing in them which I thought unworthy of a follower of the Lord Jesus Christ. I know this is saying a great deal, but it is no more than I believe to be the truth.

How then is righteousness to be obtained? To gain the "treasure hid in a field," the man "selleth all that he hath." What does this mean for us? I have not overstated the excellence of the treasure—that is impossible—and I will not intentionally understate the price that we have to pay. We must sell *all*.

This means, first, that we must give up all known sin. Most men who neglect to seek the kingdom do so, not because they do not think it valuable, but because they are not willing to pay the price—to give up sin. I cannot, of course, enumerate in particular all the sins which keep men out of the kingdom. I will mention some of them.

Very often it is *dishonesty*. I cannot tell whether this is keeping any of you back, but as a faithful preacher I am bound to look at the possibility of this. Let me suppose then that I am addressing one who has acted dishonestly. You have defrauded your neighbour; or, what is the same thing, you have defrauded the revenue of your country. I say it amounts to the same thing, because, sooner or later, the Government gets all the money that it requires ; and therefore for every dishonest man who pays less than his share, some honest man pays more than his share. Whoever robs the Government as certainly robs his neighbour,

as if he took the money out of his neighbour's pocket or
till. If you have been dishonest in the past, you must give
up your dishonesty, if you want to enter the kingdom. You
must do another thing. You must *make restitution to the
utmost of your power.* There is no salvation for you without
repentance; and here there is no repentance without restitution. Three hundred years ago Hugh Latimer preached
restitution. Some people were very angry with him, and
said, "Why cannot he preach contrition, and let restitution
alone?" but Latimer said, "I must preach restitution; and
to the dishonest man I say, *Restitution or damnation.* You
may take which you please, but there must be one or the
other." His preaching was so effectual, that one of his
hearers brought him more than £500, which he had kept
back from the king's treasury, and which Latimer with his
own hands paid over—a sum probably equal to £5,000 in
the present time.

Another sin which keeps many a man out of the kingdom
is *unchastity*. You must give up that sin. I was told very
lately of a man who attended one of our chapels—alas! an
old man too—who was often seen to weep under the sermon
and in the prayer-meeting; but he did not find peace with
God. Why not? He was living in unchastity. Nothing
can be clearer than the testimony of the word of God on
this point. You will find it in the sixth chapter of the First
Epistle to the Corinthians.

The sin may be *intemperance;* it may be *worldly ambition;*
it may be a *wrathful, envious, revengeful spirit.* In a word,
whatever evil course of life you are living in, you must turn
from it with unfeigned repentance, or you will never find
your way into the kingdom.

You must give up all *your own righteousness.* How many
stumble at this stumbling-stone! They are decent, moral
people. Repentance, they think, is necessary for the pro-

fane, dishonest, intemperate, licentious, but not for them !
But no; to receive the kingdom, we must " sell all," even
our confidence in our own righteousness, and must come as
humble suppliants for mercy.

Last of all, and most difficult of all, we must renounce
ourselves. We must resolve that the rule of our life shall
be: Our own way in nothing, when it is opposed to the
way of Christ; our own will in nothing, when it is opposed
to the will of Christ. When we thus resolve, we may be
said to ' sell all that we have '; but never till then.

I am not only a preacher, I am also a witness ; and as
such I claim your credence. I would not knowingly for a
thousand pounds, or for ten thousand, or for any bribe you
could offer, say what I did not believe to be true; and I
say this : Christ has bestowed on me pardon and peace,
and power over sin, and the hope of everlasting life. And I
am but one witness amongst many. You have friends and
neighbours who will tell you the same—men whom you
know to be true, men concerning whom you know that any
one of them would sooner cut off his right hand than tell
an untruth ; and these men tell you that religion makes
them happy, that it gives them power over temptation, and
sustains them under any trouble as nothing else can ; and
that what they enjoy of the religion of Christ is more to
them than all that they have in the world beside.

And then we all agree in saying another thing : We who
enjoy this happiness in religion do not look upon ourselves
as the special favourites of heaven. " God is no respecter
of persons." And just as we are sure that God has blessed
us, we are sure that He is quite willing to give what He has
given to us to every one of you.

FALLING—RETURNING.

"O Israel, return unto the Lord thy God ; for thou hast fallen by
thine iniquity."—Hos. xiv. 1.

THERE is a very instructive parallel between the
apostasy of ancient Israel and that widespread apostasy which has taken place in the Church of Christ in these
later ages. You will remember what was the origin of the
separate kingdom of Israel. It was founded by the rebel
king Jeroboam, who, among all the kings, obtained the bad
pre-eminence of the man "who made Israel to sin." The
kingdom which he set up had in it from the first the elements of its own decay ; because Jeroboam, preferring State
policy to true religion, set up in Bethel and in Dan the
golden calves, in order that his subjects might not go and
worship at Jerusalem, the capital of the rival kingdom.
Jeroboam the son of Nebat made Israel to sin, because he
corrupted the faith of the people. His sin did not consist
precisely in trying to induce the people to give up the
worship of Jehovah, but he materialized it, introducing the
worship of images unauthorized by, indeed directly contrary to, the law of God. The faith of the people was
transferred from the invisible to the visible, and their worship therefore became far less spiritual, far more sensuous.
And so it has happened since. The great apostasy which
we call the Papacy, now reviving in England in the form of
ritualism, has had a like origin. Our objection to ritualism
is not a senseless outcry of bigotry. Why do we object to
it ? Because it overlays the pure, spiritual system of Christianity with unauthorized ceremonies of man's addition. It
makes religion less a matter of faith, and more a matter of
sense ; it finds more work for the body, but less for the
soul.

The great evil of this system is, that it tends to immorality; it has produced, and will produce, the monstrous result of a religion divorced from morality. Do you ask the proofs? I point to the history of France, of Spain, of Italy. I point you to Louis XIV., and to others like him.

Hear the words of John Milton on this matter. " They began to draw down all the Divine intercourse betwixt God and the soul, yea, the very shape of God Himself, into an exterior and bodily form, urgently pretending a necessity and obligement of joining the body in a formal reverence, and worship circumscribed. They hallowed it, they fumed it, they sprinkled it, they bedecked it— not in robes of pure innocence, but of pure linen, with other deformed and fantastic dresses, in palls and mitres, gold, and gewgaws fetched from Aaron's old wardrobe or the Flamen's vestry. Then was the priest set to con his motions and his postures, his liturgies and his lurries,[1] till the soul, by this means of overbodying herself, given up justly to fleshly delights, bated her wing apace downwards; and finding the ease she had from her visible and sensuous colleague, the body, in performance of religious duties, her pinions now broken and flagging, shifted off from herself the labour of high soaring any more, forgot her heavenly flight, and left the dull and droiling[2] carcase to plod on in the old road and drudging trade of outward conformity." [3]

This is how the faith of men now is shaken and corrupted. It may have been the case with some of you. I address myself to all who are conscious of having departed from God, whether secretly in the heart, or outwardly in the life; to those who, looking back upon their religious life at some

---

[1] Confused throng of words, gabblings.
[2] Drudging, grovelling.
[3] Milton : *Of Reformation in England*, bk. i.

former period, are obliged sadly to acknowledge, " It was better with me then than it is now."

There was once a time when your faith in God was simple and unshaken. But you listened to and cherished the doubts which arose in your own mind, or the doubts suggested by others—in books, or in conversation—until you had no longer the simple and strong faith that you had before. The realities of the invisible world, the God and Father reconciled in heaven, the great High Priest above ever pleading your cause, the witnessing, sanctifying in-dwelling Spirit, the endless and infinite bliss of the saved, the endless and infinite misery of the lost, became less vivid realities to you than they once were, until at last you some-times doubted whether they were realities at all. As a result of this, you took less delight in a worship purely spiritual. The intercourse of your soul with God in the silence and retirement of your own chamber became less welcome. Prayer—true prayer, communion with God— can only live in an atmosphere of faith. Unbelief chills and kills it.

Yet many a one in whom spiritual religion declines is unwilling to give up religion altogether. He changes his religion. It becomes less spiritual and more formal. It has less to do with the invisible, more with the visible. The man betakes himself to ritualism. The body is set to " con its motions and its postures," and there is a constant effort made to shift the duties of the soul to the body, until the strong language of Milton becomes true again.

There is often but a short step from a sensuous religion to a sensual life. If the senses are to be so much gratified at church, why not at home? The man wishes to live the kind of life ascribed to the rich man in the gospel. He would fain if he could—and if he can he does—' fare sumptuously every day.' Once he cared very little about the pleasures of the table; now he cares about them a great deal, and the questions, "What shall we eat? what shall we drink? wherewithal shall we be clothed?" have for him an absorbing interest. In the first instance, it may be, he keeps within moderate bounds. He indulges in what John Wesley calls "an elegant kind of sensuality." But even an elegant sensuality is quite enough to drown all spirituality of mind, and to make earnest religion impossible. But in too many instances of spiritual decline, the bounds of even worldly and conventional decorum are passed, and the man proceeds from elegant to gross sensuality. He becomes a drunkard.

When he falls so low as this, you will generally see that the whole moral strength is undermined. He is no longer the upright man of business that he once was; the keen sense of honour is gone. He is capable of taking a mean advantage of his neighbour. He can overreach and cheat. He loses his character for honesty. He loses character with the men of the world who profess no religion.

Sometimes what is still worse follows. He proves unfaithful to his marriage vows; he loses the confidence of his wife, and the respect of his children. At last he loses all respect for himself. Where is he now? He is a fallen man: fallen from grace, fallen from God, degraded, despised, miserable.

Spiritual decline sometimes takes another course. It manifests itself not in sensuality, but in intense worldliness. A man cannot divest himself of those elements of his nature which, when rightly used, make him a religious man. Man must trust, and he must worship; and if he withdraw his confidence from God, he will assuredly place it in some of God's creatures. Thus Comte, the great apostle of modern atheism, worshipped a woman. We find John Stuart Mill speaking of his wife in language which we use respecting

God, and telling us that after her death her memory served him for *a religion.*

Men often withdraw their confidence in God to place it in the great ones of this world. Israel ceased to trust in God, but put confidence in the great king of Assyria, and said, "Asshur shall save us." You know what was the issue of that. The king of Assyria was first the helper of Israel, then his master, then his destroyer.

So it happens now. A man is tempted to depart from God by the hope of some great alliance. He thinks if he can only make my Lord So-and-so, or Mr. Such-a-one, his friend, once gain the *entrée* to his house and be accepted by him as an acknowledged friend, his fortune will be made, and his happiness secure. What is the result? It often happens that he who tries to curry favour with the great does not succeed. After all his efforts the great man shows that he despises him, perhaps uses him as his tool for a time, and then casts him off.

At other times he does succeed in attaching himself to the great man's train, but his very success is his ruin. His noble friend leads him into expenses beyond his means, perhaps teaches him follies and vices that he knew not before, and leaves him at last when he most needs his help. And the man who succeeds best with his ambitious schemes always finds that whatever he gains by them, there are two things wanting—contentment and self-respect. And yet there are those who for a great man's favour forsake religion, lose the society of their best friends, lose peace of mind, and it is to be feared, too often, heaven itself.

There are others however who are far too independent to act in this way. These say to the work of their own hands, "Ye are our gods." For the essence of idolatry is to give to the creature the honour, the love, the trust due to God. With many men the supreme deity is mammon.

They seek their happiness in the possession and increase of wealth; and though often disappointed, they still hope to find the satisfaction which the soul craves in 'the abundance of the things which they possess.' And how faithfully they serve their god! They rise early, and late take rest, and eat the bread of carefulness, in the service of mammon. For their god they make many sacrifices. They not only sacrifice ease, but family and social enjoyments also; so that when away from business their minds are still full of it, and they are often like strangers in their own homes. They sacrifice health and strength, and even life; and men die premature deaths because they are too eager to obtain the means of living. In the pursuit of wealth men sacrifice honour. They lend their names and use their efforts in schemes of fraud, intended to enrich their promoters and to bring ruin on all who are their dupes. And how deplorable it is when we see one who was once a true worshipper of God, become a worshipper of mammon; so that he who once delighted in the service of God, and found a pure and exquisite joy in secret intercourse with his Maker, now knows no more ecstatic bliss than the sudden rise of some stock in which he has largely invested, or when he discovers, on making up his books, that he has a large balance on the right side!

Some of you may think perhaps that I have not described your particular case. Perhaps not; yet your own conscience tells you only too truly, that you *have* departed from God; and it tells you another thing: you are not satisfied, you are not happy.

What then are you to do? Is there no remedy? There is one, and only one. The cause of all man's misery lies in one thing—*departure from God*. The cure may be expressed in one word, *Return*.

How shall we return?

First of all, you must *return to faith.* Once a believer, you are now a doubter. You must recover your faith. This may seem to you a thing very difficult, perhaps impossible. Certainly it is not impossible. There are many instances on record of men who had given up all faith in the Bible and in God, who afterwards returned to a simple, child-like trust.

"But," you say, "it will be a long and tedious process. It will require much thought and much time." And so it may; but remember, this is a case in which life is at stake. If you were suffering from some bodily disease which threatened your life, you would spare neither pains nor money to obtain a cure; and now the welfare of your immortal soul is concerned. 'Without faith it is impossible to please God.' You will forfeit your immortal life, if you do not recover your faith. Retrace your steps. You have listened to the suggestions of unbelief; listen to the arguments of faith. You have read books on the one side; surely you can read books on the other. You have associated yourself with unbelievers; go now to godly and experienced neighbours. They have reasons which satisfy them; these may also satisfy you. By all means in your power seek to get back your forfeited faith.

Next, go to God with humble *confession of sin.* "Take with you words, and return." I advise not confession to man, but I earnestly urge confession to God. Let it be appropriate and full. If seriously, and in the presence of our Maker, we particularize our sins, not only recalling them to our thoughts, but expressing them in words, they will appear to us more hateful than before; and our resolve to forsake them will be greatly strengthened.

Plead for *present, conscious pardon.* Here it is that so many of those who are sincerely penitent utterly fail. There are some who think that evangelical preachers are very narrow-minded in insisting so much upon this one point. They blame us because we do not preach morality more, and sometimes insinuate that we are indifferent to morality. But we are not so ignorant of our proper business as such people suppose.

With the great majority the chief lack is not ignorance of what is right, but power to perform it. Now if a man only laments and confesses his sins, and goes no further, he will not gain power over sin. He will on Monday commit the very sin which he confessed and sincerely deplored on Sunday. But let him seek God's forgiveness; let him ask, expecting to receive; let him trust in Christ for present pardon, and plead with God until he receives assurance of forgiveness, and the blessed Spirit bears witness with his spirit that he is a child of God : that man will *not* go on the Monday and commit the sins pardoned on the Sunday. He will have a hatred of sin he never had before, a love of God and of holiness, a power to refuse evil and a power to do good, that he never had before. He loves God because God first loved him. He knows himself His child, and he cannot sin, because the seed of God remaineth in him.

Receiving God's pardon, *promise to consecrate your life to Him.* Returning Israel is instructed to say, "So will we render the calves of our lips." Under the old covenant calves or young bullocks were brought in sacrifice. The prophet now says, "Let your lips be the calves of your offering ; let your lips be consecrated to God."

Why the "lips"? Because by our lips we make confession of our allegiance to God. You must confess Christ your Master before men. Others have been witnesses of your rebellion ; they must be witnesses of your return to allegiance. And if you are really willing and resolved to be Christ's servant, the sooner you confess Him openly

before men the better. In some way which the world will
not mistake, which Christ will accept, say, " I am on the
Lord's side."

At the same time *renounce the world.* Israel was instructed
to say, " Asshur shall not save us ; we will not ride upon
horses : neither will we say any more to the work of our
hands, Ye are our gods. That is to say, " Assyria shall not
be our trust ; we will not rely upon a great cavalry force to
protect us ; we will not trust in the things that our own
hands have made."

Translate this into language appropriate to your own
case. Say unto God : " I am Thy servant, Thou art my
Lord; I am Thy child, Thou art my Father. Thou shalt be
my Friend for ever. I will not henceforth trust in the great
ones of the earth. I will not regard the favour and society
of the rich and great as essential to my happiness. I will
not trust in my riches, in anything that I now have or may
hope to have. I will not make a god of any friend, or any
earthly possession. I will seek, as I hope to find, my happiness in Thee. Thou art the refuge of every distressed
soul. ' In Thee the fatherless findeth mercy.' To Thee
will I betake myself when I am in trouble. The temporal
good, the friends that Thou givest, I will receive as Thy
gifts. I give Thee thanks for all. I will enjoy them in
Thee and for Thee ; and every enjoyment and pursuit
which is inconsistent with loving and serving Thee I will
henceforth and for ever reject."

In this spirit return unto God. And then you will hear
the comforting voice speaking to your heart : " I will heal
their backsliding, I will love them freely : for mine anger
is turned away from him."

Will you not return ? Remember the happy days which
you once had, when your heart was full of joy, full to over-
flowing. It seemed to you then that you were as happy as

you could live, and you could have sung with full sympathy
the rejoicing lines of Charles Wesley :

> "How happy are they
> Who the Saviour obey,
> And have laid up their treasure above!
> Tongue cannot express
> The sweet comfort and peace
> Of a soul in its earliest love."

Have you ever known anything to compensate for the
loss of this, ever had so pure and satisfying a joy? I
know you have not. When you entered into the liberty of
God's children, many rejoiced in that day. There was joy
in your father's house on earth, joy in the house of your
Father above. There was joy in the Church. How has
that joy been clouded since ! How many have mourned
your spiritual decline ! You remember perhaps when your
father, your mother, or brother died, the one deep trouble
of that departing soul was that you had wandered from God ;
and the last, most solemn, anxious charge given you was,
that you would return. Perhaps you gave the promise to
return without delay. Yet you have delayed. Think then
that my voice is to you as the voice of departed parent, wife,
husband, friend : " Return." That voice now speaks to
your conscience from the silent grave ; but there is a voice
which speaks to you from heaven. Your Saviour calls you
back. By His life of mercy, by His agony and bloody
sweat, by His cross and passion, by His death and burial,
by His ascension into heaven, by the sure promise of His
second coming to judgment, now through His Spirit in
your heart, He is saying, " O wanderer, return ! " See that
ye refuse not Him that speaketh from heaven.

INSTANTANEOUS PARDON.

IT is sometimes said that it is unreasonable to look upon the blessing of pardon as the gift of a moment. I say to you, It is unreasonable to look upon it in any other light. I appeal to you who are parents : when your children have incurred your displeasure, and have come to you for forgiveness, could you think of the child standing before you half-pardoned and half-condemned? Could you think of the work of pardon as occupying any time, as half-finished this moment, wholly finished the next? I believe you cannot. Pardon is an indivisible act. Observe, I do not say that we can always *tell the precise moment* when we first obtained mercy, or that it is at all necessary to our salvation that we should know this.

SELF-SACRIFICE IN MAN HAS ITS PATTERN IN GOD.

THE death of Christ was above all things a manifestation of God's love to man. "Herein is love, not that we loved God, but that He loved us, and sent His Son to be the propitiation for our sins." No words can set forth the infinitude of love here displayed ; but we aid our very feeble and inadequate conceptions of it when we remember that the love of God displayed in the gift of His Son is the pattern and source of all that is noblest in human nature and in human conduct.

What are the noblest deeds ever done by men? They are deeds of self-sacrificing love. Think of the life of Paul himself ; think of the noble host of confessors of Christ in former ages, who in the service of Christ and man endured privations and sufferings and the loss of life itself. Think of the noble men and women of our own time who have given themselves and are giving themselves to the service of Christ. Think of missionaries like Brainerd and Henry Martyn, and Carey, and Marshman, John Williams, John Hunt, Patteson, and others. Are there any deeds ever done which call forth higher, juster praise, or more enthusiastic admiration, than self-sacrificing zeal for the good of others?

Now when in other cases we see a noble character in man, when we see noble deeds done by him, we surely conclude that this must have its pattern in God. And strange indeed would it be if we could trace up to God every other feature of nobleness, but self-sacrificing love should not find its original in Him. But the doctrine of atonement shows the pattern of this in God, and not only the pattern, but the producing motive. Ask the noblest workers living—men and women who are devoting themselves to the good of others without stint, leading the noblest lives given to man on earth. Ask them, What leads you to act in this way? And we are certain what answer they will give. They will say, one and all, "The love of Christ constraineth us."

"BAGS WHICH WAX NOT OLD." [1]

"Provide yourselves bags which wax not old."—LUKE xii. 33.

WHERE are such bags to be found? Not in this world, because everything that is of earthly make is subject to decay, and for the things imperishable we must look to the world that is to come.

We cannot fulfil this precept of Christ, we cannot set

---

[1] A sermon preached at the missionary anniversary at York, April 16th, 1880.

ourselves in good earnest to fulfil it, unless we have a firm belief in a future state of being. It is of great practical moment to attain to what we may call a *working faith*, that is, a belief which will regulate our daily conduct in life.

If on this occasion I thought I was addressing men who had not made their election sure, it would be my duty to urge you to secure this title and to point out the way. But I will assume that you have already made your peace with God, and have a well-founded hope of everlasting life, and I now ask you to consider the question, How is it possible to increase the heavenly treasure? How may we whilst living on earth augment that weight of glory which, as we trust, will be ours when we depart hence? Because it is a plain doctrine of Scripture that those who enter into life will not be rewarded equally, but our place in the kingdom, and the measure of our bliss, will depend on our conduct here. The servant who received the one pound and by trading made it into ten, was made ruler over ten cities; and he who made his pound into five, had authority over five cities. And amongst the very latest recorded utterances of our Saviour we read, in the last chapter of the Revelation, "Behold, I come quickly; and My reward is with Me, to give every man according as his work shall be."

Possibly some one may say: "I am not ambitious. If I can only get inside heaven's gate, and occupy the lowest place there, that will be recompense enough for me." But this, which may sound like the language of humility, is in reality the utterance of slothfulness and cowardice; and to give way to the spirit which it expresses is highly dangerous, because faithful, earnest service for Christ is not an optional matter, and if we deliberately aim at less than the Master holds out to us, we are in danger of losing all.

How then may we increase the heavenly treasure ?

1. By the improvement of our personal character.

2. By using our earthly possessions for the spiritual good and salvation of others.

1. *By the improvement of our personal character.*

We are all familiar with the words, " We brought nothing into this world, and it is certain we can carry nothing out." These words are true in one sense, not in another. They are true as to all earthly possessions. The friend of a Scotch minister one day called on him, and told him with much excitement that a neighbour of theirs had just died and left £120,000 ! The minister received the announcement very coolly, and his informant was disappointed that he had not produced a stronger impression. He said to the minister, "You don't seem surprised." " No," replied the other, "I am not. Had you told me that the man had taken all that money with him to the other world, I should have been very much astonished ; but as you only said that he had left it behind him, I am not at all astonished, for men are doing the like every day." The millionaire the day after his death is poorer in earthly possessions than the workhouse pauper.

But in another sense, the words are not true. There is one thing that we shall carry with us out of the world, and which we shall possess for ever, and that will be *our personal character*. And the character which we shall have at the hour of death will be the net result of all the events and experiences of life.

During the past week we have been engaged in our daily duties, we have had various experiences of sorrow and joy. We have passed through these with a certain disposition of mind, acting on certain principles, exhibiting a certain character. It may be that we have acted on Christian principles. We have been tempted, and have overcome temptation. In the transaction of business and in all the affairs of life we have acted in the presence of others in a way which has been worthy of our profession and has brought honour to Christ. Or something very different perhaps is true. We have been tempted, and have yielded to temptation ; we have acted in such a way as to bring discredit to religion. In a religious point of view, we have either done well or ill ; and the net result of the week's transactions, as found in ourselves, is, that we are morally the better, or morally the worse than we were a week ago ; and this net moral result will enter as a factor into the whole future of our lives, making the path of virtue henceforth more easy, or more difficult. When we come to the end of life there will be the summing up of the net results of the days and years of our lives, and the total will be found in that moral character which we shall have at death ; and that character will determine our everlasting destiny. It will settle the question what we are fit for, what is to be done with us,— whether we are to be admitted into the kingdom of glory, or whether we are fit only to be cast out ; and if admitted into life, whether we are to take a higher or a lower place in the heavenly kingdom.

Considerations of this kind enable us to form a standard by which to judge of our true success in life. Success in the very highest sense depends not on whether we are improving our circumstances, but whether we are growing better ourselves. And judging by this standard, how different will be our conclusions from those of the world generally ! For example, here is a man who twenty years ago was poor. To-day he is rich, and how the world praises him ! How everybody speaks of him as an exceedingly prosperous and successful man ! and, according to a merely worldly standard, this is quite true. But judging by the

standard of everlasting truth and righteousness, how different is our verdict !   The man is richer in worldly goods,
but poorer in his souL   Twenty years ago he had much
zeal for God's glory ; to-day he has little or none.   Then
he delighted in communion with God, and in fellowship
with God's people ; now he does not.   Then he was self-
denying and generous; now he is self-pleasing and nig-
gardly.   So that whilst richer in worldly possessions, he is
poorer in spiritual enjoyment, in all that constitutes the true
worth and dignity and happiness of man.   He has more
treasure laid up on earth, and far less laid up in heaven.
He is not a man to be praised, but a man to be pitied.

Take an opposite example.   A man who twenty years
ago was rich, to-day is poor, at least, in comparison with
what he was then.   He is nothing the better for being poor,
and there are some melancholy cases where a man's spiritual
and temporal decline go together, and he becomes poorer
for both worlds at once.   But in other cases great temporal
losses are so borne that they turn into everlasting gains.

Some years ago a gentleman in Manchester was sitting at
his breakfast table opening his letters, and he came to one
which made it perfectly clear to him that he had sustained
a loss of £30,000.   The calamity was great, and wholly
unexpected ; but that gentleman said afterwards that the
loss of this money was one of the greatest blessings that
ever came to him.   Up to this time he had regarded his
increasing wealth as the simple result of his own skill and
prudence.   Now he saw that God had given him all he had,
and that what God had given He could easily take away.
From that day he held worldly wealth with a lighter grasp,
and began to give away his money more freely than he had
ever done before.   Who can doubt that that loss turned
into endless gain ?

But let no one suppose from what has now been said that

in order to lay up much treasure in heaven we must have
the control of much worldly wealth.   Hard would be the
case of many of God's servants if this were so.   But the
truth is, that our heavenly reward depends, not on how much
we have, but on the way in which we use it ; not on the
various trials we suffer, but on how we pass through them.

If you have regard only to the position in life and daily
occupations of many of God's saints, life in their case must
appear a very poor thing indeed.   Look at the daily work
of many good Christian women.   Their time is spent in
spinning, or weaving, or in some sort of household work,
in cleaning rooms and preparing the daily meal ; spent in
doing what is speedily undone, and on things which perish
in the using.

Look also on the employment of many godly men.
They plough and reap, they buy and sell and get gain ; yet
after the labour of years, to what can they point of a
permanent kind and say, "That is the fruit of my labours
during these years"?   Life in their case would be a very
poor thing if this were the whole account of the matter.
But in the case of God's servants, this never is the whole
account.   There is much more to be said.   If we live in
the true spirit of Christ's religion, the whole of our earthly
care will be a heavenly discipline.   It is possible so to pass
through the common duties of life, with so entire and cheerful a resignation to God's will, with so constant and sincere
a desire to please and glorify Him in all things, that the
commonest toil may become heavenly service, and every
event of life contribute to perfect in us that character of
goodness which we shall have for ever.

The work wrought out by the Spirit in the character of
many of God's children may be compared to the work of a
great artist on one of his masterpieces.   A painter sometimes spends several years over a single picture.   And if

you went from time to time to that artist's studio, you would probably be much impressed with two things. First, with the cheapness of the materials which he employs. We see a piece of canvas, a few brushes and paints ; cheap in themselves, but when placed in the hands of a man of genius attaining a priceless value. Then you would be struck with another thing. If you visited the studio at the interval of a month, you would be ready to say : " How slowly the man works ! He has done nothing since I was here last ! " But the artist knows better. He has corrected one line here and another there, altered a light here and a shadow there. He works slowly, but he works surely ; and he will work on until he has produced a thing of perfect beauty, which will be placed in some glorious gallery, where it will last for centuries and delight the eyes of millions of men.

So it is in the life of one of God's saints under the transforming power of the Spirit of God. How poor often the substratum of natural character on which He works ! How varied, and often how seemingly trivial, are the incidents in our lives which He employs ! At one time it is an arduous labour, in which we put forth all the energies of body and mind ; another time it is an act of kindness which costs us very little, but is worth much to him to whom it is shown. Sometimes it is enforced rest, which comes very unwelcome, but is patiently submitted to ; now it is a deep sorrow, and now an exultant joy ; now an honour well deserved and generously given, now it is a reproach wholly undeserved and cruelly cast on us. But the Spirit of God, that Divine Artist, if we may reverently call Him so, makes use of all—of our labour and rest, and sorrow and joy, and honour and dishonour ; and He will work on until He has finished His work, and moulded it at last into a thing of perfect moral beauty, which, when finished, shall be transported to the palace of the King of kings, and, bright with the radiance of a heavenly virtue, shall shine as the stars for ever and ever.

2. A second way in which we can lay up treasure in heaven is *by benefiting others.*

The verse of which my text is a part shows that, by using our worldly wealth for the benefit of others, we may increase our own heavenly treasure. We do so, because we never seek to benefit others from pure Christian motives but we do good to ourselves, we make ourselves better for evermore. But, further than this, we may so use our worldly possessions as to contribute to the spiritual good and salvation of other men ; and these saved men, owing their salvation directly or indirectly to us, will be a cause of rejoicing to us for evermore.

We contribute to such blessed results, for example, by building places of worship.

More than 1,250 years ago, this famous city of York was a mission station. The name of the missionary was Paulinus ; and where the Minster now stands he baptized King Edwin, and built his first wooden church. How insignificant the cost of that church would seem to us now! Yet that was the beginning of a good work which has lasted till this day ; and the work of Methodism in this city, and that done by the missionaries whom you have sent forth from this very place, connects itself in an unbroken chain of sequence with the work of Paulinus twelve centuries and a half ago.[1]

When the house in which we worship was built, a good work was done, the blessed results of which will never end. Some of you in the building, or in the maintenance of this

---

[1] The Rev. Dr. Lyth in his *Glimpses of Early Methodism in York* (pub. 1885) gives the names of no less than nineteen Wesleyan missionaries who have gone out from that city.—EDS.

place, have made sacrifices. They were perhaps not great in the eyes of others, but they were sacrifices to you. But when you have worshipped here, and the Master Himself has graciously manifested His presence; when you have felt constrained to say, "Master, it is good to be here, because Thou art here"; when, best of all, the Master has repeated here in a spiritual sense His deeds of power, and the blind eyes have been opened and the deaf ears unstopped, and men have been raised from the death of sin to the new life of righteousness, and you have witnessed the beginnings of that new spiritual life which shall last for ever;—you have not then regretted the sacrifices which you had made, but have rejoiced that you were led to consecrate wealth in such a way as would contribute to results so blessed and permanent as these.

To-day God gives you the opportunity of putting money into bags which wax not old. You are asked to contribute to the funds of a society which, in common with other missionary societies, is doing the noblest work which is ever done in the world. And what is done by the agents whom you send out and support is, in a secondary but very important sense, done by *you*. What are they doing? They are carrying to others that gospel which has brought peace and joy to us. They are kindling the light of life among those who "sit in darkness and in the shadow of death." They are the means of bringing peace to troubled consciences, of raising men from the deep moral degradation of heathenism to the purity of Christian life. They are founding Christian Churches and schools, diffusing a pure and sanctifying literature, leading to the establishment of happy Christian homes, where husband and wife, parents and children will be blessed with the sanctifying influences which you have known, and will have all their joys heightened and all their sorrows soothed by the blessings

and consolations of the gospel of Christ And the good
work done to-day will never cease.   It will perpetuate itself
through generation after generation, down to the end of time.
When you walk around your stately Minster, your eyes
behold glorious work done by hands which mouldered into
dust six centuries ago.   But the work remains ; and long
may it remain !   You can do a work more lasting.   You
can help to gather in the living stones of that spiritual
temple which will outlast the world.

What then shall we do ?   Here is this precept of Christ :
" Sell that ye have and give alms ; provide yourselves bags
which wax not old, a treasure in the heavens that faileth
not, where no thief approacheth, neither moth corrupteth."
This is Christ's precept : what will you do with it ?   Some
people treat a saying of Christ after this fashion : they
say, " The language of this verse is highly figurative, somewhat parabolical."   And when they have gone through this
piece of criticism, they seem to think they have done with
the whole matter.   I grant that the language of this verse is
highly figurative, somewhat parabolical if you like.   Still, it
means something.   It means something to you, if you are a
professed servant of Jesus Christ.

I am not going to suggest what you ought to give.   I
will not even suggest any scale of giving.   But I say this :
You must take care to satisfy the Master.   You have a
certain amount of income.   Some of this you must spend
for your own maintenance and for those dependent on you.
Some of it you must in prudence reserve for the future, for
you and yours.   All this is unquestionable.   What will you
do with the remainder?   You can do one of two things.
You can use it selfishly, or you can use it Christianly.   You
may use it to feed your vanity, to gratify your pride, to build
a mansion, and fill it with rich furniture, to buy costly books
and pictures, and in other ways to gratify self, with small

regard to the claims of Christ, and with little or no pity for the millions of men who are perishing for lack of knowledge. And what will be the result? By keeping back from Christ what He would have you consecrate to His cause, you will degrade your own souls, and be continually sinking lower and lower in the judgment of God and of all good men. If your self-love and self-indulgence do not shut you out of the kingdom, you will not have the place there that you might have had, if you had been more faithful to the trust committed to your care.

But I hope better things of those to whom I speak. I may without flattery say to you as Paul says to the Corinthians, I know your forwardness in this matter. Do as you have done; but where possible, do more abundantly. What will be the result? Every act of sacrifice will bring a present reward in increased nobility of soul and vigour of spiritual life. It will bring a permanent reward in making you more capable of noble living through all the time to come. The good that you will do to others you cannot fully know. But in lands far remote from this, among peoples you have never seen, the happy results will be found in the lives of converted heathen, in their blessed and triumphant deaths, and in their endless happiness in the life to come.

We have to choose between using wealth for self and using it for Christ. You can take which course you please. But remember, life centred in self and devoted to self is full of unrest and disappointment, and never separable from meanness: but life centred in Christ is full of peace and joy; it is a life of growing dignity and moral power, of usefulness and blessing, and a life for Christ on earth will issue in a life with Christ for ever.

"WHATSOEVER HE DOETH SHALL PROSPER."

THESE words complete the picture given in the first Psalm of the happiness of the good man.

Some will be ready to dispute and deny the truth of this text. But we hold it to be absolutely true. What, it will be said, does everything that every good man does prosper? Nay, I have not said that; the text does not say it. This psalm is not a description of every good man, but of *the* good man—the ideal, the model good man. The character here described is without a flaw; it is absolutely perfect. You may say then, What is the use of it to us, seeing we are none of us absolutely perfect? Much every way. *The promises of Scripture are given not so much to individuals as to character;* and this promise belongs to you and me so far as we possess the character, and no farther. Read the history of David. Can we say that everything that David did "prospered"? Certainly not. What then? Did this promise fail David? Nay, but David failed to correspond to this character. All that he did consistently with this character prospered; but in the things in which he departed therefrom he did not prosper. Well, some will say, after all, it seems to us that there are some religious men, some who really seem to be good men, who never prosper. The explanations are many. The man is a good man now, but he is paying the penalty of the sins of his youth. Or it may be that he is a good man in many respects, but he has one serious fault; and that very fault stands in the way of his prosperity. He is perhaps a good man in every respect *but one;* but that is a serious fault, he is somewhat lazy. Or perhaps he has tried to grow rich by speculation, and has lost in an hour of folly the honest gains of many years. In other words, he

H.   27

has not been true to his own character; and he pays the just penalty.

It may be, however, that you are mistaken. The man is getting on in reality, but not according to your standard. He is not rapidly growing rich; and perhaps for this very reason, that his conscience will not allow him to use those means of growing rich which other men less scrupulous adopt. The man is inflexibly honest. His integrity is beyond all suspicion, and as the fruit of this he has a world of happiness in the very consciousness of integrity, which he would be a fool to barter for the wealth of the richest man living. He "prospers." He rules well his own house; his children love him, his neighbours respect him; he is a counsellor and a comforter of many. He knows that he is the child of a King and the inheritor of a kingdom, and that he is travelling on to an eternal house above. When he dies he may not be able to leave his children much wealth, but he will leave them what is far better—a memory which they will reverence, an example which they may safely follow, and a heritage of love which many will show them for their father's sake. Say not of such a man that he does not prosper. Yes, it is true, and always true of the good man here described, "whatsoever he doeth shall prosper."

DAILY FOOD.[1]

THE happiness of religion is further seen in this, that it purifies and therefore heightens all the common joys of life.

---

[1] From a sermon on Prov. iii. 17.

It gives us greater enjoyment of *our daily food.* Some of you perhaps may be surprised that I should refer to such a topic. But the partaking of daily food is to none a matter of indifference. Remember the large amount of men's time spent in procuring food, or in obtaining the wages that buy food ; think of the amount of time and care spent in the preparation of the daily meals ; think of the time spent in actually partaking of them ;—and you will see that it is mere affectation and hypocrisy for any one to pretend that his daily food is a matter of little concern to him. Besides, have you never noticed that in the record given in the Acts of the Apostles of the results of the day of Pentecost, it is said of the new converts that "they did eat their meat with gladness and singleness of heart"? It may be said that men enjoy their food very much without religion. That is true, but there are often many drawbacks. Religion saves from the evils of intemperance, which so often mar and ruin the happiness of households. Besides, if you study the Book of Proverbs, you find that the wise king had seen what many others have seen since, that the enjoyment of a bountiful feast may be destroyed by want of harmony amongst the household : " Better is a dry morsel, and quietness therewith, than an house full of sacrifices with strife." Religion blesses our daily life by causing men to be of one mind in a house, by banishing the sin and folly and misery of intemperance, by enabling us to take our daily food apart from the burden of sin and guilt and care, by giving peaceful consciences and happy countenances, and by uniting all our innocent earthly enjoyments with thoughts of God and hopes of endless life.

THE SLUGGARD.

"The sluggard will not plough by reason of the cold ; therefore shall he beg in harvest, and have nothing."—PROV. xx. 4.

THERE were many sluggards in the days of Solomon, as, alas ! there are many now. This class of persons attracted the special attention of the wise king. He closely observed their character, watched their course, saw the evil results of their slothfulness, and has left his observations for our instruction, treasured up for ever in the pages of inspiration.

I propose to call your attention, first of all, to the particular sluggard mentioned in the text, and then to some others who are like him.

The sluggard mentioned here is a ploughman, at least he ought to be one. He would have been, if he had not been a sluggard. The picture of the text is in outline. A little exercise of the imagination will enable us to fill it up. You may be sure that in the early morning, after his more industrious neighbour has risen, has driven his team afield, and has done a good stroke towards his day's work, the sluggard is still upon his bed. And if any one should go to him to rouse him from his slumbers, he resents as an injury what was meant for a kindness. His language is, "Yet a little sleep, a little slumber, a little folding of the hands to sleep" (Prov. vi. 10). Or to give it in the language of Dr. Watts, with which so many children are familiar :

"'Tis the voice of the sluggard ; I heard him complain,
'You have waked me too soon, I must slumber again.'"

But now, as the sun rises in the heavens, even the sluggard is at last ashamed to lie on his bed any longer. He rises, and goes to the door of his house to see what weather it is without, and he finds that it is very cold. His resolution to go to plough fails him. He says within himself, "I will not go to plough to-day; I will wait till to-morrow; perhaps then it will not be quite so cold." And so, instead of going forth to plough his field, he seats himself by the fireside and idles away that day. To-morrow comes, and it is still cold. He says, "I will not plough to-day; I will wait till to-morrow." And thus he wastes day after day, until the whole season of ploughing is gone by, and it is useless to think of ploughing now. So his field remains uncultivated, given over to weeds.

But let us pass from the time of sowing to the time of reaping. The harvest season has come, and the diligent man who ploughed his field during the winter's cold rejoices to reap it in the time of autumn; and he that sowed it and he that reaps it rejoice together; and when the whole field has been reaped, and the last sheaf has been gathered in, the farmer and his workmen rejoice all together, and cheerfully celebrate their harvest home with plentiful harvest fare.

But what will the sluggard do now? You picture him to yourself as he passes slowly along by the rich harvest field of another, and how gladly now would he put his sickle into the corn and reap, if he might! but he has sown nothing, and he can reap nothing. His only resource is to beg. Well, let him beg, and see with what success he meets. He begs in harvest, and has nothing. He goes to the farmer who is keeping his harvest feast, but he obtains nothing but rebuke. The farmer will not grudge to give of his plenty to the poor and helpless, to the orphan and the widow; but he will not give to the sluggard, and just because he is a sluggard—a man that can work, but will not. And now the poor wretch sees everybody else happy whilst he is miserable ; others are feasting while he is starving ; and that which intensifies his misery most of all is the thought, " I might have been happy ; I, too, might have reaped my own field, if I had not been a sluggard."

Now let us leave this sluggard, to think of some others who are like him.

First, there is the sluggard at school—in the Sunday school and in the day school. I have sometimes seen such an one. His whole device is to get through the school hours with the least possible amount of work and the greatest possible amount of idleness ; and whilst doing this he thinks himself very clever, and despises his more industrious schoolfellows as if they were dull drudges. For there is one thing in the sluggard that is very remarkable : he is always full of conceit ; and whatever else he lacks, of that he has plenty. So that, though very strange, it is very true, that "the sluggard is wiser in his own conceit than seven men that can render a reason." And so he trifles away day after day, week after week, and year after year, until the precious seedtime of school life comes to an end. Then he begins to find the evil results of his slothfulness. He has learned nothing valuable to him. He cannot read well, he cannot write his own name in a creditable manner ; he cannot do a difficult sum in arithmetic ; he has mastered no science ; he has not thoroughly learned any foreign language ; he is not master of his own. What now shall be done with such a lad ? His father or his friends want to put him to some trade or some profession. But the difficulty is to get him a master. A good master does not like sluggards about him ; and so perhaps, if he gets a master, it is one who is almost as great a sluggard as himself—like master, like man—and they make one another worse, and help to pull one another down into the slough of despond.

And now the worst results of his slothfulness begin to show themselves. He learned whilst at school nothing very valuable, but he learned much that was injurious; for nothing is more certain than this—that where the ground of the heart is not occupied with good, it will be taken possession of by evil; if no good grain is sown, weeds will surely spring up. And now the lad is pushed out into the great world of temptation, and is perhaps removed from under his father's roof. He has formed no good habits, but plenty of bad ones; he is assailed by powerful temptations, temptations to dishonesty, untruthfulness, intemperance, unchastity, and he finds in himself no power to resist. He readily learns the evil ways of older sinners, and rapidly goes from bad to worse. What is often the end of such a sluggard? Too often he finds his way to the prison, or, if he escapes that, becomes the prey of vice; and before he reaches middle life is bankrupt in fortune, ruined in health, ruined in character; a grief to his father, a reproach to his mother. He comes to an untimely and dishonoured end; and as to this world, and the world to come, makes shipwreck of his hopes.

But now I will tell you of another sluggard. He is a sluggard, and yet he is not. He rises early, he late takes rest, he eats the bread of carefulness. He is diligent in his business, and is a prosperous man. He is adding house to house and field to field, or he is adding pound to pound and hundred to hundred. How can such a man be a sluggard? Yet he is. There is no saying more frequent in his mouth than this, *Business must be attended to;* and still he constantly neglects the most important business of all. The man has a soul to save. He has to make his peace with God; he has to make sure his calling and election to eternal life. But to this business he does not attend. He knows that he has broken God's law, and that a long

catalogue of sin and transgressions is written down against
him in the book of God's remembrance all unpardoned.
Christ, the Lord of the harvest, the gracious Saviour, who
has given Himself for him, is constantly saying to him
through the Word and through the Spirit, "Go, work
to-day in My vineyard ; put thy hand to My plough." But
still the man refuses. He knows that, were he to die to-day,
as he now is, he would die unpardoned, unsaved, and
perish in his sins for ever ; yet he delays to seek his peace
with God. And in this greatest business of life he does,
what he never does in his other affairs, he waits for fine
weather. He "will not plough by reason of the cold." He
has certain evil habits which he knows he must give up if
he would become a servant of Jesus Christ, dishonest but
gainful ways, habits of sinful self-indulgence ; and he says,
"If I must give up all this, I will not enter Christ's service
—at least not at present." He looks at the services which
he must render, and the sacrifices which he must make, if
he become anything more than a nominal Christian. "It
will cost me time and money ; it will cost too much."
And so, for these and other reasons, he delays, and hopes—
how vainly hopes!—that he shall be able some day to plough
when it will not be cold, that he can become a good
Christian without self-denial. Such a day never comes ; but
by-and-by the last day of life comes. It often surprises
him in the midst of his busy schemes : the grand house that
he was building is only half finished ; the contract that
was to bring in so much is not complete; the time bargain
that was to prove so lucky will never mature for him. He
knows that before the sun, which is now high in the heavens,
has reached the western horizon his own day of life will be
ended, and, alas ! the whole business of life remains undone.
What is left him but to cry out in despair, "The harvest is
past, the summer is ended, and I am not saved "? This

also is no mere fancy picture. There are busy men and rich men dying thus hopelessly, I fear, almost every day; and, what is worst of all, descending to the chambers of eternal darkness from the midst of the full light of gospel day. And surely if there is one thought more unspeakably distressing than another, that will enhance all the misery of the lost, it will be the thought that the loss of heaven, the punishment of hell, are only the result of their own slothfulness. If any of you should at last perish in your sins, how it will wring your heart with misery when you know that the companions of your youth, and of your more mature age, friends, neighbours, parents, brothers, sisters are happy for ever with Christ in His glorious kingdom, and that you might have been among them, if you had not been sluggards!

But now we will think no more of the sluggards. Some of you are not slothful. You have diligently set about the great business of life. You have sought and found peace with God through our Lord Jesus Christ. You have put your hand to God's plough, and intend never to look back.

Let me try to encourage you in your toil. Let us for a while anticipate that which in scriptural language is called "the joy of harvest." This joy, in the literal sense of the words, is often very great. Most of us can remember some delightful harvest days. The too fierce heat of summer was already gone by, and the cold of winter had not begun; the plentiful harvest was all around us, the very air seemed balm, and the sower and the reaper rejoiced together to bring in the sheaves that crowned the labour of the year. But raise your thoughts to that glorious harvest which shall be gathered when "the reapers are the angels, and the harvest is the end of the world." You may be sure that Christ's reapers will do His work so well, that they will not want any

to glean after them.   Not one precious soul shall be overlooked.   There shall be gathered together the pure and
good, the noble and the wise of all ages.   And then will be
fulfilled, in a sense in which it never can be fulfilled till then,
the saying that "he that soweth and he that reapeth shall
rejoice together."   Righteous Abel will rejoice to see the
blessed fruit of his own righteous example running through
all the ages ; and the last man who shall look upon the
natural sun and look by faith upon the Sun of righteousness shall acknowledge himself the better for Abel's faith
and Enoch's walk with God.   And how will the brave and
hardy ploughmen of God's field rejoice to see the accumulated fruit of their unflinching toil?   Think of the
Apostle Paul.   You remember what sort of ploughing his
was.   It was no holiday work.   He had to encounter perils
by land and by sea, in the wilderness and in the city.
Stoning, stripes, imprisonment, death, all came to him as
the result of his ploughing ; but every succeeding age has
been the better for his labours, his writings, and his example.
And in the great day he will rejoice to see that his sufferings
at Lystra, at Philippi, at Jerusalem, at Rome, have been
bearing fruit ever since.

   Let us not forget famous ploughmen who have laboured in
our own land, and who by toils and suffering and martyrdom
have won the blessings we now enjoy.   Think of glorious
William Tyndale, the man who by God's blessing gave to
us our English Bible.   When shall all the harvest springing
from his labours be gathered in?   It is growing every day ;
it will grow till the end of the world, and the blessed result
shall abide for ever and ever.   We think of labourers that
came after : good Hugh Latimer, and Cranmer, and Ridley,
and Hooper ; we think of Baxter and Howe and Owen, of
Wesley and Whitfield, and of Carey and Marshman, and
Hunt, and Burns, and Livingstone—men that have done

work which will fill the world with blessing as long as the world lasts.

But, above all, let us think of Christ Himself. In the time of harvest, however great the joy of others, the owner of the field has the greatest joy, because all the harvest is his own. How great will be the joy of Christ in that day ! He rejoices "over one sinner that repenteth "; and, blessed be God ! we are well warranted to think that our Saviour's is an ever-growing joy. Never since the world began were there so many living on earth who honour and love Christ. But the heart of Christ is fixed on the day of His full and perfect triumph, when the number of His elect shall be complete, and when there shall be gathered into one glorious company those that have come out of every nation and kindred and tribe, who will have washed their robes and made them white in His own blood, and will ascribe all their salvation to Him for ever. Then shall He see of the travail of His soul, and His own infinite desire shall be satisfied. When we think of all this, we are ready to take up the language of John Bunyan, who, when he had conducted his pilgrims to the gates of the heavenly Jerusalem, and had caught through the open gates a glimpse of the glory which was within, and heard the strains of heavenly music, says, "Which when I had heard and seen, I wished myself among them."

You may have a part in that glorious harvest joy, but you must be willing to work in God's field to-day. " Let us not be weary in well doing : for in due season we shall reap, if we faint not." You who are Sunday-school teachers, do not refuse to "plough " because of the "cold." Make up your mind that you will have hard work sometimes. Reckon on self-denial and labour ; but when you are tempted to grow weary, think of the harvest. Though I do not profess to be a prophet, I think I can foresee what will be in many cases

the fruit of your toil. There is that girl who sometimes
tries your patience and your temper, and on whose account
you seem to labour in vain. But have patience. The good
seed is already lodged in her heart. It will one day spring
up and bear fruit. Look forward. She is now the mother
of a family, her hands full of business, her mind filled with
domestic cares. She has her share in those sorrows and
joys which the heart of a woman alone knows. But in the
midst of all there is a deep peace. It lessens every sorrow,
heightens every joy, purifies every affection; and she will
often tell that under God she owes it all to you.

And there is that boy who seems so unpromising. Look
forward a few years. A happy vision rises before me. He
has gone to the Western States of America, or to Australia.
He perhaps is the founder of the township in which he
lives, and has called it after the name of his native place.
He is now an old man, venerable with years and virtue,
the pillar of his church, and an ornament to society. He is
telling to his children, and to his children's children, the
story of his life ; and recollection travels back to his Sunday school, and he says to those who listen to him so
lovingly, " I owe all to God ; I owe all to religion ; and I
owe my religion to the dear teacher who so faithfully and
patiently taught me the way to the kingdom."

God may call some of you boys to preach His gospel. If
so, first make sure that He has called you, and then be sure
you do not refuse. You may have to labour at home. And
if so, you will have a sphere which any man may covet.
You will be helping to lift English society higher in purity
and goodness, and whatever is done for England is done
for the world.

Or you may have nobler work still. You may become a
missionary to the heathen, not building on any other man's
foundation, but yourself a foundation-builder. You may be

called to preach the everlasting gospel in a tongue which you have never heard, to a people whose name has never yet reached you. You may have to lay down life in some far-off land, and find your last resting-place by some wide river and beneath some mighty tree of tropical lands. But if you labour faithfully, yours will be no unhonoured grave. It will be often visited ; and the men of future ages as they gather around it will speak of you as the man who first kindled the light of life among them and opened to them the path that leads to the city of God.

Work while it is day. Put your hand to the plough. Endure the cold. Think sometimes of the joy of harvest, and cheer yourself with the Divine assurance : "He that goeth forth and weepeth, bearing precious seed, shall doubtless come again with rejoicing, bringing his sheaves with him."

THE CENTURION WHO BUILT THE SYNAGOGUE.

"Now when He had ended all His sayings in the audience of the people, He entered into Capernaum. And a certain centurion's servant, who was dear unto him, was sick, and ready to die.   And they that they were sent, returning to the house, found the servant whole that had been sick."—LUKE vii. 1-10.

1. THIS centurion was *a good master*. He was very strict in requiring obedience to his commands. This belongs to the character of a good master. The Greek historian Xenophon tells of a Greek general named Clearchus who strongly inspired his soldiers with the conviction that *Clearchus must be obeyed*. On this principle also our own Sir Henry Lawrence acted in India ; so did this centurion. The worst kind of masters are those who issue commands without requiring them to be obeyed. If they are unreasonable commands, they are very foolish in giving

them ; if reasonable, it is weak and blamable not to have
them obeyed.

This man was "under authority." He knew that he had
to obey his superior officers ; and he really could not do
this unless others obeyed him. What use for the tribunes
to bid him lead his century to any place, if he had not
drilled his men to obedience ?

But whilst he was very firm, he was very kind. He had
a servant who in this case was also a slave. No doubt
he was a good servant, otherwise it would never have been
said that he "was dear" to his master. Servants must not
expect that their masters will value them highly, unless
they give them some good reason for doing so. When this
slave fell ill, the master was anxious to do all he could for
him, and he sought the help of the best physician anywhere
to be found. What a reproof his conduct affords to many
masters who profess and call themselves Christians ! Ask
some of these, "Do you *love* the men in your employ?"
They will probably think it a very strange question, and say :
"I neither love them nor hate them, like them nor dislike
them. All I care about is, that they earn well the wages
I give them." Very true ; that is all you do care about,
but it is not all you ought to care about. God in His providence has placed you in a position where you can command the services of others ; and He requires that you
should make use of that position for the good of those
who serve you. Some masters show their want of kindness
especially when their servants are ill. The trouble of sickness, hard to bear in itself, is followed by dismissal. They
send their servants to the workhouse or to the parish, anywhere to get rid of them. There are other masters who
act in a more Christian way ; and I have heard of some who
take old servants into their houses, and make their own
homes houses of recovery, where the servants receive every

care and attention. Our Master in heaven is well pleased with those who do this. Let all Christian masters learn a lesson from this Roman soldier.

2. He was *a very generous man.* He had built the synagogue at Capernaum at his own sole cost. Some may say that a Jewish synagogue in a provincial town would not be a very costly affair, and therefore it was no great thing to build one. But remember, the man was in all probability comparatively poor. His pay as a centurion would be less than one shilling a day ; and he could not build a synagogue without making some sacrifices. He did what in other places was done by a whole congregation. Brought up in heathenism, and converted to the Jewish religion, he had in his zeal for his new faith erected this synagogue. He little thought that in the house which he built wonderful works would be wrought, which would be told of as long as the world should last ; and that there discourses would be delivered which would be heard again in all the languages of the earth, down to the end of time ! He is the prototype of many generous men since, who have done the like. I am far from saying that it is always best that a church should be built by the few rather than the many ; but I am glad that in our own day there are men who have it in their power, and have it in their heart, to build a church at their sole cost.

This was done by Lord Haddo. He built a church in the East End of London, which cost him £10,000—more than three times his annual income. So careful was he in all this to seek God's glory, that he would not allow his name or even his initials to appear on any part of the building ; and when the church was opened, though he attended the first service, only the clergyman and the builder knew he was there.[1]

---

[1] See Elliott's *Memoir of Lord Haddo,* chapter iii.

3. This centurion was *a true gentleman.* He was anxious not to give needless trouble. He sent a message to our Lord saying, " Trouble not Thyself."

There are many good Christian people who are like him. There are others very unlike him, who put on those about them a great deal of needless trouble, and for the service which they receive give neither thanks nor pay. They act as if they thought no one could do too much for them, and that they should be excused from exerting themselves to do anything for others.

4. He was *a very humble man.* He had most exalted views of Christ, and therefore he had lowly views of himself. He said that he was not worthy that Christ should come under his roof; but while he said this of himself, his fellow townsmen said of him that he *was* worthy, and Christ Himself said that he had greater faith than any man in Israel. He is an example of the truly humble people, whose neighbours will say of them better things than they will ever say of themselves; and a contrast to those who will say of themselves better things than any one else can say. Happy for us when we are little in our own eyes, highly prized by our friends, and commended by the Master Himself !

5. But above all, this centurion is to be commended for *his faith.* This is what Christ commends. No doubt He took account of the centurion's other virtues; but this He praises, this He admires, this He holds up as an example for others; and it was the centurion's faith that obtained the servant's cure. Had he possessed all the other virtues, but had wanted faith in Christ, the blessing of healing would not have been given. When shall we understand the importance of faith ! See what wonders it works ! Let faith be present, and the great work is wrought; let faith be absent, and no miracle is wrought. How plainly the Scrip-

tures teach this! and yet how slow we are to learn! "If ye have faith as a grain of mustard seed, ye shall say unto this mountain, Remove hence to yonder place ; and it shall remove ; and nothing shall be impossible unto you."[1] Again, "If thou canst believe, all things are possible to him that believeth."[2] And again, "He did not many mighty works there because of their unbelief."[3]

Notice Christ's *hearty admiration* for the centurion. I am glad we have this on record, because it contains a lesson to some people who think themselves very wise, and who admire nothing. Show them a very fine building ; they say nothing about its grandeur, but point out its defects, or what they think to be defects. Let them hear a grand musical composition well rendered ; they have no praise for composer or performer, but if there are one or two false notes in a long piece they are sure to notice them. If they hear a good sermon, they have no commendation for the preacher, but say it was too short, or too long, or had too few illustrations, or too many, or had some fault or other. These are very uncomfortable people to have to do with, and I should think they are not very happy in themselves. Not so with Christ. He thoroughly admired the man, and He said so. Did He see no faults in the centurion ? No doubt He did ; but he admired him for what was admirable, notwithstanding his faults. If we reserve all praise until we meet with people absolutely perfect, I am afraid we shall possess a faculty which will decay for want of use.

I hope you who are parents sometimes praise your children, and you who are masters sometimes praise your servants. I hope you who are husbands sometimes praise your wives. A friend of mine once told me that the highest

---

[1] Matt. xvii. 20.   [2] Mark ix. 23.   [3] Matt. xiii. 58.

praise his mother ever gave him was this : "That and *better* will do." Children and servants and wives too make great efforts to please us ; and they are often greatly disappointed, because they are hungry for the praise which never comes. Is it wonderful if their efforts to please us become fewer ?

Christ not only admired, but *praised*. He did not think that well deserved praise would do the man harm. I wish some of the Lord's servants were more like their Master in this respect.

It is related in an old legend that once upon a time a dead dog lay by the roadside, exposed to the contemptuous comments of every passer by. "What a wretched mongrel ! " cried one. "Doubtless he deserved his bad end," said another. "How loathsome an object ! " added a third. At last there came one who looked upon him and said, "Pearls cannot equal the whiteness of his teeth." And those who heard said one to another : "This must be Jesus of Nazareth. None but He would find anything to praise in a dead dog." [1]

"*A PECULIAR PEOPLE.*"

"Who gave Himself for us, that He might redeem us from all iniquity, and purify unto Himself a peculiar people, zealous of goo works."—TIT. ii. 14.

ALTHOUGH, as a general rule, it is one of the most unprofitable of occupations for a preacher to spend much time in setting forth what his text does *not* mean, yet this is sometimes necessary. The words of the text have

---

[1] This apologue occurs in its oriental dress in a poem entitled *The Treasury of Secrets*, written in 1157 A.D. by the Persian poet Nizámi. —EDS.

been very often misunderstood, because the word "peculiar" has, since the year 1611, almost entirely lost one of the meanings which it had then. It is derived from a Latin word, meaning "money" or "property,"[1] and the text really means that the Lord's people are His property or His possession. So in the Revised Version we read here, "A people for His own possession."

The misunderstanding of this word has led to serious practical mistakes. Men have thought it a sign of religion to be singular, to depart from the generality of their neighbours in outward things which are purely indifferent. We all know to what an extent this was the case with the Society of Friends. There was once, and is still to a certain limited extent, a Quaker dress, and there are Quaker colours. So amongst the early Methodists it was often thought a piece of religion to wear a coat, hat, or bonnet of a particular shape, and a piece of irreligion not to do so. I cannot see any reason for this; and these notions are now generally abandoned, except, strange to say, in the case of ministers of religion. There is still a clerical costume, which I think is to be regretted, although the evil is now less than it was; for the distinctions are mostly reduced to a minimum, and every sensible man knows that nobody is a whit the better because he wears gaiters, or lawn sleeves, or a white neckcloth.

There is a more serious evil still remaining. There are oddities of voice, for instance. The poet Cowper in the last century very properly ridiculed "the nasal twang heard in conventicle."[2] That has passed away, but we still have the clerical voice heard in reading prayers and reading Scripture; and some people still, in talking about religion, use a style of voice not heard at other times. These are

---

[1] *Peculium.*   [2] *The Task,* bk. ii.

serious evils, because they all tend to keep up the delusion, which has been the source of infinite mischief, that the religion of Christ is in some way distinct and apart from our ordinary life; instead of the true view, that, when we live as Christians should, religion is inseparably connected with every part of life.

What then is the true view taught in this text? It is a most weighty one. *True Christians are the purchased possession of the Lord Jesus Christ,*—a truth frequently expressed in Scripture, but much overlooked. One reason of this is the frequent use of language which is *not* scriptural. Good people often in prayers and sermons speak of what Christ "has purchased for His people." It must also be acknowledged that our own excellent hymn-book gives sanction in a few instances to this mode of speaking. Still it is unscriptural. The Scriptures never speak of what Christ has *bought for us*, but they often remind us that He has *bought us for Himself.*

Now look at the practical consequences which follow from this truth. Because Christ has purchased us for His own possession, we have no absolute property in ourselves, we "are not our own." There are many powerful arguments against suicide; this is the most conclusive of all. If my body, my life, is the property of another, I cannot have any right to dispose of it according to my own will, and against the ordinance of the great Proprietor. Not only is this view conclusive against suicide in the ordinary sense, but against every kind of conduct which may be said to amount to slow suicide. The careless, reckless sinner sometimes says, "If I choose to have a short life and a merry one, who has a right to interfere?" The answer is, *Your Creator and your Redeemer.* You have no right to destroy that for which Christ died. Christians do wrong when by ill-guided zeal they shorten life, even in doing good

service. Is the Master well pleased when His servants quit
too soon a post of usefulness, which might have been occupied longer ? Again, we have no right to maim the body
by adherence to any evil fashion. The Chinese women are
to be condemned for adherence to a fashion which makes
them cripples. And we have no need to go to China to
find people whom fashion leads to do serious injury to their
bodies. Such things are sins against Christ.

This principle also is conclusive against drunkenness.
There are many powerful arguments against drunkenness
and intemperance of all degrees. To the Christian mind
the most powerful is, the body is the Lord's. As such
it ought to be kept as a ready and fit instrument for the
Lord's service. How severely men reflect on a doctor, if
he is ever found in a state of intoxication when one of his
patients urgently requires his services, and he has made
himself unfit to render the service required ! How infinitely displeasing it must be to the Lord Jesus Christ,
when any one of His professed servants reduces himself
to a condition in which he cannot do the work which
his Lord requires of him ! This too is the most powerful
argument which the Apostle Paul can urge against the sin
of fornication and all uncleanness : " The body is
for the Lord."

Of course, as all men are the Lord's creatures, as all have
been redeemed by Christ, everything that is valid against
injuring our own bodies is a valid reason against injuring
the body of another. I own that this is a powerful argument against *warfare in general.* Though I have never
been able to go to the extent to which the Society of
Friends go on this question, it is plain that nothing can
justify war to any of us, unless we have an earnest, honest
conviction that God Himself sanctions, in certain great emer-
gencies, man's taking away the life of his fellow man.

Further, this principle implies that we are under an obligation to make the best use of all the faculties with which God has endowed us. It condemns *idleness* and *slothfulness.* No child has a right to neglect the diligent improvement of his faculties, and no parent can be right in encouraging or allowing such neglect. The neglect to obtain for our children a good education, when it is in our power to procure it, is a grievous sin.

It is well for us to consider, both young and old, whether we have in times past cultivated, whether we are now cultivating, our powers to the utmost. Are not some of you self-condemned for past neglect? You perhaps might have been a good musician, and are not. You ought to have been a good artist, and are not. You might have been a good linguist, chemist, or botanist, you might have been a first-rate master of some handicraft, a mason, joiner, or blacksmith: and you have allowed the opportunity to go by. You may have been endowed with uncommon intellectual powers, which, if cultivated, would have given you a high place, or at least a useful place, in the ranks of men of science or literature, in medicine, law, or politics. What account will you give to your Lord of this neglect?

HAPPINESS AS AN END.

WE are sometimes told that men do not err in making happiness the supreme end of life, but only in seeking the wrong kind of happiness, and searching for it in forbidden paths. "Seek happiness in religion," it is said. "Make your peace with God; make your calling and election to eternal life sure; find your enjoyment here in religious services and benevolent work, and aim at the happiness of heaven hereafter, and you follow the course of the highest wisdom." All this sounds very plausible, and it may be thought by some to have the support of Scripture. Do we not read in the first psalm, "Happy is the man that walketh not in the counsel of the ungodly"? Does not Christ begin His Sermon on the Mount by saying, "Happy are the poor in spirit"? Are not the Beatitudes, taken all together, a perfect scheme of a happy life? But a more careful examination of the subject will convince us that these passages are intended to show that happiness *results* from virtue, when virtue itself is first chosen. "Happy are the pure in heart": but those who attain to purity of heart desire the *purity itself,* even more than the happiness which it brings. "Seek *first* the kingdom of God and His righteousness."

When by religious people happiness is made the chief end, and virtue valued only as it leads to that end, there results a religion which is not of the highest kind. Men adopting this view of life think too much of their privileges, and too little of their duties; they are too anxious to be *happy,* and not sufficiently careful to be *holy,* and often sacrifice the supreme end to what is only a means. One of our religious magazines lately contained an account of a very pious chapel-keeper. He was so zealous, that he would attend all the special religious services held in his own neighbourhood. Very pleasant for him; but it had this disadvantage: whilst he was away enjoying himself, his wife had to do his work in addition to her own.

It leads men to sing about heaven, and express their desire for it, when it is evident to others that they are not sufficiently careful to be made "*meet* for the inheritance of the saints in light." It leads to quite sensuous views of heaven itself, as a place where we shall "gather at the river," and ramble through "sweet fields beyond the swelling flood"; and it reduces the infinitely exalted abode of

God and angels and glorified saints to some pleasant resting-place " over there."

What *is* the supreme purpose of life? I give as the answer to this question the words of the Apostle Paul: " Whether therefore ye eat, or drink, or whatsoever ye do, do all to the glory of God."

THE SECOND GREAT COMMANDMENT

" And the second is like unto it, Thou shalt love thy neighbour as thyself."—MATT. xxii. 39.

IT is like the first great commandment in its brevity, like it in its comprehensiveness, like it in clearness, like it in the prominence which it gives to the great principle of love.

It differs from it in this respect: that whilst the first requires love to the Creator, this requires love to the creature. It differs from it also as the stream does from the fountain, for from true love to God springs true love to our neighbour.

It is remarkable that whilst the love of God is the real source of the love of our neighbour, the rule by which we are to regulate this last is the love of ourselves, or, as Lord Bacon has pithily expressed it, " Divinity maketh the love of ourselves the pattern: but the love of our neighbours the portraiture." [1] Hence it follows that there is a love of ourselves which is commendable and justifiable. We may define it to be a proper care for our true interest. But what is our true interest? and what is a proper care for it? Our true interest is to be what God would have us be, and

---

[1] Essay XIII. : *Of Goodness, and Goodness of Nature.*

do what He would have us do ; so to live here that we
may attain eternal life hereafter.   And a proper care for our
true interest is, to seek the accomplishment of all God's
blessed will in us and by us, according to the teaching of
His word.   Thus to act is to love ourselves with a true and
wise self-love.   And it is easy to see that this love of self is
consistent with the love of God, on the one hand, and the
love of our neighbour, on the other.   If we love God with
all our heart, we shall earnestly desire that the will of God
may be done in us ; but we shall desire also that it may be
done in others : and if we are satisfied that our own highest
happiness consists in conformity to God's will, we shall
easily and safely conclude that the happiness of every other
human creature does also.   In one word : to love ourselves
rightly is to desire the accomplishment of God's will in
ourselves ; to love our neighbour rightly is to desire the
accomplishment of God's will in him ; and the more
enlightened our love of self, the more enlightened will be
our love to our neighbour.

"CHILDREN, OBEY YOUR PARENTS."

" Children, obey your parents in the Lord: for this is right."—
EPH. vi. 1.

I AM addressing myself to those who are converted,
who are " in the Lord."   And I say,—St. Paul says,—
God says, " Children, obey your parents."   There are many
good reasons for this ; but weigh first the one given in the
text : " *For this is right.*"   It is a duty founded in nature.
Under God, you owe to your parents your existence in this
world, and a thousand benefits besides.   I speak now to the
generality of children ; I speak of the generality of parents.

It is a sorrowful fact that there are some parents who are a disgrace to the name, who show less love to their offspring than do the brutes that perish. But such persons are monsters; the general voice rightly designates them as unnatural, and we would fain hope, for the credit of our common nature, that such instances are rare. But when *you* were quite incapable of taking any care of yourselves, your parents cared for you; and to supply all your wants, to protect you from harm, to secure your health and strength and good bringing up, has cost them many, many hours of toil, of self-sacrifice, much sorrow it may be, and very many cares and anxieties.

You owe them a debt which you can never discharge; and the least that you can do is to yield a prompt and ready obedience to their commands. I know that this is much easier in some cases than in others. Some of you Christian children may have unconverted parents; perhaps they are harsh, perhaps they are sometimes unreasonable in the commands which they lay upon you. Yet they are your parents still; and you owe it to them, and you owe it to Christ, to obey them in everything, unless they lay any commands upon you which you cannot obey without disobeying Christ. In such a case, disobedience to parents becomes a duty. But even then I say, Never plead conscience as a reason for disobedience, unless the case is unmistakably clear.

Christian children must not be satisfied with mere obedience; to this they must join *honour* "Honour thy father and thy mother." I have seen many beautiful examples of obedience to this precept. I have known men, having children of their own, who have treated their aged parents with the honour and respect which they gave them when they were children; and when I have seen this, I have always felt the most profound respect for such children.

Again, I have seen children who have rendered to their parents very scant honour indeed. They have appeared to pride themselves on their superior attainments, which very attainments they owed to the self-sacrificing love of their parents, and have scarcely treated their father and mother with common civility. However brilliant and clever such young people may be, I can never feel for them one atom of respect, I will never reckon them in my list of friends, I will gladly escape from their company.

Not only honour your parents, but, where need is, supply their wants. To many of you this will never be a duty. Your parents provide for themselves, and lay up for you. You will never feel the obligation, you will never have the happiness, of ministering to them when they are in need. With others the case is different. Your parents are poor, and need your help. Shame on the children who in such a case *can* help, but will not !

I heard of one man of this sort, a lawyer. He became wealthy. At his death he left a wife, but no children. His father survived him, and was poor. The will showed that all the property was left to the man's wife. To his aged father he left not one penny. What did his father say? This: "I did not think my son would have acted so. His mother and I have often gone almost without the necessaries of life to provide for his education." Now I tell you, I would rather die a pauper in a workhouse than act as that son did.

I will tell you another example. S. W. is a lawyer. He is still living ; and when he had earned some money by his profession he presented his father with £1,000 to repay the cost of his education. Can you doubt that our Father in heaven would approve an act like that ?

"*BE CAREFUL FOR NOTHING.*"[1]

"Be careful for nothing; but in everything by prayer and supplication with thanksgiving let your requests be made known unto God. And the peace of God, which passeth all understanding, shall keep your hearts and minds through Christ Jesus."—PHIL. iv. 6, 7.

IN this text we see an evil to be avoided, a duty to be performed, and a blessing to be obtained. The evil, *much care ;* the duty, *much prayer ;* the blessing, *much peace.*

I. "Be careful for nothing." Had you no authority for these words higher than that of the present preacher, you would some of you be ready to exclaim, What impracticable advice! I can well imagine a commercial man saying: "The preacher clearly knows nothing about business. In these days of foreign competition and depressed trade, it is only by *incessant care* that we can pay our way at all." And I can imagine the anxious mother of a family, one who perhaps has many mouths to feed and little to feed them with, I can imagine her saying: "The preacher knows little about my life. My life is one of *constant anxiety and fore-thought.* I have to care for everybody and everything in my household ; and if I did not, no one else would." And then there is the poor invalid, seldom perhaps if ever quite free from pain, who says in the evening, "Would God it were morning !" and in the morning, "Would God it were evening !"—such an one might easily say, "To bid me cease from *care* seems almost a cruel satire on my suffering."

And yet all these objections are hushed when we remember who it was that spoke the words.

St. Paul was now a prisoner in Rome ; of worldly possessions he had none ; his liberty was taken from him ; he was the subject of an incurable bodily affliction ; little but his

---

[1] In the absence of a recent MS., we have reproduced this sermon partly from memory.—EDS.

life was now left to him, and for all he knew the morrow might see him led forth for execution. You who speak of the anxieties connected with your temporal affairs, was it easier for Paul to have no care than it is for you? Think too of what his life had been. " In labours more abundant, in stripes above measure, in prisons more frequent, in deaths oft. Of the Jews five times received I forty stripes save one. Thrice was I beaten with rods, once was I stoned, thrice I suffered shipwreck, a night and a day I have been in the deep ; in journeyings often, in perils of waters, in perils of robbers, in perils by mine own countrymen, in perils by the heathen, in perils in the city, in perils in the wilderness, in perils in the sea, in perils among false brethren ; in weariness and painfulness, in watchings often, in hunger and thirst, in fastings often, in cold and naked-ness. Beside those things that are without, that which cometh upon me daily, the care of all the Churches."[1]

Think of what all this mean. Take one single thing : " Thrice was I beaten with rods." Imagine the prisoner stripped to the skin, beaten with heavy rods by the strong arm of a Roman soldier till the blood ran down and the prisoner could bear no more ; then see him thrown fainting and wounded into a noisome dungeon ; and all this repeated three times. Think of him deserted by most of his friends, and saddened too often by the news that some of the con-verts in the Churches he loved so well were burning with unholy strife, or had gone back to heathenism ! Tell me, are your family cares worse than this? And tell me, even you poor sufferer on your sick-bed, are you not willing to listen to the voice of Paul, as one who had more to suffer than you?

Yet another class of objectors might say : " This advice is

---

[1] 2 Cor. xi. 23–2S.

dangerous. Those who are careful for nothing *must be care-less;* and carelessness is sin." Let the logicians attend to the verbal fallacy ; the practical answer we proceed to give.

There are *two sorts of carefulness,* a right and a wrong. The first is enjoined in Scripture, the latter forbidden. The right carefulness is a *carefulness about duty,* the other is *anxiety about consequences.*

The care of the farmer to see that his ground is well ploughed and good seed duly sown in it, is right care, it is wise carefulness. The care of the farmer who, having done this, should perpetually trouble himself with the question, "Will the seed grow?" and should visit his field every day, and many times in the day, to see if the crop were springing up, would be absurd and wrong. It could not make one seed to grow, or cause any to grow the faster. All that care is wrong and hurtful which is useless, which does not tend to secure some good result, or to ward off some threatened evil. Neglect not to use the means likely to secure success ; but, having done this, leave the result with God.

Never be careful for anything in such a way that your carefulness shall be a practical denial of God's good providence over you. A child that would please his parents must indeed strive in everything to fulfil their wishes, and must use diligence and thoughtfulness that he may do everything his parents require, in the best possible way. But suppose that a child of yours, having done all this, becomes anxious as to the continued supply of his daily food, although he has never lacked ; or anxious as to how the clothes he wears will be provided in the future ; or doubtful whether a week hence he will still have the shelter of your roof, although you have always made the home happy for him : would you not be angry with him? would you not say : "This carefulness of yours is ingratitude to me. You do me a great wrong in doubting my continued kindness." But have you never given your heavenly Father occasion to reason thus with you?

If you make it your chief business to do the will of your Father who is in heaven, do you not think it likely that He will look after your temporal affairs? Has His good providence ever failed you in times past? Has He not given you His word for it, that He will provide things needful for you in the future? Are we not taught in the Sermon on the Mount that the reason why *we* ought not to be careful about the things of this life is, that our heavenly Father " knoweth that we have need of all these things "?

II. " Be careful for nothing, *but*——" This little word deserves our attention. Much of the instruction of Scripture is given in the form of antithesis. A thing to be done is set against a thing not to be done, a blessing against a curse. So here we better understand what is forbidden by observing what is commanded. The duty is the antidote for the evil, the cure for the disease. The command is this, *Be careful for nothing yourselves, but get the Lord to care for you ;* or, as we read in the twenty-second verse of Psalm lv. :. "Cast thy burden upon the Lord, and He shall sustain thee." " In everything by prayer and supplication with thanksgiving let your requests be made known unto God." " No," say some ; " not in *everything*. I can manage all my small affairs and all my little troubles very well myself. I will not trouble the Lord with these. I will only take the great ones to Him." Are you sure that you can manage little affairs and your little troubles by yourself? What was it that led you to indulge that bad temper? Was it a heavy loss in business? or was it some trifle that would long ago have been forgotten, had it been met in a right spirit? What was it made you speak unadvisedly with your lips? Was it some vile slander on your reputation? or was it the carelessness of a child or of a servant? Experience teaches

us that we are not able to do anything, great or small,
without God's grace.

Again, you say you will not go to God in prayer with
your small concerns, because they are not worthy of His
notice.   But are your *great* ones so worthy?   Is there one
of your concerns worthy of the attention of the Infinite?
To the Infinite mind nothing is great, and nothing is
small; it is only our own littleness that makes us think
otherwise.   Surely the words of Christ settle all doubt on
this question: "Are not two sparrows sold for a farthing?
and one of them shall not fall on the ground without your
Father.   But the very hairs of your head are all numbered."

How great is the privilege afforded to the children of
God!   None but those who have tried it can have an idea
of the value of prayer.   Trials will often come upon a man
so peculiar and secret in their nature that he cannot fully
communicate them to his dearest earthly friend; but there
is a heavenly Friend to whom he may at any time make
known any trial, and do so in perfect confidence of obtaining help.   It is true that he cannot always be sure that
his trial will be removed.   He would not think it right
to ask this in every case; but he may be sure of gaining
renewed strength to bear the trial, if it remains.   Happy
the man who knows his privilege and uses it well!

But whilst we make known our requests, it must be
with thanksgiving.   Thankfulness is as much a duty as
prayer.   We cannot expect God to bestow new blessings
if we make no acknowledgment of those already received.
Some men's hearts are like the desert sands, which swallow
up every drop of rain that falls upon them, but yield
nothing in return.

A certain rich man had a poor neighbour living upon
his estate.   The rich man was exceedingly generous to the
poor man.   He did so much for him, that not a day passed

in which the poor man did not receive some benefaction from his generous friend. And yet no word of gratitude was ever given in return, everything was received as a matter of course ; and if at any time the poor man failed to receive what he wished for, he would be heard to accuse the other of hardness and neglect. "What ingratitude!" you cry. "If he should never again receive anything more from the rich man's hands, it would be a just requital for his unthankfulness." True : and *thou* art the man !

And again, a thankful spirit is a happy spirit. How is it that many professing Christians have little joy ? One great reason is, that they are so unmindful of the unspeakable blessings already bestowed upon them, and of those still richer ones treasured up in heaven. If such persons would dwell less on their troubles, and more on their blessings, they would find an increase of happiness which would be surprising to themselves. If you doubt it, make the trial.

It was thus, in prayer and supplication and thanksgiving, that David wrote his psalms in his time of sorrow ; for "he set his troubles to music, and played them off upon his harp." It was thus that Paul Gerhardt, banished from Berlin, and plunged into the deepest need and sorrow, wrote the hymn, beginning

> "Commit thou all thy griefs
> And ways into His hands."

And God did not suffer him to be forsaken.[1]

Yet two things are necessary that you may comply with these conditions. Firstly, you must be, as the Philippians were, "saints in Christ." These words are not for the enemies, but for the friends of Christ ; and if you are not reconciled to God, you must seek reconciliation. Then,

---

[1] See *The Methodist Hymn-book, Illustrated,* by G. J. Stevenson, for an account of the circumstances here referred to.—EDS.

and not till then, will the duty here enjoined be practicable ; then only will this great privilege be within your
reach.   And, secondly, the fulfilment of this duty implies
an entire surrender of ourselves to God.   You cannot cast
all your care upon God, unless you are willing to cease
caring for those objects which God disapproves.   You
may cast all honest and honourable cares upon God, not
dishonourable ones ; bad debts made in business, not bad
debts made by gambling or reckless speculation.   Nor
must you bring a request for the fulfilment of a desire
of which you are ashamed.   The murderer, the adulterer,
the robber, can never make his requests known to God
in prayer.   How great is the practical advantage of making
this our rule !   The very attempt to bring a request to
God will cause us to abandon it, if it be unlawful.   And
here is the very question of questions.   Here lies the
secret of a happy life.   And you have to make your choice.
Resolve to do everything for God ; to touch nothing,
attempt nothing, desire nothing on which you cannot ask
God's blessing.   And, again, resolve that whatever you
do you will commend to Him ; and you will find the secret
of happiness.   You will have peaceful days and tranquil
nights, and a joyful spirit ; and you will greatly glorify God.
Reject this counsel ; and then, with all your striving, you
will never be truly happy, you will never have the bliss
which God gives His own.

    III. And, lastly, to those who fulfil the conditions, who
are "careful for nothing, but who in everything by prayer
and supplication with thanksgiving let their requests be made
known unto God," to them, and to them alone, there is
given "*the peace of God*, which passeth all understanding,"
to keep their "hearts and minds through Christ Jesus" (or
rather, "*in* Christ Jesus ").

    The peace of God is not a blessing above consciousness ;

if so, it would not be known. It is the peace which God gives, and the stream resembles its source. It implies *peace with God*, the peace which arises from the absence of guilt and fear and care. It is a peace which rises above " every understanding," which a man can indeed feel, but cannot explain to another. This peace is a fountain which no human vessel can exhaust, a sea which no line can fathom. It is wide as infinity and lasting as eternity; and to know the uttermost of it shall surpass the power of every saint for ever and ever.

In Christ Jesus are they kept. Kept as in a citadel, kept as a garrison keeps a fortress. The peace is full and constant, while they cleave closely to Him.

We have known some who, to a high degree at least, have fulfilled the duty and enjoyed the blessing of the text. See them! How distinguished they are! They are heaven's own nobility. The storms of sin and strife and passion and care are raging all around them. These come near, and touch and strike them; but, like strongly fortified and well-garrisoned cities, they stand unmoved amidst it all. There are legions of foes battering at the gates; but they never win an entrance within the walls. And why? These men have not the citadel of their souls in their own keeping; God has supreme and undisputed control, and He keeps them in perfect peace.

REST

NOW beyond this present life there remains for the people of God a perfecting and a perpetuation for ever of all that is most blessed in the earthly rest. Some of God's best people on earth are hard-working men; and though they richly enjoy the Sabbath rest, they sometimes sigh when they think that they must bear the heavy burden of their toil till the end of life. To such I say, Courage, fellow Christians! God may, very likely will, give you on earth an eventide of rest at the end of life; but if not, there is sweet rest in heaven. "Be thou faithful unto death," and then the last day of life will be the last day of labour; and as on the Saturday night you now feel that you have done with the toils of the week, and that there is a Sabbath rest before you, so then you will feel that toil is ended for ever, and that you are about to enter upon a Sabbath that knows no end.

There are others who have to bear the burden of bodily weakness and pain. To you the Sabbath day does not bring complete rest, though it often brings many alleviations, and shines for you the brightest day of the seven. But there remaineth a perfect rest for you. The burden which you bear you shall not carry always. You may not have to carry it long. A little more patient waiting, and you will lay aside the feeble body for ever; "this corruptible must put on incorruption." You will dwell in a country 'the inhabitants' of which 'never say that they are sick'; where there is no death and no decay, but the vigour and the bloom of a glorious youth for evermore.

And thou, fellow Christian, much perplexed with care, much harassed with doubt, sometimes struggling hard with the difficulties of religious faith and practice, only be faithful in trial, meet mental difficulties as you meet others, humbly, honestly, prayerfully; and in due time you too shall enter into rest, in the place where doubt and perplexity cannot arise, but where there abide "quietness and assurance for ever." Amen.

Butler & Tanner, The Selwood Printing Works, Frome, and London.